THE GAMES LOVERS PLAY

A CYNSTER NEXT GENERATION NOVEL

STEPHANIE LAURENS

ABOUT THE GAMES LOVERS PLAY

#1 New York Times *bestselling author Stephanie Laurens returns to the Cynsters' next generation with an evocative tale of two people striving to overcome unusual hurdles in order to claim true love.*

A nobleman wedded to the lady he loves strives to overwrite five years of masterful pretence and open his wife's eyes to the fact that he loves her as much as she loves him.

Lord Devlin Cader, Earl of Alverton, married Therese Cynster five years ago. What he didn't tell her then and has assiduously hidden ever since—for what seemed excellent reasons at the time—is that he loves her every bit as much as she loves him.

For her own misguided reasons, Therese had decided that the adage that Cynsters always marry for love did not necessarily mean said Cynsters were loved in return. She accepted that was usually so, but being universally viewed by gentlemen as too managing, bossy, and opinionated, she believed she would never be loved for herself. Consequently, after falling irrevocably in love with Devlin, when he made it plain he didn't love her yet wanted her to wife, she accepted the half love-match he offered, and once they were wed, set about organizing to make their marriage the very best it could be.

Now, five years later, they are an established couple within the haut ton, have three young children, and Devlin is making a name for himself in business and political circles. There's only one problem. Having attended numerous Cynster weddings and family gatherings and spent time with Therese's increasingly married cousins, who with their spouses all embrace the Cynster ideal of marriage based on mutually acknowledged love, Devlin is no longer content with the half love-match he himself engineered. No fool, he sees and comprehends what the craven act of denying his love is costing both him and Therese and feels compelled to rectify his fault. He wants for them what all Therese's married cousins enjoy—the rich and myriad benefits of marriages based on acknowledged mutual love.

Love, he's discovered, is too powerful a force to deny, leaving him wrestling with the conundrum of finding a way to convincingly reveal to Therese that he loves her without wrecking everything—especially the mutual trust—they've built over the past five years.

A classic historical romance set amid the glittering world of the London haut ton. A Cynster Next Generation novel—a full-length historical romance of 110,000 words.

OTHER TITLES BY STEPHANIE LAURENS

Beyond Seduction

The Edge of Desire

Mastered by Love

Black Cobra Quartet

The Untamed Bride

The Elusive Bride

The Brazen Bride

The Reckless Bride

The Adventurers Quartet

The Lady's Command

A Buccaneer at Heart

The Daredevil Snared

Lord of the Privateers

The Cavanaughs

The Designs of Lord Randolph Cavanaugh

The Pursuits of Lord Kit Cavanaugh

The Beguilement of Lady Eustacia Cavanaugh

The Obsessions of Lord Godfrey Cavanaugh

Other Novels

The Lady Risks All

The Legend of Nimway Hall – 1750: Jacqueline

Medieval (As M.S.Laurens)

Desire's Prize

Novellas

Melting Ice – from the anthologies *Rough Around the Edges* and *Scandalous Brides*

Rose in Bloom – from the anthology *Scottish Brides*

Scandalous Lord Dere – from the anthology *Secrets of a Perfect Night*

Lost and Found – from the anthology *Hero, Come Back*

THE GAMES LOVERS PLAY

THE GAMES LOVERS PLAY

Copyright © 2021 by Savdek Management Proprietary Limited

ISBN: 978-1-925559-46-0

Cover design by Savdek Management Pty. Ltd.

Cover couple photography by Period Images © 2021

First print publication: March, 2021

Savdek Management Proprietary Limited, Melbourne, Australia.

www.stephanielaurens.com

Email: admin@stephanielaurens.com

The names Stephanie Laurens and the Cynsters and the SL Logo are registered trademarks of Savdek Management Proprietary Ltd.

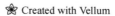 Created with Vellum

CHAPTER 1

OCTOBER 5, 1851. ALVERTON HOUSE, MAYFAIR.

I have to leave. Lord Devlin Cader, seventh Earl of Alverton, lay slumped in his wife's bed, with satiation a warm blanket, one imbued with the aftermath of sensual pleasure, lying heavy over his limbs.

He did not want to move—not now, not ever. But...

On a primal level, he was reassured by the warmth of his wife's body, stretched alongside his, and his reckless inner self insisted that there was no good reason he couldn't remain where he was and let the cards fall as they may.

Yet while his muscles lay lax and unmoving, his mind had come alive, driven by the knowledge that, courtesy of his unwise and impulsive words of yesterday, there was a degree of urgency in deciding what came next, and thinking rationally while lying beside Therese, with the perfume that rose from her hair and warm skin wreathing his senses, was next to impossible.

Aside from all else, if she woke and, with dawn approaching, found him still there, she would be surprised and would question him, and he had no idea what to say.

No idea what it would be safe to say or how to explain that, for the past five years, he'd practiced on her and everyone else what some might call the ultimate deception—not that he'd pretended to love her when he hadn't, but that he'd allowed everyone including her to believe that he didn't love her when he did.

That challenge and the stark realization that he had no idea how to respond to it had him easing away from her. Luckily for him, she was deeply asleep.

He turned onto his back and stared upward, unseeing, at the darkened canopy of the four-poster bed. The words she and he had exchanged yesterday afternoon, at her oldest brother's wedding breakfast, rang clearly in his head.

"I am so utterly in charity with dear Christopher. I'd virtually given up all hope that he would ever be sensible enough to choose a lady like Ellen as his bride—that he would recognize the possibilities, the prospects, even were she to appear before him, pressed upon his notice as, indeed, I gather occurred."

It hadn't been the words so much as her smugly proud tone and the depth of satisfaction in her consequent sigh that had unexpectedly pricked him on the raw and resulted in his unwise riposte: *"Perhaps your dear Christopher finally opened his eyes and took his cue from me."*

He'd immediately bitten his unruly tongue, but of course, that had been too late.

She'd taken umbrage and sought to set him right, reminding him that, as all the ton knew, she'd had to badger and hound him to the altar—or so she still believed.

He could have smoothed things over by smilingly agreeing and ascribing his gaffe to a faulty memory; she'd been expecting that and would have accepted such a retreat with nothing more than a haughty sniff. Except he'd glimpsed a species of hurt swimming behind the nearly reflective silver blue of her remarkable eyes...and he hadn't been able to stop himself from responding.

"Oops."

Such a small, inconsequential, even nonsensical word, yet given the context, his faintly taunting delivery, and her character, it had been tantamount to a red-rag invitation to pursue—to doggedly investigate his meaning until she'd uncovered all and had satisfied herself that she truly understood him. Him and their marriage.

He was confident that lure would fix her interest unswervingly on him and allow him to lead her step by carefully judged step forward until she uncovered all he'd kept hidden.

She would believe it more readily if she discovered it for herself rather than through him trying to convince her of it.

Such was his reasoning, albeit assembled after the fact.

Reviewing the events of yesterday, he realized her comment regarding Christopher having had the sense and the courage to seize love when he'd found it had been merely the last straw that had tipped Devlin over the edge of the precipice on which he'd already been teetering. Therese had been the first of her generation of Cynsters to marry, and consequently, over the past four years, he and she had attended a string of Cynster weddings up and down the country. He and she were now one of a group of couples who regularly met at family events such as Christopher and Ellen's wedding. When he'd embarked on his deception, he hadn't anticipated the impact that being surrounded by couples united in marriages based on openly acknowledged love would have on him, much less that it would rescript his view of what he wanted from his and Therese's marriage.

More than anything else, viewing the contemporary Cynster marriages against the backdrop of those of the older Cynster generation had brought home to him that, as he and Therese would inevitably grow old, he wanted to grow old like that—in an openly loving relationship.

In a marriage acknowledged as being based on reciprocated love.

Although his change of heart and mind had happened prior to yesterday, he hadn't made any definite decision about how to correct Therese's belief. He'd been vacillating for months, and yesterday afternoon, his reckless inner self, having grown increasingly impatient to the point of revolt, had seized the opportunity and taken over his tongue, resulting in his uncharacteristically impulsive pseudo revelation.

Deep inside, he'd known he'd been dragging his heels for no valid reason, and his reckless self had resolved to act for his own good. Over the years, that had happened twice in business dealings, and in both instances, his inner self had been correct; his reticence over acting was a weakness of sorts—when he knew he should do something, but kept putting it off.

He turned his head on the pillow and looked at Therese, letting his gaze linger on her features, currently relaxed in sleep.

He'd said enough to engage her legendary inquisitiveness, then aided by circumstance, had frustrated her every attempt to learn more immediately; because they'd had their children with them, she'd declared that they wouldn't stay, even overnight, at her childhood home, Walkhurst Manor in Kent, given that the bridal couple had intended to retreat there and the manor wasn't that large. Along with most of the Cynster couples attending, he, she, and the children had driven back to town, and because of the children, they'd been among the first to leave. They'd broken their journey to dine at Sevenoaks, then continued to London, arriving at Alverton House just before midnight.

Courtesy of the children and the ever-present staff, Therese hadn't been able to question him regarding what she no doubt considered his inexplicable comments, and after settling the children, she and he had retired to their respective rooms, then later, as he usually did, he'd joined her there, in her bed. In doing so, he'd made very sure that from the moment he'd walked through the door, she'd been sufficiently distracted to be unable to form coherent questions and, later, that she'd been drained of all energy and inclination to do so.

He could hear the soft sough of her breathing, quiet and steady, much as she was. Capable, reliable, steadfast, loyal; she was that and so much more.

From the instant he'd first set eyes on her—across Lady Hendricks's ballroom—he'd recognized that she had epitomized everything he wanted and needed in a wife, and so it had proved. When he'd first looked into her silver-blue eyes, he'd known beyond question that his life had, in that moment, irrevocably and inescapably changed. He'd loved her—had fallen in love with her—completely and utterly, just as, thank all the saints, she had fallen in love with him.

He blinked into the darkness. Arrogant of him, wasn't it, to be so certain of that? He'd never encouraged her to say the words, given he'd been so set on not admitting to the same sentiment in return, yet...

While he couldn't know with absolute certainty what she currently felt for him, his knowledge of the female of the species assured him that the glory they habitually shared in that very bed—an outcome that, despite his extensive prior experience, he'd only ever attained with her— was a manifestation of the emotion that, regardless of his deception and her obliviousness of his truth, lived inside them both.

Now that he'd cracked open the door on his most deeply held secret and invited her to explore, in the same way that he'd initially plotted to keep her—his otherwise highly observant wife—from perceiving his true state, he was going to have to tread warily in crafting their way forward.

The first step in any such plan was, unquestionably, to get up and leave her bed. Now, before she awoke and found him still there. As part of his pretense that, on his part, their marriage was entirely conventional rather than a love-match, he'd never been there, beside her, when she woke. He always left her sleeping, and as far as she knew, he spent the better part of every night in his own bed. As she slept soundly and he always made sure she was boneless and pleasurably enervated prior to her slipping into slumber, she had no idea that he rarely left her side until dawn drew near.

While the sun had yet to rise, dawn wasn't that far off. He forced himself to adhere to the script he'd written and ease from the bed. Immediately, he regretted the loss of her warmth. Lips setting, he shrugged on his robe and belted it, then quietly left via the connecting door that led to his apartments.

Once in his bedroom, rather than crawl between his cold sheets, he walked to the window, drew back the heavy curtains, and looked across Park Lane to the trees in the park beyond. Leaves still clung to the branches of the old oaks, and a fine mist was slowly thickening, draping the nearly skeletal canopies with insubstantial wisps.

He stared out at the chilly sight while the reasons that had driven him to conceal his love scrolled through his mind. His parents and their marriage. And more recently, that of his best friend. At the time of his and Therese's wedding, his reasons had seemed sound, undeniable, and self-evident, and the decision he'd made incontrovertibly correct.

As a young boy, he believed he'd seen first-hand the injuries that could be inflicted on a man, even one of strong character, who, having fallen in love with a lady of resolutely determined personality, made the mistake of acknowledging that love to its object. To his younger self, his parents' marriage had served as a stark lesson in what could happen to a gentleman unwise enough to admit that he loved a strong-willed wife of managing disposition. In his eyes, his mother had lorded it over his father, taking his love, regard, and support for granted and frequently riding roughshod over his pride and his standing, belittling and diminishing him before their staff and their children. His father had never protested or reined his mother in, and times without number, Devlin had seen him swallow his pride and accede to her dictates. Devlin had been forced to stand and watch, impotent to do anything to lessen the impact as, in his eyes, his mother's undermining had only grown worse and more hurtful with the years, albeit only in private. To the world, the previous Earl and Countess of Alverton had been a devoted couple.

Then Devlin's close friend James, Viscount Hemmings, had married a virago, purely and openly for love. Despite the fact that everyone agreed James and Veronica were madly in love, they never ceased sniping at each other. If Devlin had needed a further lesson in the dangers inherent in a marriage between a gentleman of his ilk and a strong-willed lady being openly anchored in love, the Hemmingses had provided it.

His experience of his parents' marriage and his observation of the Hemmingses' union would have made him eschew the institution of marriage altogether, except that then, he'd succeeded to the earldom, and all the ton had expected him to marry and secure the succession. Admittedly, if he'd remained a bachelor until he died, his younger brother, Melrose, seven years his junior, would have stepped into the earl's shoes, but neither Devlin nor Melrose nor, indeed, anyone else had deemed that a wise course to follow; currently twenty-nine years old, Melrose had shown no sign of settling down or becoming serious about anything at all.

Consequently, when Devlin had first locked eyes with Therese and recognized that she held out the promise of all he would ever want and need in a wife, he'd seized her. Despite her already well-established reputation of being strong-willed to the point of ruthlessness, despite her being in every possible way the epitome of the sort of lady he'd been determined above all others to avoid. Despite her being the very last lady he should have considered offering for, with one look—one fateful look —she'd changed his mind.

But she hadn't changed his mind about allowing her to know that he loved her.

Prior to yesterday, he'd never let her glimpse even the slightest hint of his true regard.

Staring at the mist now blanketing the park, he grimaced. He'd thought himself so very clever, and indeed, he had been. He'd used her own self-conviction to steer her beliefs, subtly guiding her interpretation of what she saw. She was so confident in her own abilities to observe, understand, and manage, it had never occurred to her that, in him, she'd met her master—or at least, someone equally adept and rather more duplicitous.

Now, he faced unpicking and reforging the web of beliefs he'd encouraged her to create, the framework of understanding on which their marriage was based. And he had to—absolutely had to—manage that task without destabilizing the edifice that now rested upon that foundation. He did not want to damage—not in any way—what they already had, both the ease of interaction that had evolved over the years and the calm, ordered, settled existence that he, she, their children, and their households enjoyed. He was well aware the latter owed much to Therese's managing disposition; she was adept at organizing so that everyone and everything ran smoothly and efficiently, to the point that the tranquil atmosphere that prevailed within his households was the envy of many of his peers.

In moving forward, impulsively or otherwise, he didn't want to risk harming the relationship they already had, yet if he'd learned anything from his years of successfully investing in new industries, it was that, sometimes, risks were well worth taking.

His exposure to the marriages of her cousins, his awareness of the benefits that flowed from the acknowledgment of mutual love—the joy, the unfettered happiness and unrestrained sharing, the closeness that was so much more evocative and enthralling—had tempted, then seduced, until he'd finally swallowed his pride, accepted his innermost truth, and admitted that if there was any chance of claiming that sort of marriage for himself and Therese, then he was willing to fight for it, willing to sacrifice to achieve that goal.

How much, if anything, he might have to sacrifice wasn't at all clear, but with his unwise words of yesterday, he'd taken the first irretrievable step toward claiming the sort of marriage that, were it not for his reservations over admitting to love, might have been theirs for the past five years.

Eyes narrowing, he gazed out at the fog that now obscured the park. He hadn't had to woo Therese; instead, he'd manipulated her into persuading him to the altar. It would be up to him to manage this transition as well, and as he wished to succeed in that delicate endeavor, he was going to need a plan—a carefully thought-out campaign to convince his wife of five years that he loved her as much as she loved him.

The morning was well advanced when Therese finally opened her eyes. She blinked, then turned onto her back, confirming that, as always, Devlin had left long ago; when she passed her palm over the sheet, it held no lingering warmth.

On a nevertheless sated sigh, with the memories of shared pleasures making her smile, she stretched her arms over her head, then snuggled them back beneath the covers. Staring up at the canopy of lilac silk, she reviewed the events of the previous day. Her smile widened as she remembered Christopher and Ellen's transparent happiness; she'd been so delighted to see the pair so patently in love.

Then she recalled Devlin's odd comments. Her smile faded as she re-examined them. She ended frowning.

On the journey back to London, she'd replayed those comments countless times and still had no clue what he'd meant.

She knew her husband; he wasn't given to making abstruse comments. "So what the devil did he mean?"

In her mind, she recreated those moments when he and she had stood by the side of the Bigfield House ballroom. She'd been fondly observing Christopher and Ellen moving among the crowd. Devlin had been standing beside her—now she thought of it, he'd stuck by her side through most of the day—so he'd been there to hear her sigh happily and commend Christopher on his good sense in recognizing the possibilities for happiness that Ellen represented and acting and marrying her.

Looking back...it seemed that something about either her sigh or her comment had provoked Devlin into saying, *"Perhaps your dear Christopher finally opened his eyes and took his cue from me."*

She frowned direfully at the lilac silk. "That still makes absolutely no sense."

After examining the words yet again, along with his intonation and every other little clue she'd learned over the past five years that could help clarify her husband's thinking, she still found herself utterly at sea.

"Nonsense." She wrestled the covers more tightly about her and frowned even harder. Not only was she confused, she was confused over being confused; normally, she encountered no difficulty interpreting Devlin's utterances.

Even more discombobulating had been his response when she'd challenged him to explain. Instead of laughingly admitting he'd forgotten that it had been she who had dragged him to the altar rather than the other way around, he'd met her gaze and, with an odd light in his greeny-hazel eyes, had smiled in a rather strange way and, quite deliberately, said, *"Oops."*

Therese heard that single syllable resonate in her mind and narrowed her eyes to slits. Abruptly, she shook her head, thrust back the covers, and electing to consign her handsome husband's almost certainly deliberately confusing utterances to the darkest recess of her mind, all but leapt from the bed.

The chill of the late-autumn morning struck through the fine silk of her nightgown, and she grabbed her robe from the chair on which it lay. Shrugging into the woolen robe, she hurried across the carpeted floor to the bellpull and tugged it, summoning Parker, her dresser, with her washing water.

Therese belted the robe and went to the window. Grasping the curtains in both hands, she drew them wide, revealing a view over the rose garden at the side of the house. It was foggy outside. She stared down at what was usually a calming sight and heard in her mind, once again, *"Oops."*

Their children frequently used the word, as did Devlin when dealing with them. Invariably, he used it to denote a mistake, often a deliberate or cheeky one.

Therese folded her arms beneath her breasts. "So where in that short exchange did he make a mistake of that nature?"

In suggesting an equivalence between how their marriage and Christopher's had come about?

Judging by the bare words, that seemed the obvious answer, but no matter how often she replayed the words as Devlin had said them, especially the way he'd said that *oops* with that certain light in his eyes, she couldn't convince herself that was what he'd meant.

Every word that had fallen from his lips had been definite and deliberate, and he'd been watching her intently throughout. No, he'd meant something other than the obvious, and she was increasingly certain that his *oops* hadn't been any indication that he was backing down or resiling from what he had said.

"Annoying man!" Especially as, the more she replayed that *oops* in her head, the more it sounded like a leading comment. A teasing lure, an invitation to play some game with him, but she had no idea what game that might be, and she wasn't at all happy about that.

A tap fell on the door, and Parker came in, followed by the tweeny hefting a porcelain jug of hot water.

By the time Parker looked Therese's way, she'd wiped the frown from her face. She nodded equably to the dresser. "I've an at-home this morning and two this afternoon. My rose-silk day gown might be best."

Banishing her husband's annoying *oops* from her mind, she focused on getting ready to face her day.

∾

Therese walked into the breakfast parlor and wasn't surprised to find it empty.

Portland, the butler, held her usual chair for her. As she sat, he murmured, "His lordship breakfasted earlier, ma'am, and has gone riding in the park."

Having expected as much, she picked up her napkin and flicked it out. "Thank you, Portland." She glanced at the well-stocked sideboard. "Just tea and toast, please." She weakened and added, "And perhaps some of Cook's strawberry jam."

"Of course, ma'am."

While Portland whisked away to fetch her tea, she found herself gazing at Devlin's empty chair. She wished now that she'd held firm to her intention of the previous night and questioned him the instant he'd entered her room. Unfortunately, when that moment had come, it hadn't seemed an appropriate one in which to commence a wifely interrogation. Aside from all else, she still found Devlin, nude, immensely distracting, so even if she'd managed to get a question out, she would likely not have remembered his answer.

Portland returned with the teapot, a rack of warm toast, a dish of creamy butter, and another holding rich strawberry jam. She smiled and thanked him, poured herself a cup of tea, then set about slathering a slice of toast with butter and jam.

Lifting the slice to her lips, she crunched, chewed, and staring unseeing across the table, reminded herself of the reality of her marriage.

Although from their first meeting she'd recognized that Devlin was attracted to her, she'd never deceived herself by imagining he loved her. Nor had she assumed that he would somehow, over time, come to love her; she'd viewed that as unlikely, and nothing over the past five years had changed her mind.

She'd approached finding a husband—the right husband for her—in her customary, organized, methodical fashion. She'd accepted that being a Cynster, it was possible, even likely, that she would be struck by what her brothers and male cousins labeled "the Cynster curse," an apparently inescapable compulsion that ensured that every Cynster married for love. Consequently, from her first forays into society, she had evaluated every likely gentleman who crossed her path, expecting that, eventually, she would find the right man and fall in love.

While the Cynster curse was assumed to result in a mutual love-match, and she knew it most often had, as far as she could see, there was nothing in the words "a Cynster always marries for love" that stated that said love was guaranteed to be returned. She'd gone into her own search with an open mind, but by the time, at age twenty-one, she'd embarked on her third Season, she'd learned a great deal about herself and about how the gentlemen of the ton viewed her. She'd overheard enough comments, and over the years, those comments had only grown more definite and accepted; she was too prickly, too strong-willed, too much her own person, and most damaging of all, too managing. She'd been considered "too" in far too many ways to be viewed by tonnish gentlemen as a desirable parti; she'd never been destined to be a comfortable wife.

But then she'd met Devlin and had been smitten by a force so powerful that not for one minute had she doubted what it was. She'd fallen in love in a minute—in a blink, truth be told—and that had been that. And while she'd never fooled herself that he'd loved her—certainly not in the same compulsive, ungovernable way that she'd loved him—in every other respect, he'd been more than eligible, and from that first meeting, she'd set about convincing him that she was the perfect wife for him.

He'd required months of persuading, of her hunting and hounding him and, eventually, badgering him, but eventually, he'd agreed to wed her, and ever since, they had—as she'd predicted—rubbed along very well. He might not love her, but he was fond of her and invariably treated her with a gentle, sometimes faintly amused, but always steadfast affection that she found soothing and comforting. Over time, to her, he'd come to represent a safe harbor against all of life's storms.

That was how their marriage had come about, so why had Devlin suggested that Christopher's motivation in marrying Ellen had mirrored Devlin's in marrying Therese?

She frowned and crunched the last of her toast. "That makes no sense." She blinked. "Unless…"

Unless in comparing Christopher to himself, Devlin had been referring to some other attribute of marriage.

"Of course." In her mind, Therese once again replayed the scene at the wedding breakfast, heard again Devlin's words, and finally felt the irritation of not knowing what he'd meant dissipate. "That's it!" Satisfied, she picked up her teacup, sat back, and sipped.

Devlin had been referring to the undeniable benefits of a ton marriage —having a hostess, someone to run his households, a mother for his children, and so on—all the reasons that had contributed to him marrying her. As a married gentleman who hadn't been motivated by love, of course he'd focused on those other incentives.

With her gaze fixed on his empty chair across the table, she sipped again, then nodded sagely. "That explains his *oops*." He hadn't been referring to a mistake he'd made but the mistake *she'd* made in thinking his comment referred to love.

She ran his comments through her mind one last time, studying them through the prism of her new insight, and nodded decisively. "That fits."

Feeling as if she'd finally fought free of a constricting web, she set down the teacup and turned her mind to her day.

In reviewing her schedule, she had to admit that in terms of the material and concomitant benefits of marriage, by any yardstick, as Devlin's wife, she had no grounds for complaint—and he'd never suggested he was in any way dissatisfied, either. Overall, in all ways, her life was proceeding exactly as she'd fashioned it, with the reins firmly in her grasp.

Except, of course, for Devlin himself. Somehow, he always contrived to remain just beyond her managing reach. She knew it and knew he did, too. Sometimes, she surprised a look on his face that made her think he viewed her efforts to manage him—for of course, she still tried—with fond amusement, as if her seeking to direct him made him strangely content even while he thwarted every attempt except for those with which he agreed, to which he readily acquiesced.

She huffed and sat up. One thing she'd learned over the past five years was that her handsome husband was a law unto himself. She'd concluded that she simply didn't understand him well enough to properly manage him, yet he always treated her, their children, the staff, and all their people well, and regarding his overall behavior, she had no wish to change anything.

She frowned and pushed back her chair. She just wished he hadn't spoken so cryptically. She'd wasted a great deal of time and energy puzzling over a comment that, now she understood it, would normally have caused her not a moment of bother.

At least all that was behind her. As Portland drew back her chair, she rose, smiled her thanks, and headed for the morning room to deal with the first duties of her day.

~

As she often did, Therese joined the children in the nursery while they ate their luncheon. She didn't manage it every day, but the children looked forward to her being there so they could share the excitements of their morning's activities while, under Nanny Sprockett's instruction, they attempted to feed themselves with something approaching acceptable table manners.

Balancing little Horatia—named for her great-grandmother and known as Horry by all—on her knee, Therese gently guided the eighteen-month-old poppet's hand as she stubbornly fought to master a fork.

"My hoop went fastest!" Spencer, a robust four-year-old, declared, puffing out his chest.

Rupert, Spencer's junior by a year, smiled at his brother and amiably added, "Mine was right behind."

Therese smiled at her sons. Along with their nursemaids, the trio had returned from an outing in the park only minutes before, and their chubby cheeks were still rosy from the cold, and their hair was tousled and windswept. Both boys had inherited their father's coloring—hazel eyes and dark-brown hair—while Therese had been informed by her mother and aunts that Horry was an exact copy of Therese at that age, with still-baby-fluffy golden-blond curls, porcelain cheeks, and large pale-blue eyes.

While encouraging the trio to eat, Therese listened to their prattle and endeavored to keep her attention fixed on them and not allow her mind to slide sideways and continue to poke and pick at her conclusions regarding Devlin's irritating comment. It was driving her demented. She'd solved the puzzle, so why wouldn't her mind simply let the exasperating incident go?

Suddenly, the boys looked across at the open door, and their faces lit with eagerness. Therese knew what caused that look; she turned her head and watched as Devlin, smiling at them all, strolled into the room.

It truly was unfair; even after five years of marriage, he still effort-lessly compelled her awareness. Her gaze skated avidly over his face—the aristocratic planes and distractingly mobile lips—and down over his tall, lean frame, dwelling on the ineffable elegance of his coat, waistcoat, and trousers and drinking in the predatory grace that was an intrinsic part of him.

He crossed to where she, the children, and Nanny Sprockett sat about the low table. He directed a vague nod at the hovering nursemaids, then ruffled both boys' hair before crouching beside them.

He grinned at Horry, who was bouncing up and down in Therese's lap, chanting, "Da, da, da" and manically waving her chubby, sticky hands. Devlin reached out and, adroitly avoiding her grabby fingers, ran the back of one finger down his daughter's soft cheek, setting the little girl gurgling with happiness, then he turned to his sons and asked what adventures they'd had that morning.

Therese seized the moment to encourage Horry to finish her chicken and chase down the last of her peas.

After listening to his sons' report, Devlin glanced at Therese, then said to the boys, "Eat up now, because I've been sent to steal your mama away for her own luncheon, and you know she'll be happier if you can show her clean plates before she leaves."

Both boys shot Therese a grin and obligingly fell to, quickly polishing off their main courses before moving on to devour their puddings.

Therese concentrated on helping Horry spoon the gooey blancmange into her small mouth while wondering if Devlin's words meant that he would be joining her for luncheon. She assumed so. He didn't often eat luncheon at home but, apparently, intended to do so today.

She considered using the opportunity to confirm her conclusions regarding his exasperating comment and what had occasioned his *oops*, but perversely, given her continuing obsession with those comments, something in her shied from addressing his meaning directly with him—as if questioning him on that subject might make him think that she was wondering anew about the basis of their marriage. About whether that had changed.

But she knew it hadn't, and she didn't need to hear him say so.

Thrusting all such thoughts deep, she beamed at Horry, who was delighted to have uncovered the bottom of her pudding bowl and was hitting it enthusiastically with her spoon. Therese cooed and deftly removed the spoon and dropped it into the bowl, then she pressed a kiss to Horry's curls and, catching the eye of one of the nursemaids, hefted Horry up and handed the little girl, now happily squealing, into the nursemaid's care.

While chatting with his sons, Devlin had been watching Therese closely. He'd seen the shifting hues crossing the silvery blue of her eyes; like shadows passing over a reflective surface, they indicated that, despite her occupation, she was thinking of other things.

He hoped she was thinking of his comment of yesterday and, most especially, his *oops*.

Across their sons' heads, he met her eyes and smiled, then he rose, patted heads all around, and offered her his hand.

She placed her fingers in his, and he reminded himself not to seize too firmly. He closed his hand and, in ordinary, gentlemanly fashion, drew her to her feet. Once upright, she retrieved her hand, and he was forced to release it. After shaking her skirts straight, she farewelled the boys, blew a kiss to Horry, then preceded him to the open door.

He followed her into the corridor, and they strolled side by side toward the main stairs. "Portland assured me that the soup would remain warm, but I gather he and the staff are waiting."

"I hadn't realized it was so late. I'd forgotten that, given the season, I'd moved the time for luncheon forward."

He glanced at her and waited. When she gave no sign of seizing the moment to launch into an inquisition, he cast about for some innocuous topic. "What are your plans for the rest of the day?"

They reached the stairs and started down.

Head high, she replied, "This afternoon, I have two at-homes that I must show my face at, and after that, if the weather holds, I'll probably spend a short time in the park."

"And this evening?"

"Thankfully, the balls are tapering off, but Lady Walton is hosting a soirée that she'll expect me to attend."

He guessed, "She's a friend of your mother's?"

"More a close acquaintance. But Mama mentioned the soirée and, as she's at Somersham, suggested I should go and wave the flag, as it were."

"I see." He recalled meeting Lord Walton at a railway investors' meeting.

They reached the front hall, stepped off the stairs, and turned toward the family dining parlor—a far smaller, more intimate room than the house's main dining room, which could easily seat fifty.

Devlin saw Therese to her chair at the nearer end of the six-person table, then moved to claim the carver at its head. As soon as he sat, Portland, who had been hovering, swooped in with the soup tureen.

When, assured that one serving would be sufficient for each of them, Portland departed to carry the tureen back to the kitchen, leaving them with only Dennis, the footman, as witness, Devlin glanced down the table and waited for Therese to marshal her thoughts and commence her interrogation. He was perfectly aware that, when it came to anything to do with him, her curiosity was unbounded.

She was silent for so long, he started to wonder if something else was wrong, but then she looked up and met his eyes. "I've been meaning to ask..."

At last! He widened his eyes in invitation.

"Whether you've concluded your business dealings with the firms at the exhibition." She set down her soupspoon, laced her fingers, and looked at him inquiringly. "It's supposed to end soon, isn't it?"

He blinked, then acknowledged that the so-called Great Exhibition currently filling Joseph Paxton's Crystal Palace, presently sited within Hyde Park, was due to shut its doors in ten days' time.

"I heard they intend to dismantle the palace and move it. Is that true?"

He nodded. "To Sydenham. Paxton designed the structure so it could easily be taken apart and reassembled." And why was he discussing engineering with his wife, who ought to have been curious about something quite different?

Her expression in no way suggested she was overwhelmed by personal curiosity. "I daresay there'll be a great deal of activity in the park over the following days." She tipped her head as if considering the prospect, then looked up as Portland returned bearing a platter of sliced roast beef. "I must remember to mention the dismantling of the palace to Nanny. I'm sure the boys would like to see it."

Portland smiled benevolently and offered Devlin the platter.

Devlin helped himself to the meat and to the vegetables Dennis duly offered. Then he followed Therese's lead and addressed the food on his plate, but he was having trouble swallowing the notion that his avidly inquisitive wife was entirely uninterested in pursuing his deliberately provocative comments of the previous day.

While they ate, via a series of adroit questions, she steered the conversation down various avenues connected with the exhibition. He held up his end of the exchange, but as it went on, he felt increasingly off balance.

He hadn't expected her to take this tack. He knew beyond question that she wouldn't have forgotten what he'd said; he hadn't imagined he might have to prompt her to address it.

The meal ended without him detecting the slightest sign that she was battling to suppress an urge to question him. She rose, and he joined her, and they strolled toward the front hall.

She smiled serenely as if she had not a care in the world. "I'd better head off on my afternoon calls."

Devlin halted. Realizing he'd stopped, she halted and looked at him, her brows rising in transparently mild query.

He managed not to clench his jaw. "I realize that yesterday, at the wedding breakfast, I replied to a question of yours in a rather elliptical manner."

Her chin rose a fraction; in the dimmer light of the corridor, he couldn't read her eyes. "Ah—your *oops?*"

He nodded, and his uneasiness grew as a tight, rather sharp smile curved her lips.

"You thought I'd be bothered by it, enough to be insatiably curious?" She still sounded unperturbed, almost faintly amused.

He suddenly felt on uncertain ground and didn't appreciate the sensation. After a moment, he admitted, "Curious, at least."

Her expression dissolved into a more relaxed smile, one he wasn't sure he believed. Reaching out, she patted his arm reassuringly. "I don't need to wonder and speculate, especially not about our marriage." She met his eyes, and hers held what appeared to be genuine assurance. "I know exactly what you meant."

He eyed her with increasing trepidation. "You do?"

She nodded. "Clearly, you thought that in marrying Ellen, Christopher had been driven by the same reasons that motivated you to marry me, namely to secure the generally acknowledged benefits of the married state." Her lashes veiled her eyes, and she arched her brows. "As we both know how our marriage came about, obviously, my subsequent questions —my assumption—was the *oops*, the mistake to which you referred. I'd misread what you were alluding to as the motivating force that drove Christopher to marriage."

His mind racing, Devlin searched for some way of salvaging his first step.

Therese's smile returned, and she leaned closer to confide, "Don't worry. You didn't flummox me—I worked it out." She patted his arm again, then turned away. "And now I must be off, or I'll be late to Lady Kettering's at-home."

In a state of utter disbelief, Devlin stood in the corridor and watched as, with a swish of her silk skirts, his exasperating wife swanned off.

∽

Devlin stalked into his study and carefully shut the door. After a moment, he walked to the large leather chair behind the desk and dropped into it.

Faintly stunned, he reviewed what had just occurred. "Damn!" He was looking at the complete and utter failure of what he'd fondly imagined would be an easy, if impulsively instigated, first step in guiding Therese along the path to realizing that he loved her.

"Huh."

Although her interpretation of his words hadn't occurred to him, he could see how she'd come to her conclusion. Unfortunately, that she'd sought and found a different explanation rather than even suspect his truth didn't bode well for her readily following any subtle hints he might make.

Oops.

He'd made a mistake, true enough. He'd thought he would be able to use the same approach he'd employed five years ago and, by giving her a tantalizingly oblique clue and engaging her curiosity, lead her to ferret out the truth. He knew he was correct in thinking she would believe in his love if she uncovered it herself, but clearly, that approach was doomed.

Doomed by his success in convincing her that he *didn't* love her.

In his mind's eye, he replayed the recent scene. Something about it had made him uneasy. Several minutes passed before he identified what that was—her tone and the way she hadn't quite met his eyes while she'd explained what he'd meant by his unwise, impulsive words.

Brittle was the description that leapt to mind. That, along with a certain vulnerability.

He shifted in the chair. He didn't like to think he might have hurt her in any way yet... He forced himself to look again, to relive the moment and look deeply and searchingly, then softly swore.

He closed his eyes. He'd acted impulsively and hadn't thought his actions through. By essentially forcing her to examine the reasons she believed were behind their marriage, he'd forced her to face and acknowledge what she thought was the truth, namely that he didn't love her.

Vulnerable. He'd made her feel vulnerable; that was what had been behind the brittleness he'd sensed.

He knew all about the vulnerability caused by love, by owning to love; at base, such love-induced vulnerability was the reason he had for so long refused to admit that he loved her.

Ironic, perhaps, but where did that leave them? Leave him?

"Obviously," he muttered, "I'm going to have to be much more careful and exercise more caution over triggering any adverse feelings." *That* was going to require a greater degree of finesse and attention to detail than he'd hitherto employed.

After he'd spent several minutes castigating himself over his clumsiness in provoking that unintended reaction, it occurred to him that her still feeling vulnerable over her belief that he didn't love her was, in fact, reassuring. "At least she still loves me." If she didn't, she wouldn't feel that way.

One positive outcome from my first disastrous attempt to rescript our relationship.

He considered anew. Although the fragility he'd sensed beneath her customary steely armor haunted him, given it arose out of her love for him, it wasn't, of itself, something he wanted to change. It wasn't a symptom he wished to eradicate, not that he could.

What he did wish to erase was the cause, namely, her entrenched belief that he didn't love her in return. Once he'd achieved that, her current wariness and uncertainty over openly showing her love for him would vanish, along, he hoped, with that dreadful vulnerability.

He'd already constructed a mental picture of what success would look like—Therese gloriously confident in her love for him and openly showing it, bolstered and supported by the absolute and unassailable knowledge that her love was fully and completely reciprocated, that he loved her as she loved him.

Essentially, him and her in a Cynster-style marriage.

That was the goal he was determined to achieve, to claim for them both.

He looked inward and found nothing but rock-solid determination and unflinching resolve.

He drew in a breath and shifted to a more comfortable position. "So, how?"

In theory, he could sit her down and explain the truth of his feelings for her. In essence, that was what his ill-fated *oops* had been about—getting her to question him and drag the truth from him.

That, she would have believed. Him simply telling her...wouldn't work. He'd done too good a job of convincing her that she knew his mind and, more importantly, his heart regarding her. Overwriting a belief he'd spent more than five years instilling and underscoring couldn't be done with mere words.

If he tried to simply tell her his truth...not only did he doubt she would believe him, but worse, such an attempt would almost certainly lead her to distrust him. She would unquestionably wonder what he was up to, and he shuddered to think what she might conclude.

While he might have deceived her by omission, by all the things he hadn't said, he'd never directly lied to her, and he would infinitely prefer to keep it that way.

His fingers found a pencil, and he idly tapped the end on his blotter. "So if words aren't a viable way forward…"

Eyes narrowing, he thought and imagined, weighing the possibilities. Given it had been he who had shaped their marriage into its current form, if he wanted that form to change, then plainly, it fell to him to do whatever was needed. "Whatever I need to do to open her eyes to the truth that I love her and always have."

Hearing the words helped him focus. He could, he decided, leave the somewhat damning revelation of *when* he'd fallen in love with her until later. The essential first step to achieving his desired goal was to convince his wife of the past five years that he loved her *now*. Today.

Given her character and his, the only approach that might work, that held any real hope of convincing her that her view of his feelings toward her was wrong, was to show her—to demonstrate the reality. She was highly observant and needle-witted; she would believe what she could unequivocally see.

He considered the prospect for several long minutes, then, resolved, tapped the pencil one last time and let it fall. "Actions always speak louder and truer than words."

CHAPTER 2

*J*ust after nine o'clock that evening, Therese finished greeting Lord and Lady Walton and moved on into their drawing room.

Therese paused and swiftly scanned the crowd. Her ladyship was well known for inviting a wide range of interesting people to her events. From social mavens to parliamentarians, from critics and bluestockings to masters of finance and business leaders, one never knew whom one might meet at Walton House. Tonight, there were few faces to which Therese couldn't put a name. The chandeliers threw soft light over glossy heads and elegant gowns, striking gleams from jewels and laying a subtle luster on countless pearls, all set against the backdrop of the severe black of gentlemen's evening coats. All in all, the sight left her feeling comfortable and assured, and the ambiance beckoned.

It was in no way unusual for matrons of her age and station to attend such events without their husbands or other companions. In her gown of figured lilac silk, with her hair swept up but allowed to softly frame her face and with the Alverton diamonds blazing about her throat and dangling from her earlobes, she was entirely as one with the crowd, and with a confident smile curving her lips, she glided through the guests to join a group of other young matrons whose lives were similar to her own.

She arrived in time to hear Georgiana, Lady Sheldrake, say, "My Thomas has just discovered the joy of tugging—he races around pulling every rope, cord, string, or tie he can reach. He's even taken to escaping the nursery to find more things to pull. My butler despairs. Every time he walks into a room, it's to discover the curtain cords have vanished."

"Better something so innocuous as curtain cords," Emily, Lady Pritchard, replied. "I still have nightmares over the months during which Cedric became obsessed with tugging necklines and trying to peer inside. You can imagine how that played out when my mother-in-law brought her bosom-bows to visit to show off her eldest grandson."

The other ladies laughed, which Emily took as her due, then she blandly added, "I did ask Pritchard whether he'd been teaching his heir bad habits, but he denied it."

Everyone chuckled, and the conversation rolled on; initially a running commentary on their children and households, gradually, the shared observations shifted focus to those of the ton still in London, what the latest gossip regarding political maneuverings was, and whether anyone had heard more about the latest scandal engulfing the business world.

Eventually, satisfied that she'd learned all her closest acquaintances could tell her and having contributed various social tidbits of her own, Therese left the group and wended through the knots of guests to join another circle of acquaintances. She paused beside a tallish lady with burnished brown hair and tapped her arm.

Veronica, Viscountess Hemmings, turned her head, saw Therese, and her face lit. "Therese, my dear! Well met."

Therese smiled as she and Veronica clasped fingers. "I wondered if I might find you here."

The tall, rakishly handsome gentleman on Veronica's other side leaned forward to smile and half bow. "Therese."

Still smiling, Therese nodded back. "My lord." James, Viscount Hemmings, was one of Devlin's oldest friends, and somewhat to Therese's surprise—and possibly James's as well—given he'd married Veronica, with whom Therese had been acquainted since girlhood, she, James, and Veronica had become established friends.

James glanced over the heads in the direction from which Therese had come. "No Devlin, I take it."

"I believe he's attending a business dinner in the City," Therese replied. Devlin occasionally attended social events, usually by her side, but by and large, he preferred to leave it to her to maintain their wider social presence, a normal arrangement for couples of their standing. Smiling easily as she acknowledged the other two ladies and three gentlemen in their circle, she shrugged aside the niggling thought that she wouldn't have minded Devlin making time to attend more social func-tions—and that she was just a touch jealous of the way James was constantly to be found at Veronica's side.

Admittedly, James's hovering came with repercussions of which Therese was well aware, but a relationship that landed midway between overly possessive and distant would, she thought, be rather nice.

There were often times in social situations when she wished Devlin was beside her to share observations and insights; strange to say, he was the person whose views most closely mirrored her own.

Such unproductive mooning was something she rarely indulged in; that wasn't how their marriage worked.

Her social smile firmly in place, she turned to the gentleman on her right, who had just joined their circle.

She didn't recognize him, not at all, which was unusual enough to make her take extra note. He was tall—as tall as Devlin—with a similar lean and rangy build. His features were blatantly aristocratic, with a patri-cian nose, well-defined cheekbones, and a squarish chin. Glossy, light-brown hair fell in fashionably cut waves, and his eyes, as they briefly met hers, were a curious shade of amber.

Well dressed, aristocratic—Therese felt she should know him.

The stranger's gaze had fixed on James; he nodded as James glanced his way. "Hemmings."

A light, social smile on his lips, one that told Therese absolutely noth-ing, James inclined his head. "Child."

Therese blinked and looked again at the stranger. *Child?* Her mind raced, assembling everything she knew about the noble family who held the Duchy of Ancaster and whose principal seat bordered that of the earldom of Alverton.

As if aware of her scrutiny and the reasons behind it, Child threw a faintly amused look her way as he said, clearly speaking to Hemmings, "Perhaps, old son, you might do the honors and introduce me."

"Of course." Smoothly, James named those in the circle, commencing with Therese, then Veronica, and continuing until he reached Child and said, "Allow me to present Lord Grayson Child."

Various bells clanged in Therese's head.

Child exchanged nods with the gentlemen and half bowed to Veronica and the other two ladies, then turned the full force of his undoubted charm on Therese and bowed with a touch more deference. "Countess."

Therese smiled serenely and gave him her hand. As he took it and bowed again, she said, "I'm acquainted with your parents."

Child straightened a fraction more quickly than elegance dictated.

Before he could decide how to reply, she arched her brows. "Am I to take it the prodigal son has returned?"

Veronica was listening, as was James. The rest of the circle had started chatting about something else.

Child assumed an easy, self-deprecating smile. "I'm not sure I warrant the label of prodigal. I merely departed for greener pastures, and after several years spent in America, I decided it was time to return." He glanced around. "I have to say that, despite my lengthy absence, I'm relieved to discover that I still feel quite at home in this milieu."

Therese returned his smile. "How reassuring for you. I have to admit I'm quite curious as to what prompted your departure. It was, if memory serves, more than a mere 'several years' ago."

Having had it confirmed which Child he was, she was intrigued. Grayson Child had been Devlin's closest childhood friend. As noble neighbors of the same age, the pair had grown up together, attended Eton together, and subsequently gone to Oxford, although there, they'd attended different colleges and, she understood, had drifted apart. James and Cedric Marshall, now Devlin's closest friends, had been at Eton, too, and had attended Balliol alongside Devlin.

"Well," Child allowed, "I suppose it was…" His brows rose as if he was calculating, then he looked faintly surprised. "Nine years ago."

That explained why Therese had never met him; she'd still been in the schoolroom nine years ago.

"And you've been in America for all those years?" She recalled whispers that Child's and Devlin's rivalry had been intense and had extended into their twenties, through the years they'd spent as well-heeled bachelors on the town; she could imagine how such a rivalry might have played out.

Child focused on her face, a hint of wariness sliding behind his eyes. "More or less."

"What drew you there?" She kept her tone light, couching her questions as if they were merely the usual social exchange. "Given you remained for so long, presumably you found much to hold your interest."

He paused for a second, then smiled, overtly charming once again. "As to what drew me there, that's easily answered—adventure and the promise of a sort of excitement quite different to what one finds here. As to what I found of interest, in a country blazing so many new frontiers, there was always some new venture afoot, and I discovered I thrived on a diet of fresh challenges."

The last words were said with an undercurrent of meaning that Therese pretended not to hear.

But before she could respond and tease out more information, Child glibly inquired, "Speaking of challenges, I see you've taken on the role of Devlin's countess."

Therese wasn't about to discuss her marriage, not in any fashion, with a gentleman who might still see himself as her husband's rival. "Indeed," she replied repressively, then continued in social vein, "The duke and duchess must have been delighted to welcome you home. Did you find them well?"

With her gaze fixed on Child's face, she caught the momentary flash of chagrin before he hid it behind a faintly bored mask.

"I have to admit," he said, "that I've only just arrived in the country, and although I did travel to Ancaster Park, my parents are away in Scotland, so the fatted calf has yet to be slain."

"And you returned to town?" Therese widened her eyes. "Given the season and your years overseas, I would have thought you might have indulged in some country pursuits—for instance, some shooting and hunting."

She all but saw the notion of saying he was, in fact, hunting pass through his mind. She leapt in to suggest, "But perhaps the exhibits at the Crystal Palace lured you back to town?"

A slight widening of his eyes told her that she'd guessed aright even before he inclined his head. "Just so. It seemed foolish to pass up the opportunity to assess what new ideas the world has to offer. Prince Albert is to be commended for backing such an undertaking."

"Were there any exhibits you found of especial interest?" Therese was fairly certain Devlin would be interested in knowing. James was listening avidly, too.

Looking faintly harassed, Child opened his mouth, then his gaze went past Therese, and he paused. A second later, a smile of genuine delight curved his lips. "Devlin's just arrived."

Therese blinked. "He has?" She turned to look.

Child hadn't been mistaken; Devlin was making his way across the room, stopping here and there to exchange greetings, but not dallying in beating what was clearly a deliberate path to her side.

When, with Cedric Marshall trailing behind in his usual languid fashion, Devlin neared, Therese met his eyes and inclined her head. "My lord."

He claimed the hand she offered, smoothly raised her gloved fingers, and lightly brushed them with his lips. "My lady."

Therese had spent half a lifetime observing the behaviors of men like her husband and his friends; she exchanged a very nearly eye-rolling glance with Veronica as Devlin, retaining possession of her hand, wound her arm in his and settled by her side, effectively ousting Child from that position.

With a deceptively mild expression on his face, Devlin regarded his old friend. "Child. I had no idea I might find you here. How delightful."

The last comment, delivered in Devlin's most depressive drawl, did nothing to dampen Child's enthusiasm. He continued to smile in what seemed to be sincere delight. "Devlin, old man. I've been getting acquainted with your lovely countess, and I was just thinking what a pity it was that you weren't here."

Therese arched a cynical brow and, ignoring Child, asked Devlin, "How went the dinner?"

The question drew Devlin's gaze from Child's face to hers. After a second, he replied, "As expected, but out of it, I realized there were some gentlemen I should speak with about one of the issues that have arisen. As I suspect they'll be here, I thought to look them up."

Somewhat to her surprise, Therese wasn't sure any of that was true, but her powerful husband could make it so. She glanced past him at Child. "Lord Child was about to tell us, in light of his lengthy sojourn in America, which of the exhibits at the Great Exhibition he found of most interest."

Every pair of eyes—Therese's, Devlin's, Veronica's, James's, Cedric's, and even two of the other gentlemen's—locked on Child. The look he bent on Therese was not entirely friendly, but when the silence lengthened, he was forced to concede. "I thought the new machinery for mining was rather intriguing."

Devlin's brows rose. "Do you think they can actually deliver the results they claim?"

Child blinked, and his attention shifted to Devlin. "It's possible, but I'd like to get my hands on the data they say they have. Without that, who can tell? It might be all pie in the sky."

Devlin nodded. "My thoughts exactly." He looked at Child with rather less antagonism. "But what brought you back to England?"

Therese judged that a far from idle question, and curiously, Child responded with an airy, "It simply seemed time," which convinced no one and only served to heighten interest on that point.

Therese noticed Cedric, who had joined the circle on James's other side, look from Child to Devlin and back again, then Cedric murmured his excuses and quietly slipped away.

Veronica had stepped in to further question Child, but he was determinedly clinging to evasion.

Therese had to wonder what he was so intent on hiding, although even on such short acquaintance, she judged Child to be the sort who might avoid answering simply to appear interesting. Interesting to ton ladies such as her and Veronica, who liked to know everything about all who moved in their sphere.

She wasn't surprised when Devlin, patently losing interest in Child's prevarications, made their excuses to the group and, stepping away, drew her with him. She *was* surprised when he made no move to quit her side but, instead, asked her several shrewd questions about some of the other guests, both male and female, and capped her replies with observations of his own while he steered her toward a group of older gentlemen, who had congregated in the far corner of the room.

The five men were very pleased to welcome her, along with Devlin. She quickly discovered that two of their number were the gentlemen Devlin had wished to contact regarding one of the railway ventures in which he was involved. While Devlin and the pair discussed something to do with loads and margins, Therese set herself to engage and entertain the other three gentlemen.

Once they'd satisfied themselves as to their mutual business, Devlin and the other two joined the discussion Therese had instigated regarding the current crop of plays. When that subject was exhausted, Devlin excused them and, once again, remained by her side as he guided her on a random course that had them idly mingling with many of their peers.

After one encounter, as they moved on, Devlin softly snorted. "I suspect we'll soon be hearing a tale of how Lord Charley's eldest son has contracted a marriage with a mill owner's daughter."

Therese's lips twitched. Lord Charley was famous for speaking disparagingly about those of the aristocracy who stooped to rescue their estates by marrying for money amassed via trade. "So the rumors are true, and he's fast approaching *point non-plus*?"

"Oh, I suspect he's well past that point and sliding into a pit so deep there'll be no getting out of it other than through an advantageous marriage. Assuming, of course, that his son will oblige, which, as I understand it, is by no means certain." Devlin paused, then added, "He mentioned his latest great investment to me at the time. I looked into it, but thought it decidedly…iffy."

Therese smiled. She had every confidence that, when it came to investing in industry, Devlin knew what he was doing. She glanced at his face. "Old Lady Morrisey mentioned that her husband had spoken to you about investing in a steamship company."

Devlin nodded. "He spoke with me. I believe he decided to go ahead with the investment."

Lady Fairchild intercepted them, plainly intrigued that Devlin had chosen to appear at the soirée. Therese deftly steered the conversation toward her ladyship's twin daughters, both of whom were, it was rumored, poised to make excellent matches in the near future.

Her ladyship was delighted to be questioned, but coy as to the details. "You will hear more soon, my dear Lady Alverton, I do assure you."

Therese smiled, and they moved on, leaving her ladyship preening, but no further forward in learning why Devlin was there.

Smiling, Devlin dipped his head to murmur in Therese's ear. "Thank you. It's comforting to know that success in the Marriage Mart still trumps interest in my activities."

She chuckled, and they continued to circulate amongst the guests.

He'd forgotten this—wending through a haut ton crowd with her, trading quips, observations, and shrewdly cynical remarks. Her naturally observant nature and often-acid wit closely mirrored his own; he'd forgotten that they matched so well and could entertain each other in such a pleasant fashion.

Fifteen minutes later, by his estimation, they'd done their duty by Lady Walton and remained for long enough.

When he'd walked in and seen Child standing beside Therese, he'd had to fight not to stride too rapidly to her. Admittedly, he'd come there intending to spend time with her to assess the possibilities of—dare he say it?— wooing her in such a setting, but discovering that his old friend was present and had already found his way to her had given him even more reason to cling to her side.

He held few illusions about Child's ability—or his readiness—to throw a spanner in Devlin's works. It was more than possible that Child might think it an excellent idea to pretend to seduce Therese. Not that he would actually do so, but that he would think it great sport to play the part just to get a rise out of Devlin.

That was the sort of relationship he and his old childhood friend had. Always had had, truth be told.

But at this particular time, the last thing he needed was to have Child queering his pitch. The fact that after nine years away, Child had chosen now—this month—to return to England felt very much as if Fate was laughing at Devlin. And if, heaven help him, Child got any inkling of the delicate quest Devlin had embarked on, after laughing himself silly, Child wouldn't be able to stop himself from interfering, and God alone knew where that might end.

As a second son and with his much older brother the fond father of two healthy sons, Child was significantly far down the ladder of the ducal succession. Consequently, in many arenas, Child had always enjoyed greater freedom than Devlin, on whom the mantle of heir and the attendant responsibilities had always weighed heavily. From a young age, Child had grown adept at exploiting the constraints Devlin's position placed on him to score points in the never-ending game between them.

Devlin had to admit that after nine years apart, he couldn't know for certain how Child would behave now, but when it came to Therese and their marriage, he wasn't about to take any risks.

They'd reached one side of the room when Therese slowed, then halted.

Devlin halted beside her, looked into her face, and saw a slight frown in her eyes. "What is it?"

She glanced at him, then leaned a little more heavily on his arm and lowered her voice. "Child—you must know a great deal about him."

Devlin fought not to tense. "I daresay I do." He eyed her warily. "What do you want to know?" *And why?*

"I was just thinking…well, our exchange with Lady Fairchild nudged my mind in that direction." She met his eyes. "Child is the same age as you, isn't he?"

"I'm a month older—hence his 'old man' reference."

She smiled like a cat sighting an oblivious canary. "And he's unmarried." She threw him an arch look. "Don't you think it's about time Lord Child found himself a wife?"

For one glorious instant, Devlin imagined what a magnificent weapon-cum-partner Therese would be in effectively countering Child... then he saw the crater opening at his feet. If he encouraged Therese to practice her matchmaking wiles on Child, it was entirely possible that Child might misconstrue both her interest and Devlin's acquiescence...

"Ah..." He refocused on Therese's face. "Actually, if you think about it, although he is from a ducal family, Child is quite distant from the succession, and given he's come home unexpectedly, who knows what parlous state his finances might be in?" He paused; he knew better than to simply tell her it wouldn't be a good idea. "It might be better to wait until you've had a chance to speak with his mother."

That, he was pleased to see, had been the right thing to say. Therese's expression, which had been darkening, cleared. "You're right. I wouldn't want to steer some suitable lady his way, only to discover he's penniless." She glanced across the room. "Given Lord Charley's experience, there seems to be quite a bit of that affliction going around."

"Exactly." Devlin breathed freely again. He glanced around, then met Therese's questioning look. "I've spoken with everyone I came to see. Is there anyone you wish to speak with before we leave?"

She blinked, then glanced at the guests. "No—I've met all those I'd hoped to encounter. And you're right. We've been here long enough."

He was relieved to be able to close his hand over hers where it rested on his sleeve and steer her to where Lady Walton was holding court. Her ladyship and her cronies certainly took note of him leaving with his wife —eagle-eyed as they were, they'd no doubt noticed how much time he'd spent by her side—but although they might be curious, he knew he hadn't yet done enough to trigger any definite speculation.

Child's return had added an element of urgency to his need to redefine Therese's view of their marriage. He'd come there tonight with the sole purpose of assessing what avenues might exist to further his cause in such a setting. Sadly, he could only do so much without attracting the attention of the gossipmongers and setting their tongues wagging, which was the last thing he wished to do.

Not only would he not appreciate being the focus of ton attention, but Therese would hate that, too.

So he had to be careful. That didn't mean that, once they'd taken leave of their hostess and descended, arm in arm, to the front hall, he couldn't help Therese don her evening cloak—and incidentally allow his fingertips to brush lightly over the bare skin of her shoulders.

After collecting his hat, he led her down the steps to the pavement, then gripped her hand to help her into the carriage and followed her up without releasing her fingers. He sat alongside her in the shadowed dark as the carriage rolled through Mayfair, and during the short journey, allowed his thumb to lightly stroke the back of her hand.

From the flash of her silvery eyes as she cast him a swift, sidelong glance, she was very much aware of his tactics.

When the carriage pulled up outside Alverton House, he perforce had to release her as he stepped down, but he reclaimed her hand to assist her to the ground and retained it in a firm clasp as they walked side by side up the steps. When they reached the porch, Portland opened the door and ushered them inside.

Devlin moved to forestall the butler by releasing Therese's hand and stepping behind her—close behind her—to grip the collar of her velvet cloak and lift it away, once again bestowing an elusive caress that, this time, had her catching her breath.

He knew better than to smile smugly. Instead, after handing over his hat, he closed his hand about hers and drew her to the stairs.

He had to release her to allow her to use both hands to manage her skirts, but as they climbed the stairs, he allowed his palm to possessively cruise the back of her waist.

When she stepped off the stairs, she paused, released her skirts, raised her head, and drew in a breath—then flung him a speaking, transparently come-hither look.

He slowly smiled and waved her on. "After you, my lady."

His voice had deepened. He heard the slight stutter in her breathing, then head high, she led the way down the corridor to their rooms; his apartments occupied the space along one side of the corridor while hers lay behind the door at the end.

She paused before her door and, from beneath her lashes, glanced at him.

He caught and held her gaze, then moving slowly, deliberately, reached past her, opened the door, and sent it swinging wide.

His voice even deeper than before, he repeated, "After you, my lady."

She walked in, and he followed.

He closed the door behind him. On the chest along one wall, a lamp had been left burning, shedding soft light over much of the room—over the inviting sight of the commodious four-poster bed decked out in silks in ivory and shades of lilac. One quick glance around assured him that her dresser wasn't waiting to assist her out of her gown. Tonight, that pleasure would be his. He focused on her and all but purred in anticipation.

She'd halted and turned to watch him.

He reached for her, and with a fleeting smile, she came into his arms —readily, eagerly.

He crushed his lips to hers, and avidly, she met him, matched him— challenged him—until he swung her around, pressed her back against the door, angled his head, and devoured.

Passion ignited. It was always there, simmering between them, ready to burst into flame at his call. In an instant, the flaring heat caught them, compelling and demanding.

Desire, hot and scorching, greedily licked over his skin and hers, teasing, taunting, luring. In this arena, there'd never been any question about the mutuality of their feelings. Of their mutual hunger. From the first, it had been there, real, potent, and indescribably addictive.

He'd fallen victim to it from the moment he'd touched her, a fever like no other, an affliction from which he never wished to recover.

But they'd long ago learned to savor—to stretch out the moments and, together, squeeze every last ounce of pleasure they could from the searing flames.

Therese raised her hands and framed Devlin's face, the better to meet the questing demands of his voracious tongue. Something within her rejoiced, and all thoughts and restraints melted away as she devoted every wit she possessed to kissing him. To exploring and engaging and urging him on and taking her pleasure from his response. At the low growl that purled from his throat, she laughed inside, feeling gloriously wanton.

He was magnificent, this husband of hers; in this arena, she seriously doubted any man could match him. His expertise and his focus—on her, on bringing her pleasure and taking his pleasure in her—were, she felt sure, impossible to beat.

His hands skated over her curves, knowingly caressing. He cupped one breast and kneaded, and her flesh heated and swelled, and she thrust the heavy mound eagerly into his palm, impatient for more. Long, skillful fingers obliged, seeking, finding, and squeezing her nipple, his evocative touch screened by the now-too-tight silk of her bodice.

Although their lips remained hungry, and they continued to savor the evocative delights of their passionate kiss, they'd both reached the state of being highly aware of every inch of their bodies. Of every pulse that sent heat surging beneath their skins.

She drew in a much-needed breath, seized the reins, and lowered her hands to his chest, then skated them up to wind her arms about his neck. She leaned into him, pushing away from the door—wordlessly urging him toward the bed. He took half a step back, and his hands swept down and around to possessively cup her derriere. He drew her hard against him, letting the rigid rod of his erection boldly press against her stomach, then he flexed his fingers before releasing his hold and raising his hands to the line of buttons running down her spine.

He didn't rush—of course he didn't—despite the insistent tattoo that beat so compellingly in her veins and, she knew, in his. One by one, with slow deliberation, he slid each button free, allowing the halves of her gown to gape, revealing bare skin down to the back of her light corset.

Impatience welled and swelled. The instant the last button was free, she broke from the kiss, stepped back, drew her arms from the gown's sleeves, and stripped off the bodice, then pushed the garment, skirts and all, floorward. As the silk slithered down her legs, she started to reach back to unfasten her petticoats, but he caught her hips and spun her around.

One of his hands flattened over her waist, and he drew her against him, her back to his chest, the swell of her hips meeting the hard columns of his thighs. He dipped his head and planted a line of hot kisses from her shoulder to just below her ear, then breathed, "Allow me."

More order than request. Feeling his fingers in the small of her back, deftly unpicking the laces of her petticoats, lashes lowering, she smiled and reached up and back and ran her fingers through his thick hair in encouragement and assent.

Seconds later, her ruffled petticoats sank to join her gown in a puddle about her feet. Devlin settled behind her, anchored and immovable, and she leaned back against him, aware of the prickling rasp of his trousers against the fine silk of her drawers and her silk stockings.

She'd left her arms draped up and back, her forearms resting on his shoulders. Expectation leapt and anticipation rose as his hands skated across and down over her hips, shielded by her corset, then lower to rest for a tantalizing instant, his palms a brand burning through the silk sheathing her upper thighs.

Then he swept his hands up to possessively cup her breasts, swollen and aching behind the restraining material, then set his artful fingers to the hooks running down the front of her corset.

Given the tension investing the hard body at her back, given her own rising urgency, she knew nothing but relief when the last hook gave and the corset finally peeled away. He grasped the garment and tossed it aside. She tensed to turn, but one steely arm clamped about her waist and held her as she was. "No. Like this."

His free hand rose to claim her breast, her heated skin now screened only by the gossamer silk of her chemise. His fingers closed, and he kneaded, and she closed her eyes and shuddered. He played, skilled and forceful, knowing just how much pressure to exert, and she tipped back her head on a soft moan and sagged against him.

He knew what he was doing—*exactly* what he was doing—and she gave herself up to the orchestrated pleasure. Like the master he was in this sphere, he played on her senses, on the sensitive nerve endings, leaving her skin flushed and desperation mounting.

Eyes closed the better to savor the tactile pleasure he lavished upon her, she dropped one hand to his thigh and sank her nails deep in wordless entreaty.

They knew how to read each other well, there, wreathed in the soft glow of intimacy. It was as if some conduit opened between them, one born of sensation and pleasure, of delight and need.

Passion beat steadily around them as, finally, his hands dipped beneath the hem of her barely there chemise and rose, skimming tantalizingly over her silk drawers and higher, trailing fire over her sensitized skin and setting her nerves ablaze.

Almost languidly, he caressed and traced, exploring a landscape with which he was very familiar yet, plainly, had yet to grow weary of. Every sense she possessed was unwaveringly focused on the play of his fingers as they drifted so knowingly over her body. Inevitably, her inner tension rose, desire coiling deep inside—tighter, then tighter still.

She moved restlessly, shifting her hips against his thighs. His fingers paused for a second, then he dipped his head and set his lips cruising the column of her throat while his hands drifted lower. One grasped her hip, holding her immobile, while with the other, he reached farther, fingertips lazily stroking down her belly, then finding the slit in her drawers and threading through the soft curls at the apex of her thighs, before dipping inward and reaching farther still.

Yes! He touched her intimately, and she arched against him. He caressed her, knowing fingertips playing in the hot slickness he'd drawn forth, and she forgot how to breathe.

Her nerves tightened, and if she could have, she would have moved, but he held her fast, a captive to his ministrations as he delved and pushed her on.

She wanted to see him, wanted to explore him as he had her. She fully expected to get her wish, but for now, this…this was for her, and she gave herself up to the surging sensations that built and swelled and grew, until her senses overloaded and that first sharp spike of ecstasy shattered them, leaving her panting, heated and languorous, yet still wanting—still empty and needy—in his arms.

They rose around her, steely and strong, and he pressed a soft kiss to her temple. Even in her semi-wrecked state, she felt the curve of his lips; he was smiling smugly.

She was smiling herself as, with practiced ease, he stripped away her chemise, drawers, stockings, and slippers, then swung her up and carried her to the bed. He laid her on the silk coverlet and stepped back.

Therese opened her eyes and watched a sight she would never tire of —her husband disrobing in soft lamplight. She let her gaze dwell on the heavy muscles that banded his chest and bunched in his arms as he stripped off his shirt. Let her eyes trace the sculpted lines of his lean and powerful body. A body she knew intimately, in every possible connotation of the word.

She felt like a cat as she stretched in anticipation, then lay back and visually devoured.

As if feeling her heated perusal, he met her gaze, his eyes dark with desire, his features harsh, etched with passion. He unbuttoned his trousers and underdrawers and let them fall, and she smiled delightedly and held out her arms.

The corners of his lips twitched upward, then he knelt on the bed. He came into her arms in a prowling rush, and she embraced him boldly, fearlessly, then lost her breath in joyous welcome as he let his body down upon hers.

Devlin clung to the reins of the galloping horses of need and greedy want. Having her climax in his arms ranked as one of his life's greatest pleasures, but having her climax while he was buried deep inside her eclipsed even that. With every part of his mind focused unrelentingly on achieving that pinnacle of pleasure, he devoted himself to setting the stage.

First by accommodating her wish—her need—to touch him. It had never been an easy task to hold back his own ravenous desires enough to allow her to fully satisfy hers, but he'd learned to manage it, because seeing the open joy and delight that flowed across her face as she seduced him, as she wove a sensual web that ensnared his senses and pandered to his sexual hunger, spoke to something buried deep in his possessively passionate soul.

When she'd reduced them both to shuddering need and her hands slowed, he took control again, guiding them both into and through that exquisite moment when she lay open and yearning, and he thrust into her scalding sheath, and she gasped softly and clamped about him and held him deep.

Then he seized the reins in an unbreakable grip and rode her, allowing his body to evocatively plunder hers, and as always, she rose and matched him, and as geysering desire drove them compulsively on, he bent his head and took her lips, her mouth. With their hearts thundering, they raced on and up, through the conflagration of their raging passions, through the brilliant, many-splendored glory of an ecstasy so powerful it seized them both and stopped their breaths, and, ultimately, on.

Into satiation deep and profound where, bodies fused, wrapped in each other's arms, they floated on oblivion's sea.

Devlin finally summoned enough strength to ease back and disengage from his deeply somnolent wife, then slumped into the cushioning softness beside her.

More asleep than awake, she murmured and turned to snuggle against his side. He shifted onto his back, raised his arm to settle her with her cheek on his chest, then lowered that arm, anchoring her in place, and relaxed.

His heart was still thudding, deep and sure; he waited while it slowed, and satiation spread through his every muscle.

As his mental faculties realigned, he thought back over the interlude. From their very first engagement, on their wedding night, she'd been enthusiastic and willing; he'd been entirely happy to teach her everything she'd wanted to know, and she'd proved an apt and eager pupil.

Five years on, and this aspect of their marriage was as perfect as it could possibly be.

His lips curved in wry resignation. It would have been helpful to have been able to use the language of lovemaking to demonstrate what he truly felt for her—except he always had.

In this arena, he'd never had to conceal his feelings; from the first, he'd been able to allow his love for her free rein, letting it infuse his actions, guide him, and inform all he did. Through their lovemaking, he'd been able to freely express what he felt for her without fear of exposure— without any risk that she would see and guess his abiding truth. He'd always encouraged her to physically demonstrate her love for him to the top of her bent, and he'd responded in the same fashion.

Given he'd been her first and remained her only lover, she had no idea that what they shared in this sphere was in any way special. In any way extraordinary. He was as certain as he could be that she thought the degree of intimate connection they shared was something all married couples, all lovers, enjoyed.

How would she know otherwise? *He* hadn't known that such a state existed until the first time they'd made love and the reality had blindsided him. He'd already known everything there was to know about sexual congress between a man and a woman and had practiced the art for decades, yet he hadn't known, hadn't even suspected, that adding love, mutual love, to the mix could create such a dramatic and fundamental transformation.

She had no standard against which to judge the depth of his devotion to her pleasure, no experience to open her eyes to the fact that his sexual worship of her wasn't something that occurred between every man and woman. Yet from their wedding night, she'd welcomed him with open arms and an innocent eagerness that had ripped his breath from his lungs, and he hadn't been able to hold himself back from seizing what she so freely offered and, in return, giving her all that he was, all he was capable of lavishing on her.

Including his love. It had always been there, a potent and powerful element in their lovemaking.

And that, he admitted as sleep drew inexorably nearer, was something he would fight to keep exactly as it was.

His lids grew heavy, and he closed his eyes. In this arena at least, he'd always been transparent. In rescripting their marriage, nothing in this sphere would have to change.

∼

Devlin's limbs felt like lead when, an hour or so before dawn, he forced them out of Therese's warm bed. He sat on the edge and, turning his head, studied her, taking in the spill of her silken hair, the delicate, evocative curve of her spine partly revealed by the disarranged covers.

He looked, then forced himself to his feet. He leaned over and rearranged the covers so she wouldn't feel the cold.

He wanted to stay. After the past hours, the visceral tug had only grown stronger, but when it came to it, he didn't dare.

Not yet.

Stifling a sigh, he swiped up his discarded clothes and headed for the door to his apartments.

Before he could stay and enjoy a dawn beside her, he needed to convince her that he loved her—and he still had a long way to go.

CHAPTER 3

*W*ith his greatcoat sheathing his shoulders, his hat on his head, and his cane in one hand, Devlin strolled, apparently idly, across the lawns of Hyde Park. With the glass-and-steel edifice of the Crystal Palace at his back, he angled across the expanse as if heading for his house on Park Lane.

James and Cedric paced alongside him, discussing an agricultural treatment, touted by one of the exhibitors, that James was considering with an eye to improving his acres. Devlin ceased listening in favor of dwelling on the unexpected opportunity that had fallen into his lap as he'd ambled down the central row in the main exhibition hall. He'd been on his way to discuss a deal with a Swedish engineering firm on behalf of the board of one of the companies he was currently involved with when he'd noticed that a figurine Therese had admired on the exhibition's opening day was still for sale.

Hardly surprising given the price the Russian jeweler was asking for the eight-inch-tall, solid-gold statue of a rearing dragon, gorgeously enameled and jewel-encrusted though it was. But he knew without asking that Therese had truly craved the little dragon; he'd seen it in her face and in the way she'd handled the delicate figurine. Given the figurine had been so prominently displayed and knowing the exhibition was ending soon, he'd assumed the jeweler was keen to sell; on impulse, he'd halted and put in a bid for the dragon, offering a little over half the price asked.

The head of the firm hadn't been on site, and Devlin had left his card and walked on, praying that the jeweler would accept the offer and he would have the figurine for Therese's birthday later in the month.

Buoyed by the prospect of what he hoped would be an unexpected stroke of luck, he swung his cane and looked ahead, scanning the carriages lining the avenue that led into the park from the Grosvenor Gate. As one of the more highly regarded, fashionable matrons in the ton, at this hour, Therese could usually be found in the Alverton barouche somewhere along that graveled path, participating in the ritual of the afternoon promenade with her peers and the rest of the haut ton thus inclined.

After his appearance at Lady Walton's the previous evening and his demonstrated preference for his wife's company, Devlin accepted that he would need to exercise greater caution—greater invention—in approaching Therese in public and spending time beside her while under the gossipmongers' eyes.

Luckily, he'd had a perfectly legitimate reason for visiting the exhibition that afternoon and, therefore, subsequently crossing the park. Cedric and James had elected to accompany him, and he'd readily agreed, reasoning that their presence would afford him additional cover.

He spotted the Alverton barouche with Therese and two other ladies seated inside about a hundred yards ahead, more or less in a direct line south of his current position.

Returning his attention to Cedric and James's conversation, he realized James had moved on to his recurring plaint about Veronica.

"It's utterly ridiculous, the way she badgers me to attend this dinner or that." James's lips were set in a thin line. "I swear, she's pushing me into becoming one of those old duffers who haunts his club day and night!"

Devlin bit his tongue against the urge to suggest James should try just that, if nothing else to see if Veronica muted her shrewish tendencies, but it was an old argument, and given James had married Veronica over six years ago, if he hadn't acted yet, Devlin doubted he ever would.

Cedric, as usual, murmured soothing platitudes.

Devlin returned a vague response—given his quest, marital discord was the last subject he wished to think about—and unobtrusively steered their steps away from his supposed destination and toward his wife's barouche.

To distract his friends from their wayward direction, he asked James, "Has Veronica ever said why she wishes you to attend these events? At this point, it seems unlikely that she feels any need of your social support."

His gaze on the ground before his feet, James grumpily huffed. After several seconds, he admitted, "She says I ought to pay more attention politically. I might not sit in the Lords yet, but ultimately, I will, and she's determined I should be ready to make my mark."

Devlin swallowed the observation that, all in all, that wasn't such a silly idea; James's father was no spring chicken.

Predictably, Cedric, who would never shoulder the responsibility of governing, made noises supporting James's resistance.

Looking ahead, Devlin inwardly smiled as they reached the edge of the avenue.

He halted, and James and Cedric halted beside him. Both looked around in mild surprise, and Devlin pretended to do the same.

"Huh—it appears we've gone astray." Cedric stepped back onto the verge and waved toward the Grosvenor Gate, now some distance away. "Shall we?"

Along with James, Devlin nodded, and the three of them set off.

Then James tugged his sleeve. When Devlin glanced his way, James nodded to the carriage just ahead. "That's your carriage, along with your wife."

Devlin looked and endeavored to keep his expression unrevealing. "So it is." He paused, then lowered his voice. "Impossible to simply walk by—we'll have to stop."

Therese had been conversing with Georgiana Sheldrake and Emily Pritchard, both of whom had been walking the lawns and had joined her in her carriage, when Devlin, James, and Cedric strolled up.

Smiling, the three halted, doffed their hats, and half bowed. As all of them were acquainted, no introductions were required, and hands were promptly offered and fingers pressed.

After acknowledging the other ladies, Devlin met Therese's eyes. "I needed to confer with one of the exhibitors and was on my way home." Still smiling, he shifted his gaze to Georgiana and Emily. "Have you ladies had a pleasant afternoon?"

Georgiana shot Therese a mischievous look and brightly replied, "We have, indeed, my lord. You've just missed your old friend, Lord Child. He spent quite a few minutes entertaining us."

Emily smiled serenely at Devlin. "He was thoroughly charming and so full of stories from his travels that the time quite flew."

Therese didn't miss the fractional tightening of Devlin's jaw, although she doubted anyone else detected any hint of reaction through the languidly relaxed mask he kept firmly in place. She also caught the faintly wary looks James and Cedric threw him. But "Is that so?" uttered in a bland and disinterested tone was all the reply her husband made.

Deciding she didn't need Emily and Georgiana to poke the bear any further, Therese blithely declared, "Did you hear that Lord Monk is threatening to cut off his son without a penny?"

"Hector?" James said. "That will put the cat among the pigeons."

"We've heard that Hector is deep in the clutches of some money-lender," Cedric confided. "Is his father's ire due to that?" He looked at all three ladies. "Or something else?"

Georgiana smiled conspiratorially. "We all suspect it's 'something else,' but exactly what—"

"Or should we say whom?" Emily put in.

"—no one knows." Georgiana looked hopefully at the three men.

Devlin leaned a shoulder against the carriage's side. "Given his lordship's widely known penchant for opera dancers, that seems a trifle like the pot calling the kettle black."

"Indeed," Therese agreed, pleased to have succeeded in diverting everyone from the subject of Child. "But when the gentleman in question is his heir, his lordship apparently takes quite a different view."

The company continued exchanging observations on a succession of ton topics, then the bells rang out for four o'clock, and Emily and Georgiana gathered their reticules and pressed Therese's fingers, assuring her they would see her at Lady Wicklow's picnic the next day.

While Cedric held the carriage door, Devlin gallantly handed the pair down to the verge. Georgiana and Emily took their leave of the gentlemen, waved to Therese, then hurried to where Georgiana's small carriage stood waiting farther along the avenue.

Therese saw Cedric and James look questioningly at Devlin, but he waved them on. "I'll go in the carriage—it'll be faster for you two to continue down to the Stanhope Gate."

James and Cedric agreed. They farewelled Therese, then strode across the avenue and continued south while Devlin climbed up and sat beside Therese.

After the mention of Child, Therese wasn't surprised; it seemed the specter of his childhood friend held the power to stir Devlin's possessiveness.

The observation intrigued her; until Child, she'd rarely glimpsed this side of Devlin. Then again, she couldn't imagine that, pre-Child, he'd seen any need; being entirely comfortable in her marriage—as he knew her to be—she'd never been inclined to encourage any gentleman, but apparently, no encouragement was needed to have Child dance attendance on her.

She wondered if the time might come when she would have to put her foot down about that.

Having claimed the seat beside Therese, Devlin donned his hat, then gave their coachman, Munns, the word to head home.

The barouche rolled smoothly forward to join the queue of fashionable carriages waiting to quit the park. Alverton House stood on the corner of Park Lane and Upper Grosvenor Street, more or less directly opposite the Grosvenor Gate.

Thinking to excuse deserting his friends' company for hers, Devlin murmured, "I have to admit I find James harping on about Veronica's behavior wearying."

"Oh?"

He glanced at Therese and saw she was smiling as if she knew something he didn't. He thought, then pressed, "If James is so unhappy, I can't see why he doesn't do something about it—at least talk to his wife, if nothing else."

Therese's smile widened, and she softly chuckled. "But James isn't unhappy—at least not about his marriage. In all ways that matter, he's perfectly content, which, strange though it may seem, is a large part of his problem."

Fascinated, Devlin stared at her. After a moment, he asked, "As you see it, what is his problem?"

"Well"—she tipped her head—"not just his but Veronica's, too. As yet, neither has come to terms with the fact that James is deeply in love with Veronica and she with him." Her smile deepened. "Apparently, that was not what either was expecting when they wed, and I gather the 'falling in love' part rather snuck up on them, which is why, despite the years, they've seemed to be getting worse."

Devlin was silent as he digested that, then thought back over the months of James's carping. Eventually, he grunted and muttered, "Trust James to fall on his feet."

After a moment, Therese glanced at him, her expression faintly puzzled.

Mentally scrambling, he offered, "I saw Lady Kilroy, Mrs. Marshland, and the old Dowager Duchess of Larwood at the exhibition."

From the corner of his eye, he watched Therese debate whether to quiz him about his comment regarding James or follow the carrot he'd dangled...

Eventually, she faced forward and asked, "What was the dowager up to? She must be quite ancient."

He promptly told her about the patented foot warmer the old lady had been examining. "As for the other two, they seemed merely to be swanning about, more to be seen than to see, so to speak."

"I can't imagine either being all that interested in any exhibits," Therese returned. After a moment, she glanced at him. "How did your business with the exhibitor go? Were they foreign or local?"

"Swedish." Devlin proceeded to share the details of his negotiations with her. Early in their marriage, he'd learned that Therese, being Therese, heard many things related to all sorts of topics from all sorts of sources, and sometimes, she was able to provide significant and even powerful information.

Therese found Devlin's observations of the Swedes and how they had approached the negotiations illuminating, instructive, and also entertaining. When it came to studying people, his eye was as keen as hers, and his sense of the absurd aligned closely with hers.

She was smiling as they approached the Grosvenor Gate. Looking ahead, she saw a familiar gentleman come striding through the smaller pedestrian gate to the side of the carriageway. Still smiling, she sat up and raised a hand. "There's Gregory."

Her brother had paused, clearly scanning the carriages. He saw them and strode toward them.

Devlin ordered Munns to draw up by the verge, and Gregory came to the side of the carriage. He took off his hat, nodded to Devlin, then focused on Therese. "I'm glad I caught you. I was coming to find you to let you know that Martin's arrived in town. His ship docked yesterday morning. I don't know where he is at the moment, but I met him earlier, and we had lunch and caught up."

Therese studied Gregory's face; his expression told her little. "And?" she prompted. "What do you think?"

Gregory pressed his lips together, then shrugged. "His tale sounds genuine—I can certainly see him doing all he says he did. But to be perfectly candid, I'm reserving judgment, at least for the nonce." Gregory glanced at Devlin. "You should hear his story directly from him and make your own assessment." Gregory returned his gaze to her. "He said he intended to look you up, so expect to see him, possibly tomorrow."

Therese nodded. "Thank you for the warning."

Smiling wryly, Gregory stepped back and saluted them both. "What are older brothers for?"

Therese sniffed, but she and Gregory were both smiling as he resettled his hat, then with a last wave, walked away.

Devlin ordered Munns to drive on. As the carriage rocked into motion, he glanced at Therese and saw that she'd grown pensive. After a moment, he said, "All I know about your mysterious younger brother is what I heard at Christopher and Ellen's wedding breakfast—that he'd vanished years ago and has only now turned up." When she looked at him, he added, "Until then, I didn't even know you had a younger brother."

She grimaced lightly. "We all thought he must be dead." She sighed and leaned back as the carriage slowed to ease through the gate. "Martin vanished in the summer of '43. He was in his last year at Eton and was supposed to come home to Walkhurst Manor for the holidays. Only he never arrived. Of course, the family went looking, and we eventually learned that he'd been in the company of two close school friends, and all three had disappeared without trace."

She paused, then went on, "Naturally, the family didn't stop searching, but no one ever found any clue as to what had happened to the three. As far as we heard, none of them turned up again. As the years went by, we were forced to conclude that the worst had occurred and that Martin had somehow met his end." She glanced at him. "That's why you never heard him mentioned—we'd all assumed he'd died."

"How old was he at the time?"

"Seventeen."

The carriage rocked as it turned in to Park Lane. Therese continued, "You can imagine Mama and Papa's shock when they attended a soirée in Chicago and discovered their lost lamb gracing the drawing room and being fêted as a highly successful and eligible gentleman!"

Devlin blinked. "That must have gone down well with your father. And your mother, come to that."

"Indeed." Therese shook her head. "You can imagine how it must have played out, but apparently, when Martin explained all to Mama and Papa, they understood and forgave him. And then the very next morning, they received word about Christopher's wedding. After making Martin promise to follow as fast as he could, they had to rush to get home in time."

Devlin frowned as Munns turned in to the Alverton House drive. "He —Martin—wasn't at the wedding."

Therese shook her head. "Papa said that Martin had interests to sell up and obligations to settle before he could leave, but he'd sworn to follow them as soon as possible." She paused as the carriage rocked to a halt on the gravel before the steps leading up to their front door, then went on, "It appears he's kept that promise, at least." She glanced at Devlin as he reached past her to open the carriage door. "Given he couldn't make it to the wedding, Mama and Papa decided not to announce his return until after the ceremony, but of course, they had to tell Christopher and Ellen before they—Mama and Papa—left. That was the first I—and you, too— heard about it."

Devlin nodded. He descended from the carriage and turned to hand her down.

She placed her gloved fingers in his.

He caught her eye as she joined him on the gravel. "I can't imagine you approve of his behavior—vanishing like that."

"No, of course not." Then she frowned. After a second of cogitation, she said, "But knowing him—at least the him as he then was— I can imagine how it might have come about. He was always quite...*uncertain* over how he fitted into the family—the fourth child, the third son. It seemed there wasn't any role for him to fill, not like the rest of us, all of whom had"—she tipped her head—"I suppose you might say, some reason for being." She paused, her gaze distant, then confessed, "It might seem strange, but I can, indeed, imagine that, at seventeen, Martin might have thought it a good idea to go out and make his own way, entirely separate from the family."

Devlin knew that by "the family," she was referring to the Cynster clan as a whole, not just her branch of it. He studied her expression as, taking her arm, he steadied her up the porch steps and concluded that, black sheep or not, she was keen to see her younger brother again. Of her three brothers, Martin was, it seemed, closest to her in age—just two years younger if Devlin's calculation was correct.

Knowing her character as he now did, Devlin also suspected that, of her brothers, Therese would be most protective of Martin as well.

Portland opened the door, and Devlin released Therese's arm and followed her over the threshold.

He just hoped her prodigal younger brother didn't distract her or try to claim too much of her time.

Portland bowed them inside, then closed the door and came to take Devlin's hat and cane. "You have a visitor, my lord, my lady."

"Oh?" Therese had laid aside her bonnet and was busy undoing her pelisse. She fixed Portland with an inquiring look.

"A Mr. Martin Cynster, ma'am—not the older gentleman, but I assumed he was a relative." Portland deftly gathered the greatcoat Devlin shrugged from his shoulders. "I've put him in the drawing room."

He's eager. Devlin saw anticipation leap in Therese's eyes. He caught her gaze and arched a brow. "Shall we?"

At least Martin Cynster's timing allowed Devlin to accompany Therese to the unexpected reunion, one he was keen to witness.

Therese hurriedly handed her pelisse to the senior footman, Morton, then shook out the skirts of her burgundy carriage gown. She cast a swift glance at the mirror on the wall, tucked a stray lock of hair into her chignon, then walked purposefully to the drawing room door, waited for Portland to open it, and head rising, walked through.

Devlin followed at her heels. Looking over her shoulder, he saw a long-legged, dark-haired gentleman hurriedly get to his feet. A faint memory stirred, but Devlin couldn't imagine where he might have previously met the much younger man. He decided the sense of familiarity was simply due to Martin being so obviously a Cynster, with features that unequivocally proclaimed him one of that breed.

As Devlin watched, Martin straightened to his full, slightly lanky height, somewhere north of six feet. His gaze had fixed on Therese, a mixture of hope and uncertainty plain in his face.

Therese slowed and halted, five paces into the room.

Devlin halted beside her, the palm of one hand resting lightly, supportively, on her back.

Therese stared, then he sensed her drawing in a huge breath. He glanced at her and saw a smile of unabashed joy break across her face.

The same emotion rang in her voice as she exclaimed, "Martin! It truly is you!"

Then she flew across the intervening space and flung her arms around her brother.

Hugely relieved and also faintly bemused, Martin managed to free his arms and gently hugged her back. After a second, he raised his gaze and, with rather wise wariness, met Devlin's gaze. "I didn't know…"

"What? Whether I would berate you like a fishwife?" With her head still pressed to his chest, Therese shook him—or tried to—then sniffed and said, "Don't worry—I fully intend to, but I need a moment to convince myself that you truly are here."

Martin's gaze lowered to her face. "I'm sorry." Faint panic edged into his voice. "By all means berate me, but for God's sake, don't cry."

"I'm not." Therese pulled back enough to swipe her knuckles across her cheeks. "Or at least, they're only happy tears—you don't need to panic."

She clearly knew her brother well, because there had definitely been incipient panic in his expression as well as his tone.

Then she stepped back, and Martin's arms fell from her. She searched his face. "My God, Martin—you put us through such a *terrible* time."

His face fell, and he held up a hand in a fencer's gesture of surrender. "I know—well, I know now, and I'm sorry. I never thought…" He broke off and grimaced. "But you know that. Back then, I didn't think things through all that well."

Martin had forgotten Devlin, and Devlin was in no hurry to make his presence felt. He studied the younger man critically as Martin met Therese's eyes.

"I never meant for anyone to worry about me, but…" He gestured vaguely. "The longer I was over there, the harder it became to even think of contacting anyone here—and at first, I was too ashamed."

Sincerity rang in his tone. Seeing the genuine contrition in Martin's face, Devlin felt respect—faint but definite—stir. Coming back from the dead—rescripting a belief that, it seemed, he'd fostered by omission— wouldn't be easy.

Devlin realized he could testify to that.

"Well," Therese said, "at least you're here now, and as Mama and Papa have forgiven you, everyone else will, too." She glanced at Devlin, then with her lips lifting in a smile, looked back at Martin. "As you vanished before our wedding"—she waved at Devlin—"you've yet to meet Alverton."

Responding to the hopeful look she threw him, Devlin walked forward.

Her smile encouraging, Therese continued, "Devlin, allow me to present my errant little brother, Martin Cynster."

Adopting an easy expression that didn't quite mask his reservations, Devlin nodded. "Cynster." He halted beside Therese and offered his hand. Martin grasped it and lightly grimaced. "Please—Martin." He glanced at Therese. "We are family, after all." There was a definite question in that statement.

Devlin wasn't surprised when Therese responded with an approving smile. "Indeed, we are, and you would do well to remember that from now on."

Martin released Devlin's hand, and as Therese moved to the sofa and sat, Devlin waved Martin to the armchair opposite. "And as you just heard, I'm Devlin."

He waited until Therese had settled her skirts, then sat beside her and waited for her to commence her interrogation, which she promptly did.

"Now—tell me. What exactly did you do? Start when you and the other two left Eton."

As Devlin had noted earlier, Martin clearly knew his sister; he'd come prepared to answer her questions. For all that his answers sounded well-rehearsed—undoubtedly, he would have already given them to Vane and Patience and probably Gregory as well—Devlin found the tale illuminating.

"Yes, I know it was the height of foolishness now," Martin replied to Therese's exclamation over his and his friends' plan to seek their fortune by running away to sea. "But at the time, it seemed like"—he gestured—"a great adventure."

Therese primmed her lips, then asked, "So what happened?"

"Instead of heading to London, we went to Southampton. It was easy enough to hire on as deckhands on a ship bound for New York. We worked our passage across—that wasn't so bad. But then we reached New York, and Lionel fell ill. Eric and I stayed with him, of course, but even pooling our funds, we didn't have all that much, and we couldn't find a doctor." Martin paused and looked down at his tightly clasped hands. Eventually, he went on, "Lionel died. After that, Eric and I found work here and there, but it was rather rough, and Eric decided he'd had enough adventure, and he took a ship home. We'd agreed for him to take news of Lionel's death to his family, but—" Martin paused, then glanced fleetingly at Therese. "I made him promise not to tell anyone anything about me."

Puzzled, Therese asked, "Why? If you needed help—"

"*That* was why." Grimly, Martin shook his head. "By then...well, I understood what I'd done. But the whole point of running away in the first place was to forge a life that wasn't dependent on the family—on being a Cynster." He waved dismissively. "Christopher's the eldest and will inherit Walkhurst. Gregory's the spare, and something will surely come his way. You"—he glanced at her and tipped his head toward Devlin—"are the dynastic connection. You all have roles to fill, but me? I'm the unnecessary third son, which is why I went looking for…a life."

He paused, then went on, "By the time Eric left, I'd realized that running away had been the wrong thing to do, but coming back seemed pointless. What was there for me here? Finish at Eton, go to Oxford, and then what? Sit quietly in a corner?"

Devlin couldn't imagine the man seated opposite doing any such thing, and a sidelong glance at Therese's expression showed she thought the same.

"So what did you do?" she asked.

Martin dragged in a breath and replied, "I decided I was going to make a go of it and build some sort of successful life, enough to prove to everyone that I wasn't any sort of cipher—the third and forgettable son."

"Mama and Papa and all the rest of us never thought of you that way."

He paused, then tipped his head. "Perhaps not, but back then, it certainly felt like that." After a moment, he went on, "Eventually, I hired out to a man running an import-export business. He…saw my potential, I suppose you could say. He showed me how best to use what he termed 'the skills God gave me' in the pursuit of business. Because of my accent and my manners and the obvious benefits of my years at school, he made me his assistant and took me with him to all his meetings. He taught me everything there was to know about wheeling and dealing in commerce and in goods. Ultimately, he brought me in as a partner, and subsequently, I went to Chicago and established an office there, dealing with all the goods trafficked via the Great Lakes and brought in from the western states." His lips lifted faintly, and pride edged his tone as he said, "I built the Chicago business into a critical hub for commerce of all sorts."

Watching him and plainly intrigued, Therese prompted, "And that was where Mama and Papa found you."

Martin's expression changed; for an instant, he looked stricken, then he nodded. "Yes. I hadn't changed my name, although I'd never made anything of it—never even alluded to the ducal connection." He blinked, then met Therese's gaze. "Meeting Mama and Papa after all that time…"

The emotion that must have invested those moments seemed to hover in the room.

Martin drew in a tight breath and went on, "They—their reaction—brought home to me how completely misguided I'd been and that they cared about me as much as they did any of you three."

He paused, then said, "We sat down and talked for hours." His lips twisted wryly. "No holds barred. But by the end of it, I saw that coming back was the right thing for me to do now. I'd achieved what I'd wanted—needed—to achieve, and"—his face softened in a self-deprecating smile—"despite my reservations, I missed England, and most of all, I missed the family."

He met Therese's gaze. "Sometimes, you don't realize what's truly important until you leave it behind."

Therese smiled encouragingly. "So you've come back for good?"

Martin nodded. "I sold up my share in the business. I owned most of the shares in the Chicago concern, so that wasn't something I could arrange overnight. I'm sorry I missed Chris's wedding—aside from all else, it would have been an easy way to meet all the family at once—but I'll go down and see him and meet Ellen in a few weeks, once I've got settled here."

"You plan to live in London?" Devlin asked.

Martin nodded. "At least to begin with." He looked at Therese. "I'm staying in Arlington Street at present."

While Therese inquired about Martin's living arrangements, with questions Martin largely and rather adroitly deflected, Devlin considered the prospect that, with the more senior members of the Cynster family—those of Martin's parents' generation, including the Duke and Duchess of St. Ives—having already retreated to the country and being unlikely to return until the Season next year, and with Christopher and Ellen fixed in Kent, Martin would, perforce, have to rely on Therese to facilitate his resurrection among the ton in order to re-establish himself in the upper echelons of London society.

Devlin wasn't sure how he felt about that. He wasn't even sure that was what Martin wanted.

He'd thought to refrain from grilling Martin on his intentions until he could engineer a private meeting, but then Therese sat back and, fixing her brother with a very direct look, asked, "So, what are your plans?"

Of course, she would want to know as well. Devlin crossed his legs and folded his hands and listened as she proceeded to tug at Martin's plans—vague strand by vague strand—until finally, he held up his hands in defeat.

"To be perfectly honest, I really don't know, Tee—I'm going to have to study and evaluate the opportunities here and form my plans accordingly. The business landscape is very different here, and until I know more, I can't even guess at my principal direction, let alone how that might play out socially." He returned her gaze pointedly. "I'll be sure to ask you for your opinion once I've learned enough to know what to ask."

Therese softly humphed, but seemed mollified by that declaration. "Just so you know, I will take it very badly if you don't let me help you."

Martin flashed her a smile—and Devlin's memory jolted, and a recently seen image crystallized in his mind.

"You were at the exhibition earlier today." When Martin looked at him, Devlin went on, "I was there, too, and I saw you talking to an exhibitor..." He narrowed his eyes, bringing the scene into sharper focus. "An American firm—something to do with pumps and hydraulics."

Martin nodded. "They're interested in importing machinery for mining, but haven't had much luck making the necessary local contacts." He paused, then added, "I know something of their products. Although the business I worked in was initially purely import-export, I eventually expanded into directly investing in companies making new products I felt had potential."

Devlin's interest grew. "How long were you working for that business?"

"More than seven years." Martin smiled, his confidence showing. "I learned a lot over that time."

Devlin was starting to believe that. Several further business-orientated questions confirmed that Therese's errant little brother hadn't wasted his years away from the fold.

Growing bored with such talk, Therese ruthlessly refocused the conversation on Martin's life in New York and Chicago; while Devlin got the distinct impression she was seeking to learn whether her little brother had developed any socially unacceptable habits—gambling and woman-izing being at the top of her list—apparently oblivious of her tack, Martin steadfastly maintained that he'd led, if not the life of a monk, then a close approximation thereto.

"Honestly, Tee, I wasn't interested in getting caught up in their version of the Marriage Mart, which, let me tell you, is just as dangerous as it is over here. I kept my head down and concentrated on doing what

I'd gone there to do—which was learn all the ins and outs of running a business and expanding the Chicago office's assets."

She narrowed her eyes at him. "Mama and Papa found you at a soirée."

"Yes, they did, but that was one of those invitations I couldn't afford to decline. The hostess's husband was one of our biggest customers." He paused, then conceded, "And yes, all right, they—the ladies—had started to target me with their schemes, but that only gave me even more incentive to steer clear of them and their daughters, which I assiduously did."

"Hmm." Therese regarded him through still-narrowed eyes. "I hope you remember how to waltz."

Resigned, Martin said, "It wasn't completely uncivilized, you know."

Having had nearly an hour to assess the connection between brother and sister, Devlin was now very certain that the emotional link between Therese and Martin was of a significantly different caliber to the rather vague relationship she had with Christopher and Gregory. Therese and Martin were plainly close, and Martin's well-being—and most definitely his reintegration into the family and the ton—would be of real concern to her. To Tee—Devlin had never heard anyone else call her that.

He regarded Martin; he was a decent judge of character, and it seemed to him that the younger man had been honest and open about his life since he'd left England. All Martin had said about his plans, vague though they were, had also rung true. Devlin glanced at the clock on the mantelpiece, then looked at Therese. "I don't have any engagements tonight. Do you?"

Distracted by the unexpected question, Therese blinked, then looked at the clock; it was nearly six o'clock. "No. I don't." She immediately transferred her gaze to Martin. "You should stay and dine with us. You don't have anything arranged, do you?"

Martin looked surprised by the invitation. He glanced at Devlin as if half expecting some protest, but really, it had been Devlin who had suggested it, however obliquely.

Then Martin refocused on her. "I haven't made any plans, so if it suits, I'd like that. Thank you."

"Excellent!" She beamed. "It'll just be us, so you can tell us more about America, and you and Devlin can talk more about business over dinner. But now..." She rose, bringing both men to their feet. She fixed her gaze on Martin and informed him, "You must come up to the nursery and meet your nephews and niece."

He smiled. "Mama and Papa told me. You do know they're as proud as punch over being the first of their lot to have grandchildren?"

"So I've heard." She looped her arm in his and turned toward the door. "And I predict you'll be equally besotted. They are very nice children, you know."

Martin laughed, and from the corner of her eye, she saw Devlin smile indulgently. Good. He was taking Martin's rather dramatic arrival in their lives better than she'd hoped.

Martin readily walked beside her as she made for the door. "Believe it or not, I do know enough about being an uncle to have brought presents. I left them with your butler. I didn't want to presume..."

When he left the sentence unfinished, she glanced up in time to catch the fleeting expression he immediately hid behind a distracting grin. He hadn't been certain she would welcome him; he hadn't taken her forgiveness for granted.

Oh, Martin. She smiled reassuringly and patted the arm she firmly held as she towed him into the front hall. "Come along now—there's no sense in attempting to resist."

He chuckled, and together, they made for the stairs.

Therese paused on the landing to glance back at Devlin, who had followed them from the drawing room, but hadn't started up the stairs.

He caught her questioning look and waved her on. "I need to check on a few things. I'll join you shortly."

She smiled in acquiescence, turned, and with Martin, continued up the next flight.

Devlin watched the pair go, then still smiling, ambled to the study. He checked the letters lying on his desk and glanced at the news sheets, but there was nothing urgent demanding his attention.

He left the desk and walked to his favorite armchair before the hearth. Settling into the comfort of well-padded leather, he reviewed all he'd gleaned over the past hour.

Regardless of anything he felt about the matter, Martin was destined to become a fixture in Therese's life. To Devlin's mind, there was no sense resisting the inevitable, and more to the point, with respect to his own quest regarding Therese, there might be aspects of the situation he could exploit.

Instead of being an annoying distraction, Martin's return might be a boon.

Critically, Devlin reassessed all he'd seen and sensed in Martin

Cynster and had to admit that, instead of the skeptical wariness he'd expected to feel regarding the younger man, he saw potential—a potentially valuable ally business-wise and another gentleman who, while being close to Therese, could be relied on to have her best interests and her safety at heart.

More, a man who had already thought about what being an uncle meant.

Devlin pondered that, along with Therese's transparent fondness for her younger brother, then rose and headed for the nursery.

He paused in the front hall to confirm with Portland that dinner would be served at seven o'clock, then climbed the stairs to the third floor. Helping Therese re-establish Martin in society would, among other things, give him a highly-acceptable-to-Therese reason for keeping her company at various events at which he would not normally appear.

And given Martin's business interests, introducing him to British business circles might well bear all sorts of profitable fruit.

Most importantly of all, helping Martin would firmly anchor Devlin in his wife's good graces.

Smiling to himself, he strolled to the open nursery door and looked in.

Somewhat to his surprise, Martin was sitting cross-legged on the floor, telling the children some story. Even Horry, firmly ensconced in her usual place on Therese's lap, was silent and looked spellbound.

Devlin watched for several minutes, until the story came to an end and his sons clapped and cheered and Spencer asked a question. Observing the way that Martin responded and the manner in which his children were beaming, Devlin felt all lingering doubts regarding the younger man fade. From experience, he knew that children rarely failed to see straight through adults' façades, and his three clearly found their new uncle fascinating and not the sort of person they needed to treat with caution.

Then Rupert noticed Devlin and leapt up, closely followed by Spencer. The boys rushed to take Devlin's hands. Grinning at their excited, non-stop prattle, he allowed them to tow him into the room. He crouched and paid all due attention while they showed off the presents Martin had brought for them—a carved wooden train of locomotive and three carriages for Spencer and a horse on wheels, also finely carved, for Rupert. Horry, meanwhile, waved a wooden-headed doll at Devlin, then when he reached as if to take it, she clutched the doll tight and chortled— whether to it or him, he wasn't sure.

He straightened and smiled benignly on the gathering, then allowed his expression to grow serious. "I'm afraid I've come to report that it's almost time for dinner to be served downstairs." The big clock on the wall stood at fifteen minutes to the hour, but he knew how long any farewell would take.

The boys instantly turned their gazes on Therese, but she met their beseeching looks with a firm "You've already been allowed to stay up later than usual. Now you need to say goodnight to your Uncle Martin and thank him for your presents, then you should take your new toys and put them safely in the playroom before going off to your beds."

Both boys' shoulders slumped, but they dutifully turned and thanked Martin, not just for the toys but also for telling them stories.

Watching her brothers, Horry wasn't sure whether to be grumpy or not. Before she could decide, Devlin took Therese's arm and helped her to her feet, then plucked Horry from Therese's hands and tossed the little girl up in the air and caught her—sending her into fits of giggles—then he noisily bussed her cheek, resulting in yet more hysterical giggles. Therese pressed close and kissed the other downy cheek, then Devlin handed his daughter to Gillian, one of the nursemaids.

Nanny Sprockett had come up to take charge of the boys. Devlin crouched again, and the pair hugged him. He closed his arms and hugged them back, then released them and rose. He looked down into their faces and ruffled their hair. "Off to bed, now."

The boys sent resigned smiles his way, turned to Therese for their goodnight kisses, then with a last wave to Martin, clutching their new toys, they allowed Nanny Sprocket to take their free hands and lead them off.

Devlin watched the children go, vaguely aware he had a faintly besotted look on his face, then waved Therese and Martin to the door.

Beside Martin, he walked along the short corridor in Therese's wake. They reached the head of the stairs and started down, with Therese leading the way.

His gaze resting on his wife's head, Devlin inquired, "Are you intending to attend the Countess of Wicklow's event tomorrow?"

Continuing to slowly descend, Therese glanced back at him in obvious surprise.

When she didn't immediately reply, he continued, "I heard it's to be quite a large affair. Several members at the club mentioned it and that they planned to go. I gather they hope to use the opportunity to discuss some of the bills we're expecting to see introduced in the current parliamentary session in a more private, relaxed, and convivial setting."

Therese's expression lightened, and facing forward, she nodded. "I can see the sense in that. It's to be a picnic, and the Wicklow House grounds are extensive, so finding places and moments in which to conduct confidential discussions won't be difficult."

"Indeed," Devlin returned. "As I would appreciate being able to assess the mood regarding several specific bills and her ladyship's event seems such an ideal venue, I was thinking of attending myself."

"Oh?"

He could imagine her asking herself why he couldn't achieve the same result via his clubs, as he usually did; before she could follow that thought any further, he glanced at Martin and added, "I also thought that given many gentlemen will, it seems, be attending, if Martin was to join us, the event might prove useful in terms of him reconnecting with society."

Therese immediately saw her husband's point. "That's an excellent notion." She looked at Martin. "Are you free? I can guarantee that the countess will be thrilled to have you come as well."

Somewhat wryly, Martin glanced from Therese to Devlin, then back again. "Tee, I only arrived in London yesterday. I haven't had time to make social plans." He glanced again at Devlin. "And this picnic does sound like an ideal opportunity to at least show my face."

"So you're free?" she pressed.

He nodded.

She was rather surprised by the easy victory; she'd expected to have to persuade him.

"We can take you up with us," Devlin said as they stepped onto the tiles of the front hall. "Unless you wish to drive yourself?"

Martin pulled a face. "Would that I could, but I haven't yet had time to look into getting a curricle and team or even a hack." He halted and looked at Therese. "Papa told me that Uncle Harry and Aunt Felicity have more or less retired from the horse breeding and racing business, and that Pru married and is now living in Ireland, so which of our cousins would it be best to ask about horses?"

"Oh, you want Toby for that," she replied. "He's the most knowledgeable about both horses and carriages. Nowadays, everyone in the family asks him."

Martin nodded. "I'll look him up, but in the meantime"—he turned to Devlin and smiled—"if it's no trouble, I'll take you up on that offer."

Therese assured him that he was very welcome to accompany them, and after further discussion, they agreed that Martin should present himself at Alverton House by ten o'clock the next morning.

With that decided and Portland pointedly hovering, Therese beamed and led her brother and husband into the dining room.

Devlin waved Martin ahead and, smiling himself, followed. His newfound brother-in-law was already proving useful. With Martin in their carriage, distracting Therese simply by being there, Devlin would have nothing to fear through the hours required to travel back and forth from Surrey, in a closed carriage, with his far-too-observant and potentially—certainly by the return journey—suspicious wife.

CHAPTER 4

$\mathcal{I}$t was a glorious autumn day, with the sun shining from a clear blue sky, when at noon, Therese strolled on Devlin's arm, with Martin on her other side, across the lush lawns at the side of Wicklow House toward where Lady Wicklow was waiting to welcome her guests.

Said guests were arriving in a steady stream and, judging by the groups already gracing the wide lawn at the rear of the house, had been for some time.

His gaze on those already there, Devlin murmured, "No wonder we had to leave our carriage so far down the drive."

"Just as well we left London when we did," Therese returned. It had been she who had insisted on the ten o'clock start; both men had thought —clearly mistakenly—that arriving later wouldn't have been a problem.

They joined the short line waiting to greet her ladyship, who was one of the older hostesses and had a wide acquaintance within the ton.

The instant the couple in front of them moved on, Therese smiled brightly and stepped up to offer Lady Wicklow her hand. "Good afternoon, Lady Wicklow. What a glorious day!"

With her gaze switching from Devlin to Martin, then back again— before returning to Martin—her ladyship was clearly in two minds over which of the pair was the more unexpected. Somewhat blindly, she grasped Therese's fingers. "I'm so glad you could come, countess."

Blithely, Therese waved at her husband. "I'm sure you remember Alverton."

Therese retrieved her fingers from her ladyship's lax grasp and waited while her husband smoothly exchanged the customary courtesies. Then she gestured to Martin. "I doubt you'll have met my brother Martin before. He's been overseas for several years and has only just returned to these shores."

Her ladyship's rather protuberant eyes slowly widened, then flared. "Oh! Oh yes—of course. You're *that* Martin Cynster. The one who... well, I see."

Therese had never seen Lady Wicklow—an experienced hostess of long standing—flustered before.

Martin duly bowed, charmingly commented on having heard of the extensive web of her ladyship's acquaintance, and voiced his hope that her ladyship would not be inconvenienced by his using her event to make his first appearance within the ton.

Delight combined with avid curiosity poured from Lady Wicklow, and she flapped her fingers. "Of course not, my dear. You're most definitely welcome."

Therese promptly stepped in. Confident that her stock with the old hostess had risen considerably given that she'd brought not one but two personable and interesting gentlemen in her train, she caught one of her ladyship's hands and gently squeezed. "Thank you, your ladyship. We'd best move on."

Leaving Lady Wicklow, still hungry for more, to satisfy the curiosity of the next guests in line, drawing Devlin and Martin with her, Therese glided toward the wide lawn where the guests were congregating. "That was nicely done," she murmured to Martin, "but just be thankful that with other guests waiting, she couldn't keep you there while she extracted your complete life history from you."

Martin glanced at her. "That's supposed to make me feel more relaxed?"

"No. That's supposed to put you on your guard." She slid her arm from Devlin's and linked her other arm with Martin's. "Now come along —there are several other hostesses here to whom you need to make your bow. Don't worry—I won't desert you."

Devlin halted. "I, however, will." When brother and sister paused to look his way, he saluted them and met Therese's eyes. "I'll catch up with you later. Enjoy yourselves."

She grinned. "I will."

Martin sighed. "I won't, but I suppose I'll have to gird my loins and get this over with." More quietly, he muttered, "At least it's a picnic and not a damned ball."

"Come on." Therese towed him toward a gathering of ladies who had already noticed them and were, albeit covertly, staring.

Devlin watched the pair go, then still smiling, walked across the lawn toward where several of his peers from the Lords were chatting in a loose group with their backs to a high hedge.

He felt rather smug over how well his prediction of Martin providing the perfect distraction for his own activities was playing out. Not only had Martin's presence in the carriage provided both Devlin and Therese with nearly inexhaustible fodder for questions, resulting in an entertaining and illuminating journey, but Martin's appearance on the lawns had succeeded in deflecting the combined attentions of the assembled ladies from the unexpected sight of Devlin himself.

Nearing the other gentlemen, Devlin glanced back and saw Martin chatting with apparent ease with a coterie of older matrons, all of whom seemed to be hanging on his every word.

Therese, Devlin noted, was looking on with a pleased smile. He, in turn, was pleased that Martin appeared to be making the most of Therese's efforts on his behalf.

Returning his gaze to the gentlemen congregating by the hedge, Devlin confirmed that there were several present with whom he wouldn't mind having a quiet word; his excuse for accompanying Therese hadn't been entirely fictitious.

During the next half hour, he moved among the gentlemen, exchanging and canvassing views on such topics as the ongoing discussions regarding the property qualification for members of Parliament and the recent unrest in France. The Great Exhibition, or more particularly, the potential consequences for British industry, dominated the minds of many.

He was standing with a group listening to Lord Carmichael expound on the possibilities for more rapid expansion of the railway network when a burnished-brown head caught Devlin's eye.

Child. Instantly distracted, Devlin watched Child—who, given the direction from which he'd strolled up, had only recently arrived—weave through the guests. Although he paused here and there to exchange greetings, he avoided being detained and continued deeper into the crowd. From the intent expression on his face, Child had someone in his sights, and Devlin was prepared to wager a considerable sum as to whom that someone was.

Without losing sight of Child, he excused himself and, leaving the group, slowly walked along the hedge to where a large beech spread branches over the top of the clipped green wall, creating a pool of dense shadow.

Child would never imagine that Devlin would attend such an event. Devlin hadn't expected Child to attend, either. Devlin halted in the shade and continued to visually track Child—until Child finally found his target.

Devlin clenched his jaw as Child halted beside Therese. She and Martin were chatting with three matrons who, between them, had four marriageable daughters in tow. Devlin narrowed his eyes at the sight of Child catching Therese's attention. She smiled and greeted him, then promptly introduced him to the others in the circle.

That made Devlin grin. Child was immediately thrown on the defensive; given his age and that he was the second son of a duke, Child ranked far higher in the eligible-husband stakes than a well-born twenty-five-year-old recently returned from America.

Child was forced to dally by Therese's side as she focused her attention on Martin, who appeared to have distracted the ladies, young and old, with one of his tales of his time abroad.

Reflecting that, in this setting, Therese was more than a match for Child, Devlin remained where he was, safely cloaked in shadow twenty yards away, and watched as his childhood friend grew increasingly restive. *Move on, Gray—she's not for you.*

Then Devlin saw Therese cast Child a sidelong glance—one Devlin recognized. She gave Child another minute to take himself off. When he remained stubbornly fixed by her side, leaving Martin to fend for himself, she excused herself to the ladies and stepped back from the group—and Child, of course, glibly did the same.

Devlin tensed, intending to emerge from the shadows and rescue— reclaim—his wife, but then he caught sight of her face and paused.

If Child had been able to interpret her expression, he would have artfully disengaged and fled, but the idiot was focused on engaging Therese, chatting in a no doubt charming manner, and hadn't looked at where she was leading him.

Devlin relaxed and settled to observe and appreciate Therese's command of the social weapons available to her.

She fetched up beside a bevy of ladies—all well-born matrons of the ton. Devlin and any of his ilk would have recognized the danger, but Child, being recently returned to London, did not. The ladies smiled delightedly as Therese introduced him, and Child responded with his usual flair.

Only to discover that, of all the ladies of the ton, that particular group considered gentlemen like him fair game. Every member of the group was rumored to take, exhaust, then discard lovers with quite staggering regularity. Within seconds, two of the group had wound an arm with one of Child's, effectively trapping him.

Therese met his widening eyes with a delighted smile and—it seemed to Devlin—commended him to the ladies' keeping and blithely took herself off.

Devlin could almost feel sorry for Child, left to defend his honor from a handful of the most voracious ladies in the ton.

Therese, meanwhile, walked across to pay her respects to a group of grandes dames—ladies even Child would recognize and want to avoid at all costs.

Reassured that there were no flies on his wife, not in this sphere, Devlin cast one last, amused glance at Child, smiled at his efforts to disengage, then looked for and located Martin.

Therese's little brother was still with the group of matrons and their daughters with whom Therese had left him. He was managing—just—but was starting to develop a hunted look. Recognizing the signs, Devlin decided that it behooved him to rescue his brother-in-law.

Ambling out from the beech's shadow, apparently idly, he wended his way between the clusters of guests and, eventually, fetched up beside Martin.

He greeted the matrons, who were known to him, and they introduced their daughters. After nodding in distant fashion—being already married, he held no interest for any of the ladies in that group—he exchanged the standard comments on the weather and their surroundings, then announced, "Ladies, I fear I'm here to steal my brother-in-law away." He looked at Martin, who was manfully endeavoring to hide his relief. "There are some business acquaintances here that I rather think you would do well to meet." He glanced at the ladies and smiled. "If you'll excuse us?"

The matrons exchanged a look, then one quickly assured him, "Of course, my lord."

Another added, "It's heartening to see younger gentlemen paying more attention to such matters."

Martin duly made his farewells, and without more ado, Devlin bore him away, steering him toward the edge of the crowd.

"Phew." As they stepped out of the ruck and beyond the ready reach of anyone else's ears, Martin glanced back. "Thank you—that was getting a trifle sticky."

Devlin chuckled. "I'm not so long married that I can't remember how that feels."

Frowning slightly, Martin studied the group he'd just escaped. "Actually, given the direction in which the conversation was heading, I'm rather surprised they acquiesced so readily to letting you spirit me away."

"Ah. That was because I said the magic words."

"Oh?" Martin looked at him questioningly. "And what were those?"

"For that company, 'business acquaintances' and suggesting I was there to take you to meet them."

Martin's frown deepened. "Why did that do the trick?"

"Because you and, more specifically, your fortune is, as yet, an unknown quantity, and therefore, any prospect of you benefiting financially from some business deal is to be encouraged." Devlin met Martin's gaze with amused resignation. "They know your family is sound, but that you've only recently returned to the country. Better for their ambitions that you establish some form of income, and these days, business is where the money is."

Martin grimaced. "I see." After a moment, in a much more cynical tone, he said, "I'd forgotten how much money counts for in the ton."

"Money and name, be it familial or an acquired reputation." Devlin considered, then added, "And believe it or not, these days, talent and achievement." He glanced at Martin measuringly. "Unless I'm reading you quite wrongly, while you unquestionably possess at least one of the first two requirements, you also have at least one of the latter two."

Martin's lips quirked, but while he didn't deny the accuracy of Devlin's assessment, he also didn't rush to admit to anything, nudging Devlin's respect for him a notch higher.

Looking ahead, Devlin continued, "Unless you want to find yourself beating off the matchmakers, I would strongly advise you to keep your financial doings under your hat—or at least hidden from those involved in the Marriage Mart—for as long as humanly possible."

Martin nodded rather grimly. "I intend to."

Devlin inclined his head, then indicated a group of gentlemen gathered by the side of the lawn. "The gentleman over there, in the blue coat, is Lord Randolph Cavanaugh. He manages a very large group of investors and is the sort of gentleman I suspect you should know. As it happens, he's also a connection of yours."

Martin frowned as if dredging his memory. "Via Mary's husband?"

Devlin nodded. "Yes, Raventhorne. Rand is Ryder's half brother. Come, I'll introduce you."

With Martin in tow, Devlin joined the group. As, over the years, he'd become known as a successful investor in railways and in industrial manufactories, he was welcomed with interest. In introducing Martin, Devlin merely described him as having recently returned from America, adding that the younger man was seeking to learn the local ropes, leaving it to Martin to decide how much to reveal.

In that respect, Devlin was unsurprised when Martin used his youth to say very little while listening intently. When, however, after agreeing to meet with Rand later in the week to discuss several firms in which they shared an interest, Devlin made his and Martin's excuses and moved on, Martin was quick to pose a range of insightful and pertinent questions regarding the companies and funds the circle had discussed.

Devlin replied as well as he could and made mental notes to follow up several of the points Martin raised.

Intrigued, Devlin repeated the exercise, introducing Martin to another select group of gentlemen investors, with much the same result. Martin listened and observed, then once he and Devlin quit the group, posed questions and made comments that confirmed that Therese's younger brother was as observant and as intelligent as she was and also had a good and, in some ways, experienced head for business. He was also transparently genuinely intent on building his understanding of ton connections as pertained to investing; Devlin could almost see Martin compiling a list of who had what fingers in which pies.

Eventually, Devlin introduced Martin to Somersby, who was one of the secretaries at the Board of Trade. On learning that Martin had recently returned from America and had been involved in the import-export business there, Somersby grew quite animated, outlining the department's current views on trade with America and endeavoring to solicit Martin's opinions. Devlin stood back, watched, and listened and, once again, was impressed by Martin's acumen in offering just enough of his own thoughts to keep Somersby engaged and willing to reveal more.

When they finally parted from Somersby, leaving that gentleman keen to maintain a connection with Martin and Devlin as well, Devlin waited until he and Martin were out of others' hearing, then said, "I get the impression that you've already got some notion of what arena of activity, for want of a better phrase, you intend to pursue in this new life of yours."

Martin threw him a brief, sharp, sidelong glance, then looked down. They walked on, ambling around the edge of the crowd, for several moments before he tipped his head in acknowledgment and replied, "Machinery. The manufacturing of it."

Devlin cocked his head. "Supplying which area?"

Martin smiled intently. "Whichever area needs machines." He met Devlin's puzzled gaze. "Take, for instance, the factories that make Britain's railway carriages. They use machinery to make the carriages, but from where does that machinery come?"

Devlin frowned. "I'm not sure."

"It's mostly imported from either America or Germany, and that holds true for most of the factories that make almost anything. But"— Martin gestured—"the cost of importing such heavy machinery is significant, let alone the cost in time, and there's really no reason we can't make much of what we need here. Decades ago, the first steam-powered looms were made here, along with some of the first locomotives, and in many industries, the most efficient designs for any sort of machines are those that arise locally." Martin paused, then said, "One of the truisms I learned in America is that those who make the most profit from any new product are those who provide the means to produce it. They take much less risk, but tend to walk away with a large and assured slice of the profits."

Devlin felt as if he'd been struck by an epiphany. "I see your point." After a moment, he said, "Rand has always been interested in automobiles, and while I can't see the government changing its stance on that anytime soon, if I understand you correctly, you wouldn't be interested in making the automobiles themselves but in supplying the machinery necessary to make them."

Martin nodded. "Exactly."

Devlin halted and faced his brother-in-law. "What sort of structure do you think such a machinery-making business might have?"

"Well..." Martin drew in a deep breath and said, "First, it would need..."

Ignoring all the encouraging looks directed their way, Devlin gave his full attention to Martin as the younger man described what was plainly his dream.

Therese had been circulating among the guests, doing her duty by paying her respects to the older ladies present as well as sharing moments with her friends and close acquaintances.

After quitting a group of fashionable matrons of much her own age, she paused by the side of the lawn to consider her options. She had, she estimated, at least twenty minutes to fill before Lady Wicklow declared it was time for the "picnic." Given the wrought iron tables and chairs Therese had spied set up on the eastern lawn, it would be more correct to term the event an alfresco luncheon. She surveyed the guests before her, idly wondering how Devlin and Martin were faring—

"There you are."

She swung around to find Child settling by her elbow. At the sight of the smile he directed her way, she decided to immediately take charge. "I trust, my lord, that you've been finding the company entertaining?"

He waved noncommittally. "I admit I've refreshed my knowledge of the ladies currently gracing the ton. However, none incite my interest to the level you do."

She arched her brows. "Because I'm Alverton's countess?"

Child blinked. He hadn't expected her to be so direct. "Well…"

"Tell me, my lord, for how long have you known my husband?"

He wasn't pleased by the question, but replied, "Since we were infants, so essentially all our lives."

"But of course, over the years, you and he lost touch." She fixed Child with an inquiring look. "How would you describe the relationship between you and Devlin now?"

Child's expression had grown increasingly impassive. "Why do you ask?"

She smiled, allowing a hint of her own intent to show in her eyes. "Quite obviously, because I would like to know."

When she waited, her gaze on his face, he shifted fractionally, then offered, "I suppose we would still be considered friends—friends rather than close acquaintances, certainly."

Again, she arched her brows. "Perhaps the sort of friends who understand each other without words?"

Guardedly, he nodded. "We were very close, once upon a time—all through our formative years, as it were."

"Indeed. And friendships forged from childhood do tend to last, don't they?" Before he could respond, she rolled on, "As you've yet to speak with your parents, you might not yet have heard how devoted I am to Devlin and all his works. Consequently, I take a real and natural interest in the return of a very old friend." Let him read into that what he might. Still smiling, she tipped her head and studied him. "You are back to stay, aren't you?"

The sudden shift in topic made him blink again. "That is my intention."

"Excellent! In that case"—boldly, she took his arm and turned him toward the other guests—"allow me to assist you to further reconnect with society. It's the least I can do for such an old friend of my husband's."

She felt the tension leap in the arm through which she'd wound hers, but she gave him no chance to break and run as, with a bright smile, she determinedly steered him to a group of five unmarried young ladies, all of whom were in their second or later year in society and, therefore, no longer expected to remain beside their mothers.

The young ladies saw her and Child approaching and, with bright, welcoming smiles of their own, readily parted to accommodate them. Blithely, Therese introduced Child, who was forced to adopt his charming façade—she'd already noticed how effortlessly he donned the easygoing, entertaining persona she viewed as a mask—and respond as she stated the young ladies' names and they exchanged bows and curtsies.

Having perforce released her hold on him, before Child could even think of sliding away, Therese announced, "Having only just returned from nearly a decade abroad, Lord Child is woefully out of touch with the entertainments London has to offer. I'm sure he would be grateful for any hints you ladies might share."

Thus encouraged, all five ladies were quick to engage, and within minutes, Child was ensnared in a discussion of the amenities of London compared to those of New York and Boston, where he admitted he'd spent some years.

Therese listened and learned something of Child's travels herself. Under the glare of the younger ladies' focused attention, he grew restive, but the five kept up a barrage of questions, allowing him no chance to step back.

She was listening to the young ladies grill Child on his preferences in drama and the style and quality of performances he'd attended in America when her senses—always alert where Devlin was concerned—informed her he was nearing.

She glanced over her right shoulder and saw him heading her way. His gaze locked on her face, and she smiled delightedly, allowing her thoroughly smug self-satisfaction to show.

Devlin took in the quality of Therese's smile and felt the grimness that had gripped him ease. He slowed his determined pace to a more acceptable, loose-limbed stride and let his features—until then rather stony—soften.

Her smile deepening, she extended her hand, which he promptly took and proprietorially tucked into the crook of his arm. He didn't wait for her to introduce him but nodded to the young ladies, all of whom he vaguely suspected he'd met before. "Ladies."

With murmurs of "Lord Alverton" and "My lord," the five curtsied.

Sadly, the momentary distraction gave Child—who, at least to Devlin, was plainly desperate to escape—an opening.

Before Devlin could even look his way, Child drawled, "So you are here, Alverton."

As Devlin's attention snapped to Child, his old tormentor beamed a smile around the circle and said, "Now the earl is here to escort his wife, I fear you ladies must excuse me."

With a half bow to the younger ladies, a brief but elegant nod to Therese, and a fleeting, triumphant glance at Devlin, Child stepped back and quickly moved away—or more accurately, fled. That was certainly how Devlin saw Child's too-rapid retreat, but courtesy of his parting shot, most especially his tone, Child had managed to suggest that there had been something in his squiring of Therese to which Devlin might take exception.

His gaze on Child's back, Devlin fought not to clench his jaw. From the corner of his eye, he saw that the implication of Child's words hadn't been missed by the young ladies. Several pairs of eyes had widened, and at least one lady ineffectually smothered a titter.

What the devil is the damned idiot up to?

Therese ignored the titter and stared—first at Child's departing back, then at her husband's face. As usual, Devlin's expression wasn't exactly readable, but the muscle that tightened in his jaw testified to his temper.

What are the pair of them playing at? And why am I in the middle?

Child had admitted he saw himself as Devlin's friend—one old and close enough to understand him without the need for words. She knew they were old rivals of sorts, but Devlin had already won her. Surely Child couldn't be so deluded as to think he might lure her away, into some form of clandestine liaison? She was fairly certain not, but then why was Devlin reacting with...such tightly leashed aggression?

She was suddenly certain that was what she sensed pouring from him.

With murmured excuses, the young ladies took themselves off. Therese made no attempt to detain them, and with his eyes still on Child, Devlin barely tipped his head their way.

The instant the five were out of earshot, Devlin switched his hazel gaze to her. "What did Child want with you?"

He'd endeavored to keep his tone to one indicating a merely interested query, yet Therese sensed a certain trepidatious undercurrent. She smiled, allowing her genuine delight over her commandeering of Child to show. "I have no idea, because rather than listen to whatever it was, I seized the opportunity to do my good deed for the day and introduce him to those young ladies and encourage them to nurture his acquaintance."

Devlin regarded her for a second, then she felt the tension that had gripped him fade. "I take it all five are unmarried?"

She opened her eyes wide and wound her arm with his. "Of course."

He smiled at her then, one of those slow, devastating smiles that still held the power to weaken her knees. "How kind of you. I'm sure Child appreciated your assistance."

"Well"—she tipped her head—"I don't know about him, but the young ladies certainly did."

Studying Therese's expression, drinking in the smug self-satisfaction not to say gloating that shone in her silvery eyes, Devlin was relieved on more than one account. With any luck, his wife's propensity to matchmake—clearly already engaged where Child was concerned—would serve to keep his erstwhile rival out of her orbit.

Feeling significantly more relaxed, he settled her hand on his sleeve and mildly inquired, "Where are you off to next?"

She glanced around, then indicated a mixed group of gentlemen and ladies of much their age, and he willingly escorted her to join that circle.

A bare five minutes later, Lady Wicklow clapped her hands and announced that luncheon was served. Devlin seized the chance to remain beside Therese as they joined the shuffling queue leading to the long buffet set up on the side terrace of the old house. It had been some years since he'd had occasion to help her fill her plate, but he discovered he hadn't forgotten her preferences and dislikes.

When, knowing they were one of her favorites, he deposited two shrimp patties on her plate, she looked at him rather strangely. Eventually, plates in hand, they turned away from the table, descended the steps to the lawn, and having spotted an empty table in the shade of a towering oak, he guided her in that direction.

They reached the table and set down their plates, and he held one of the six wrought iron chairs for her. Once she'd settled, he caught the eye of a roving footman and lifted two glasses of champagne from the man's tray. After setting one glass in front of her, he took a sip, then drew out the chair beside hers and sat.

She'd watched him throughout the entire performance. Now, she leaned closer and murmured, "You do know that at an event such as this, dancing attendance on your wife is considered *most* unfashionable."

He met her gaze and arched his brows. "And when have I ever cared what the ton thinks of my behavior?"

As he said the words, he realized they were true; the only person whose opinion had ever mattered to him was her.

She sat back as if much struck. Regarding him as if having only just seen him, she slowly nodded and said, "Now you mention it, you have made a habit of being a law unto yourself."

Then she smiled and chuckled. "Please don't think I'm complaining." With her fork, she gestured to the plate he'd helped her fill, then circled the implement to include the prime table and her glass of champagne. "Being waited on by someone I don't have to direct is rather pleasant."

Good. Feeling as if he'd achieved a minor goal, he returned her smile, and they settled to savor the delicacies provided by Lady Wicklow's much-lauded French chef.

They were comparing the flavors of several canapés Therese thought their own chef might reproduce when Martin approached, his own loaded plate and glass in hand. He gestured to the empty chairs. "Mind if I join you?"

"Of course not!" Therese waved him to the chair on her other side, but Martin didn't move until Devlin also smiled and nodded.

Martin's stock with Devlin continued to rise.

A few minutes later, another couple of their acquaintance joined them, and once Martin had been introduced, the conversation turned general. Given there was one vacant chair at their table, Devlin kept expecting

Child to appear and join them, but although Devlin scanned the tables all around, he caught not a glimpse of his nemesis.

That left him feeling rather more in charity with the world. All in all, the day had thus far been a success. As he had hoped, the wide range of guests had excused his presence, allowing him to spend hours with Therese—more or less wooing her as he hadn't before.

Once their plates were empty, the guests rose again and, at Lady Wicklow's recommendation, commenced ambling down the many paths that led deeper into the extensive gardens.

Devlin had had time to consider his best way forward. After he'd helped Therese to her feet, he, she, and Martin parted from the other couple. Before Martin could think of taking himself off, Devlin caught Therese's eye. "The groups wandering the gardens will be rather smaller than on the lawn, and the exchanges less formal, more relaxed. Perhaps you and I should escort Martin around. You can deal with the female half of society, while I pave his way with the men, both socially and business-wise."

Therese's face lit. "What a wonderful notion." She linked her arm with his and looked at Martin. "This truly is a superb venue at which to further your resurrection within the ton. We really should make the most of it."

Martin looked from one to the other, then smiling, inclined his head. "When it comes to managing my return to the ton, I place myself in your hands."

Therese beamed. "Excellent. Now!" She surveyed the guests departing down the various paths. "I suspect the path to the lake will prove most fruitful. Come along!"

Martin grinned and gestured for Devlin and Therese to precede him. Smiling, Devlin escorted his wife on, in pursuit of what was transparently to be her latest social campaign, and Martin fell in behind them.

CHAPTER 5

The following morning, Devlin left Alverton House and set off to walk to St. James. He was too experienced to cling to Therese's side through every hour of every day; there was a limit to her blindness, especially regarding him, and he wasn't yet ready to lay down his cards in the game of revelation that, did she but know it, he was playing with her.

Despite Child sticking in his oar, yesterday had gone very well. On the journey back, while Martin distracted Therese with questions about those he had met, Devlin had used the time to consider what else—what other situations—he could engineer to advance his cause. To woo his wife without alerting the entire ton to that fact. As a consequence, later in the evening, he had penned several letters and, despite the hour, had dispatched footmen to deliver them.

While those irons were in the fire, he'd decided that concentrating his efforts in areas that he knew would please her would be the most sensible use of his time. He was, therefore, on his way to meet Martin, to further his brother-in-law's introduction to the ton.

They'd arranged to meet at eleven o'clock outside White's on St. James Street. When Devlin hove in sight of that august club's portal, he was pleased to see Martin leaning against the wall of the building next to the club. While transparently waiting for someone, the younger man was using the time to study who went in and out of the club as well as taking note of the gentlemen strolling past.

As Devlin approached, Martin straightened from the wall. He nodded in greeting as Devlin halted beside him, then tipped his head toward White's door. "Is it still as stuffy as it was?"

Devlin pretended to consider, then nodded. "At least." He eyed Martin. "I'm sure your father will put your name down and you'll be admitted, but for your purposes, being a member of White's is unlikely to be of much help." He looked down the street. "That's why I suggested I show you around the more useful venues."

Given Martin's focus on establishing a machinery manufacturing business and Devlin's interest in business investment, he knew which clubs had memberships most amenable to making the right connections.

Martin waved down the street. "By all means, lead on. Where to first?"

With his cane, Devlin pointed across the street. "Boodle's."

As a member himself, Devlin led Martin inside, introduced him to the doorman and concierge, then gave Martin a quick tour of the rooms.

From there, they proceeded down St. James Street, stopping in at Brooks's for a similar tour before entering Arthur's. On leading Martin into the club's library, Devlin scanned the room. Only a few of the comfortable leather armchairs, arranged in groups of three and four about the room, were occupied. Quietly, he said, "We're a trifle early for the usual crowd, but of all the clubs in town, this is the one favored by most of my peers and also many of your in-laws and connections, at least those of our generation."

Martin glanced shrewdly at Devlin. "Your favorite club?"

"Yes." He paused, then went on, "I'm a member of six clubs, and as you'll have gathered from what I said at Boodle's and Brooks's, each has a distinct...flavor, I suppose you might say. I use each club for what it offers. If I need information on politics, I'll call in at the Reform and, these days, perhaps White's. For some types of business, the Oriental is best, but Boodle's and Brooks's can also be useful. On almost any subject of interest, be it social, business, politics, or government, there's a decent chance you'll learn something at Arthur's. It might not be in the same depth as you might find via one of the other venues, but it'll be enough to set you on the right track."

Looking around, Martin nodded. "So this is a central clearinghouse for information of all sorts."

"Among our set, yes." Devlin gestured across the hall. "Let's take a look in the smoking room. That's the room for conversations and discussions. Despite the hour, we might find more members there."

Sure enough, there were quite a few groups of gentlemen scattered about the long room, which was actually three rooms joined together with various alcoves on both sides. And as if to confirm Devlin's earlier words, Henry Cynster, Jason Cynster, and George Rawlings were seated idly chatting in one of the alcoves; with respect to Martin, the first two were cousins of sorts, and George was a connection, and all three were close to Martin in age.

George happened to glance up, saw Devlin, and nodded, then his gaze moved on to Martin. George blinked, then sat straighter and said, "I say, Alverton, isn't that…?"

The other two looked up, recognized Martin, and hailed him. Devlin accompanied his brother-in-law over and, amused, watched and listened as Henry, Jason, and George pumped Martin's hand, insisted he join them, and proceeded to bombard him with questions as to where he'd been and why and what he was planning now he'd come back.

Having glimpsed James and Cedric farther down the room, Devlin clapped Martin on the shoulder and interrupted his replies to say, "I'm going to talk to some others. Come and fetch me when you're ready to go on."

Smiling, Martin nodded, then returned to satisfying his long-ago friends' curiosities.

Devlin ambled down the room. Even before he reached the armchairs James and Cedric occupied, he knew from the look on Cedric's face that James, who was speaking animatedly, was relating the latest episode in the apparently never-ending saga of his marriage. The melodrama that perennially invested James and Veronica's clashes would have done credit to a Haymarket stage.

As Devlin neared, Cedric looked up, and after following his gaze, James broke from his monologue to observe, "You're out early."

"I could say the same for you two." Devlin dropped into the third chair in the grouping.

James huffed. "I'm sure you, at least, haven't been driven from your home. My wife is driving me demented!"

Unseen by James, Cedric rolled his eyes.

Knowing what was expected of him, good friend that he was, Devlin inquired, "Oh?"

He settled and resigned himself to spending the next ten minutes pretending to listen to a litany of James's complaints, but the insight into the Hemmingses' marriage that Therese had offered on their drive home from the park rose in his mind, and he found himself listening rather more attentively, searching for—and finding—numerous indications that, as usual in such matters, Therese had been right.

James wasn't really complaining at all, although he dressed up his concerns, his uncomfortableness over loving his wife, in those terms. James had been taken by surprise and was still struggling to accept and adjust to the reality that he loved his wife. He'd yet to grapple meaningfully with rescripting his expectations and finding ways to cope with a situation he had never imagined happening to him.

For the first time since James had started railing about his marriage, Devlin grasped the genesis of James's problem.

Given it wasn't a problem he shared, his blindness until now wasn't all that surprising. From the first moment he'd met Therese, he'd known and accepted—inwardly if not outwardly—that he loved her. He'd loved her in that first instant and, even then, hadn't doubted, hadn't questioned, hadn't underestimated the magnitude of the force that had erupted and gripped him. Not for a minute had he thought of attempting to resist such an all-consuming passion; he'd never imagined that excising it from his soul was a viable option. Instead, he'd embraced it—wholly and completely. He'd concealed his state from everyone else, especially Therese, but he'd never attempted to deny or defy the emotion that was now such a fundamental part of him or pretend that it was less than it was.

The latter was what James was still actively attempting to do, predictably to no avail.

Devlin could have told James not to waste his time, not to exhaust himself in such a futile endeavor. Indeed, the impulse to tell James that fighting love was impossible set words burning the tip of Devlin's tongue, but he swallowed them. Until James stopped trying to deny that he was in love with his wife, recommendations of how to cope with that emotion would fall on deaf ears. Until James was ready to listen, there was no point speaking.

Eventually, as he always did, James ran down, ending somewhat dejectedly staring at the toes of his boots. Then James raised his gaze and focused on Cedric. "But enough about me and the sorry state of my life. Devlin, as usual, is busy juggling his family, business, and politics, but what about you, old son? What are you up to?"

"Well." Cedric leaned back in the chair and folded his hands across his stomach. "I'm tossing up whether to take up my uncle Maxwell's annual invitation to shoot grouse in Scotland. And there's a sale at Tattersalls that I wouldn't mind attending."

With James, Devlin listened as Cedric outlined the events likely to fill his calendar over the coming months. Although Devlin remained outwardly relaxed, he felt...restless and impatient on his friend's behalf. A life like Cedric's would—in James's words—drive Devlin demented. Admittedly, from his earliest years, he'd been raised to manage a large and wealthy estate and shoulder the responsibility of providing for not just his family but also all those who depended on the earldom of Alverton.

To drift through life as Cedric was doing, with a complete lack of any meaningful goal... Devlin would find such an existence crippling.

He glanced at James, then returned his gaze to Cedric and gave mute thanks for his present life and his current course. The prospect of, with Therese, building something lasting and meaningful from the building blocks he'd inherited was the foundation stone of Devlin's purpose, the engine that drove him through life. He wouldn't be him—the man he was and the man he wanted and hoped to be—without it.

Viewing the roiling morass of James's life and the aimlessness of Cedric's reaffirmed for Devlin that his latest tack was not just worth pursuing but an endeavor he needed to push to a successful conclusion. Having Therese join with him in harnessing the power he now knew love brought to a marriage was, beyond question, the right path for him.

Cedric was still verbally ambling through his uninspiring prospects for the coming weeks when Martin walked up. Cedric broke off, and Devlin introduced his youngest brother-in-law, glibly referring to Martin's return from America as if it was in no way remarkable.

Martin shook hands with James and Cedric, and Devlin rose. He arranged to meet James and Cedric for dinner at Boodle's that evening, then farewelled them and, with Martin, quit the club.

Devlin resettled his hat, then with his cane, waved down the street. "Right—let's head to the Reform Club in Pall Mall, and on the way, we might as well look in at the Carlton Club."

Martin acquiesced with a nod, and they set off down the street.

After conducting an attentive, interested, and observant Martin around the two most-notable clubs in Pall Mall, Devlin hailed a hackney, and they traveled north to Hanover Square and the Oriental Club.

Standing on the pavement outside the club and looking up at its imposing façade, Devlin explained, "The club was originally established for those who had served in or who had visited and had business interests in India and the East Indies. The majority of the members would still fit that description, but others, such as myself, are connected to the East purely via business interests." Devlin glanced at Martin. "These days, the Oriental is an excellent place to meet gentlemen with experience in the business of importing."

Martin met Devlin's eyes. "Whether from the East or the West?"

Devlin smiled and inclined his head. "Indeed. The club is also known for having an excellent chef and a superb cellar." He gestured to the door. "Come. I'll stand you lunch."

While showing Martin around the club, Devlin was stopped by three different gentlemen, two of whom had snippets of business information to impart, and the third solicited Devlin's advice about a milling business in the Midlands.

Martin kept silent and listened and, when they parted from the third gentleman, murmured, "And that's why you're a member here."

"Exactly." Devlin gestured toward an archway. "The dining room's through there."

The club's butler welcomed them and showed them to a table in an alcove. They settled and proceeded to enjoy an excellent goat curry, served with various strange but tasty accompaniments.

Devlin waved his fork at the dishes. "The fare does tend to be oriental in nature, I suspect along the lines of stirring fond memories."

Martin huffed, then admitted, "I suppose I can understand that." He went on to describe some of the unusual foods he'd come across in America, and Devlin learned that, although his brother-in-law had spent most of his time in New York and Chicago, he'd also traveled to cities farther south.

Inevitably, the talk turned to business, and it became clear that Martin was devoting considerable time and mental energy toward refining his idea of establishing a machinery manufactory.

While Devlin knew little about machines themselves—gears and so forth—he recalled that Rand's brother-in-law, William John Throgmorton, was a brilliant inventor of steam-driven machinery. He told Martin of the connection. "You might look up William John—" He broke off, then went on, "Actually, I've just remembered. It's Rand's wife, Felicia, you should speak with. Their late father—hers and William John's—was the brilliant scientist-inventor whom Rand originally backed. Inventing-wise, both Felicia and William John are chips off the old block, but it's she— believe it or not—who is the organized one who ensures that things get done. William John is undoubtedly brilliant, but also eccentric. You might talk to him and think you had agreed on something, only to discover he'd actually been thinking about some cog or valve and hadn't been paying attention." Devlin refocused on Martin. "Given your interests, I would strongly urge you to speak with Felicia Cavanaugh."

Martin slowly nodded. "At the picnic, Rand gave me his card and told me to call if I needed advice on securing funding. I'll follow that up, explain my interest in machinery, and ask him to introduce me to his wife."

Devlin grinned. "Strange to say, he'll be happy to do that. Felicia's always on the lookout for new inventions or, as I understand it, industrial processes in need of improvement."

Martin nodded decisively. "She sounds like the sort of person I should contact. I need to learn which industries are most in need of modernization as well as what the prospects for entirely new processes are."

They talked further regarding his evolving ideas and departed the club in definite charity with each other.

Devlin detoured along Oxford Street to show Martin the Portland Club on the corner of Stratford Place. They halted on the pavement outside the club. "It's the most acceptable venue for enthusiasts of card games, but you won't find much else discussed in the rooms."

Martin glanced at him. "A purely social venue?"

Devlin nodded. "I've rarely been inside, but you might well hear of it or be invited to accompany someone else there, so best you know. The play is often deep. Against that, you won't find any Captain Sharps in residence."

"Duly noted."

Together, they turned away from the building. With his cane, Devlin gestured across the street, and they crossed and continued south along Davies Street, walking with easy strides into the heart of Mayfair.

"And that concludes your tour of the cream of London's gentlemen's clubs." Devlin glanced at Martin. "As I'm sure your cousins and any friends you may stumble across while in the capital will tell you, there are countless other establishments catering to every vice under the sun to be found in London's streets, but you'll need advice from someone your own age as to which are safe to patronize." He paused, then added, "What I wouldn't advise is making that assessment on your own—appearances can be deceiving, especially when it comes to anything to do with the ton."

Martin snorted. "*That*, I already know."

After a moment, Devlin felt Martin's gaze as the younger man swiftly searched his face.

Then Martin said, "I'm grateful to you for steering me in the right direction, not just with the clubs but with business as well, so don't take this question amiss, but you're already well-established and successfully settled in your business endeavors, while I'm your wife's errant, black-sheep, prodigal little brother. Why are you being so helpful?"

Devlin continued to stroll as he thought about that; it was a fair question, and the answer wasn't all that hard to find. He paused for a second, debating how truthful to be, then met Martin's gaze. "I might say that I feel duty bound, or that I'm distantly interested in watching how you evolve your ideas."

Martin's gaze sharpened. "But?"

Devlin inclined his head and halted; they'd reached the corner of Brooks Street. He swung to face Martin, who had halted as well. "But the most accurate answer is that Therese wants to see you happy, meaning that seeing you find your feet within the ton and succeed in business will make *her* happy. That being so, I'm happy to—willing and ready to—assist you in achieving your goals in whatever way I can."

Martin scrutinized his expression.

Unperturbed, Devlin smiled. "Your sister couldn't have shown you around the clubs, and while Gregory might, he's not focused on the business world, and he's also not as well-connected, socially or business-wise, as I am." Then Devlin caught Martin's gaze and, still smiling, quietly said, "You might remember that, in all this, my principal motivation is to see Therese happy."

The implication that he would be very *un*happy were Therese to cease to be content rang clearly in the simple words.

Martin read the warning in Devlin's eyes and dipped his head. "I'll bear that in mind." He looked away. After a second, he added, "Thank you for telling me."

Smoothly, Devlin inclined his head and, in lighter vein, asked what Martin's plans were for the rest of the day.

He learned that the younger man intended to return to the house in

Arlington Street where he was currently staying before following up one of the business contacts he'd made at the exhibition.

"After that, I'm going to meet Henry, Jason, and some of their friends for dinner." Martin threw Devlin a mischievous smile that reminded him forcibly of Therese. "I suspect they'll want to introduce me to some of those other clubs you mentioned."

Devlin grunted. "Very likely." Somewhat to his own surprise, he felt confident Martin had more than enough sense to keep himself out of trouble. "Just remember what I said."

Martin chuckled. "I will."

With that, they parted, and Devlin headed west along the north side of Grosvenor Square, leaving Martin walking on toward Piccadilly and Arlington Street beyond.

～

Five minutes later, Devlin let himself into the front hall of Alverton House. Portland came forward to relieve him of his hat, cane, and greatcoat. After consigning all three items into his butler's care, Devlin inquired, "I take it the mail has arrived?"

"Indeed, my lord, some hours ago. Her ladyship collected all that were hers, and subsequently, I placed the remaining missives on your desk."

"Thank you." Devlin proceeded to the study. He shut the door, then crossed to the desk, sat behind it, picked up his letter knife, and settled to open the small mountain of missives stacked on his blotter.

He was sunk in analyzing the information sent by his various stewards regarding the harvests thus far when Portland tapped and, at Devlin's mumbled "Come," entered.

Devlin glanced up to see a thick envelope in the butler's hand.

"A couriered delivery, my lord."

"Excellent!" Devlin pushed aside his stewards' letters and held out a hand. It appeared one of his contacts had managed the impossible.

He took the packet, wielded the letter knife, and shattered the seal. He spread the packet's contents on his blotter, revealing a letter and an ornate voucher. The sight of the latter made him smile.

"Will there be anything else, my lord?"

Devlin glanced at the clock on the mantelpiece, then looked at Portland. "Has her ladyship taken the barouche?" Although overcast, the day had remained dry.

"Indeed, my lord. I overheard the countess give Munns orders to drive to the park."

It was past three-thirty. "Very good." Devlin restacked the stewards' letters and glanced briefly at the others that had arrived; none required his urgent attention, and he set the lot aside. Then he opened the top drawer to his right and put the letter and the voucher inside, shut the drawer, and rose.

Still smiling, he met Portland's eyes. "I believe, Portland, that I'll take a walk."

As he'd hoped, Devlin found Therese in her carriage, drawn into the verge along the avenue. Lady Finlay and her unmarried daughter were seated in the open carriage with Therese, and a group of three ladies and two gentlemen had paused on the lawn beside the barouche, and the five were chatting animatedly with the three occupants.

Therese was the first to see him approaching, and for a second, she stared. Then she was forced to return her attention to the conversation before her, but Devlin was aware that, from the corner of her eye, she kept him in sight as he strolled nearer.

He did nothing to conceal his intention of joining her; he had an excellent excuse for wishing to speak with her. That said, he saw no reason to cut short her entertainment; he was well aware that she found guiding younger ladies through the shoals of the Marriage Mart diverting.

So when he paused by the carriage and, still faintly surprised, she tipped her head his way and said, "My lord," he nodded back in relaxed fashion and, smiling benevolently on the small gathering, asked her to introduce him.

Once the introductions were complete, he smoothly apologized for interrupting the conversation and, with a languid wave, said, "Don't mind me. Do carry on."

After a fractional hesitation, the group obliged, somewhat warily at first, but when he gave no sign of doing anything other than listening, their animation returned, and they continued their discussion of their social calendars and the events they expected to be the highlights of the coming weeks.

With very little interest in that subject, Devlin seized the moment to indulge himself by watching Therese in her element. There was something about the way she so commandingly managed the conversational reins that he found quite...entrancing.

Arousing, truth be told; watching her was akin to studying a master of social manipulation wielding their magic.

But the shadows were lengthening, and a brisk breeze sprang up, making several ladies shiver. One of the gentlemen consulted his timepiece and declared it was nearly four o'clock, and in a rush, the group walking made their farewells and departed.

Lady Finlay briefly eyed Devlin, then turned to Therese. "Dulcimea and I had better be on our way as well, dear Lady Alverton. Thank you so much for your wise counsel—Dulcimea will be sure to bear your words in mind."

Devlin waved Dennis, his young footman, back and opened and held the carriage door. He offered his hand and assisted Lady Finlay and her daughter to descend.

"Thank you, my lord." Lady Finlay waited for Dulcimea to curtsy, then wound her arm in her daughter's. Then her ladyship looked at Devlin and faintly smiled. "And for being so patient." She cut a glance at Therese and inclined her head graciously. "We'll leave you to your delightful wife's company."

With that, the pair turned and set off across the lawn.

Devlin watched until they were out of earshot, then climbed the steps and joined Therese in the carriage.

She studied him as he settled elegantly on the seat beside her and Dennis shut the carriage door.

Without looking around, Munns asked, "My lord?"

"Home, Munns." Devlin looked at Therese and more quietly verified, "I take it that was your intention?"

She was still regarding him with something close to fascination. "It was." She waited until the carriage rocked into motion, then drew breath and said, "If I might ask, to what do I owe this unexpected pleasure?"

He smiled; he'd been waiting for her to inquire. "First, it occurred to me that this relatively fine weather is unlikely to last much longer, and then early next month, we'll up stakes and head to the Priory. I wondered if we shouldn't seize the moment to indulge the children and take them to the zoo. They haven't been since April, and you know how they love to see their favorite animals."

She was already nodding. "That's an excellent idea. Especially as, once we leave, we won't be back until early March, if not later."

"Indeed. And with the exhibition entering its final week, most visitors to the capital, and many Londoners, too, are flocking there, so with luck, the zoo won't be overly crowded."

"I agree." She turned to look at him. "When were you thinking of going?"

He shrugged lightly and met her gaze. "Are you doing anything tomorrow morning?"

"Thursday morning..." She frowned as if mentally consulting a diary, then her face cleared. "I have nothing I absolutely need to attend." After a second, she added, "We could go early—say at ten o'clock—and be back for a late luncheon. That way, we'll be able to keep our afternoon appointments."

He nodded. "Good. That's settled, then. We'll leave at ten o'clock." He smoothly rolled on, "And the other subject on which I wished to consult you was whether you would like to attend the opera on Friday evening."

She stared at him. "*This* Friday?"

He nodded. "The chance of a box on that night has come my way, and I wondered if you would be interested in viewing the current production."

The expression of stunned wonder that filled her face was all and more than he'd hoped for.

Therese could barely believe her ears. Indeed, she felt compelled to clarify, "You are talking of the Vienna Opera's performance of *William Tell* to be held at the Royal Italian Opera House in Covent Garden? The one that was all but immediately sold out from the moment it was announced—that's the performance you're referring to?"

"So I believe—Friday evening at the Royal Italian Opera House in Covent Garden."

She expelled the breath she'd been holding. "Good Lord! How on earth did you manage to secure tickets, let alone a box? Most of London's hostesses would kill for a box."

Her exasperating husband grinned at her. "I take it that's a yes?"

"That's a Good Lord Almighty yes!" Still stunned, she stared at him. "I can't believe you snagged a box. How did you manage it?"

He shrugged lightly and looked ahead. "A friend of a business acquaintance has reason to want to butter me up. You know how it goes."

She did. She sat back against the seat and, as the carriage rolled smoothly through the park gates and turned onto Park Lane, marveled at such a remarkable stroke of good fortune. Unable to stop smiling, she envisioned the event, then cast a curious glance at Devlin. "Do you plan on attending?"

Attending the opera was by no means his favorite pastime, but occasionally, he accompanied her, more to show his face and connect with other gentlemen than from any wish to experience a performance.

He tilted his head and appeared to weigh the matter, then slowly nodded. "Given the chance came via a business associate, I suspect it will be politic to be there myself, to demonstrate that I appreciate the opportunity directed my way."

That made sense. As they rolled through the open gates of Alverton House, Therese reflected that, regardless of his reasons for accompanying her, the prospect of having him by her side added an extra fillip to her already soaring expectations of the evening.

～

The following morning dawned fine and clear, with a brisk breeze swirling the fallen leaves in Regent's Park.

By the time Devlin and Therese guided their brood through the ornate wrought iron gates of the Zoological Gardens, the sun had been up for some time and, although weak, together with the breeze had managed to dry the gravel and the grass verges bordering the paths.

As usual, Spencer and Rupert ran ahead, closely but unobtrusively shadowed by Dennis, the footman. With Nanny Sprockett and Patty, one of the nursemaids, Dennis had been brought along to help shepherd the children.

Little Horry had insisted on walking and was toddling along, clutching Therese's hand. Devlin strolled beside his daughter, smiling as he watched his sons make a beeline for the camel enclosure.

The zoo had opened to the public only four years ago, but from that time, Devlin and Therese had made a point of taking the children there at least twice a year, and it had become one of the boys' most anticipated excursions. There were thirty or so exhibits, but the boys, of course, had their favorites. The camels, the lions and tigers, the giraffes, and the elephants were always on their must-see list.

After duly pausing to admire the camels, they walked on, skirting the large enclosure that housed a flock of pelicans. Abruptly, Horry stopped, drew her hand from Therese's, and clapped excitedly, then she chortled and rushed to press her little face to the bars.

Therese crouched beside Horry and peered at the little girl's rapt expression.

Horry pointed at the pelicans. "Birdies! Birdies!"

Therese smiled. "Yes, sweetheart. Big white birds."

Devlin leaned down and, when Horry looked excitedly at him, smiled. "They're called pelicans."

Horry screwed up her little mouth and managed, "Peri-cans." When Devlin's smile deepened, she looked back at the birds and pointed. "Peri-cans! Peri-cans!"

Therese laughed, rose, and held out her hand. "Yes, indeed. And you can keep looking at them as we walk along, but we need to catch up with your brothers."

Horry's rosebud lips formed an O, and she obediently let Therese take her hand and lead her on. Horry searched the paths ahead, plainly looking for her siblings. "Where?"

Devlin, who had kept the boys in sight, reached down and took Horry's other hand. "They're looking at the lions and tigers in their cages." He pointed. "Can you see them?"

Horry's little face looked worried, but then she spotted Spencer and Rupert, and her expression lit. Then she stopped, tugged her hands free, faced Devlin, and held up her arms. "Up! Up!"

Smiling, he dutifully scooped her up and settled her in his arms. He'd known that was coming. Not only could she see better from that vantage point, but Horry wasn't all that enamored with the lions and tigers, who occasionally roared.

She jigged in his arms as he carried her along, but when they approached the cages, she quieted and leaned against his chest. He halted several yards behind his sons. The boys were standing a few feet from the brick base of the main cage and staring in wonder at the large male lion prowling back and forth on the other side of the bars.

With Horry tucking her head beneath his chin, Devlin glanced at Therese.

She smiled, patted Horry, then went forward to crouch between Spencer and Rupert and talk to them about the big cats.

With his arms full of the soft weight of his daughter, Devlin watched Therese and his sons and felt richly satisfied. He'd suggested the outing in order to distract Therese from thinking too much about the opera tomorrow night, specifically about how, at such a late date, he came by a box for an event that had been sold out for so long and for which many among the ton remained fervently eager to snap up any stray tickets.

Therese rose and, with the boys, moved to the next cage, where a tiger snoozed, barely deigning to open one eye. Devlin smiled as Rupert—the tigers were his favorite—started to explain something to Therese, and she listened with encouraging interest. He was pleased his diversion was working and also because it was a pleasant interlude in the family's otherwise structured ton existence.

At the zoo, the children were freer to run and shout and point and exclaim. Indeed, *he* was conscious of being free from others' eyes, too; in that setting, he didn't need to keep an eye peeled for Child or anyone else and could largely be himself without restraint.

The boys finally moved on from the tiger and headed for the giraffes' enclosure. Therese went with them. Devlin looked at Horry and arched his brows in question, and she smiled and wriggled. "Down."

Obediently, he bent and deposited her on her feet, then followed as she raced after her brothers.

Horry rushed past Therese to catch Rupert's arm and steady herself, then with her brothers, she stared at the long-legged, brown-spotted orange beasts stalking on cloven hooves about the space behind the railings.

After confirming that all three children were absorbed, Therese glanced around and smiled as Devlin ambled up to halt beside her. She watched as his gaze rested on the children, saw the expression of contentment that softened his sharply cut, aristocratic features, and felt appreciation well.

She experienced that emotion, one of gladness and gratitude, quite often when out with him and the children. As a maven of society, she knew very well that few of his peers would ever even think of accompanying their children on such outings. Children were to be seen and not heard—and even then, the seeing was severely restricted and regimented. Gentlemen like Devlin hired others to raise their children, yet to his credit and her real relief, he'd never been of that mind.

He'd never been a distant father, although she strongly suspected his own father had been. From the moment that, as squalling newborns, each of their children had been placed in his arms, he'd embraced them as if they were the gifts she herself thought them, gifts it was his duty and pleasure to protect and guide through life.

Growing bored with the stately giraffes, the children ran on to where the two elephants were stamping and tossing hay about their enclosure. Whether the animals were engaged in some game or a disagreement wasn't clear, but the boys applauded the action and cheered the beasts on, and Horry jumped up and down and enthusiastically added her voice to the chorus.

Devlin chuckled, Therese smiled and linked her arm with his, and they strolled in their offsprings' wakes.

Although Nanny Sprockett, Patty, and Dennis hovered, ready to assist if required, Therese and Devlin took it upon themselves to herd the children around the paths and along the fronts of the enclosures. They had arrived soon after the gardens had opened, and as the morning wore on, more families appeared. When they reached the monkeys, Devlin took the boys' hands and held them back until others departed and a suitable opening appeared, then went forward with them, while Therese lifted Horry and carried her to where she could look into the cages over her brothers' heads.

The monkeys chattered noisily, and the boys grinned, then Rupert asked whether monkeys ate only monkey nuts. "And why," Spencer added, "are they called 'monkey nuts' when we eat them, too?"

Therese briefly met Devlin's eyes and left that for him to answer—which he did, explaining that other people called the nuts different names, for instance, peanuts, but that as the British first learned of the nuts as monkeys' favorite food, the name "monkey nut" had stuck in their country.

"As for what monkeys eat"—Devlin looked at Rupert—"I know they eat bananas and other types of fruit."

"But not eggs or bacon or sausages?" Rupert asked.

Devlin ruffled Rupert's hair. "I'm not sure that anyone has ever offered them eggs, bacon, or sausages, but I suspect they wouldn't like them. I think they're herbivores, which means animals that eat only leaves, fruits, nuts, and vegetables."

"We're not herbivores," Spencer declared. Then he looked up at Devlin, faintly puzzled. "What are we?"

"I think"—Devlin met Therese's eyes and widened his in a plea for help; they'd discovered that giving incorrect answers could sometimes rebound in unexpected ways and in unhelpful company—"that as we eat meat of all sorts, we're carnivores."

Therese promptly stepped in. "*However,* because we also eat our vegetables—and you know Nanny Sprockett is forever telling you how important that is—then we're actually, technically, omnivores."

Devlin nodded. "*Omni* means 'all' in Latin, and *vores* comes from the Latin verb *vorare*, which means"—he widened his eyes at the boys and raised both hands like claws—"'to devour!' Argh!"

The boys shrieked and giggled as Devlin pounced on them both and pretended to roar like a beast.

Therese couldn't stop smiling. She couldn't imagine any other earl making a fool of himself in public just to make his children laugh.

They finally waved goodbye to the monkeys. With all three children starting to flag, Therese caught Devlin's eye and tipped her head toward the exit, and he nodded and steered their tribe in that direction.

Wise in the ways of young children, Nanny Sprockett had brought biscuits; once she'd distributed her treats, the children walked rather slower as they munched, allowing the adults to stroll in more leisurely fashion.

With her arm wound in Devlin's, with him, Therese followed their trio and inwardly acknowledged how content she was with the way the morning had gone. The truth was she treasured the moments such excursions gave rise to—the interactions, the often-wordless communication, the sense of acting together to protect and nurture the three little people they both held so dear.

In dealing with their children, she and Devlin had always been something of a team, but today, that partnership had seemed…smoother. Easier. More instinctive and practiced. The closeness, the sense of togetherness the morning had engendered, reminded her of how they'd worked together in reintroducing Martin to the ton at Lady Wicklow's event two days before. There, too, she'd sensed a drawing closer, at least in terms of their understanding of each other, of how the other thought and would behave.

Whatever the subtle change, or perhaps a deepening of something that had already existed, Devlin seemed as amenable to embracing it as she was.

She glanced at him; he was watching the children, and she seized the moment to drink in his relaxed, easygoing expression. Looking ahead again, she revised her assessment; he wasn't passively accepting the change she'd sensed but actively inviting and encouraging it.

They'd been married for over five years. Such a change—a deepening connection—was, she supposed, to be expected of a maturing relationship.

Not having any similar relationship with which to compare, she couldn't be sure, but she resolved to keep her eyes open and her wits about her during their upcoming joint engagements to see what other signs of evolution she might detect.

Her mind returned to the hour and more she'd spent with Devlin after Lady Wicklow's picnic had been consumed, when they'd banded together in furthering Martin's cause. She'd enjoyed those minutes more than she'd expected; she'd derived more satisfaction from those moments than she had through any similar interlude at a ton event.

And her delight hadn't been solely due to her pleasure over helping Martin. She'd found herself engrossed with what she'd learned about Devlin and his various interests, as with her on his arm, he'd weaved through the guests and sought to make her brother known to those who might be useful to Martin in reclaiming his place in the ton.

Somewhat to her surprise, she'd had a role to play, too; several times, Devlin had thrown her a certain look, which—correctly, as it had turned out—she'd interpreted as an appeal for her to distract one or more gentlemen while he and Martin conversed with another. She'd discovered that her years in society had left her more than able to engage with such men and divert their attention from Devlin and Martin's more private discussions.

That had been…a novel challenge, and meeting it had left her feeling buoyed.

Looking back on those moments, thinking of the deepening connection between her and Devlin and imagining what might lie ahead, she acknowledged that, now the children were growing and she'd consolidated her control over the various Alverton households, she was rather keen to take what seemed to be shaping up as her next step, namely to fulfill the role of Devlin's countess on a wider, business-inclusive, possibly politics-inclusive stage.

The more she dwelled on all she'd sensed and felt over the past days, it definitely seemed that Devlin was ready and willing and even happy to invite her deeper into his life.

At the thought, she felt hope, anticipation, and eagerness soar. She was definitely ready to take on that challenge.

"Mama! Mama!" Rupert pointed, then turned big eyes up to her face. "Did you see the g'rilla scratching himself?"

She'd missed the performance, but duly glanced at the gorilla's cage as they strolled past, then turned to her expectant sons and said, "And now you know why gentlemen who behave like that are said to be no better than apes!"

From the corner of her eye, she saw Devlin struggling to hold back a laugh. She shifted her gaze, for an instant limpid with innocence, to his face, then she smiled, chuckled, and tipped her head lightly against his shoulder before facing forward and settling her arm more comfortably in his as, together, with the children running ahead, they walked toward the exit.

CHAPTER 6

$\mathcal{O}$n Friday evening, Devlin sat draped in shadows alongside Therese in a prime box at the Royal Italian Opera House and watched his wife's face. On the stage, the tenor was delivering an aria with passion and verve, but for Devlin, the expressions that flitted over Therese's fine features were infinitely more mesmerizing.

Even the downpour outside, a torrential storm with which they'd had to contend to reach the Opera House's foyer, hadn't dimmed her mood, her transparent expectation of enjoyment. Anticipation had glowed in her eyes and lit her entire countenance.

On the way to Covent Garden, she'd admitted that she'd considered inviting others to join them in the box, but given the invitation would have been at such short notice, she'd decided against it.

He hadn't thought of that possibility and appreciated her restraint. Being able to drink in her expressions without anyone else being close enough to notice his absorption was his notion of a just reward.

He was dimly, distantly aware of the activity on the stage, but his attention remained riveted on Therese, on the play of emotions ranging from tense to rapturous that, as the music swelled and built and the soloists' voices combined in a duet, flowed across her features.

She'd always enjoyed musical performances. He'd learned that shortly after they'd first met, when he'd been forced to inveigle an invitation from one of his aunts to a musical evening held by said aunt's closest friend by pretending to an interest in the talents of some Italian tenor, purely in order to continue to cross Miss Therese Cynster's path. It had, however, been several years since he'd accompanied her to an opera; he'd forgotten how completely the dramatic music could enthrall her and sweep her away. Sweep her consciousness from this world and leave her reactions visible for anyone to see.

Of course, the vast majority of the ladies and even the gentlemen occupying the boxes to either side were similarly affected, which left him to enjoy the sight of Therese's changing expressions without fear of being observed.

In the grip of a fascination he could rarely indulge, he didn't stir or redirect his gaze until the curtains swished closed and the attendants rushed about, turning up the gaslights for the main intermission.

The visiting Vienna Court Opera had elected to perform the shortened version of Rossini's *William Tell*, which comprised three acts. The interval between the first two acts had been of only a few minutes' duration, just long enough to allow the scenery to be changed and those who had secured seats for the highly anticipated performance to look around and take note of who else had managed the feat and smile and nod and catch the eye of those they wished to impress by their presence.

Devlin had seized the moment to ask Therese what she'd thought of the production to that point and had happily listened to her rhapsodize until the lights had dimmed and expectant silence had descended on the auditorium once more.

Now, Therese sighed and turned to Devlin. "Thus far, this has been a tour de force." She glanced past him at the occupants of the next box, then swept her gaze around the circle. "The audience seems to be more heavily weighted to the diplomatic set than the usual ton gathering."

Elegantly, Devlin uncrossed his long legs. "I suspect that's an outcome of so many visiting dignitaries having congregated in the city for the final week of the exhibition."

He rose as an attendant opened the door to the box and wheeled in a trolley bearing a large platter of canapés, glasses, and an ice bucket in which resided an open bottle of champagne. After closing the door, the attendant parked the trolley against the rear wall, then at Devlin's signal, poured two glasses of the wine.

Devlin took the glasses and offered one to her.

Still seated, she accepted it with a quizzical lift to her brows. "Is this your doing or our benefactor's?"

He sipped and glanced at the attendant, who was readying the platter of canapés. "Mine." He looked back at her and smiled. "It seemed the least I could do to add to the ambiance, given the box fell into my lap."

He raised his glass to her, and smiling, she returned the salute and sipped.

The attendant came forward to offer the canapés, and she chose a small pastry. She barely had time to savor it before the first knock fell on the box door.

At Devlin's nod, the attendant opened the door, inquired of the persons without, then stood back and announced, "Lord and Lady Hardcastle, Lady Poulson, and Miss Nagley."

Therese rose as Lady Hardcastle, a matron with whom she had a passing acquaintance, swept into the box and, barely glancing at Devlin, bore down on her.

"My dear countess, I might have known you would be here! Such a splendid performance, don't you think?"

Therese recalled that Lady Hardcastle considered herself something of a musical aficionado. "Indeed. I can't remember hearing better. The tenor, in particular, was superb."

"Wonderful delivery! But of course, they are foreigners, and one has to admit they do seem to manage Italian better than our local performers."

Lord Hardcastle had greeted Devlin, who arranged for glasses of champagne to be poured for their guests. Lord Hardcastle duly arrived to thrust a glass under his wife's nose. "Deuced good stuff, m'dear. But then, it's Alverton, of course. He's always had a knowing palate."

Lady Hardcastle accepted the glass with a flash of annoyance. "Thank you, dear." She turned to salute Devlin. "My lord."

Devlin half bowed, then turned to greet Lord and Lady Cremorne, who were old friends of his family.

Lady Poulson seized Lady Hardcastle's distraction to push forward. "My dear Lady Alverton, you must allow me to present my niece." She gestured to the brown-haired young lady hovering in her shadow. "Miss Frances Nagley."

Despite Lady Poulson's sadly horselike features and her bluff, blustery manner, Therese knew that her ladyship had a heart of gold; she had a definite soft spot for the older lady. Therese knew for a certainty that Miss Nagley—who did not look that young—hadn't been presented during the Season earlier that year, which suggested that the young woman was one of those daughters of gentry of lesser standing as well as lesser fortune who, during the weeks when a select portion of the ton returned to the capital for the autumn session of Parliament, came hoping to make their mark in quieter social times and, hopefully, attract a suitable gentleman.

Smiling encouragingly, Therese offered her hand. "Miss Nagley. Have you been in town long?"

Miss Nagley touched fingers and curtsied, a touch more deeply than required, yet with enviable grace. "Lady Alverton. I've only recently arrived." She directed a sweet smile at Lady Poulson. "My aunt has very kindly offered to show me around."

"Yes, well." Lady Poulson accepted a glass from the attendant, although Miss Nagley declined. "Frances here was supposed to come to me in early September, but my sister took ill, so the poor gel only arrived last week. We've been visiting modistes ever since." Her ladyship sipped and glanced around the box. "This is Frances's first real outing among the ton."

"I see." Therese focused on Miss Nagley. "Are you enjoying the performance thus far?"

Miss Nagley's eyes were a lovely shade of cornflower blue, and her gaze was direct and refreshingly free of guile. "To be perfectly honest, Lady Alverton, this is the first opera I've attended. I'm finding it remarkably interesting, but also a trifle overwhelming."

Therese laughed. "Such a lauded troupe performing at Covent Garden is rather jumping in at the deep end."

Miss Nagley smiled, and tiny dimples flashed.

Lord and Lady Cremorne were patently waiting to speak with Therese.

Lady Poulson noticed, edged closer to Therese, and lowered her voice. "My dear countess, I was hoping to ask your advice on how best to introduce Frances to the ton, given it's so late in the Season."

Therese met Lady Poulson's eyes and decided that helping Miss Nagley might be entertaining; given the circumstances, finding the girl a suitable husband would be a challenge, and she rather thrived on those. Therese looked at Miss Nagley. "Perhaps you might both call on me tomorrow? Shall we say at two o'clock?"

"Thank you, my dear." Lady Poulson patted Therese's hand. "As I told Frances, we need a good plan of campaign, and I know of no one I would rather ask."

Therese smiled. "I'll put on my thinking cap." She nodded in farewell. "We can discuss the possibilities tomorrow."

Miss Nagley's gratitude shone in her eyes. She curtsied prettily, then retreated with her aunt. But Lady Poulson halted at the rear of the box to accost the tall gentleman who had just stepped inside.

Child.

Although Therese approved of Miss Nagley, she doubted the young lady would hold any appeal for Child. Nevertheless, she wished Lady Poulson joy of the encounter; nothing ventured, nothing gained.

She smiled at Lord and Lady Cremorne. "Good evening. Have you been enjoying the performance?"

Two other gentlemen had entered and were discussing something earnestly with Devlin on the other side of the box. Before Therese could do more than exchange first opinions with the Cremornes, whom she often met at musical evenings, Child fetched up before her, with an elegant flourish bowed over her hand, then settled to join the group.

Lady Cremorne, in her late forties and quite formidable in her own right, arched a cynical brow at Child. "I daresay, my lord, that your parents will be delighted to see you back. Do you intend remaining in England, or is this merely a visit?"

Plainly impervious to such an attack, Child smiled charmingly. "I decided I'd had enough of foreign climes, so yes, I'm home for good." With a glance that indicated their surroundings, he continued, "It's refreshing to be back in civilization—I hadn't realized how much I missed it."

Somewhat mollified, her ladyship asked for his opinion on the production thus far.

Therese wasn't surprised to hear Child deftly avoid answering, deferring instead to her ladyship's judgment. He then seized the conversational reins by complimenting her ladyship on her elaborate headdress and her dark-bronze silk-taffeta gown, which, of course, gave him license to compliment Therese on her gown of lavender-rose silk, with its froth of rich lace at neckline and cuffs and figured-silk underskirt.

"And"—greatly daring, he raised a hand and tapped a finger to the large stone that blazed from amid the lace beneath the hollow of her throat—"one has to say that the Alverton diamonds complement the whole perfectly." With an openly appreciative glint in his eyes, he dipped his head to her. "Quite stunning, my dear countess."

As a piece of outrageously flirtatious flattery, that skated close to the line, but not over it.

Acknowledging as much, Lady Cremorne snorted. "'Ware, Child, or you'll make enemies." When Child glanced at her, she tipped her head across the box toward Devlin.

Child smiled delightedly. "I rather count on that, you know."

Lady Cremorne huffed and shook her head. "Back to your old ways, I see. Some things never change."

Therese wished she could have dragged her ladyship aside and inquired further—as to what things, presumably things between Child and Devlin, hadn't changed—but more people had pushed into the box, which was becoming rather crowded.

With Child beside her, she found herself with her back to the balcony railing in one front corner while, surrounded by gentlemen, Devlin held court on the other side of the small chamber. Lady Poulson and Miss Nagley were chatting with young Lord Swan. In his mid-twenties and with a burgeoning reputation as a connoisseur of music, Swan was a favorite of Therese's, and she definitely wished to speak with him. Lady Poulson's son, Jonathon, had arrived, presumably in search of his mother and her charge, but, on seeing Devlin, had diverted to join the group about him.

Lady Cremorne noticed Swan and, with a nod to Therese and Child, drifted to join the conversation with the young lordling, while with a similar nod to Therese and Child, Lord Cremorne went to join the others around Devlin.

Before any newcomers could claim her attention, Child turned to Therese and arched a brow. "And what's your opinion on the performance, my lady?"

Yours or the players'? Therese was tempted to ask, but instead replied, "I'm enjoying the opera immensely. Tell me, how long has it been since you attended an opera?"

Child waved dismissively. "Some years."

"Any musical event?"

Child's gaze sharpened while his contrived expression suggested he couldn't quite remember.

Despite the people around them, Therese felt Devlin's gaze. She glanced his way and saw that although he appeared to be listening to the comments of the gentlemen about him, his gaze was, indeed, locked on her and held a quality, an intensity of focus, that sent a slight but pleasurable shiver down her spine.

Returning her attention to Child, she smiled knowingly. "Alverton only attends musical events under duress or with some other motivation.

Perhaps your difficulty in remembering is due to your 'years' being, in fact, decades?"

Child feigned hurt. "You wound me, countess. I'll have you know I'm excessively civilized. At least," he amended, with a provocative glint in his eye, "in all the ways that matter."

She laughed. "I daresay that's true, but I'll have you know, I'm very fond of music. Speaking of which, have you met Miss Conningham?" She smiled invitingly at Lady Conningham and her pretty, if sadly freckle-faced, daughter, who had been waiting to approach.

After introducing Child, as he straightened from bowing over Miss Julia Conningham's hand, Therese glibly added, "Lord Child has been sadly absent from ton drawing rooms and even more from music rooms for many years. I was just telling him he needs to improve his under-standing of musical performance, and here is your Julia, who is such an accomplished pianist."

Lady Conningham needed no further encouragement; she immedi-ately buttonholed Child, inquiring as to his plans now that he'd returned to England's shores.

Therese stood back, watched, and declined to assist him. Child threw her a surreptitious look of betrayal, then with an adroitness she had to reluctantly admire, extricated himself and weaved across the box to seek refuge beside her husband.

Quite what Child thought was going on between Devlin and himself, Therese had no idea, but she was faintly annoyed that he had thought to use her to bait her husband in any way whatsoever. She was not a pawn to be used by Child to poke at Devlin.

Relieved of Child's presence, she smiled on Miss Conningham and her mother and, drawing both with her, joined the widening circle about Lord Swan.

Devlin had closely observed Child's interaction with Therese and had resignedly concluded that via his attentions to her, in his inimitable and rather predictable fashion, Child was deliberately trying to provoke him. He'd mentally applauded when Therese had serenely introduced Child to the Conninghams—a more definite fobbing off was hard to imagine. Soon enough, it would dawn on Child that Therese's only interest in him was to foster a suitable match between him and some young lady. Devlin couldn't think of a situation more likely to make Child keep his distance.

Reassured by that understanding—anchored in his knowledge of both Child and Therese—when Child, having picked up a glass of champagne along the way, joined the group about Devlin, he acknowledged Child's nod with one of mild curiosity rather than the bristling Child had hoped to trigger.

From childhood, Child had been court jester to Devlin's more serious nature. Child had always delighted in poking at him just to get a reaction.

Plainly, after nearly a decade apart, neither of them had changed.

Devlin and the other gentlemen, including Cremorne, had been idly discussing the hunting and shooting they expected to enjoy over the coming months. Child sipped and listened, but as he had only just returned to England, no one expected him to contribute, and he didn't.

Shortly after, Lady Cremorne summoned her husband and left, and the other gentlemen departed. Poulson nodded a farewell to Devlin and Child and crossed to join his mother and her charge.

Devlin seized the moment to arch a brow at Child. "You dislike opera as much as I do." He tipped his head toward his wife. "She's my reason for being here. What's yours?" He seriously doubted the prospect of poking at him would have provided sufficient motivation to get Child through the Opera House's doors.

Broodingly staring across the box, Child sipped, then muttered, "My paternal aunt, Lady Matcham. She has a box and insisted I show my face." He shrugged lightly. "I have to start somewhere, I suppose, and at least this is a rather select event."

Lady Matcham was an avid aficionado of all things musical. Devlin followed Child's brooding gaze to Therese and murmured, "You do realize you're giving Therese ideas?"

Child blinked; he hadn't expected what he interpreted as a direct attack. "I…have no idea what you mean."

"Oh, I think you do." Devlin kept his tone light. He was tempted to drag out Child's discomfiture—for all that he delighted in teasing Devlin, Devlin knew Child would never genuinely attempt to harm him or his marriage—but the consternation he glimpsed forming in Child's eyes had him weakening and letting him off the hook. "Therese is one of the most prominent matrons in the ton. I've heard other ladies describe her as a grande-dame-in-the-making. Simply by being you and spending time in her orbit, you're triggering her matchmaking tendencies." He met Child's eyes and arched a brow. "For instance, with Miss Conningham."

Child shuddered and gulped champagne. "For God's sake, don't encourage her."

Devlin couldn't—didn't try to—mute his grin. "Trust me when I say that she's an unstoppable force of nature—even her family call her that."

Child grumbled, "She did try just now and at that damned picnic." He swallowed another mouthful of champagne, then complained, "Why is it that ton matrons such as your countess so adamantly believe that bachelors like me must be in need of a wife?"

Devlin pretended to give the question ten seconds' serious thought, then opined, "Possibly because it's true."

Interestingly, the deliberate statement didn't provoke a "Bah" or any similar dismissal; instead, Child, his gaze on Therese, looked increasingly uncertain.

And *that* fixed Devlin's attention. *Oh, ho!* It seemed his childhood friend had reached a predictable personal crossroads. Reflecting that watching Child look for a wife would almost certainly be hugely entertaining, Devlin relaxed even more.

Cedric Marshall stepped into the box. He looked first at Therese, still chatting with Lord Swan and the Poulson party. After observing the sight for several moments, Cedric drew his gaze away, spotted Devlin, smiled, and walked over.

Child drained his glass, mumbled a farewell, and after exchanging nods with Cedric, departed.

Devlin welcomed Cedric with a smile. "I'm surprised to see you here. I didn't think you appreciated opera any more than I do."

Cedric faintly grimaced and shifted to stand alongside Devlin. "I'd heard about this event from so many people, I wondered what all the fuss was about. Thought I'd come and take a look." Cedric's gaze had drifted across the box to rest once more on the group talking animatedly on the other side. Then Cedric pulled a pained face. "Sadly, by that time, I could only just squeeze into the pit."

Devlin waved at the extra chairs lining the box. "You're welcome to join us for the rest of the performance, if you wish."

Cedric's gaze had settled on the young lady standing beside Lady Poulson; it took several telltale seconds for Cedric to register what Devlin had said.

To Devlin's amusement, Cedric blinked and lightly shook himself. "Oh. Yes." He glanced around, noting the prime position of the box and the view of the stage and the audience it afforded. "Thank you. That will"—Cedric's gaze returned to the other group, this time to rest on Therese—"help."

Intrigued, Devlin studied Cedric. While as interested in ladies as the next man, Cedric resolutely eschewed tangling with the well-born variety.

The bells throughout the theater started ringing, pealing out a warning to the audience to return to their seats.

Devlin strolled to join Therese in farewelling Lord Swan and the Poulson party. Cedric, however, hung back, merely exchanging nods with the group.

Once the others had left, Cedric bowed over Therese's hand and, with Devlin, rearranged the chairs.

The three of them sat across the front of the box, with Devlin on Therese's left and Cedric on her right. As the lights dimmed, from the corner of his eye, Devlin saw Cedric, his gaze on Therese, hesitate, then Cedric leaned closer to Therese and whispered, "That young lady who was here with Lady Poulson."

Therese turned to regard Cedric with awakening interest. "Miss Nagley?"

Cedric nodded. "I wondered if you knew much about her. I thought I recognized her. Where does she hail from?"

Reflecting that such a weak excuse for his interest had no chance of pulling any sort of wool over Therese's sharp eyes, Devlin, cloaked in the deepening shadows, grinned and sat back in the expectation of enjoying the rest of the performance even more than he'd expected.

As the low murmur of Therese's reply and Cedric's subsequent questions continued while the orchestra finished tuning their instruments, Devlin felt utterly content.

If there was any development likely to increase his wife's enjoyment of the evening, his good friend Cedric had just provided it.

It was still pouring when they left the Opera House, and the rain drummed so noisily on the carriage roof that it was impossible to converse as they traveled the slick streets back to Park Lane.

Not that Therese required words to convey her delight. Her face all but glowing, she sat beside Devlin and positively radiated her pleasure.

His satisfaction was commensurately great.

When the carriage rocked to a halt outside Alverton House, footmen holding umbrellas ran out and shielded them from the deluge as they descended from the carriage and hurried up the front steps.

Once indoors, laughing, they shook raindrops from their cloaks, then surrendered the garments to a smiling Portland. "I take it the evening went well, my lady."

"Indeed, it did, Portland." Therese's expression said it all. "The performance was sublime!"

She whirled to face Devlin. "Even you have to admit that the final scene was utterly riveting, with so many voices soaring and weaving in such harmony."

Smiling, Devlin strolled to join her. "I will admit to being entranced." His smile widened, and he looked into her eyes. "Satisfied?"

She tipped her head in thought, then with her lips irrepressibly curving, replied, "For the moment." With her dazzling eyes and a plainly inviting look, she drew him with her as she started for the stairs.

Buoyed on a wave of unalloyed happiness, as they climbed, leaving the bustle in the hall behind, Therese linked her arm with Devlin's. She felt as if the music was still swirling in her mind, a compulsive harmony running through her veins.

They reached the head of the stairs, and as they turned down the corridor to their apartments, she pressed the side of her head against his shoulder. "Thank you." Raising her gaze, she met his eyes. "This evening will live in my memory as one of my most fabulous experiences."

He smiled. "I'm glad you enjoyed it."

They were nearing the door to his room. Eyeing the panel, she heaved a mock-disaffected sigh. "Devlin, 'enjoy' is far too mild a word." Slipping her arm from his, she seized his hand and drew him on—past his door toward hers at the corridor's end. Looking over her shoulder, she caught his eye and mischievously grinned. "I didn't just enjoy it—I *reveled* in it."

She faced forward, opened the door to her room, towed him through, and paused. She waited only until, his gaze locked on her, he reached behind him and pushed the door closed before flinging herself at him, into his arms.

He caught her, and as she'd hoped, he stepped back to catch his balance, and his shoulders hit the panel. Immediately, she pressed her body to his, reached up and, with both hands, framed his face, then smiling entirely unrestrainedly, in a sultry tone, purred, "Now, my lord, let me show you just how much I gloried in the music."

She set her lips to his, noting that his lips were, initially, as curved as hers had been, but as she pressed a flagrantly enticing kiss upon him, his lips firmed as—as always happened—her desire ignited his. She felt the flame take hold in the irrefutable change in his body and the corresponding reaction of hers.

In open challenge, she parted her lips in blatant invitation, an invitation he seized. He took over the kiss, and his tongue surged into her mouth—licking, stroking—and claimed.

Pleasure leapt, spiked, then swelled between them, a heady, intoxicating, familiar brew. Desire, passion, and unshielded need were always there, essential elements of their intercourse—potent, ravenous, and compelling.

With their mouths fused, they lavished and ravished in an escalating dance of give and take; in her head, she could almost hear the welling beat of their shared dance, could almost sense the swirling, evocative strains as the moment fully ensnared them both.

She didn't know how he'd managed to secure the box, and she didn't truly care. At that moment, all she cared about was making clear to him the depth of her appreciation for the wonders of the evening thus far.

By creating wonders of a different kind.

As a reward, as encouragement.

She'd done this before—taken the initiative in an encounter—for much the same reason. And as before, he not only allowed it, but with his hands on her body, with his lips on hers, actively encouraged her to do her worst.

Or her best, as the case might be.

Through the scorching, drugging kiss, she made her intentions clear, then doing her level best to ignore the flaring sensations his hard, possessive hands, roving her curves, sent surging through her, drew her hands from his face and turned her attention to unbuttoning his evening coat.

That accomplished, she deftly undid the large buttons of his waistcoat, then fell on his knotted silk cravat.

By the time the silk hung free, he'd managed to wrest control of the kiss from her and, with knowing hands, set fires burning beneath her skin, and the entrancing, uplifting melody playing in her head threatened to sweep her away.

But she wasn't willing to let the reins go; pressing and stroking her silk-clad curves against the muscled planes of his body, she snared his attention, momentarily captured it, while as rapidly as she could, she slipped free the buttons on the placket of his shirt.

She tugged the hem of the shirt from his waistband, found and undid the last button, then in triumph, drew back from the fiery kiss, grasped the gaping sides of the shirt, and wrenched them wide.

Her gaze fell on his magnificent chest, and her breathing suspended, then she forced in a breath, raised her gaze to his, sent her tongue skating over her lips, and placed both hands, palms flat, on his heated skin.

It was his turn to stop breathing—just for an instant—then his eyes flared dark, and he reached for her as she swept her hands wide and ducked her head and pressed her lips to the center of his chest.

His arms still closed about her, but gently—as if he wanted to seize but didn't want to distract her. As she continued, with touch and the trail of her lips and subtle licks and flicks of her tongue, to pay homage to what was, in truth, a most devotion-worthy expanse, he stilled, then gradually leaned against the door, tipped his head back, and—when she suckled one flat nipple—clenched his jaw in a vain attempt to stifle a groan.

She took the sound as encouragement and increased the intensity—the intimacy—of her sensual ministrations.

She'd always known that beneath his fashionable and quietly elegant clothes, he was the Adonis of most women's dreams. The truth had rung clearly in the effortless yet harnessed strength he commanded, in the ineffable grace with which he moved.

In all she'd uncovered and explored on their wedding night.

Finally, she raised her head, stretched up against him, and when he tipped his head down to look at her, pressed her lips to his again, while with her hands, she wrestled coat, waistcoat, and cravat from him. Successively letting each piece drop to the floor, she pushed the shirt off his shoulders; while continuing to fully participate in the kiss, he reached around her to free his hands from the shirt's cuffs, then allowed her to strip the garment away.

Blindly, she flung it aside, reached for the waistband of his trousers, and flicked the buttons undone.

After five years, she was achingly familiar with every contour of his body, but there was one appendage that continued to fascinate; she reached within his loosened trousers, slid her fingers through the slit in his underdrawers, and the hot, rigid rod all but leapt to her hand.

She closed her fingers lovingly, and he drew back from the kiss on a muted groan. She heard a soft *thunk* as the back of his head met the door, and she would have smiled, but her attention had fallen to the thick, corded, velvet-soft member in her hand. Enthralled as ever by his reactions, she stroked, then ran her thumb over the flaring bulbous head, encased in what was, quite definitely, the softest skin she'd ever felt, even softer and finer than a baby's.

Her hand was too small to fully encircle him, but she knew how to employ her nails to best effect. When he groaned again, she decided not to linger overlong, or she might push him into prematurely taking charge.

She suspected that, like most gentlemen of his kind, he assumed that, when comparing notes with other married ladies, she shied from sharing the details of what transpired in their marriage bed. While such discussions might be limited to a small and trusted circle, like most of the assumptions men made about their wives, that one, too, was untrue; she'd learned quite a lot—sought and received clarification and ideas—from her female cousins and her male cousins' wives.

Of course, when she'd experimented and, afterward, Devlin had asked where she'd learned of the variation, she'd told him she'd come across it in some book.

What she had in mind for her performance tonight was an act she'd employed several times before, always with excellent results. She'd experimented and learned and was entirely confident in her ability to pleasure him to the very edge of surrender—which was as far as he ever allowed her to push him, but she was perfectly happy with that outcome, and the resulting engagement was inevitably stunningly satisfying for them both.

Letting her other hand slide to his hip, she edged back—and he realized her intention.

He lifted his head and looked at her as one of his hands closed on her wrist. "Therese—"

He never stopped her, but he always questioned—always gave her a chance to change her mind—even though she knew just how much he enjoyed the act; she'd accepted long ago that he needed to be reassured. As some of her coterie of confidantes had explained, some gentlemen seemed to think that their wives wouldn't truly want to pander to their desires in such a way.

She was already salivating.

She swallowed, looked up, met his eyes, then licked her heated lips. "I want…" Where were her wits when she needed them?

"What?"

The words appeared on her tongue. "I want to give you as much pleasure as the music—the opera—gave me."

His face taut, he searched her eyes, then he eased his grip and growled, "In that case, consider me and my poor body at your disposal."

She laughed, then leaned in and pressed a quick, hard, hungry kiss to his lips. "Thank you," she breathed, then kicking her skirts out of the way, she sank to her knees.

It was the work of an instant to push aside his clothing and take his straining erection between her hands.

She planted a kiss on the flushed tip, then ran her tongue around the edge, then from nearer the base, slowly licked upward and heard his breathing hitch.

Then she parted her lips and took him in, deep, then deeper. Then she suckled and felt his fingers blindly slide through her hair and tighten on her head. Not in any way to discourage her.

She smiled and set to work to reduce him to that mindless state of wanting to which he so often pushed her. This was her moment to give him pleasure, and she seized it for all she was worth.

Devlin felt as if a vise was locked about his chest and steadily cranking tighter; he could barely breathe as Therese suckled, licked, stroked, and with her fingers, knowingly squeezed. Over the years, she'd paid attention and knew all too well what most weakened his knees; he was grateful for the solid panel at his back as with her customary single-minded determination, she lavished pleasure upon pleasure on him.

She was thorough and talented. Even while he closed his eyes and clenched his jaw and strove to hold back his raging libido—adamantly denying the impulse to grip her head between both hands and thrust into the scalding haven of her mouth—she pressed sensual delight on already overstimulated nerves.

Then she angled her head and took him deeper yet, and he saw stars.

His hands convulsed on her head, then he hauled in a massive breath, seized every rein he could find in a death grip, and forced himself to slide a thumb past the corner of her lips and withdraw his now agonizingly throbbing member from her mouth.

She blinked somewhat dazedly up at him. "Already?"

He would have sworn disappointment tinged the word. In reply, he closed his hands about her shoulders, lifted her to her feet, then swept her into his arms and, after pausing only to free his feet from his trousers, underdrawers, and shoes and kick the tangling garments aside, carried her across the room to her bed.

She obligingly toed her high-heeled evening slippers off along the way, and each clattered to the polished boards.

"I don't know about you"—he halted by the side of the bed and tossed her onto the lilac counterpane—"but I'm definitely more than ready."

On a delighted laugh, she landed in a froth of silk skirts and ruffled petticoats.

Like a ravening beast, he fell on her and, with her help, wrestled her out of her gown and petticoats, then efficiently dealt with her corset, chemise, and drawers. But when it came to her garters and stockings, he paused.

He raised his gaze and met her eyes, then slowly smiled. "Lie back," he murmured, "and close your eyes."

She did as he'd ordered, but he knew that, ultimately, she would peek; she always did.

He settled beside her, his shoulders level with her thighs, and rested his palm on her stomach. The muscles beneath the fine skin fluttered under his touch, and his smile grew more intent.

He set himself to lingeringly trace her curves, first with his fingers, then with his lips and tongue. He didn't hurry—rushing was for men who knew no better—but held himself to a slow exploration, knowing how the anticipation of his next touch ratcheted her sexual tension higher. Then higher.

After sculpting her hips and the tops of her thighs, he turned his attention to her garters and stockings. He peeled each away—slowly exposing her knees and the long, sleek curves of her calves. Her ankles, the bones so delicate, had always fascinated him, and he spent minutes tracing and caressing while she grew ever more restive and needy.

Then continuing to move to the same, torturously slow beat, he reversed direction, working from the perfect arches of her feet upward. Her breathing grew steadily more choppy as he progressed; by the time he closed his hands above her knees and parted her thighs, her chest was rising and falling dramatically, and from beneath the arm she'd draped over her face, he caught the glint of her eyes.

He smiled at her. "You can watch if you like." Then he lowered his head and licked—and she tried valiantly to muffle her shriek as her body reacted and bucked.

He held her firmly and proceeded to return every iota of pleasure she'd earlier lavished on him.

She writhed and sobbed and moaned; the sounds she made fell like music on his ears—a music he cherished far more than anything else he'd ever heard.

He wielded decades of expertise honed over the past years to serve one ultimate aim—to bring her the most joy and sensual pleasure he was capable of bestowing. In those heated moments as he pushed her on, holding her down as he used his tongue to pleasure her to climax, as he reached up and, finally, closed his hand about one of her swollen breasts and circled, then squeezed, her nipple, eliciting another breathless shriek, he knew nothing beyond the drive to devote himself to her, to her fulfillment.

Her tension peaked, then shattered, and her climax rolled over her in a long, rolling wave. It took her under, scrambled her mind, and more of her nectar, the most glorious ambrosia, hit his tongue. Slowly, he lapped and waited.

Eventually, the wave receded and left her temporarily wrung out, limp and splayed upon her bed.

He drew back and, with considerable pride, looked upon what he'd wrought.

The pleasure he derived from seeing her thus was immense and undeniable.

Then she stirred and held out a hand. Her eyes glinted from beneath her heavy lids. "Come."

The murmured order was a command from a deity at whose altar he was more than ready to worship.

He crawled up her body and let himself down upon her, settling his hips between her widespread thighs, which she readily adjusted to accommodate him.

He fitted the head of his rock-hard erection to her slick entrance, then paused and caught her gaze. "I might not be the master of any musical instrument, but I adore making your body sing."

Because in so many ways, you sing to my soul.

He saw her eyes widen, and he thrust into her scalding sheath and watched her lids fall. He saw her lips soften on a pleasured gasp, and satisfied, reassured, he closed his eyes and thrust fully home, and she clamped tight about him.

For several heartbeats, she held him there as if savoring the moment, then she eased her muscles, and he responded and withdrew, then thrust again, hard and sure, and they started dancing to the music they knew so well.

The analogy flooded his mind as their passions surged and desire soared and the rhythm of their joining built in a crescendo.

But he and she were not novices; he slowed, and together, they eased back, changed the tempo, and embarked on a second act in which, united and as one, they rode through a swirling symphony of their senses.

He lowered his head, and she raised hers, and their lips met again and held.

They moved together, bodies sliding, gripping, holding, needing, their skins growing heated and slick.

He orchestrated the interlude as far as he was able, searching for different elements—different notes—to add to the recurrent theme. She bent one knee and hooked her calf over his hip, altering the angle, and both of them gasped, then forged on.

Heat grew, desire swelled, and need grew claws and raked them, and ultimately, the compulsions of driving passion and a hunger too desperate to deny sent them plunging, racing, and with all reins long cindered, they careened up and over the peak, soaring into that moment of ecstasy that seared both body and mind.

Pleasure as bright as any star burst across his senses and obliterated all ability to think.

The moment held, extending like spun gold in their minds, then the threads thinned and faded, and the release of all tension left them help-lessly spiraling from the heights into satiation's sea.

It was still raining; if Devlin strained his ears, he could hear the distant patter on the roofs. He lay slumped beside Therese and marveled at the depth of contentment that filled him.

After long minutes of simply wallowing, he raised his head and glanced toward the window. When, earlier, he'd stirred enough to lift his weight from Therese's limp and sleeping form, he'd realized they'd left a lamp burning and had got out of bed and turned the wick down. Then he'd thought and had crossed to the window and drawn back the curtains before returning to the warmth of his sated wife's bed.

Where he belonged.

Confirming that it was still deepest night, but that the moon had trav-eled a good way across the heavens, he inwardly sighed. He thought back over the evening and their engagement on their return; if there was any lesson to be taken from the way they'd come together, the way they'd both set themselves to lavish pleasure on the other, it was surely that they were already lovers in all the ways that actually mattered. They always had been and always would be; no matter what he'd allowed her to believe, that was their reality.

One he needed to openly acknowledge.

That was what he was working to achieve.

Thinking back over recent days and reviewing the events of the evening, he accepted that he hadn't yet accomplished enough in terms of rescripting her perceptions to be able to risk revealing his truth.

Not yet.

He'd advanced several steps, yet was still some way from his goal.

Although that fact was unpalatable, he swallowed it and, despite being tempted to stay longer, forced himself to draw away from Therese's warmth and slide from the bed.

After collecting his discarded clothes, he walked across the room, then paused at the door leading to his apartments. He looked back at Therese, snuggled down in her bed, then forced himself to turn, open the door, and leave.

Soon, but not yet.

CHAPTER 7

*A*t Devlin's suggestion, the following afternoon, they indulged the children with a walk in the park, their ultimate destination being the Serpentine, where they would feed the ducks.

As arm in arm with her husband, Therese followed the children—attended by their nursemaids, Gillian and Patty, and the household's youngest footman, Dennis—across the lawns, it occurred to her to ask, "Did you come out to feed the ducks when you were a boy?"

A smile touched his lips. "Less often than I wished, but at least every few weeks." He paused, then added, "Of course, after Marcella fell in the water, my visits were curtailed, then I grew too old to view feeding the ducks as a desirable outing."

Marcella was his sister, five years his junior. Therese studied his face. "How old was Marcella at the time?"

He screwed up his face in thought, then offered, "Three? Something like that."

"Good Lord! Was she all right?"

"Of course! I fished her out straightaway, but sadly, having demonstrably been close enough to do so, that only weakened my subsequent protestations of innocence."

She eyed his relaxed expression. "Were you innocent?"

He nodded. "On that occasion, entirely. As to the time she fell in the lake at the Priory—do remember the water is only a foot or so deep, and she was seven at the time—I reserve my defense." He mock frowned and shook his head. "She was an annoying chit back then, and after Melrose came along, she grew even worse."

Melrose was Devlin's brother, currently twenty-nine years old; Therese considered him the idler in the family—he never seemed to be interested in achieving anything. As for Marcella, she was married to Lord Corncrake and lived in Scotland with their four children. Marcella and Melrose occasionally dropped in on Devlin and Therese, and Marcella and her family visited Alverton Priory in early January every year—when the snows lay deep in Perthshire.

Prompted by the realization that she knew few details of Devlin's childhood exploits, Therese asked, "What other childhood outings did you enjoy while in London?" Given that his father had been the earl and, like Devlin, active in politics, he would have spent much of the year in the Park Lane house. When he looked at her quizzically, she added, "If you enjoyed some particular activity, it's likely your sons and possibly your daughter will as well."

A high-pitched shriek drew their gazes to where Spencer and Rupert were gamboling ahead; the frustrated shriek had emanated from Horry, who was struggling to keep up on her much-shorter legs.

Dennis swooped in, picked Horry up, ran with her almost to where her brothers had paused, then set the little girl, now beaming, back on her feet. The boys grinned, turned, and took off again, while Horry, chortling, resumed her chase.

Devlin wondered if Child had said something to start Therese wondering about his childhood. Regardless, he was willing to follow her tack and see where it led—where it might get them. "The zoo wasn't at Regent's Park then, of course, but instead, we visited the Royal Menagerie in the Tower. Then there was Gunter's for ices during the warmer months and, of course, once I was old enough, Noah's Ark toy shop in High Holborn."

"Hmm. While I wouldn't want to take Horry to Noah's Ark yet—she would be overwhelmed—perhaps we can take the boys next year. They'll be old enough then, don't you think?"

By the time they returned to London in the new year, Spencer would be almost five years old, and Rupert would be nearly four. Devlin nodded. "We should make a point of taking them when we return. They can pick out presents for their birthdays."

"That's an excellent idea! I used to do that when I was a girl."

He grinned and met her eyes. "Some of my fondest memories are of walking the aisles of Noah's Ark with my eyes wide, not being sure where to look next."

She laughed and nodded. "Mine as well."

They shared a smile, then looked ahead, to where their children were fast closing on the shores of the Serpentine. As the emotions evoked by his memories rolled through him, Devlin recognized just how happy the earlier years of his childhood had been. He had never harbored any doubt that his parents had loved all their children. Regardless of what he'd come to view as their toxic relationship vis-à-vis each other, in the matter of their offspring, both his father and his mother had been loving and fiercely protective.

Now he had his own brood, he could look back, see, and appreciate that.

"So as a youngster, when your parents were here, at Alverton House, you were mostly on your own?"

He thought back. "Yes and no. There were other young boys about—Child and others as well. Sons of the nobility. Our mothers were acquainted and arranged for our nurses to walk us in the park at the same time." More memories stirred, and his lips lifted irrepressibly. "When we were a bit older, some of those other boys and I, along with our maids and footmen, would go on day trips to Greenwich. That was always fun—seeing all the boats and flying kites in the park there." He met her gaze. "You can imagine how some of those outings went. Young boys—most of whom were lords—allowed to run amok can be…"

"Little heathens?"

He chuckled and dipped his head in acknowledgment. "At times, that might have been an accurate description."

They'd been happy times, now he thought of them. He glanced her way. "But what about you? You spent at least some part of each year in London, didn't you?"

"Yes, but nowhere near as much as you. Most of the year, we remained at Walkhurst. Mama and Papa used to come up for the Season, of course, but only when each of us was very young did they bring us to town, too. Once we were old enough, they'd leave us at Walkhurst, given we had tutors and governesses and horses and more to keep us occupied there." She tipped her head. "That held true through my years of being in the schoolroom, so over that period of my life, I only rarely visited London."

Therese thought back over the years. "At Walkhurst, we were very much a local gentry family. There, we grew up largely unfettered by ton constraints. I recall rambling all about the fields and lanes, often in Christopher and Gregory's wake, with no groom or governess in sight."

She lifted her face, remembering the play of country sunshine over her skin. "We led a very active childhood—we spent as much of our free hours outside as we could." She looked ahead and located the children, now tramping the banks of the lake, and grinned. "I was rather like Horry —or more accurately, she takes after me. I always enjoyed doing things. I never was one to sit and play with dolls."

"So that's where Horry comes by her intrepidity."

Therese's smile deepened. "We rambled and, later, rode everywhere. All the neighbors knew us, especially Ellen's uncle and aunt at Bigfield House. They had no children, but loved to have us visit, and her uncle had his goats, even then, and they always provided some form of entertainment."

She felt Devlin's gaze, softly curious, pass over her features.

"I have difficulty," he murmured, "imagining you getting into any mischief, even as a young girl."

She chuckled and conceded the point with a tip of her head. "From a young age, I learned to stand back and let Christopher and Gregory take the lead in any endeavor that might land us in trouble." Her expression turning coy, she admitted, "I might, once or twice, have alluded to the activity first, but if there were repercussions, I always let them claim credit, which, being male, they invariably did, as by then, they usually believed whatever it was had, in fact, been their idea from the first. I was merely the little sister who tagged along behind them."

He laughed, then asked, "Did they ever realize?"

"As far as I'm aware, they remain oblivious to this day."

Smiling, he looked at their three, now clustered by the bank and busy tossing bread crumbs to a flotilla of greedy ducks. "I wonder if I should warn Spencer and Rupert what they have to look forward to."

She squeezed his arm. "No, you shouldn't. It's one of those things they have to learn for themselves." Her gaze rested on Horry, who was trying her best to hurl bread crumbs at the ducks. "Or not, as the case may be."

They joined the children. Devlin crouched between the boys and engaged them in a discussion of the behavior of individual ducks, while Therese bent over Horry and endeavored to help her daughter improve her throwing.

Given the season, the overcast skies, and the hour, there were few others in that section of the park—mostly nursemaids and children, with a few courting couples with eyes only for each other. No one interrupted their pleasant family interlude, and it passed off without drama. Throughout the moments, as Therese and Devlin shared the tasks of answering questions and directing bright eyes and attentions, she sensed, once again, a softening in their interaction, a relaxed closeness—not so much a physical one as on the mental plane—that she couldn't recall being there months before.

Once the children had fed the hungry ducks every last crumb they'd brought, the flotilla lost interest and paddled off. Satisfied, the children stood and watched them go, and when Therese suggested it was time to head home, the three willingly turned toward the house.

Smiling, Therese took the arm Devlin offered her, and they strolled slowly in their flagging children's wake, with the staff flanking the youngsters on either side.

Free to ponder, Therese's mind returned to that curious closeness; now she thought of it, the feeling wasn't so very novel, just novel in this setting. She recognized the sense of sharing—of shared purpose, shared emotions—as the same feeling she experienced with Devlin in her bedroom, in her bed. Considering that, she decided it was more a case of a subtle shield—one he didn't maintain between them in the intimacy of the bedroom—lowering in other settings.

Until now, while out of the bedroom, he'd kept that shield in place, but she knew she wasn't wrong in sensing a change.

Yet another indication of our maturing relationship.

Deciding she very much approved, she tightened her hold on Devlin's arm. When he glanced at her, she flung him a smile. "I was just thinking that, although as a child, you spent more time in London than I, and consequently, our childhood experiences were somewhat different, those experiences had one element in common." Catching his gaze, she tipped her head. "We were always *doing* something."

Devlin followed her thinking, then arched his brows. "Active rather than passive?"

"Exactly." Therese looked at the children; the boys were each holding one of Horry's hands, and the trio were talking quietly. "And those three are the same."

Devlin grunted. "Something for us to bear in mind in the years to come."

She nodded, and they continued to stroll, taking a more direct line toward the Grosvenor Gate than the route they'd followed to the Serpentine.

Glancing surreptitiously at Therese, noting the small, satisfied smile playing about her lips, Devlin was very aware that she was relaxed, entirely comfortable, and that courtesy of tightening her hold on his arm, she was walking a fraction closer to him than was usual in public.

He'd told Martin that his principal motivation in helping Martin take his place in society was a wish to make Therese happy. Taking her to the opera had also made her happy, as had this excursion, minor though it had been.

And as he'd hoped, she was drawing closer, nearer, turning to him more openly.

His campaign was working, yet at this point, it was still very much a case of one small step at a time.

As they neared the Grosvenor Gate, he looked ahead and, through the trees, studied the graceful bulk of Alverton House. They'd been speaking of their childhoods; was there an opening there for him to mention his parents' marriage and how his view of it had colored his own expectations of the married state?

He glanced at Therese's face—at the relaxed pleasure infusing her features—and decided that such a revelation was too difficult, too deeply personal to introduce at that point.

As it happened, I thought my parents' love-match of a marriage was a disaster, at least for my father, so I decided that such a marriage was the last sort of relationship I would ever engage in. But...

Lips firming, he looked ahead. No, this was definitely not the time.

His success to date—steady and sure—confirmed that his best way forward was to focus on the present and what he wanted for their future and, at least for now, to leave the past well alone.

The dinner that evening at Fortescue House was a must-attend event for both Devlin and Therese. While Devlin stood beside Therese in the Fortescues' overly ornate drawing room and, with one corner of his mind, paid attention to the conversation of the group he and she had joined, the better part of his faculties were employed in scanning the room and assessing the social and, more importantly, political implications of who was there.

Thankfully, neither the Prime Minister nor his nemesis, Palmerston, was present. Russell's ministry stood on shaky ground, and more often than not, it was the ambitious and headstrong Palmerston behind the quaking.

The Marquess of Lansdowne, President of the Council and Leader of the House of Lords, was chatting to Grey, the Home Secretary, and Auckland, the First Lord of the Admiralty. Noting that he had caught Devlin's attention, Lansdowne nodded. Devlin nodded back, subtly agreeing to have a word with the marquess at some point. Although getting on in years, Lansdowne was one of the longest-serving parliamentarians and, as one of the most senior Whigs, tended to keep an eye on those younger peers, such as Devlin, who had similar legislative concerns.

There were a few other cabinet ministers present, along with several secretaries and undersecretaries. Devlin was aware that his and Therese's inclusion on Lady Fortescue's guest list was due to both their social prominence and his standing as a nobleman with a real interest in the political issues of the day and the furthering of the same, yet with no ambition to wield power directly, at least not for the foreseeable future.

His was a vote many in the various parties and factions saw value in courting.

It didn't hurt that other members in both the Lords and the Commons had taken to following his lead.

While he was willing to actively support those causes he deemed worthy—popular education, for one—he was leery over joining any of the established factions, preferring, like Lansdowne, to make up his own mind.

In that, perhaps unsurprisingly, he was strongly supported by Therese. Devlin doubted she'd ever done anything other than make up her own mind about any issue in her life.

Consequently, she stood beside him and aided and abetted him in observing and eliciting opinions from all those with whom they spoke.

She'd done so previously, in similar situations, yet tonight, she seemed...more focused. More transparently, more openly acting to further his interests.

When they parted from one group, before they joined the next, she tipped her head his way and murmured, "When do you think to speak with Lansdowne?" She glanced at him. "I assume you wish to."

He met her eyes and nodded. "But it might be more useful if we approach him after dinner. By then, he'll have had time to digest what he's extracted from Grey and Auckland."

She nodded in agreement, then surprised him by leaning closer and quietly asking, "Is Palmerston likely to bring down Russell?"

She'd picked that up, had she? Devlin dipped his head to murmur, "I would say it's very likely."

"With the only question being not if but when?" She met his eyes. "That's certainly what I've sensed from most of those we've spoken with tonight."

Interesting. But he merely nodded as they neared another group of political and social mavens.

On reaching the far end of the room, Devlin glanced over the heads of those they'd already spent time with and was surprised and a touch intrigued to discover that Child had joined the gathering.

As far as he knew, his childhood friend and present-day nemesis had never had the slightest interest in politics. *Maybe Child's years away have given him a deeper insight.*

Devlin returned his attention to the ongoing discussion of the blight of continuing slavery in some of the far-flung sections of the empire.

"And from what I've heard from m'brother," Lord Kennedy said, "there's some bounder on some island off the coast of Sierra Leone still actively trafficking in slaves!"

"The government needs to take more decisive action," Devlin stated. "Slavery was supposed to have been outlawed in '33, when Parliament passed the act. Bad enough it took until '43 and another act to cease the vile practice continuing under the East India Company, but eighteen years on, to still have slaves existing anywhere under British rule doesn't show government of whatever stripe in any favorable light."

Others around the circle nodded, and several murmured, "Hear, hear."

Lord Kennedy shifted closer to Devlin and caught his eye. "I assume you'll be having a word with Lansdowne. See if you can drop a word in his ear about the Sierra Leone situation, will you? M'brother says he believes it to be quite serious, and it might well impact our ability to deal with some of the native groups, what?"

Lord Kennedy's brother was the governor of Sierra Leone. Devlin nodded. "I'll see what I can do."

"Good man." His lordship smiled at Therese, who was standing on

Devlin's other side. "Good to see you here, m'dear, listening and taking note. I suppose you want to steer Alverton on, heh?"

Therese smiled charmingly. "I do think we should circulate." She regally tipped her head. "Until later, my lord."

With a nod to Kennedy and the others in the group, Devlin obediently stepped back and allowed Therese to guide him to the next group of guests. Early in their marriage, he'd learned that her social timing was impeccable, and that proved once more to be the case when they joined a circle including the Duchess of Lewes, a senior political hostess.

The duchess smiled approvingly upon them, and they joined the conversation, which revolved about the establishment of schools for workers' children in the Midlands, a particular interest of Devlin's that Therese had chosen to especially champion. Soon after, however, Lady Fortescue's butler announced that dinner was served, and her ladyship rapidly directed her guests into their proper marching order, then led the way to her dining room.

As Devlin escorted the ageing Lady Morpeth—a favorite of his— through the front hall, he overheard two ladies just ahead commenting in approving tones on Therese's behavior.

"Day by day, she seems to be stepping more definitely into the wider role of Alverton's countess." Lady Kilgardie went on, "That's heartening, given none of us are getting any younger. We need more like her, of her age and status, willing to stand up and, in the years to come, take our place."

"Very true," Lady Finchley murmured. "And given the countess's wider connections, she's certainly one we should encourage."

Devlin hid a pleased smile and made a mental note to share that exchange with Therese.

On being escorted to the table by Lord Cromwell, Therese discovered that Lady Fortescue had sat Child on her left. Devlin, meanwhile, was seated diagonally to her right, on the other side of the table. As in such settings it was permissible to talk across the board, that suited her very well.

After chatting to Lord Cromwell over the soup course, she dutifully turned her attention to Child. "I have to confess that I'm surprised to see you at an event such as this, my lord." Therese took a sip of her wine and, over the rim of her glass, met Child's charming smile with appropriate skepticism. Lowering the glass, she murmured, "I would have thought the conversation too serious for your liking."

With his hand rising to his chest, Child sat back, a look of mock dismay on his face. "You wound me, countess." Then he grinned. "The truth is my father wrote and asked me to stand in for him tonight. I suspect that he and the mater are hoping that exposure to this side of ton life might instill something approaching the seriousness which"—he tipped his glass her way—"so many believe I lack."

Therese detected an undercurrent of bitterness beneath Child's deliberately playful tone. She studied his face, then asked, "Do you think that's likely?"

He glanced around the table, his gaze dwelling on Devlin for an instant before moving on. "If this gathering had more to do with investing, I might summon up some interest, but as I'm a second son and the political baton will pass to my brother, I see little point in developing an interest in this sphere."

She tipped her head, trying to decide what it was that she'd glimpsed in Child's amber eyes. "You could always stand for your own seat."

He blinked at her, then stared as if just noticing some distant vista. After a moment, he returned to the present and more moodily raised his glass. "Perhaps." He sipped, then more firmly stated, "Perhaps once I've rediscovered all I've forgotten about life in the ton, I might look in a political direction."

Deciding to leave that thought to simmer in his mind, she turned the conversation to the opera, asking what he'd thought of the final act. She soon verified that, as she'd suspected, Child had even less understanding or appreciation of operatic performance than Devlin, and when the lady on Child's other side leaned forward to engage him, Therese drew back and turned her attention to her husband.

While the courses came and went, she devoted her considerable skill to directing the conversations that engaged that section of the table, encouraging those she knew Devlin wished to sound out to air their views on various topics.

Immediately understanding what she was attempting, Devlin was quick to pose questions in support. To Therese's delight, he and she formed a satisfyingly effective team.

She was doubly delighted when she realized that Child had leaned forward and was listening to the exchanges with apparent interest.

At one point, under cover of a remark by Lord Philpott, Child murmured to Therese, "I can't decide—is your awareness of such topics driven by personal interest, or are you exerting yourself on Devlin's behalf?"

The question took her by surprise. After a second's thought, she replied, "Can't it be both?" Then she conceded, "Although I doubt I would be so interested—would know enough to be so interested—if being around Devlin and listening to him discuss the issues with others hadn't opened my eyes."

A comment drew her attention back to Lord Cromwell, who was conversing earnestly with Devlin and those flanking him. The lady on Lord Cromwell's other side was also contributing.

When a few minutes later, a noisy discussion farther up the table drew all eyes, Child tweaked Therese's sleeve and, when she glanced at him, said, "I noticed earlier that in this company, you remain by Devlin's side more than, for instance, at a social event."

She shrugged. "At purely social events, no encounter is likely to be of major significance with respect to how we live our lives. Here, it's...I suppose you might say business of a sort, and sometimes, I see and hear things—glean insights—that Devlin, being male, simply doesn't notice." She met Child's eyes. "Being with him and forming an opinion is a way in which I can help him, so I do."

Once again, the conversation to her right drew her attention.

Child sat back and pondered what she'd said, just then and in reply to his earlier question.

He was trying to understand what was going on between his old child-hood friend and his friend's wife. Knowing Devlin as he did, ever since he'd met Therese, Child's curiosity had steadily escalated, yet he simply couldn't figure the pair out, and the more situations in which he saw them together only left him even more intrigued.

He glanced at Therese, then looked across the table at Devlin and, as he had on several occasions, saw an adroit passing of the conversational ball between the pair.

All he had observed that evening spoke of a working partnership, one based on both parties' strengths, and yet...he remained convinced there was something not quite settled between Devlin and Therese.

Lady Fortescue tapped a spoon to her glass and, when everyone glanced her way, smiled and rose, bringing all the diners to their feet. After graciously reminding the gentlemen not to dally overlong, she led the ladies from the room, leaving the men to pass the decanters and continue their discussions.

Entirely content with what she'd achieved by way of assisting Devlin thus far, Therese strolled with the other ladies, listening to Mrs. Holbrook, who was a firm advocate of schooling for the masses, with unfeigned interest. Therese and Devlin had already set up schools for the local village and workers' children on the Alverton estates.

As one of the younger ladies attending, she took up a position standing beside the fireplace. Other ladies also remained standing, leaving the chairs to those who needed them. Therese fell to chatting with two ladies of similar age to herself, who were also still finding their feet at social events of political bent. But other than accompanying their politically established husbands, neither lady had much understanding of politics and policies herself.

Therese found that disappointing and rather odd. She couldn't imagine not learning the details of Devlin's position on every subject that came up; how could she effectively assist him if she didn't know and understand his views?

Eventually, she parted from those ladies and crossed to where old Lady Morpeth sat; Therese had known her ladyship virtually since birth.

After inquiring as to Therese's parents and family, Lady Morpeth patted Therese's hand. "You are doing very well, my dear. Keep it up!"

Although unclear on exactly what behavior her ladyship sought to encourage, Therese smiled and promised to persevere and moved on. She was drifting around the edge of the gathering when, to her surprise, Lady Kilgardie and Lady Finchley planted themselves in her path.

Both were widows, but had been highly regarded political hostesses in their day. Therese halted and courteously greeted the pair.

Lady Kilgardie nodded approvingly, but her gaze remained sharp. "My dear countess, I wished to mention how heartening it is to see you so actively engaged with political matters."

"Alongside your husband," Lady Finchley put in.

"Indeed." Lady Kilgardie continued, "The government—indeed, the country—needs new blood and fresh ideas and people with energy to carry policies forward."

"To ensure that the right policies are put into practice such that our nation prospers," Lady Finchley clarified.

Unsure what—if anything—was being asked of her, Therese nevertheless inclined her head. "I'm sure Devlin will endeavor to support the most helpful policies, and as his wife, I will, of course, stand by his side."

Apparently, that was the right thing to say; both ladies beamed.

"Excellent, my dear!" Lady Kilgardie tapped her cane on the floor for emphasis. "Be certain we will watch your progress with interest."

Lady Finchley patted Therese's arm, much as Lady Morpeth had. "Never forget, dear, that all gentlemen of a political stripe require the assistance of a devoted lady, especially to help them perceive the wider view."

"Jolly good." Lady Kilgardie pointed with her cane. "Come along, Emma. We've yet to speak with your goddaughter."

With nods to Therese, the pair continued around the room. Somewhat bemused, she watched them proceed to buttonhole one of the younger matrons with whom she'd previously spoken.

Then a stir about the door drew her attention, and she watched with a certain relief as the gentlemen ambled in to rejoin the ladies.

She spotted Devlin and smiled.

As if informed by some sixth sense, on crossing the threshold, Devlin found his gaze drawn to his wife. He took in the warmth of her smile and, responding to that beacon of welcome, corrected his course and strolled to her side.

She immediately looped her arm in his and, leaning closer, confided, "Several of the older hostesses have gone out of their way to encourage me." She sent a laughing look his way. "I'm going to take that as a minor triumph."

He smiled back. "You should. You know as well as I that they don't bestow approval all that readily."

The glow in her face delighted him. Then she glanced around the room. "Who's next?" She located Lansdowne. "The marquess?"

Devlin considered the older statesman. "I suspect we should."

Together, they approached Lansdowne, and as Devlin had suspected, the government leader in the Lords wished to sound him out regarding his likely voting intentions.

To that end, Lansdowne excused the three of them from the others with whom he'd been conversing and, with Devlin and Therese, stepped back from the crowd, giving them a modicum of privacy.

Discussions of this sort were what dinners at houses such as the Fortescues' were intended to facilitate.

"Now then, Devlin." Lansdowne's gaze went past him to Therese, and his lordship inclined his head. "Countess." Without further ado, the marquess launched into an outline of several upcoming bills and the amendments already proposed for each.

Devlin paid attention. The planned bills embodied changes that were more than superficial to the mechanisms behind the movement of capital and, as such, would likely have an impact on their family's wealth and that of most of the upper classes and would ultimately affect the prosperity of those dependent on the Alverton estates and all similar land-holdings.

While Devlin listened carefully, he was reassured by the knowledge that anything he might miss or forget, the lady beside him was sure to remember. Honed by the exercise of correctly remembering all the far-flung twigs on the family trees of the noble houses that made up the haut ton, Therese's memory was, in his opinion, second to none.

When Lansdowne completed his exposition, Devlin put several questions. He was amused when Therese, not intimidated by Lansdowne but being careful to pander to the older man's expectations, rather than pose her own questions, couched them as thoughts and musings, which nevertheless drew the required information from the marquess.

Devlin had to wonder if Lansdowne was even aware he was being managed.

Regardless, as the evening progressed, Devlin continued to be exceedingly grateful as well as pleased that he had Therese by his side.

～

The following morning, Devlin elected to accompany his wife to Sunday service at St. George's Church in Hanover Square.

He sat alongside Therese in a pleasantly relaxed state and allowed the sermon to wash over him. He couldn't be said to be a regular churchgoer, but in common with most gentlemen of his ilk, he showed his face occasionally—in his case, whenever he wished to take advantage of the habitual post-service gathering on the church porch to make contact with his politically or business-minded peers. Not that they always attended, either, yet the venue was a useful one at which to exchange information of the sort that might not be discussed in more formal settings.

Today, however, he was there purely for the chance to spend more socially sanctioned time with his wife. What was more, he could rest assured that he would not have to contend with any distractions posed by either Child or Martin; neither, he judged, was likely to appear within the hallowed precinct.

The service rolled on, undemanding; he responded to the minister's prompts by rote. When the congregation rose to sing the final hymn, he shared a smile with Therese as they stood, then indulged himself by listening to her clear alto voice melding with the organ, the choir, and the other parishioners in a stately paean to the heavens.

After the final extended note faded, the minister raised his hands, and the congregation bowed their heads for the benediction. Once that was bestowed, the minister led the way up the aisle, and Devlin roused his mind from its contented, near-somnolent state and proceeded to escort Therese up the aisle in the minister's wake.

Delighted to have Devlin beside her, Therese smiled and nodded graciously to this lady and that couple as she and Devlin progressed in the usual slow shuffle up the nave. She always appreciated having his arm to lean on, his protective presence by her side, yet many matrons attended Sunday service without their husbands, especially during the Season, and now, in October, with quite half the ton's families having already retreated to the country, the congregation at St. George's, the ton's favored church, had thinned, and she was pleased to have Devlin's company, although she seriously doubted his purpose in being there was in any way connected with the care of his soul.

As they neared the main door and the minister, she dipped her head toward Devlin and murmured sotto voce, "Is there someone specific you hope to see?"

She assumed that was why he was there, and after the encouragement she'd received the previous evening—from everyone, but most importantly from him—to further develop her interest in his political career, she was eager to pursue that path and learn more.

To her surprise, he murmured back, "Not really."

She shot him a faintly startled look, and glancing ahead, he smoothly added, "But if we come upon any of my peers from the Lords, that would be an added bonus."

They'd reached the door, and it was their turn to greet the minister. She was forced to face forward and smile and extend her hand and exchange the usual pleasantries, even while the question *A bonus added to what?* echoed in her mind.

Devlin dragged his wits from their satisfied wallowing and, while shaking hands with the minister and commending him on his sermon, ruthlessly refocused on his campaign.

Smiling urbanely, he turned from the minister, grasped Therese's elbow, and steered her to one side of the colonnaded porch. Rapidly scanning the crowd, he dipped his head and murmured, "There's Kilroy with his wife. I'd rather like to have a word in his ear about some of Lansdowne's ideas."

He released her, assuming she would seize the opportunity to talk with some of her female acquaintances, but instead, she laid her hand on his sleeve and walked by his side to where Lord and Lady Kilroy were chatting with two other ladies.

All three ladies recognized Therese, which made it a simple matter for her to breezily make the introductions, then take command and engage the ladies in a discussion of the latest style of headdress. A quick glance directed at Devlin plainly stated she was clearing his way and leaving Kilroy to him.

Devlin hid a grin as, entirely predictably, Kilroy turned to him in relief.

His lordship leaned closer to confide, "My compliments to your wife, Devlin—dashed if I know what to say to all these females."

Devlin smiled understandingly and launched into a brief outline of one of the subjects Lansdowne had raised. He concluded with, "The question is whether we are for or against abolishing the requirement for property ownership for election to the Commons."

"Hmm." Kilroy frowned. "That was one of the Chartists' demands, wasn't it?"

The two other ladies had just taken their leave, and Therese and the somewhat older Lady Kilroy had turned to their husbands in time to hear Kilroy's question.

"What is one of the Chartists' demands?" Lady Kilroy asked.

Briefly, Devlin explained, then continued, "While no one is proposing to adopt the entire petition, the feeling is that the government should at least be seen to be examining those reforms that patently have some merit." He gave a wry smile. "This is Russell, the reformer, after all."

Kilroy snorted. "Still, I can see the point for representation in the Commons. Can't see that it will make any odds to us in the Lords."

"True. I would assume most of us will be sitting on the fence—a vote for won't impact us in any way. The only concern I can see arising is over what such a change might mean for who governs in the lower house."

With respect to that point, Therese asked what Devlin and his lordship felt might, hypothetically, constitute a danger. "Assuming the requirement for property ownership is revoked."

Somewhat to Devlin's surprise, the answers to that led the four of them—for Lady Kilroy had been a keen observer of politics for more than a decade and wasn't backward in stating her views—into an animated and far-reaching discussion.

Lord Compton and Lord Gisborne, overhearing some remarks and made curious, came to join the group. Therese encouraged the pair to air their views, and in short order, the engagement had broadened in scope far beyond what Devlin had initially envisaged.

Far beyond, he was the first to admit, the scope it would have attained if the four peers had been left to themselves. The ladies, both of them, introduced viewpoints and possibilities the gentlemen hadn't immediately perceived.

By the time Lady Compton and Lady Gisborne swept up to reclaim their spouses, their group was among the last left standing on the porch, and none of them had noticed the time passing.

Sincerely thanking each other for their company, they parted. With Therese on his arm, Devlin walked toward where their carriage waited around the corner in the square.

"That was," Therese informed him, "invigorating."

He looked at her face, tilted up to the slight breeze, and smiled. "It was. And thank you—you were a great help."

The smile she sent his way was rich with satisfaction.

Deservedly so. He couldn't understand why he hadn't encouraged her to assist him in the political sphere long before now. Her extensive social skills made it easy for her to guide conversations, and she often accomplished the task without her interlocutors being aware of it.

Largely thanks to her assistance—and that of Lady Kilroy, too—he now had a much deeper understanding of the likely issues that might arise in bringing forward some of the bills the Prime Minister was hoping to introduce. When next he spoke with Lansdowne, he would have quite a bit to report.

They reached the carriage, where Dennis the footman was proudly holding open the door. With a flourish, Devlin offered Therese his hand. With a beaming smile that declared she was entirely delighted with her morning, she placed her fingers in his and, smiling in much the same way, he handed her up, then followed.

～

In the small hours of the following morning, Devlin lay sprawled beside Therese in the comfortably rumpled expanse of her bed.

From the soft, steady huff of her breathing, from the bonelessness of her limbs, she was still sunk deep in the oblivious sleep of extreme satiation.

A state in which Devlin, too, had been immersed, until a persistent, nagging question had speared through the pleasured fogs and dragged him to awareness.

He didn't know what had brought it to the fore or why it seemed so important, but *Does she love me?* suddenly blazed in his mind.

He couldn't stop himself from reacting—from rapidly reviewing their past, especially their interludes over recent weeks, most especially their activities over the past hours.

As the memories scrolled through his mind, the unforgiving tension that had, out of nowhere, gripped him eased and fell away. Given how she'd behaved over the past hours, only a highly insecure man could possibly doubt that she loved him, and surely he wasn't such a man?

She loved him. She had that night, through the past weeks, through the past months, for the past five years and more. She'd given him her love from the first; he'd always known that. Why, then, the question?

He honestly didn't know, and that left him just a touch uneasy.

Hoping to banish the unsettling feeling, he turned his mind to assessing the progress he'd made in his campaign. He'd drawn closer to her socially, finding ways to spend more time by her side. He'd helped her with Martin, and she was openly happy over how well he and her younger brother were getting on. And—admittedly somewhat to his surprise—he'd found it easy to interest her in the business and political aspects of his life; indeed, he could foresee them functioning as a much closer partnership in those arenas from now on.

All those small but deliberate steps had gone better than he'd hoped, and he'd been able to deliver an unexpected gift in arranging for her to see the special performance at the opera house. That had made her exceedingly happy.

Making her happy was now the standard against which he measured any potential gift, outing, or event. If it would make her happy, excellent. If not, what was the point?

Looking back over recent weeks, he felt an undeniably deep relief that he'd been able to accomplish what he had without in any way upsetting or damaging the relationship they'd already enjoyed. He'd been able to build on that without in any way weakening it.

He turned his head and looked at Therese. She remained asleep, her expression—relaxed and unanimated by the elemental energy of her conscious mind—that of the gentlest Madonna, her face framed by the golden web of her disarranged hair.

He drew in a slow breath, conscious of the upswell of feelings that rose inside him—familiar, yet stronger, deeper, more powerful. Those feelings had always been there between them whenever they'd come together in passion, but in recent weeks, at least for him, their continuing intimacy and what, through that, they shared with each other had only grown more precious. More infused with meaning and feeling that reached to his soul.

He hoped she felt the same.

Looking at her, wondering and hoping, he allowed the question hovering in his mind to form. Was he ready to take the final step and open her eyes?

How?

He thought of the possible ways. The only one that seemed realistic was via some sort of declaration.

He tried to envision that, to formulate the words he would use to explain what he'd done and how he wished to correct his mistake, but at that point, his mind balked and halted.

Much like a horse refusing a fence.

He frowned. He wasn't yet ready; that much seemed clear.

He grimaced. While he was excellent at acting on the fly and, in pursuit of his immediate best interests, taking advantage of situations as they occurred, long-term planning wasn't his strong suit. Indeed, that weakness had significantly contributed to his current dilemma; he hadn't foreseen changing his mind over acknowledging that their marriage was, in fact, a true love-match.

Now...

The truth was that it would probably be wise to play to his strength and assume that, once he'd reached the point of being ready to declare his love to Therese, some scenario, some situation, would arise, and the necessary words and actions would occur to him. Following that approach was, usually, how he got the best, most desirable results.

He refocused on her features, then softly sighed and forced himself to ease from the bed.

After collecting his robe and shrugging into it, he crossed to the connecting door to his room, opened it, and walked through. He carefully closed the door, then went to his cold and lonely bed and climbed between the chilly sheets.

Of one thing he was very sure; he was getting exceedingly tired of greeting the dawn alone.

CHAPTER 8

*A*s she had no morning engagements, Therese elected to take her morning tea with the children in the nursery.

The large L-shaped room took up a significant portion of the attic, with the long arm running down one entire side of the house and the smaller arm stretching halfway across the front. The schoolroom, where the children spent most of their days, occupied the smaller arm, with wide windows affording an excellent view over the tops of the trees in the park. Therese glanced that way and saw the distant glass panels of the soon-to-be-dismantled Crystal Palace winking in a stray beam of autumn sun.

"See, Mama?" The boys had been drawing, and Spencer proudly held up his effort. "It's Nobbin on the lawn at the Priory."

Nobbin was Spencer's pony. Therese studied the oddly shaped lumpy brown figure with all the admiration her eldest son might expect. "It's a very good likeness, my darling. You'll be drawing as well as your great-uncle Gerrard any day now."

Spencer beamed. Therese suggested he put the sheet aside to show his father later.

Also seated at the low table beside which Therese sat, Rupert hunched over his artistic effort and heaved a disgruntled sigh. As Spencer took his drawing to set it on the wide window ledge, Rupert looked up at Therese with weary resignation. "I tried to draw Pippin, but I just can't seem to get him right."

Pippin, of course, was Rupert's pony. Therese smiled reassuringly. "Let me see."

Reluctantly, Rupert straightened, picked up his sheet, and held it out.

Therese took the drawing and studied it, in truth more closely than she had Spencer's. Although he was a year younger, Rupert's effort showed a better grasp of line and perspective than Spencer's. "You have a good if still developing eye," Therese told her second son. Making a mental note to continue to monitor Rupert's artistic progress—drawing, after all, ran in her family—she handed him the sheet. "That's enough on that one for now. Go and put it with Spencer's so your father can see it later, and then"—she collected Spencer with her gaze—"I have another challenge for you both."

Spencer hurried back to the table and sat. While waiting for Rupert to leave his sketch with Spencer's and return, Therese glanced down at Horry. Her daughter was sitting on the floor to one side of Therese's chair, being watched over by Gillian, one of the nursemaids.

At eighteen months old, Horry could barely hold a crayon, but as she sat on the floor, a large sheet of paper spread before her, with her small features contorted in a furious show of concentration as she stabbed and slashed at the paper, she seemed single-mindedly focused on making her mark.

Therese smiled, then returned her attention to her sons as Rupert returned to his chair. "Now, take another sheet of paper each." There was a stack of fresh sheets in the center of the table, and she waited while they each helped themselves to one. "Very well—I want you to draw me a tree." She held up a finger to stay them. "I don't want you to draw anything but the tree, but first, I want you to close your eyes and imagine the tree until you can see it clearly in your mind. I want you to be sure what sort of tree it is—you know enough different trees by now. I want you to think of how the branches angle out from the trunk and how the leaves hang from the twigs. Once you are absolutely sure what your tree looks like, you can open your eyes and start drawing."

Both boys had their eyes closed. A slight frown marred Rupert's brow, but even as she looked at Spencer, his face cleared, and he opened his eyes and picked up his pencil.

Rupert, however, kept his eyes shut for a full minute more before he opened them and, still frowning slightly, started to draw.

Hmm. Therese made another mental note to ask her uncle, Gerrard

Debbington, what exercises he would recommend to encourage a child who might possess a talent for drawing.

While the boys worked and Horry stabbed and slashed, Therese poured herself another cup of tea. Sitting back, she sipped. Her gaze drifted to the window, and she found her mind sliding from her children to their father.

She was now very certain that something in their relationship had changed. Not in the sense of maturing, as she'd initially assumed, but actually altered, albeit in a subtle way.

She recalled her earlier thought of a shield lowering, of some barrier being taken away, and yes, it was something along those lines, and it was Devlin who had changed, not her. He was the one removing some amorphous barrier.

So what was he revealing?

Potentially more importantly, why? Or why now? Was it something to do with Child appearing—reappearing—in Devlin's life?

She pondered that, but while Child-as-cause fitted the bill time-wise, why Devlin's childhood friend would be a catalyst for Devlin—who had known Child virtually since birth—to change with respect to her, she couldn't imagine. She certainly didn't believe jealousy had anything to do with it; Devlin knew very well that she had never been interested—not in that sense—in any other man, not even one as undeniably handsome and urbanely charming as Child.

Allowing all she'd sensed over their recent nightly interludes to flow through her mind, she felt quite sure Devlin knew precisely where he stood with her—that he was the center of her world. She had never disguised, much less attempted to conceal, what emotion drove her when it came to him. He was the man she loved, and neither she nor—she would wager the Alverton diamonds—he had ever seriously questioned that.

The boys informed her that they'd completed their trees. She drained her teacup, set it aside, and duly admired their efforts, evenhandedly praising both, although, as she'd suspected would be the case, Rupert's tree was a great deal more treelike than Spencer's.

She sent them to place the trees with their pictures of their ponies and got to her feet. When they pelted back to her, she bent and hugged them, then releasing them, straightened. "I have to go downstairs, but Gillian and Patty and Nanny Sprockett will help you with whatever game you want to play."

She glanced around as the motherly Nanny Sprockett came bustling up, a smile creasing her comfortable face.

"It'll be lunchtime in a little while," Nanny Sprockett informed her charges. "Perhaps we can play Spillikins until then."

"Yay!" The boys raced off to fetch what was presently their favorite game.

Therese exchanged an understanding smile with Nanny Sprockett and made her escape.

On reaching the front hall, she noted that, as usual, Portland had left the day's mail stacked on a silver salver on the hall table. She went forward, intending to collect whatever invitations had been delivered, only to see, prominently displayed on the top of the pile, an envelope with the name "Alverton" boldly scrawled across the front in harsh black ink, with the word "Urgent" angled across one corner and underlined three times.

Therese reached out and picked up the missive, absentmindedly registering the poor quality of the paper. Normally, she wouldn't dream of opening a letter addressed to Devlin, but...even though it had been a long time since she'd seen Martin's handwriting, she was as certain as she could be that the inscription was his penmanship.

She stared at the letter, then swung on her heel and walked to Devlin's study. As she'd expected, given Portland had left the letters in the hall, Devlin wasn't there.

She walked to the bellpull and tugged it, then went to stand by the desk. When Portland arrived, she waved the letter so the butler could see which one it was. "Did his lordship say when he expected to be back?"

"No, my lady. Indeed, the earl said that he couldn't be sure when he would be home, other than that he anticipated joining you for dinner."

"I see." She tapped the letter against her fingertips. "I don't suppose he mentioned where he was going?" If it was to one of his clubs, she could send the letter with a footman.

"He said he was going to a business meeting, my lady. Unfortunately, he didn't mention where."

She grimaced. A business meeting could be held anywhere in London. Increasingly concerned, she stared, frowning, at the letter.

Portland cleared his throat. "I take it the letter is the source of some anxiety, my lady."

It wasn't exactly a question, but still staring at the envelope, she replied, "I strongly suspect it's from my brother Martin."

"The one who only recently returned to England, ma'am?"

Trust Portland to put his finger on the point that most worried her. "Exactly." Speaking slowly, she went on, "It's possible Martin's in some sort of trouble. I really can't imagine why else he would write *urgently* to Alverton."

Portland drew himself up. "I see your point, ma'am." The butler's voice gentled. "Perhaps, given the possibility of such extenuating circumstances, it might be best were you to open the note. Just in case."

With every word of their exchange, Therese's anxiety had been mounting. Without further ado, she picked up Devlin's letter knife, turned the envelope over, inserted the knife's tip beneath the anonymous red wax seal, and with a twist of her wrist, broke it.

She set down the knife and unfolded the note and read.

She scanned to halfway down, then hauled in a breath and went back to the top of the missive and forced herself to read every word.

That didn't help.

By the time she reached the end of the note, her mind was awhirl.

Lowering the letter, barely able to believe the message therein, she said, "Martin writes that he's being held by the owner of an establishment called Gentleman Jim's, which is located in a lane off Pall Mall, just past Waterloo Place, near Haymarket. Apparently, not being able to recognize him by sight, the owner and his crew are refusing to believe who Martin is, and therefore, the owner is refusing to accept Martin's IOU and is, instead, insisting that he pays all monies due before they will release him!"

She raised her head and stared at Portland. "Some blackguards are holding my little brother to ransom! *Ransom*—in London!"

Her temper surged, and she set her lips. "Nonsense!" She narrowed her eyes. "We'll see about that."

She focused on Portland. "Please order the town carriage to be brought around immediately. And I'll need my pelisse, bonnet, and reticule—at once!"

"Ah…" Portland wavered.

Therese put steel into her voice. "At *once*, Portland! I cannot risk waiting for Alverton to come home. Who knows what these blackguards might do if no one responds to Martin's plea?"

Unable to answer that, Portland bowed and hurried off.

Therese read the letter again. "Money—we might need money to pay the debt." Taking the letter with her, she ran for the stairs. Luckily, Devlin had always been generous with funds. She rushed into her room and crossed to her dressing table. She tossed Martin's letter on the top, extracted a key from its hiding place behind the mirror, unlocked the central drawer, and rifled through the contents. She retrieved a bundle of notes secured with ribbon and turned as Parker came toward her, holding her pelisse and her reticule.

Therese grabbed the reticule and stuffed the notes inside, then set the small purse down beside Martin's letter and thrust her arms into the pelisse's sleeves. Then she seized the gloves Parker held out and tugged them on, swiped up the reticule and letter, looped the reticule strings over one wrist, thrust the letter into the pocket of the pelisse, took the bonnet Parker held out to her, and rushed for the main stairs.

She was tying her bonnet ribbons and pattering down the last flight when someone rang the front doorbell.

Bonnet secure and with Martin's letter once more in her hand, Therese was on Portland's heels as he reached for the latch and swung the door wide.

She'd hoped against hope it would be Devlin, but no. "Child." Her disappointment rang in her tone.

Child's gaze raked her face, and he tensed. "What's happening?" He looked past her into the hall. "Alverton?"

"Out on business, and we don't know when he might be back." She dodged to the side. "Now, if you'll excuse me?"

Instead of stepping aside and allowing her down the steps, Child held his ground. "What's going on? Trouble?"

He'd come to see if, via his usual brand of teasing, he could extract from Devlin some indication of the situation underpinning Devlin and Therese's marriage, enough, at least, for Child to determine if what he thought might be going on was, in fact, true. But if there was trouble that in any way posed a threat to Therese…despite their long rivalry, when it came to threats from any source other than each other, he and Devlin had always stood shoulder to shoulder.

If Therese was in trouble and Devlin wasn't there…

"Tell me," he commanded.

She glared at him. "I don't have time to waste! Please stand aside."

"Tell me what's got your dander up, and I will."

"Child!" She uttered the name through clenched teeth.

Child caught the furtive look Portland threw him, then the butler glanced at Therese's hand, at the letter she clutched in her fingers. Her helpfully gloved fingers.

Child whisked the sheet from her grasp.

"What? Give that back at once!"

Child turned his shoulder to her as she tried to grab the letter, and he rapidly perused the short message. "Good Lord!"

"Exactly!" Therese snapped. "Martin's being held, and Devlin isn't here, so I'm going instead. I am not about to sit in the drawing room and twiddle my thumbs while my little brother is being held for ransom by some bully boys!" She barely paused for breath. "Ransom! Held prisoner for money! It's outrageous—and so I shall tell the wretched owner of the place."

Once again, she tried to push past him. Child had heard the carriage draw up on the gravel drive at his back and, again, held his ground. When she glared furiously at him, he met and held her gaze. "You can't go to a hell."

She blinked. "A hell? Is that what Gentleman Jim's is?" Then she refocused on his face. "Do you know it?"

"I've only just returned to London, so no, I don't, but with a name like that, in that area, I can guarantee that's the sort of establishment it is. And"—he continued as implacably as he could—"it's not a place you can barge into."

She huffed dismissively. "Perhaps not in the evening, but in the middle of the day? Yes, indeed, I can barge in. Now please, get out of my way."

When he didn't budge, she leaned closer and, locking her eyes with his, quietly yet distinctly menacingly enunciated, "You are overstepping the mark, my lord."

Child read the promise of hideous retribution in her silvery eyes. After a second of rapid calculation, he stepped to the side. "All right, but I'm coming with you."

Therese didn't pause in her headlong rush for the carriage door, just waved at him to join her. "If you are, hurry up!"

Child seized the moment to thrust the letter at Portland. "Make sure Alverton reads that the instant he returns and tell him I've gone with her."

"Indeed, my lord."

Child turned and strode down the porch steps as a footman helped Therese into the carriage.

Therese sat on the bench seat and scooted along to give Child room.

In truth, she was hugely relieved that he'd chosen to accompany her. He was as tall and nearly as physically impressive as Devlin and, being the son of a duke, could no doubt be as intimidating as her lordly husband should the situation call for it.

She would have preferred not to involve Child, but if his presence improved her chances of rescuing Martin, she would live with the consequences.

The instant Child sat, the footman shut the door, and the horses started trotting. A second later, the flap in the carriage's roof opened. "Where to, ma'am?"

Before she could reply, Child gave Munns directions to drive to Waterloo Place as fast as possible. Once the flap dropped, Child glanced at her. "At least Waterloo Place is a street down which it's acceptable for ladies to stroll. We can see how the land lies from there."

Judging by the grim look in his eyes, Therese felt sure that, once they reached Waterloo Place, he planned to make her wait in the carriage while he went to the hell.

That wouldn't work, but he would learn.

Possessing her soul with what patience she could muster, she stared ahead unseeing as the carriage rattled rapidly down Park Lane.

∼

Devlin exited the Grosvenor Gate just in time to see his town carriage turn down Park Lane.

He grimaced. He'd hoped Therese would be in for luncheon; apparently not. He'd just had a minor triumph in securing a major contract for a steelworks of which he was chairman of the board and had been hoping to share his success with his wife over a sustaining meal.

As he crossed the road, he wondered what event she was on her way to; she was the only one who might have taken the carriage out at this hour, yet although he racked his brain, he couldn't remember her mentioning any luncheon engagement.

He turned in to the Alverton House drive. Seconds later, he strode up the steps, opened the front door, stepped into his front hall—and immediately saw Portland hurrying to meet him.

"My lord! Thank heavens you're here!"

Devlin blinked in surprise, then shut the door behind him even as a chill unfurled in his chest. "What is it, Portland?"

His normally unflappable butler was in an outright flap. Portland halted before him, dug a folded paper from his pocket, and offered it.

"Her ladyship opened this letter, my lord. Given it stated the matter was urgent and she recognized her brother's hand, she grew anxious and had to see…"

Devlin took the paper, and Portland gestured weakly. "Well, of course, her ladyship felt she had to go immediately, but thankfully, Lord Child arrived in the nick of time."

"Child?" Devlin glanced up and saw Portland nod at the letter.

"His lordship left that with me and insisted I show it to you the instant you returned. Then he went with her ladyship."

Devlin returned his attention to the note as Portland went on, "Although Lord Child did his best, there was no stopping the countess."

Having reached the end of the missive, Devlin snorted. "I can imagine." The compulsion to race after Therese—*Now! Immediately!*—battered at him, eroding his control. He closed his eyes and forced himself to draw a calming breath. Panicking rarely helped, and it certainly wouldn't help Therese, much less Martin.

His mind turned over the facts as he knew them… He looked at Portland. "As I was leaving the park, I saw the town carriage drive away. Child and her ladyship were in it?"

"Yes, my lord. And I made sure Morton went as well."

Morton was their older and more experienced footman. Devlin nodded. "Good thinking."

That was something he had to do—think. Therese was safe enough; in such circumstances, he knew he could count on Child to ensure she remained unharmed. But as for the situation they were walking into… Devlin wasn't so sanguine about that or about Martin's safety.

Frowning, he studied the note. He couldn't fathom what was going on. Martin was a Cynster. The Cynster name alone should have been enough to assure anyone of his ability to pay, and Martin looked enough like his father and cousins that his claim to being one of the family shouldn't have been questioned.

Devlin narrowed his eyes, then stuffed the note into his greatcoat pocket and headed for his study.

"My lord?" Portland followed at his heels.

"Get me a fast hackney, Portland."

Devlin strode into the study. He rounded the desk and swung back the painting that graced the wall behind it, exposing the large safe. He turned to the desk and pressed the catch to release the desk's hidden drawer and withdrew the safe's heavy key. He inserted the key and turned over the massive lock, then shifted the lever handle and swung open the thick door.

A stack of banknotes rested in a corner of the bottom shelf. He lifted an inch's worth of notes from the pile, folded them, and tucked them into his inside coat pocket. Then he reached farther, deeper into the safe, and extracted the gun—one of the new revolvers—he kept there. He checked that the gun was loaded before sliding it into his greatcoat pocket, then swung the safe closed, latched it, locked it, pushed the painting back into place, and returned the key to the hidden drawer.

As he strode for the door, he struggled to keep his surging emotions locked down, locked away. His face felt like granite.

He reached the front hall to find Portland waiting; he swung open the front door. "The hackney is waiting, my lord."

Devlin nodded and walked out and went quickly down the steps. He paused with his boot on the hackney's step and looked up at the jarvey—a youngish man who looked eager to please. "The corner of Pall Mall and Waterloo Place. As fast as you can."

The jarvey grinned and saluted him. "Right you are, guv."

Devlin flung himself onto the seat, and true to his word, the jarvey cracked his whip, and with a spray of gravel, the carriage shot off down the drive.

By the time the town carriage reached Waterloo Place, Therese was in two minds over Child's presence. On the one hand, he might come in useful in dealing with the owner of Gentleman Jim's. On the other hand, he was plaguing her with suggestions that she should remain safe in the carriage while he went in to learn what was going on.

Rather than argue, she simply said, "No."

Exasperated, Child glared at her. Lips thin, he studied her face, then said, "In case you've forgotten, I've only recently returned to these shores after nearly ten years away. That means not only do I know nothing about this particular establishment, but I also can't be sure I understand how, these days, matters are dealt with within such places. I'll need to tread warily."

"You might need to do so." Therese elevated her chin. "I most certainly do not."

Child's jaw clenched so hard she thought it might crack.

The carriage rocked, then halted, and the flap in the ceiling rose. "Do you want to stop here, your ladyship?" Munns asked.

Therese peered out of the window. "Can we walk from here?" she asked Child.

He scowled. "If you're set on going in, then let's see if the carriage can get closer." He raised his voice and ordered, "Go around the block to the left. Left into Pall Mall, then left again as soon as you can. There should be a lane there. The place we're looking for is a club called Gentleman Jim's. Stop as close to the door as you can."

"Right, my lord."

The flap shut, and the carriage smoothly rolled on. It turned left, then almost immediately swung left again, into a lane barely wide enough for two carriages to pass.

While not exactly seedy, the buildings along the lane lacked the polish of those on the wider streets. The façades were definitely less well-kept.

Therese and Child peered out to either side. Although the pavements weren't particularly crowded, tradesmen, messenger boys, deliverymen, and even three flower sellers were walking along the lane. The carriage rolled past two gentlemen earnestly discussing something as they walked briskly toward Pall Mall.

Then Child pointed through the window beside him. "There it is—on the corner of an even narrower lane that must lead to Haymarket."

Therese leaned forward to look. The sign—gold letters on a black board—was mounted flat against the bare brick wall above an unprepossessing black-painted door. Munns must have spotted it; the carriage slowed and pulled into the curb, more or less opposite the place.

Her footman dropped down and opened the carriage door. Therese gathered her reticule.

Child's hand landed on her sleeve. "Therese—please!"

She shot him an aggravated, distinctly warning look, slid her arm free, and proceeded to step down from the carriage.

Child followed, but she didn't wait. Head high, she sailed across the street.

Behind her, Child softly cursed and strode after her.

She halted in front of the black-painted door, grasped the heavy knocker, and banged it peremptorily.

She released the knocker and listened. After only a few seconds, lumbering footsteps approached on the other side of the door.

From behind her, Child muttered, "At least let me—"

The door swung open, and Therese found herself staring at the unlovely visage of a man who, judging from his cauliflower ear and misshapen nose, she took to be a retired pugilist. He certainly had the brawn.

The big man regarded her in patent surprise.

Before he could recover, she tipped her head higher and, in imperious tones, stated, "I am the Countess of Alverton. I understand my brother—Mr. Martin Cynster—is currently under this roof."

Boldly, she stepped forward. Startled, the doorman—if that was what he was—all but leapt back.

Grimly determined, she swept over the threshold, forcing the man to squeeze back against the wall of the long corridor beyond the door. She glided on. Glancing to right and left, she saw dim, unlit reception rooms; all had the air of being unoccupied. She slowed.

"'Ere!" The pugilist had found his voice. "You can't just barge in 'ere!"

"I already have." She swung to face him. "Take me to my brother immediately!"

She was accustomed to managing staff and had no trouble investing her words with whiplike authority.

The doorman eyed her, then looked at Child, who had stepped through the door in her wake. Then the big man shook his head, closed the door, and lumbered forward. "I don't get paid to deal with lords 'nd ladies," he muttered. "The boss'll have to deal with this hisself."

Therese nodded approvingly. "A very wise decision." As he drew level with her, she demanded, "Now, if you please, where is my brother?"

With an unexpectedly graceful half bow, the doorman gestured down the corridor, then stepped past her and took the lead.

Therese followed. Child, who had remained obligingly silent since they'd entered, brought up the rear. At the end of the corridor, a set of carpeted stairs led up to the first floor. There, another long corridor mirrored the one beneath, and the pugilist led them to a door toward the end. He tapped, then opened the door and looked in. "Visitors, guv. The Countess of Alverton—or so she says—and another gent."

With that, the big man set the door wide and stepped back, and Therese swept into the room.

Her gaze landed on an unknown man seated behind a desk. She scanned further and found a stunned-looking Martin coming to his feet; he'd been sitting on a straight-backed chair in the corner beyond the desk.

A single comprehensive glance assured Therese that her brother was unharmed. Relief swamped her; she and her family had only just got him back—the notion of anyone attacking him now was simply not to be borne.

Another ex-pugilist, who had been standing, guard-like, behind Martin's chair, slapped a meaty hand on Martin's shoulder. "'Ere!" the thug protested.

Martin shrugged him off and remained standing. "Tee!" Eyes wide, plainly horrified, Martin stared at her. "What the devil are *you* doing here?"

Therese ignored him. She halted in the middle of the room and trained her gaze, sternly severe and unrelentingly disapproving, on the man behind the desk, who had yet to rise.

He possessed an unremarkable face and otherwise appeared average in every way, the sort of man one would pass on the street and never notice. His clothes were neat and clean and of a sufficiently passable cut; had he been pointed out to her, Therese would have taken him for a well-to-do merchant.

A few feet behind him, another ex-pugilist—the third she'd seen—stood at ease, but she ignored him in favor of impressing on the still-seated man her immense displeasure.

She said nothing, simply waited.

Everyone waited.

Finally, the man behind the desk fidgeted, cleared his throat, and slowly got to his feet. Then he hesitated, plainly unsure, but eventually, he inclined his head to her. "Countess." His hard, brown gaze slid past her to Child—who had halted to one side and slightly behind her—then returned, uncertain and also uneasy, to her face.

He cleared his throat again, but before he could speak, at her most haughty, she demanded, "Who are you?" Then she decided she didn't care. "I take it you are the owner of this establishment?"

"Er, no. I'm the manager. I run the place for the owners." He nodded again. "Lester Biggs, ma'am."

From the corner of her eye, Therese saw Martin frown and look at Biggs. Martin had written that he was being detained by the owner.

"It's 'my lady,'" Therese replied. Realizing the light in this room, too, was rather dim, she glanced at the windows, confirming they remained curtained. Frowning, she pointed at the man behind Martin, then gestured at the windows. "For goodness' sake! Open those and let some light in here. It's nearly noon, not midnight."

Uncertain, the big man glanced at Biggs, who reluctantly nodded.

Therese folded her arms and tapped her toe.

As the curtains were opened, allowing daylight to slant into the room, Biggs waved her to one of the pair of chairs facing the desk. "Please, ma —my lady. Won't you be seated?"

Until she sat, he couldn't.

"No." She met Biggs's gaze directly. "I don't plan on remaining in this insalubrious location for long. Now"—now that she could more clearly see his face—"I wish to know the names of the owners of this establishment."

Biggs's nervousness visibly increased. "Ah…I'm not sure they would want you to know who they are." He assayed a weak smile. "That's why they have a manager, you see—anonymity."

With her arms still crossed, she arched a skeptical brow. "Indeed?" Then she shook her head and lowered her arms. "Come now—you know as well as I do that it would be easy enough for my husband, or Lord Child here"—she gestured at Child and, from Biggs's startled look, realized that was the first time Child's name had been mentioned—"or even Martin to learn who the owners of this establishment are, simply by asking in the right quarters."

She took a second to study Biggs's escalating unease, then let her lips curve in a distinctly cold smile. "Or is it a case of the owners having no idea that you're holding my brother—a Cynster—for ransom?"

"*What?*" Biggs reacted as if she'd struck him. He stared at her. "Ransom?" His voice rose on the word. He swallowed and waved. "No—it's not like that! That's not what this is about at all."

She opened her eyes wide. "Is that so?" Although she'd glanced at neither her brother nor Child, she was aware both were now alert and focused, intently, on Biggs. Smoothly, she continued, "In that case, perhaps you would like to explain to me and his lordship, and my brother as well, just what this situation *is* all about."

Biggs dithered—there was no other word for it. His fingers restlessly trailed across the desktop. He shifted his weight, plainly wanting to sit in his chair, but her presence kept him on his feet.

Therese watched him, her gaze unwavering, and waited.

Biggs dragged in a breath, held it for an instant, then said, "It's like this." He glanced at Martin. "This gentleman here, who says he's Martin Cynster—"

"He is Martin Cynster," she flatly declared.

Biggs angled his head in a manner suggesting that might or might not be so. "Be that as it may, we"—he gestured toward his men—"me and my boys, we recognize our punters. In this business, you have to, don't you?"

She eyed him coldly. "I wouldn't know."

Biggs blinked, then drew breath and went on, "Well, come the end of play last night, this gentleman—"

"Martin Cynster." She wasn't going to let him off that hook.

"He ended up owing the house a ton."

Therese frowned, and from behind her, Child murmured, "A hundred pounds."

Biggs nodded. "Like the gent says." He indicated Martin. "This gentleman here owed the house a hundred, and he couldn't pay up."

"I believe," she said, "that he offered you an IOU. Isn't that normal practice?"

Biggs dipped his head. "Yes, it is, and yes, he did offer, but you see"—he glanced at Martin, she thought almost in a man-to-man appeal—"none of us here know who he is."

As if finally feeling on firmer ground, Biggs returned his gaze to Therese. "If there's no way to be sure he is who he says, then we need to hold him until someone we know can vouch for him, or how do we know we'll get the money?"

Therese stared at Biggs. "Mr. Biggs. I am Lady Therese Cader, Countess of Alverton, and that man is my brother, Mr. Martin Cynster. What more verification of his identity do you need?"

The steel in her voice was cold enough to make Biggs freeze. He stared at her, then forced a weak, shaky laugh. "But who's to say you're who you say you are?" His gaze shifted to Child. "Or him, either."

In building outrage, Therese stared at Biggs.

Faintly, he winced and held up a placating hand. "I know, I know. But you must see, my lady—"

"What I see, Mr. Biggs, is that this is the most ridiculous situation I have ever encountered!" Therese knew she had at least a hundred pounds in her reticule, but she was not at all inclined to hand it over to Biggs. Aside from all else, such an act might reflect badly on the worth of Martin's IOUs; if his sister accepted that she needed to stand as guarantor... No. She wasn't going anywhere near such a potential quagmire.

But more, despite having very little idea of the procedures that pertained in the gambling hells gentlemen of the ton frequented, she was increasingly certain that there was something rather odd going on. She glanced at Martin, then turned her head to look fleetingly at Child. Both men wore unreadable yet intent expressions, which, to her, suggested that they were thinking much the same, namely, that none of this was making sense.

Or more to the point, they were missing some vital information that would make the situation understandable.

She cast about for some way to establish at least one of their identities; she wanted to leave this place and was determined to take Martin with her. She remembered the letter. "Mr. Biggs, Lord Child and I came here in response to the note my brother"—she tipped her head at Martin —"sent from here this morning, requesting assistance from my husband, Lord Alverton. That letter was delivered to Alverton House." She glanced at Child. "The letter?"

Briefly, Child met her gaze. "I left it for Devlin."

She managed not to grimace. She returned her gaze to Biggs. "Regardless, quite obviously, that letter reached me. At Alverton House. Pray tell me, Mr. Biggs, were I not Lady Alverton, how would I have had access to that letter and known to come here, to Gentleman Jim's, in order to find my brother?"

Everyone looked at Biggs, including the three thugs... She glanced around and realized that there were now only two. Apparently, the doorman had retreated to his post.

She returned her gaze to Biggs and saw consternation crawl across his face, then desperation hardened his expression, and he offered, "Perhaps you're on the staff at Alverton House, along with your brother"—Biggs looked at Child—"and him, too, and you've all decided it would be a great game to impersonate your betters and take advantage of a place like Gentleman Jim's."

Therese could barely believe her ears. Child and Martin looked equally stunned. Her gaze sharpening and pinning Biggs, she asked, her voice even and controlled, "Are you seriously suggesting that I'm some maid dressed up in my mistress's clothes?"

Despite her best efforts, by the time she reached the final word, her delivery had more in common with a fishwife's than the wife of a peer of the realm.

"Well"—Biggs frowned—"you have to admit it's possible."

"No," Therese stated. "It's not! How *dare* you suggest such a thing?"

A stir at the door had everyone glancing in that direction.

His greatcoat flapping, Devlin strode in.

Therese almost wilted with relief. He'd come. *Thank God.* Despite her firm belief that she could manage almost any situation in the ton, this incident was proving beyond her.

Calmly, Devlin walked to her side, took her hand, and raised it to his lips. "My lady." Then he set her hand on his arm and looked at Child, then at Martin; he didn't look at Biggs or his men. "What's this about?"

His lazy, faintly bored, aristocratic drawl effortlessly exerted absolute control over the room and all its occupants.

Unsurprisingly, Therese was the least affected. "Mr. Biggs"—she indicated the manager with a wave—"acts for the owners of this place." She still felt that point was important, although she'd yet to fathom why. "Mr. Biggs refuses to accept that Martin is who he says he is and, on those grounds, has refused to accept Martin's IOU. He—Biggs—insists that he will continue to hold Martin prisoner until his identity can be vouched for by someone Biggs or his staff recognize." She drew breath and went on, "Rather than accept my word or Child's on the matter, Mr. Biggs instead questioned my identity and Child's as well on the grounds that neither he nor his men recognize us."

"I see." Rather than sounding soothing, the quietly spoken words fell into the silence like a prelude to violence.

Devlin finally looked at the manager—Biggs—and was delighted to see that the man had paled. He possessed some self-protective instincts, then.

Bad enough the situations he'd imagined on the short journey there, but on approaching the room and hearing Therese's tones of outrage, his hold over his instinctive impulses had grown even more frayed. Exceedingly aware of how close to the edge of some regrettable action he stood, Devlin captured Biggs's gaze and silkily inquired, "Do you—or your men —recognize me?"

Biggs swallowed and bobbed his head. "Yes, my lord."

"Excellent. In that case, allow me to tell you that the gentleman to your left is, indeed, Mr. Martin Cynster, of the Walkhurst branch of that family." Devlin arched a brow at Biggs. "I assume that you therefore perceive no further impediment to accepting Mr. Cynster's IOU?"

Biggs bobbed again and managed a sickly smile. "Naturally not, my lord." He cut a sidelong glance at Martin and cautiously nodded. "Always happy to extend credit to a Cynster."

Devlin resisted the urge to shake his head. There was something—many things—distinctly strange about the entire situation. A question he'd asked himself on the way from Alverton House rose in his mind. "Incidentally, how much was the debt?"

Biggs paled to a pasty hue. He glanced at Martin as if preserving Martin's privacy was suddenly high in his mind.

His expression stony, Martin supplied, "One hundred pounds."

One hundred pounds? Devlin swallowed his surprise, but clearly, his instincts hadn't lied. There was something far beyond the obvious going on.

"One last point before we leave," Devlin said, allowing veiled menace to color his voice, "just in case the question should ever arise, allow me to confirm that this gentleman"—with a languid wave, he indicated Child —"is, indeed, Lord Grayson Child, son of the Duke of Ancaster. And this lady"—he allowed his features to soften as he smiled at Therese—"is most definitely Lady Alverton, my wife."

Devlin shifted his gaze to Biggs, who now looked positively ill.

The man had the sense to bow deeply. "My apologies, my lady. My lords." He straightened and bit his lip, no doubt wisely holding back a false protestation that he couldn't have known.

For Devlin's money, the man should have known and not just about Therese and Child. But his immediate goal was to remove Therese—and Martin and Child—from the building. "Now that your lack of knowledge has been rectified, Biggs, we'll take our leave. Martin?" Devlin caught the younger man's eye.

Martin took a moment to resettle his coat, a subtly contemptuous gesture that made Devlin inwardly smile, then without a single glance at Biggs or his hulking henchmen, crossed to a side table, picked up the hat and cane that had lain there, and unhurriedly joined Devlin and Therese.

With her free hand, Therese reached out and gripped her brother's sleeve.

Smoothly, Devlin slid his arm from hers and turned, putting his back to Biggs, and waved Therese and Martin toward the door.

Therese immediately started questioning Martin on his treatment at

Biggs's hands. Child fell in beside Devlin, and they followed brother and sister from the room.

In the dim corridor, Child caught Devlin's eye and arched a skeptical brow.

Devlin shook his head and murmured, "Wait until we're outside."

CHAPTER 9

*T*herese and Martin led the way to the front door. They stepped outside, then halted on the narrow pavement.

Devlin and Child joined them, and Devlin put a hand to Therese's back. "Let's go to the carriage."

With Child and Martin following, he ushered her across the lane and around to the other side of the carriage, where the carriage's body shielded them from anyone watching from the hell's front rooms.

Therese halted and put her back to the carriage. Devlin halted beside her, and Child and Martin ranged in front of them.

"What the devil was that all about?" Child asked.

"Indeed." Devlin looked at Martin. "None of that should have happened. Certainly not over a mere one hundred pounds. Your coat is worth more than that, and that's something Biggs and his men would definitely have known."

Therese frowned. "Would they?"

Devlin glanced at her; now she was standing beside him, he could almost smile. "You don't get hired to be the manager of a hell in this neighborhood, one that specifically caters to the aristocracy, without learning to judge men—and women—by the cut of their clothes and the clarity of their speech. To Biggs and his men, all three of you should have been instantly recognizable as who you are." He looked again at Martin. "That was never the issue."

Frowning, Martin nodded. "I did wonder. I was seventeen when I left

England. I'd never visited such a place—not in England—before, so I wasn't sure what was normal, not enough to be certain of my ground."

"But...why?" Child waved across the street. "Why go to the bother of staging all that? What did Biggs get out of it?"

"That," Devlin agreed, "is the critical question." He looked at Therese. "You made a point of telling me that Biggs was the manager and not the owner. Why?"

She promptly replied, "Because earlier on, when I asked for the names of the owners, I got the distinct impression that the last thing Biggs wanted was for any hint of him holding Martin to get back to the owners." She paused, then said, "He tried to make it sound as if he was acting to protect the owners' interests, but it seemed to me that he was up to something on his own."

"I agree," Child said. "I read that exchange in the same way."

"I did, too," Martin put in.

Devlin thought for a moment, then looked at Martin. "Tell me exactly what happened after you walked into the hell yesterday evening. Who took you there? I assume someone did."

Martin slid his hands into his pockets. "My cousins, Henry and Jason Cynster, and some of their friends. As you know, I ran into Henry and Jason last week, and we met again for dinner yesterday, then the company rolled on to"—Martin tipped his head across the lane—"Gentleman Jim's." He paused, then plainly thinking back, went on, "After being shown around the tables, I settled in playing poker, then Henry and the others had to go on to some ball, and I decided to stay on." Martin shrugged. "I was winning, too. Until the last hand."

His face hardened, and he met Devlin's eyes. "I've been playing poker for the past eight years, but on that last hand, I'm as sure as I can be that the dealer dealt from the bottom of the pack."

"He cheated?" Therese was horrified. "And you didn't say anything?"

Martin glanced resignedly at her. "I only just caught it and couldn't be absolutely sure, so there was no point trying to make anything of it. It was late by then, and there was no one else at the table—well, no one who could or would back me up, anyway. Besides, even with the loss, I was only a ton down, and I assumed they would accept an IOU." He glanced at Devlin. "I'd been warned not to carry too much cash in my pockets, so I didn't have that much on me."

Devlin nodded understandingly. "Not carrying much cash is wise. And if your cousins took you to the place, presumably no one else could have known you would spend the latter part of the evening there. There-fore…" His gaze sharpened, and he refocused on Martin. "When you were in the rooms, did you see anyone—anyone at all—whom you recog-nized? Other than your cousins and their friends."

Therese watched her brother frown in thought, then he started to shake his head and stopped.

His eyes narrowed. "No acquaintances, but there were three Germans I'd met at the exhibition. We exchanged nods, so I know they saw and recognized me. And I also know they're trying to buy up a Dutch inven-tion I've been invited to invest in."

Devlin smiled like a predator sighting prey. "And if you buy in, the Germans won't be able to acquire the invention?"

Martin nodded. "I believe that's the case."

"Are you due to do something today regarding that investment?" Devlin asked.

Martin wasn't slow; he met Devlin's gaze. "I'm due to sign the deal later today. You think the Germans paid Biggs to keep me at the hell until after the meeting?"

Devlin's smile was all edges. "I'd wager a considerable sum on that. If you miss the meeting, simply fail to turn up, what will happen?"

Martin shifted. "The Dutch inventor is…not quite desperate, but he needs the deal completed. If I don't sign on, he will almost certainly have to turn to the Germans, which he doesn't want to do."

Therese caught Child's eye. "That was why Biggs was so nervous. Did you notice?" She glanced at Martin. "As soon as Child and I appeared, he started to react—"

"As if a plan of his was unraveling before his eyes." Child met Martin's gaze. "Devlin's right. The Germans will have paid Biggs hand-somely to fabricate some situation that would allow him to keep you secreted away until after this meeting of yours."

Brows arching, Devlin mused, "Biggs must have been in two minds over delivering your note."

Martin softly snorted. "Your title made him—and even more, his men —nervous, but Biggs relaxed when I asked for it to be delivered to your house—enough to make me wonder if I should have sent it somewhere else."

Devlin pointed out, "They would have assumed I would spend my day out and about town and wouldn't return home and receive the note until early evening, well after your meeting." *And that would almost certainly have been the case if I wasn't actively pursuing my wife.*

Martin nodded. "They mentioned something along those lines—that I should resign myself to having to sit tight for the day. That's why I wrote 'urgent' on the front of the note."

Devlin glanced at Therese and smiled. "Just as well you did." That "urgent" on the note in her brother's writing was what had pushed her to open the letter and react as she had. Given his own protectiveness, he could hardly throw stones and complain. His smile deepened. "Although I'm sure Biggs never expected your note to bring who it did." He met Therese's eyes. "I'm sure you made him regret his part in the scheme."

She smiled back and looped her arm in his. "Not as much as you did. I got the impression he was glad to see our backs."

Child chuckled. "True, but I rather liked your touch with the curtains, and the mention of ransom was inspired."

Martin grinned. "Not to mention the point about how, if you weren't Lady Alverton, you got hold of my note. And then he was forced to suggest you were a maid! I thought you were going to verbally skewer him."

"Ah." Devlin saw the light. "That was what Biggs had suggested that had you so incensed when I walked in."

"Indeed." Therese mock glowered. "I hope the Germans return and demand their money back. It would serve Biggs right."

"At least the way things are, I'll make my meeting this afternoon, and the Germans will be out of their money with nothing to show for it—they, after all, were the ones behind the scheme." Martin smiled at Therese, Devlin, and Child. "Thank you—all of you—for coming to my rescue."

Therese reached out and patted Child's arm. "Indeed. Thank you for coming with me. I appreciated the support and will look forward to repaying you appropriately at the next social event we both attend."

Child looked faintly alarmed. "No, no—no need to exercise your talents on my behalf." More candidly, he added, "In fact, as a reward, I'd rather you didn't."

The admission made the others laugh.

On that note, they parted, with Child—who wanted to know what Martin had been doing in America over the years he himself had been there—inviting Martin to lunch with him. With nods to the others, the pair ambled off, and Devlin waved Morton back and opened the carriage door and handed Therese in.

He followed and sat beside her.

Therese settled against the fine leather with a satisfied sigh. She waited until the carriage was rolling freely along Pall Mall to turn her head and look at her husband. "Thank you for coming to our rescue. Neither I, Child, nor Martin knew enough to work out what was really going on." She waved one hand. "Who knows what Biggs might ultimately have done? He did have those three ex-pugilists to help him."

Devlin caught her hand, drew it to his lips, and brushed a light but lingering kiss on the backs of her gloved fingers. "I seriously doubt Biggs would have risked harming you, Child, or even Martin. No matter what he said, he knew all three of you were who you said you were, and I suspect that, ultimately, you would have had his measure. Regardless, regarding my contribution, all three of you are entirely welcome." He smiled. "Indeed, I haven't enjoyed an adventure like that in a very long time."

She chuckled and relaxed against the squabs. As the carriage rolled on, Devlin continued to hold her hand as if he'd forgotten he'd grasped it. She made no move to take it back.

Reviewing the morning's events, she realized he must have returned shortly after she and Child had quit the house, and he couldn't have wasted so much as a minute in following them. She considered that and inwardly admitted it was comforting to know that she, her need, had commanded his immediate attention and compelled equally immediate action.

After a moment, she murmured, "It was lucky your business meeting ended early." She glanced at him. "I assume it did. Did it go well?"

He smiled. "Very well." He met her eyes and gently squeezed her hand; clearly, he hadn't forgotten he still held it. "Thus far, today has been one of minor triumphs."

She widened her eyes encouragingly and was gratified when, his smile deepening, he explained about the contract he'd signed that morning. Informed by what she'd recently learned through listening to discussions in various drawing rooms, she was able to ask questions that drew more details from him—details he seemed happy to share with her.

By the time the carriage turned in to the Alverton House drive, she understood enough to genuinely applaud his success of the morning. In return, with a graceful dip of his head, he paid tribute to her contribution by way of having fostered a critical discussion at Lady Wicklow's picnic.

In excellent spirits, they descended from the carriage and entered the house, to be greeted with some relief by Portland.

While endeavoring to conceal his pleasure over seeing them both safe and well behind his customary imperturbable mask, Portland lifted Therese's pelisse from her shoulders. "Nanny Sprockett mentioned that she would appreciate a quick word when you came in, my lady."

"Thank you, Portland." Therese handed over her bonnet. "I'll go straight up."

"Luncheon will be ready shortly, my lady."

She smiled at Devlin as she made for the stairs. "I'll be down in ten minutes."

Still smiling himself, he inclined his head. "I'll see you later."

As she climbed the stairs, she looked back and saw him heading down the corridor to his study.

Therese faced forward. She hadn't stopped smiling for quite a few minutes, purely because, between them, all was as it should be—and given the possibilities of what might have occurred, that was, in fact, significantly better than merely well.

That evening, when Therese and Devlin attended a dinner party hosted by their next-door neighbors, the ageing Lord and Lady Warkworth, they were the youngest couple present by a goodly number of years.

Indeed, given that she was younger than the majority of the guests' children, Therese had difficulty even pretending to an interest in the topics the ladies chose to discuss. She wasn't silly enough to attempt to introduce any topics of her own. Dealing with this company required all the social skills she'd accumulated over her twenty-seven years in the ton.

Consequently, after a torturous time over the dinner table, where she'd been flanked by gentlemen older than her father and rather less interesting, as she perched on the edge of an uncomfortable straight-backed chair in the Warkworths' drawing room and sipped tepid tea with the female half of the company as they awaited the return of the male guests, her gaze kept drifting to the drawing room door, while inwardly, she willed the gentlemen to appear.

She was aware that her nerves were just a touch tightly strung, and her senses were alert as if anticipating…something. She had no idea what. Ever since she'd come downstairs after discussing Horry's latest bout of teething with Nanny Sprockett, gaily expecting to join Devlin at the luncheon table, only to discover, via Portland, that his master had quit the house, she'd been out of sorts. Just a tad disgruntled.

According to Portland, Devlin had had business matters to attend to and had elected to lunch at one of his clubs.

For some reason, that news—which she would have found utterly unremarkable just a few weeks ago—had dimmed her mood.

Subsequently, she hadn't seen Devlin until, turned out in his customary impeccable evening attire and, therefore, appearing every inch an aristocratic Adonis, he'd joined her in the front hall just in time to leave for the Warkworths'; the short stroll around the corner and along Upper Grosvenor Street had left no time at all for even the briefest of conversations.

She wanted to go home and, somehow, assess whether she'd misread their earlier embracing of what she'd taken to mentally terming "a deeper connection" or if she'd been correct in thinking they were, in fact, growing closer and Devlin's decision to leave the house instead of sharing luncheon with her had been driven by necessity rather than inclination.

"So, my dear Lady Alverton." Ensconced on the sofa, Lady Carmichael turned and leaned closer to address Therese. "What university did your sons attend—you have two, I believe? Was it Oxford or Cambridge?"

Therese plastered on an innocent smile. "I fear my sons are still in the nursery."

Lady Carmichael's eyes widened, and she sat back. "They are?" Her ladyship's gaze swiftly surveyed Therese as if finally registering her age. "Yes, well, I suppose that's not to be wondered at, heh? Can't imagine that husband of yours being that much of a cradle snatcher, devil though he undoubtedly is."

Therese smiled weakly and prayed the gentlemen ran out of port.

Two minutes later, noises in the hall heralded the return of the men. She surreptitiously heaved a relieved sigh and waited; she was prepared to claim a headache—something she'd never done in her life—if that was what it took to get Devlin to leave expeditiously.

The gentlemen started to stream in, and finally, she spotted Devlin toward the rear of the pack, strolling in that nonchalant way that was so much a part of the languid image he projected in such company.

She'd expected to have to rise and go to him, but instead, without in any way appearing to do so, he made a beeline for her. She watched him in slight surprise.

When he neared, he trapped her gaze and widened his eyes in a look she had no difficulty interpreting as *Can we please go home?*

She fought to mask her delight. She set aside her teacup and, when he halted beside her and, with a show of solicitousness, leaned closer as if to speak with her, she promptly informed him, "Horry's teething and having a dreadful time of it." Lady Carmichael and two others were close enough to overhear. Therese fixed Devlin with an anxious-mother look. "I really think we should return home."

Hiding his relief, Devlin schooled his features to reflect appropriate concern, both for his daughter and his wife. He straightened and offered Therese his hand. "Come. I'm sure Lady Warkworth will understand that we need to leave."

Therese put her fingers in his and allowed him to draw her to her feet. He twined his arm with hers and led her to the other sofa, where Lady Warkworth was holding court. Her ladyship was all solicitousness; Devlin was grateful that it was to Therese that the inevitable questions regarding Horry's teeth and general well-being were directed. He knew Horry had teeth; he didn't know how many.

He wanted to get Therese alone, but not to discuss Horry's teeth. Or Spencer's or Rupert's.

He wanted...his wife. It really was that simple.

Since returning from the hell, he'd been plagued by the inevitable outcome of the morning's excitement. Not so much his business success, although that lesser triumph undoubtedly contributed to the compulsion simmering in his veins. He'd always known Therese engaged a protectiveness in him that he couldn't entirely rule. What he hadn't appreciated was that his push to acknowledge that he loved her would escalate that protectiveness to new heights and imbue his reaction to having said protectiveness exercised with commensurately ungovernable power.

When, at midday, they'd walked into the front hall, he'd had to wrestle the unruly demands of his baser self into submission simply to allow her to walk up the stairs and away. If she hadn't been going to the nursery, he wasn't sure he'd have managed it. He'd retreated to the study and, unable to sit, had paced.

And paced.

It hadn't helped.

Courtesy of hauling her out of that hell, his possessive instincts and all that trailed in their wake had been aroused and left hungry and not for food. The notion of sitting through a luncheon with the object of his ravenous desire within reach...

He'd had no idea what might have happened—what possibly premature revelations might have slipped past his guard in the heat of an out-of-control engagement—so he'd cravenly left to spend the afternoon and as much of the early evening as he could in his clubs.

Now, after sitting through a dinner of near-unimaginable dullness, he felt he'd regained some semblance of control. Enough, at least, to go forward and appease—or at least take the edge from—his clamorous needs.

Finally, Lady Warkworth released them, and with nods to the rest of the company, they walked into the front hall, retrieved Therese's evening cloak and his overcoat, hat, and cane, and quit the house.

As, arm in arm, they stepped down to the pavement and turned toward Park Lane and Alverton House, he asked, "Is Horry truly teething, and even if she is, is there any reason for you to go to her?"

"Yes, and no." Therese studied his face. "She is teething, but she's over the worst of it and, at this moment, is doubtless sound asleep."

"Good." His smile felt sharp with hunger. He lengthened his stride, and obligingly, Therese increased her pace as they rounded the corner, then turned in to the Alverton House drive.

Seconds later, Portland admitted them to the house.

Devlin handed over his hat and cane, then stepped behind Therese and lifted her heavy velvet cloak from her slender shoulders. She'd worn an evening gown of cornflower blue, and the wide neckline left her shoulders bare; the soft lamplight in the hall laid a pearlescent sheen over skin he knew felt like the finest silk.

His mouth watered. After handing the cloak to Portland, he let the footman take his overcoat, then walked quickly to catch up with Therese as she made for the stairs.

"Goodnight, my lord, my lady," Portland called.

"Goodnight, Portland," they chorused.

Devlin captured Therese's hand as they started up the stairs. She threw him a faintly questioning look, but uncertain of what she might see in his eyes, he kept his gaze fixed forward.

Fed by anticipation, the impulses he'd thought well-leashed were rising.

They gained the landing and turned up the second flight—and his hold on his smoldering passions snapped.

Using the grip he had on Therese's hand, he drew her to face him, stepped closer, and backed her against the panelled wall of the stairwell, then bent his head and crushed his lips to hers.

They were out of sight of Portland and the footmen locking up downstairs. Freed of restraint on that score, Therese responded instinctively to the scorching kiss, to the desire and hunger she sensed behind it, with her own almost-desperate need.

In an instant, with that one searing kiss, Devlin answered all her questions and swept away her newfound uncertainties. *This* was what now lived between them—this glorious, heady rush of passion, desire, need, and wanting, all focused on the other.

She kissed him back every bit as ardently, as heatedly, as he kissed her.

She gripped his nape and sank her fingertips into his shoulder and held him as tightly to the kiss as he, through his unbreakable grip on her hips, was holding her.

He ravaged her mouth, and she ravaged his back, equally hungry and greedy and needy.

On a gasp, he broke the kiss. They were both heated and close to breathless. Their gazes met and held. His eyes were dark pools of sinful temptation. She had no idea what he saw in hers.

He hauled in a breath, then stepped back, pulled her from the wall and, slinging a steely arm around her waist, urged her up the stairs. "Your room." His voice was a gravelly rumble.

Grinning from ear to ear, she grabbed her skirts and rushed up the stairs.

He easily kept pace, steadying her when, in her haste, she almost stumbled.

They reached the gallery and rushed along it and into the corridor leading to their rooms. But it wasn't easy to run in well-laced stays and still breathe.

When, gasping, she staggered sideways to lean against the corridor wall and catch her breath, he swooped on her and kissed her again, voracious, greedy, and with a soaring urgency that sank its claws into her and didn't let go.

She clamped her hands to the sides of his face and held him as she kissed him back, as she poured all the passion surging through her—so much more than she'd ever felt before—into the kiss, into him.

He was hungry for it, for her, and the power of that hunger, that all-consuming need, seemed so much greater than before.

I want, I want. With every pulse of her heart, the words beat through her, and she wasn't sure if they came from her or him.

Or both. Certainly, as their hands raced over their still-clothed bodies, there was no distinction between them in terms of desperation, urgency, and sheer driving need.

He pulled his lips from hers enough to insistently growl, "Your room."

Yes. Desire gave her the strength to push away from the wall. He stepped back, supporting her as she swayed.

She met his eyes, then she grinned and made a mad dash for her door.

He was on her heels as she got the door open and all but fell into the room.

One quick glance confirmed that Parker was nowhere in sight and the lamp beside the bed had been left alight.

Then Devlin kicked the door shut behind him, spun her into his arms, and she forgot about everything else—ceased to be able to think of anything beyond him, beyond them, beyond slaking their ravenous need.

Lips locking, releasing, then hungrily fusing in a long succession of searing, open-mouthed kisses, they fell on each other, hands knowingly caressing, seeking, possessing, as driven by that unrelenting need, they divested each other of their clothes, peeling each garment away to reveal the prize beneath.

When, already nude, he spun her around to attack her laces, she tipped her head up and back, trying to drag air into lungs starved of that commodity. Kissing him always took priority over mere breathing.

Eyes open, she stared upward, but couldn't focus on the ceiling. Her mind wasn't engaged, yet words leapt to her tongue. "When you didn't stay to share luncheon, I thought I'd read things—*this*"—with one hand, she waved over her shoulder, indicating what was between them —"wrongly."

His attention locked on the desperately necessary task of loosening her laces, Devlin blinked. For a second, his fingers slowed, then he huffed. "I couldn't trust myself to be in the same room." He set his fingers frantically working once more, then glanced at her face, at what he could see of her expression. "I didn't know how attached you were to that dress."

Her features eased into a delighted smile, and she laughed, a tinkling sound of sheer happiness, and something in his chest heated and swelled.

Then she said, "Not that attached." She paused, then twisted her head and glanced over her shoulder. "Next time...tell me."

There was a wealth of sexual encouragement in her tone, which, at that precise moment, he really didn't need to hear. He was rock hard and aching already.

He wrestled with the final knot at her waist. "I assure you I will, but equally, I fervently hope you won't see the need to make another excursion to a place like Gentleman Jim's."

Finally, the last closure was free, and he peeled the light corset from her and cavalierly flung it aside as, clad only in a gossamer-silk chemise, she turned toward him.

The lamplight found her eyes, the silvery blue darkened by passion to a steely shade, as she boldly stepped into him. The silk screening her curves tauntingly caressed the heated planes of his body, then she pressed closer, and the tactile impression of her barely screened flesh sent a surge of heat to his groin as she draped her arms over his shoulders and, with those mesmerizing eyes locked with his, purred, "Well...if this is the result, I'm not sure I would go so far as to offer any firm undertakings." Her lips curved provocatively as her lashes fell, and in seductive fashion, she whispered, "I certainly won't promise."

Lord, I'm well on the way to creating a monster.

He couldn't find it in him to care.

Quite the opposite.

He waited until, wishing to gauge the effect of her teasing, she raised her gaze to his face, then allowing the true extent of his possessiveness to infuse the gesture, he smiled, closed his arms tightly around her, bent his head, and kissed her.

No reins, no restraint.

What followed was nothing short of a passionate conflagration.

He ripped away her chemise, and she urged him on. Urged him to take even as she claimed him.

With single-minded determination, they stoked each other's fires. Their hands raced over already heated skin, stroking, fondling, caressing, then seizing. Possessing.

They fell on the bed, body on body, skin to skin, and the only thought in their minds was the overwhelming need to get closer yet.

Driven beyond bearing, they writhed and rolled, then taunted and teased each other's senses until the hungry, greedy flames roared, and they burned.

Breathless and aching, they joined, and the moment threatened to incinerate every last vestige of control.

His and hers.

Therese had never experienced passion's heat to this extent. Never plunged into intercourse, into intimacy, to such a deep level, to where there seemed no boundary, no barrier at all, between him as him and her as her.

They were one. Totally merged, their conscious minds subsumed by mutual need. By a hunger too elemental to deny.

Barely controlled, he thrust powerfully into her willing body, and she clamped her thighs to his flanks and rode with him. Even as the familiar landscape bloomed in their minds, that impossible-to-deny creation of their senses, she couldn't believe how much more intense every last facet, every last scintillating sensation, was.

After five and more years, how could there be so much *more*?

She had no idea, but she felt that reality to her bones.

Even while her senses whirled and spun, desperate to understand, she fought to marshal sufficient wit to focus on him as, propped on his braced arms, he hung over her. The steady rhythm of his hips between her thighs, the repetitive flexing of the long muscles of his back beneath her spread hands, anchored her in the here and now as she raised her lids enough to peek up at him. His eyes were closed. She gazed at his face, all sculpted, passion-etched, rigid planes, yet even in those unyielding lines, she could see there was more.

A deeper commitment to their pleasure, a greater striving for the ultimate in closeness.

Had anyone ever asked, she would have said with absolute certainty that from the first, they'd shared the deepest of physical connections, the most rapturous of intimacies.

She hadn't, then, known *this*.

Hadn't even imagined or dreamed that such an intense connection could exist.

Molten passion had long since claimed her, pooling and tightening at her core. Now he shifted, subtly altering the angle of his thrusts, and she gasped anew, arched and clung.

All thought—all ability to think—vanished in the hot haze of pleasured delight as together, they raced harder and faster to completion.

She surrendered to the driving compulsion, bathed in the indescribable heat, and gladly raced with him as he steered them up that ineluctable peak and straight into a nerve-shattering, mind-numbing climax.

The brilliance of ecstasy and the surge of warmth that came with its fading glow were very familiar, yet so much more profound. As she sank, willingly, into soothing satiation, he murmured something, then lifted from her.

She was nearly asleep when, slumped on his back, he gathered her to him.

Without conscious direction, her lips curved, and she pressed a warm kiss to his chest. Settling in his arms, she sleepily admitted, "I never thought that we could have more, but now we have this—and it's *glorious*."

Devlin heard her, but in the aftermath of their passion, it took several moments to register the meaning of her words. When he did, he shifted his head and squinted down at her face, but she was already asleep.

He contemplated waking her gently and asking what she'd meant, but he was fairly certain he knew. Adding smug satisfaction to the emotions coursing through him, he lay back, let his lids fall, and wallowed in the warmth, in the sensations of holding her sated body in his arms, in the relaxed state of utter completion that had swamped his limbs.

Given her last statement, it seemed the time for chancing his hand and speaking of his new direction was drawing near.

Yet…even with his mind fogged with pleasure, he lectured himself sternly that he could indulge only until it was time to haul himself up and retreat to his own bed.

Despite that first hint that she might be seeing what he wanted her to see, he was determined not to act precipitously and risk putting a foot wrong. He would wait until he was absolutely certain that the time to speak had come.

CHAPTER 10

*T*he following evening, Devlin and Therese attended Lady Cassington's ball. Despite being held so late in the year, the Cassington ball was regarded as a major haut ton event, not least because the guest list was invariably highly select.

As Devlin escorted Therese—tonight wearing a striking gown of midnight purple that set off the Alverton diamonds, blazing about her throat and at her ears, to perfection—on an ambling circuit of the long ballroom, greeting and being greeted in return, he initially gave thanks that, courtesy of the event's exclusivity, there was no fashionable crush.

Then he realized that the very space that allowed guests to freely mingle also enabled the large contingent of grandes dames present to notice him and, more specifically, take note of his constant presence by Therese's side.

And they were definitely taking note.

At an event of this nature, as the Countess of Alverton, Therese would have been expected to attend and remain for most of the evening, but beyond him escorting her to the ballroom and showing his face, few would imagine he wouldn't stroll off to chat with his peers in the card room or even leave once he deemed his duty done.

Such behavior was all very well, but the events of yesterday, morning to night, had yet to fade from his memory. Had yet to lose their potency in provoking visceral reactions within him every time the more intense moments replayed, usually unbidden, in his mind.

In setting out to make the reality of their union manifest, he hadn't considered the effect that establishing his true feelings for Therese in the forefront of his mind—freely allowing that most powerful of emotions to be the principal driver of his behavior—would have.

He hadn't expected to feel...whatever this was he was feeling. It wasn't quite jealousy, for there was no one of whom he could be jealous, but in some ways, it felt as if he teetered on the brink of surrendering to that emotion. The term "raw possessiveness" came closest to describing the compulsion that kept him by Therese's side. He'd thought that sating his escalating possessiveness, propelled to new heights by her venture into a hell, as he and she had so thoroughly last night, would, if not reduce the feeling, at least lull it somewhat, but if anything, the insistent, persistent pressure had only grown.

Therese's words of the night resonated in his brain. *"I never thought that we could have more, but now we have this—and it's* glorious. *"*

He didn't disagree. The problem was that he was greedy and wanted even more.

As he steered her through the assembled guests, stopping to chat, to exchange observations and news of their family, all of which he could do without much thought, he pondered the source of his constantly building emotions.

The simple fact was that a large part of him wanted to confess all to Therese.

He was inching closer and closer—his emotions were inexorably pushing him nearer and nearer—to revealing his truth.

The battle to hold back, to hold the line and not speak precipitously and ruin his chances, was what was making him so tense.

Ambling from group to group—giving others no chance to claim her attention for too long—seemed to alleviate the possessive pressure some-what. As he and she left another circle of ladies and gentlemen and he steered her on through the throng, she glanced up at him.

He felt her gaze briefly scan his face. He looked down, met her eyes, and arched a brow.

She searched his eyes for a second, then faced forward; her fingers tightened fleetingly on his arm as she murmured, "Just so you know, I'm delighted to have you by my side."

He wasn't sure what to make of that, but before he could ask, she flashed him a pixielike smile and, looking ahead again, went on, "The grandes dames are watching us like hawks and no doubt speculating and getting the wrong idea, but I don't want them—their attention—to frighten you off."

She looked up at him, and there was a warmth in her eyes of a sort he'd longed to see. "For the record, I like the way we've been recently, over recent weeks, with me helping you in business and with politics rather more than before." She paused, then returned her gaze to the circle they were approaching and gently gripped his sleeve as if for emphasis. "I like this new and improved version of us."

Devlin had to take a moment to breathe. If she'd looked at him then, she would have seen his dilemma in his eyes.

Tell her! Tell her!

The impulse battered him. In that instant, he wanted nothing more than to seize the moment, but the middle of a haut ton ballroom was the last place any sane gentleman would choose to reveal his heart.

But he couldn't let the moment slip. He had to say something.

Words leapt to his tongue, and he heard himself say, "Good." That would have been enough, but with the opening there, placed before him, he couldn't resist adding, "And who knows? The grandes dames' speculation might not be in error."

Even as the words fell from his lips, he wanted to close his eyes and groan.

Courtesy of his bumbling overeagerness, he'd done it again—the equivalent of speaking in tongues.

Therese heard Devlin's comment, and although she continued to glide toward the next group of guests with a suitable smile curving her lips, her mind came to a screeching halt, then scrambled to make sense of his words. Her heart—an increasingly sensitive organ where he was concerned—seemed to stutter, then race. What had he meant? His tone had sounded lighthearted, almost flippant, yet...

Even while she greeted the three couples they had joined and responded to their observations more or less by rote, she turned Devlin's words over in her mind, then sternly told herself not to be so stupid.

Doubtless he thought that, due to his recent habit of spending more time by her side, the grandes dames were speculating that he was growing more attached to her. Nothing more. For anyone who didn't know the ladies involved, that was an entirely reasonable conclusion.

But she knew every grande dame present and was prepared to wager the Alverton diamonds presently gracing her throat that *wouldn't* be what that cohort of old ladies was thinking.

No. What the grandes dames were thinking—and hoping—was that after five years of marriage, Devlin was finally falling in love with her.

For some unfathomable reason, the realization left her feeling exposed. Vulnerable.

She told herself to let the comment pass unremarked, but their marriage was central to her existence, and any occurrence impinging on it was, for her, impossible to ignore.

As they moved on to the next circle of guests, she glanced at Devlin's face, but his expression, as it usually was, especially in social settings, was unreadable. But she remembered the incident at Christopher's wedding breakfast and the hours of agitation that had caused her, purely because, at the time, she hadn't pushed Devlin for an explanation.

In her mind, she replayed his words. *"And who knows? The grandes dames' speculation might not be in error."*

Accepting that she simply had to know, she forced herself to catch his eye and quietly ask, "Regarding your earlier comment about what the grandes dames might be thinking, I assume you meant that it's impossible to say what their conjecture might be." Her tone made it clear she was asking a question rather than making a statement.

He looked ahead and hesitated—just for an instant—then a muscle in the side of his jaw tensed, and he dipped his head. "Just so."

Therese stared, then forced herself to face forward as well. Far from answering her question, he'd only compounded her confusion, because she was as sure as she could be that he'd...perhaps not *lied*, but certainly his "just so" hadn't been the whole truth. Possibly not even a part of the truth. She was learning to read the signs of prevarication in his sons; now she knew from whom they'd learned the knack.

To her annoyance, the Hemmingses approached through the increasing crowd, and she was forced to cling to her social mask when what she really wanted to do was drag Devlin into some anteroom and demand to be told precisely what he'd meant...

Gah! Even as she traded greetings and observations with James and Veronica, a fresh wave of uncertainty rose and swamped her. She couldn't help but recall how she'd overthought and overinterpreted Devlin's words at Christopher's wedding. Ten to one, she was making too much of his latest throwaway comment as well.

She had to force herself not to grit her teeth; this was the second time he'd flung her into an emotional fluster with an ambiguous incidental comment.

Determined to put the latest episode behind her, she ruthlessly focused on the tale Veronica was relating about an excursion to a fabric warehouse in pursuit of curtains for her most-recent refurbishing effort. Veronica seemed compelled to redecorate at least every second year; Therese strongly suspected that Veronica did so for reasons other than keeping up with the latest style.

Devlin was doing a passable job of listening with some degree of attention, while James, as usual, looked supremely bored and just a trifle irritated—which might have been Veronica's intention.

Keeping her social façade firmly in place and her mind focused on the task, Therese set herself to behave and react as expected of the Countess of Alverton.

Devlin cast a sidelong glance at Therese and tried to tell himself all was well, but he knew that wasn't the case. Aside from all else, beneath his polished, impenetrable veneer, his heart continued to beat too rapidly —whether in trepidation, in misplaced hope, or in expectation, he couldn't tell.

Once again, he'd muddied the waters between them. He knew perfectly well that the grandes dames, keenly perspicacious as they were, would be speculating that his attentions to Therese signaled that he was falling in love with her. Given that the Cassington ballroom was in no way an appropriate venue for any such personal revelation, he should have shut up after his "Good." If he had, all would, indeed, have been well.

Instead, in oblique and ambiguous fashion, he'd suggested the grandes dames might be correct without actually confirming anything at all.

Why he hadn't had the sense to bite his tongue, he didn't know. It was the second time he'd spoken impulsively, without due thought; he knew the fault lay with him. Within him, truth be told; from the first moment he'd met Therese, he'd recognized that the best way of managing her was to hint at facts and allow her to "discover" them for herself. That had been his habitual way of dealing with her, and no matter that after his first unhelpful attempt, he'd accepted that, in this situation, such an approach wouldn't work, his escalating impatience to seize what he wanted had tripped him into reverting to his previous ways.

He was just a touch confounded that, after all his careful planning, his impulsive self could still take charge and have him tossing out sentences like that. He'd never encountered such a problem in business or in politics; even when he'd acted impulsively in those spheres, when he spoke, he was always considered, clear, and concise.

Only with Therese had he ever lost his head and had his tongue run away with him.

He glanced at her again, but could glean nothing of what she might actually be thinking from her expression; she was as polished a social performer as he. No one observing her would imagine she had any concern beyond enjoying the ball.

Cedric Marshall arrived and joined their group, as did two other couples who were acquainted with the Hemmingses as well as with Devlin and Therese. From beside Therese, Devlin conversed and exchanged anecdotes with his customary unrufflable ease, but he continued to watch her closely and, eventually, concluded that, behind the reflective mirror of her eyes, she'd grown pensive.

She was still mulling over his words; any hope that she would shrug them aside died.

Everything had been going well; they'd both been in good spirits when they'd arrived. Now…no matter how she appeared to others, he knew she was focused inward and was no longer deriving any enjoyment from the ball.

Anger at himself for having once again destroyed her peace of mind welled.

Enough. He'd allowed the words to leave his tongue—he would view that as him having taken his first, irrevocable step toward telling her, clearly and unambiguously, that he loved her. He would master his impulse to dance around the truth and simply tell her. Tonight.

He was not going to allow a situation that was causing her any kind of distress to continue.

Unfortunately, he couldn't speak with her there, and it was still too early for them to leave.

Two minutes later, the musicians arrived and started to set up in a nearby corner. Cedric whispered something to Therese, then she turned and put a hand on Devlin's arm. "I'm going to have a word with Lady Poulson."

Meaning that Cedric wanted Therese to facilitate a meeting with her ladyship's protégée, Miss Nagley.

Devlin nodded, caught Therese's hand, and smoothly wound her arm with his. With his usual flair, he excused them to the other couples, leaving Cedric to follow suit. Devlin cast an inquiring glance at Therese. "Which way?"

She regarded him with faint suspicion, but tipped her head toward the ballroom door. "Farther along the wall."

Smiling urbanely, he steered her in that direction, with Cedric keeping pace.

Devlin breathed deeply and felt assurance and certainty well and anchor him. Tonight, he would bare his soul to his wife, and after that, all truly would be well.

~

Half an hour later, with the ball in full swing, Grayson Child stood by one side of the room and watched Devlin circle the dance floor with his wife in his arms.

In returning to London and, inevitably, to the haut ton, Gray had foreseen that one of the major dangers he would face was that of matrimonial snares. Until arriving in town, he hadn't spent much time thinking of marriage, but from experience, he'd learned to evaluate any significant threat that might arise, and stumbling unawares into an unintended marriage ranked high on his scale of potential disasters.

Given that, beneath their competitive banter, he and Devlin were alike in many, many ways, from the instant Gray had learned that his childhood friend was securely married and had been for five years, he'd taken to watching Devlin—and Therese, but mostly Devlin; who better from whom to learn of the benefits and drawbacks of the married state?

At first, it had seemed that Devlin's marriage was the epitome of the tried-and-true marriages most popular among the ton, one based on mutual respect and, if the couple was lucky, affection similar to what existed between close friends.

But the more Gray had watched, the less he'd believed, until eventually, he'd come to the startling conclusion that Devlin's marriage wasn't a conventional one at all.

Even with his deep knowledge of Devlin, it had taken Gray quite some time to convince himself of the reality of what he was seeing and what that must therefore mean.

He knew women—in his estimation, rather well—and had satisfied himself of Therese's state first. That she loved Devlin wasn't any longer a question in Gray's mind, even though, when in society, she rarely if ever allowed any sign of the depth of her devotion to show.

That, of course, hadn't told him anything about Devlin's emotions but —at least to Gray, who knew Devlin so well—had given rise to an eye-opening possibility.

Then Gray had been present and, with his own eyes, had seen Devlin's face, his expression, when he'd stalked into the manager's office at Gentleman Jim's. In that instant, no matter how shocking Gray found it, the truth had been revealed.

Nothing he'd seen or heard subsequently, as they'd left the hell or in what he'd extracted from Therese's younger brother, had done anything other than confirm Gray's assessment of Devlin's state.

Subsequently, putting that together with all he'd observed over the past weeks had left Gray facing another, even more astonishing question. Devlin was in love with his wife, but did Therese know that?

The more he'd examined and analyzed all he'd seen of the pair, the more convinced he grew that the answer was no.

Given his purpose in studying Devlin's marriage was to learn how Devlin managed the relationship, that realization had only fixed Gray's interest even more avidly.

The waltz ended, and Gray watched as Devlin raised Therese from her curtsy and, with an elegant solicitousness that didn't entirely conceal his possessiveness, looped her arm with his and, after consulting her as to her wishes, escorted her to engage with a circle of other couples.

Inwardly, Gray frowned. He'd already been in the ballroom when Devlin and Therese had arrived, but he'd hung back, playing least in sight to further observe what he mentally termed the "state of play" between the pair.

At first, he'd felt certain that Devlin must have said something to open Therese's eyes; there'd been a glow in her face and a depth of female confidence in her expression that Gray hadn't seen before.

He'd started to approach, intending to tease Devlin in his customary fashion and, perhaps, learn more. Despite the season, the ball was well attended, and Gray had taken his time wending his way through the crowd.

He'd been within a few yards of his quarry when he'd seen Therese look up and say something to Devlin, and her love for the blighter had never been more clearly on show. Assuming that meant that Devlin had finally confessed to his feelings, Gray had smiled in genuine delight and not a little anticipation of all the minutes he could look forward to, ribbing Devlin about his fall...*but* then Devlin had said something in reply, and Therese's glow had faded, then died.

Her expression had shuttered, and all the warmth that had been all but spilling out of her had vanished.

Gray had stopped short, two paces away from them; he'd stared, but neither had noticed him, and he'd turned and slipped away through the crowd.

Devlin, the damned fool, had muffed it!

In between repolishing his social skills by chatting and conversing with numerous guests while artfully avoiding the ladies who sought to detain him, Gray had continued to review all he now knew of Devlin's marriage. He tried to tell himself that it was none of his business, that it wasn't up to him to meddle, much less interfere, but some part of him wouldn't let the matter rest.

When he found himself quitting the side of the room and, as if drawn by an irresistible lure, heading toward Devlin and Therese, Gray gave up and surrendered to the inevitable. How many times had he hauled Devlin's arse out of the fire? Admittedly not as often as Devlin had rescued his, but the habit had been set in stone long ago.

He timed his approach so that he fetched up beside Therese just as the musicians once again set bow to string. When she turned and smiled at him in polite welcome, he smiled charmingly and bowed. "Lady Therese, might I have this dance?"

Therese was mildly surprised—there were any number of ladies Child might have approached instead of the very-much-married wife of his oldest friend—but she recalled the plans she had for him and decided that confirming his expertise in the waltz wouldn't go amiss. She allowed her smile to widen and offered her hand. "Indeed, my lord, you may."

Child's expression stated that he felt honored, but Therese didn't miss the sharp look he sent Devlin as the pair exchanged an outwardly cordial nod. *What was that about?*

She was aware that it was perfectly possible that Child had requested the dance purely to prod Devlin; in some respects, the pair seemed to share a relationship of schoolboyish one-upmanship. Perhaps understandably. As she allowed Child to lead her toward the area clearing in the middle of the room, over her shoulder, she threw an amused look of resignation at Devlin—and saw his rather tense posture fractionally relax.

He'd been growing increasingly tense as the evening progressed; she had no idea why.

Child reached the open space and turned to face her. She held up her hand, allowing him to grasp it, and settled her other hand on his shoulder as his palm splayed over her back. Then the music began, and they stepped out.

Within seconds, they were part of the whirling throng. Within a minute, she was sufficiently reassured that Child could waltz more than creditably.

He met her gaze and arched a weary brow. "Do my poor skills pass muster?"

She laughed. "You know very well that they do."

Before she could ask him how old he'd been when he'd quit England, the better to gauge his experience of the ton, he said, "You seemed rather pensive earlier." Far from being playful or teasing, his expression was serious when he faintly raised his brows and went on, "If it's something to do with Devlin, perhaps I can help. I have known him since childhood, after all."

Therese felt her eyes instinctively narrow. It was difficult not to question what was behind such an offer, yet...she sensed that Child was being entirely sincere. And the more she saw of him and Devlin together, the more their relationship—for all its schoolboy moments—seemed one of long, still-close, and well-weathered friendship. A friendship borne of common experience that had lasted through the decades.

Without conscious thought, she followed Child's lead, and the world continued to revolve around them as he patiently waited for her to decide.

She drew a slow breath. Given the uncertainty roiling inside her, if Child had any insight to offer, she wanted to hear it. She focused on his face. "How close were you and Devlin as children—before you both went to Eton?"

He grinned, and from his expression, she suspected he was remembering those days. "We were the only boys of our age and station in the neighborhood, so our parents encouraged our association, and whenever we had the chance, we spent our free hours together. Early in our lives, that meant a lot of our waking hours. We rambled and, later, rode and explored as avidly as boys are wont to do." He met her gaze and shrugged lightly. "We were more or less inseparable."

She nodded. "And then came Eton."

He confirmed that, explaining that they were not only in the same year, but also in the same house. "And we attended all the same classes, of course."

"More or less inseparable again?"

His smile was almost fond as he nodded. "We enjoyed ourselves more than either of us expected, and on top of that, we spent most of our holidays running wild together as well." He went on to describe some of their exploits, confirming Therese's sense of the one-upmanship that seemed to have survived to this day. When she put that to him, Child admitted it. "We might have been—might still be—close friends, but we always had an underlying sense of rivalry, too."

He met her gaze openly. "That said, we would never, ever, do anything that would...hurt the other. Our rivalry has always been of the sort that grows out of a deep and abiding understanding of each other—of what drives each other. We challenge each other, but only in the sense of making each other reach farther, do better."

She considered him for a moment, then ventured, "My brothers are a little like that—competitive in a sense—but they would always, unquestionably, have each other's back in a fight."

Child nodded. "Then you understand. Devlin and I aren't brothers by blood, but we are very definitely brothers in experience." He glanced around as he steered her through the more rapid turn at the end of the long room, then refocused on her face. "That being so, I will admit to being insatiably curious over how you and Devlin met." He arched his brows. "Was it in the ton, at a ball such as this?"

She admitted it was, and he asked how long it had been before Devlin proposed. Having more or less done the proposing herself, she skated around that point and asked if his interest was due to him assessing the possibility of marriage for himself, and while rather coyly avoiding a direct answer, he allowed her supposition to stand.

The rhythm of the music slowed, then the waltz ended. Child released her and bowed, and Therese curtsied.

As she straightened, Child nodded toward the archway leading to the refreshment room, then glanced up the now-crowded room to where they'd left Devlin, closer to the other end. "Shall we see what's available to slake our thirsts before we undertake the trek back?"

As she hadn't yet broached the question she most wanted to ask him, she inclined her head. "By all means—I'm quite parched."

He gave her his arm, and they strolled into a decent-sized anteroom. A long table was manned by Lady Cassington's staff, all busily pouring libations for thirsty guests.

Child drew her to the side of the room. "Champagne?"

"Please." She waited while he went to the table and, in short order, returned with two slim flutes. She accepted the glass he offered her. "Thank you." She took a sip, then another; she truly was parched. Then she lowered the glass and fixed her gaze on Child's face. "What can you tell me about Devlin's parents' marriage?"

She'd never thought to ask before, but she should have; it was highly likely that Devlin's parents' marriage had informed his views of that state.

Child studied her for several seconds, then without any hint of being surprised by the question, replied, "I can't actually say from my own experience—I only saw them occasionally, and often it was one or the other, not both together." He faintly grimaced. "And by the time I reached the age of possessing some degree of discernment, Devlin's father had died." Child's eyes remained steady on hers. "You know that happened as Devlin was finishing at Oxford?"

She nodded. "And his mother died the year after."

Child tipped his head in agreement. "So I had little opportunity to view their marriage first-hand." Over the rim of his glass, he held her gaze. "However, I do know how Devlin saw their marriage."

Which was precisely what she wanted to know. "Oh? How?" She ensured that her expression and her tone reflected nothing more than mild interest.

"As a love-match, of course." Child looked at her rather strangely, then added, "That was, I believe, the general consensus as well."

Therese frowned. That wasn't what she'd been expecting to hear. She'd assumed that Devlin, with his rigid adherence to the construct of conventional marriage—one founded on respect, affection, and perhaps fondness, but not love—had been following in his parents' footsteps, along a path they had forged of which he approved and with which he felt comfortable.

But if that wasn't so... Her frown deepened. What had caused Devlin to turn aside from seeking a love-match himself?

Had it been her?

The thought left her mentally floundering.

Child had been studying her. Now, with his gaze still locked on her face, in a tone she could only interpret as amazed resignation, he bluntly stated, "He hasn't told you yet—and you haven't seen it, either."

His delivery suggested he could barely believe that, yet was absolutely certain it was so.

She directed her frown at him. "Told me what?" He was as bad as Devlin in not communicating clearly. Her lips thinning, she flatly demanded, "And what haven't I seen?"

Still searching her expression, he shook his head in patent wonderment. "For two people who are normally so observant and so much in charge of everything about you..." He broke off, then continued, "You do realize you and he are strikingly similar in that respect, don't you?"

She knew that. "Get to the point," she all but growled.

He started to open his mouth, then shut his lips and looked around, his gaze raking the room in which they stood. "I will, but not here."

He reached out and plucked the half-empty glass from her fingers, then crossed to set it and his glass on a corner of the long table. Then he quickly returned to her and glanced around again; in the ballroom, another waltz was in progress, and the refreshment room had more or less emptied of guests.

Child caught her hand. "Come with me. We need somewhere more private for this." He drew her toward a minor door set into the wall near the room's corner.

Therese hesitated for only a fraction of a second before allowing her feet to comply with his direction. She needed to learn what Child knew that she didn't, and she seriously doubted he was in the mood for any illicit dalliance—or that he would target her even if he was.

She believed him when he said that there was something about Devlin that she hadn't understood—she *knew* that was true—so she followed closely as he led her through the door, into a side corridor that ran beside the ballroom.

The corridor was dimly lit and clearly not intended for the use of guests. Child started trying the doors they came upon. "There's bound to be a parlor of some sort along here."

Devlin had spent the duration of the waltz Child and Therese had shared by idly conversing with several gentlemen. Of course, once the music ceased and the dance floor cleared, he'd looked for Therese—and Child —but hadn't found them.

He had seen the archway leading to the refreshment room at the farther end of the ballroom. After counseling himself that Therese and Child would appear soon enough, he'd waited with what patience he could muster.

When the musicians had summoned the dancers for the next waltz and he'd yet to sight either his wife or Child, inwardly gritting his teeth, Devlin had excused himself to those with whom he'd been chatting and, reining in the urge to stalk down the floor, had strolled as nonchalantly as he could toward the refreshment room, having to pause here and there to avoid whirling couples.

It wasn't that he imagined anything untoward occurring between Therese and Child. He knew his wife, and she was in love with him, while Child, although Child, was, despite all, a man he inherently trusted, especially when it came to something Child knew was important to him.

No, it was the delicate situation—the critical point he'd reached in his oh-so-important campaign—that had knotted his nerves, leaving him feeling as if he was teetering on a knife edge, with something dark and powerful and not quite controllable prowling beneath his skin.

He reached the refreshment room, almost deserted, and glanced around—in time to see a fragment of deep-purple silk whisk through a narrow, minor door. The door remained ajar. Devlin regarded it for several seconds, then jaw setting, started toward it. Then he halted and scanned the room again. Perhaps Therese was on her way to the ladies' withdrawing room. But if so, where was Child?

Not in the refreshment room and not in the ballroom, either.

Jaw clenching even tighter, Devlin marched toward the door in the corner, intent on finding his wife.

After turning several corners, Child finally found a small parlor that was helpfully empty and, with some relief, towed Therese inside.

He wasn't happy about how far they'd had to go to find a spot that would afford them suitable privacy; he'd had no idea so many guests had already availed themselves of the nearer rooms. When he'd glanced in, most hadn't been talking.

He'd clearly been away from ton society for too long; he'd felt almost scandalized.

Once Therese had entered, he closed the door.

She freed her hand from his light clasp, walked four paces into the room, then swung around and fixed him with a commanding look.

"What," she demanded, "hasn't Devlin told me, and what haven't I seen?"

The moonlight streamed in through two windows to his right and lit her expression well enough for him to note and appreciate the determined set of her features. It really was a pity that Devlin had found her first.

Then again...

He held her gaze, rendered even more silvery by the moonlight, and simply said, "That he's in love with you."

Not in her wildest imaginings had Therese expected Child to say that, and the storm of emotions his words unleashed was so powerful, so overwhelming, it literally made her sway.

His eyes flaring in alarm, in two quick strides, Child closed the distance between them, gripped her shoulders, and steadied her. "Good God! Don't faint on me."

He truly was rattled.

The sight of his patently genuine concern gave her the strength to raise her chin and stiffen her spine. "I have no intention of fainting."

But her heart was still somersaulting in a disconcerting way. In near desperation, she reached for her social armor and narrowed her eyes on Child's face. "I will grant that, in many respects, you might know Devlin better than I do, but regarding his feelings toward me, you've misread him."

She made the statement with steady resolution. She tipped her chin a touch higher. "The basis of our marriage has always been entirely clear between us. He didn't marry me because he loved me." Before she could censor her tongue, she rolled on, "We married because I loved him."

Child's lips tightened, and adamantly, he shook his head. "I will allow that might have been so when the pair of you married. I don't know—I wasn't here then. But whatever was or wasn't between you when Devlin put his ring on your finger"—he dipped his head so that his eyes bored directly into hers—"trust me when I say that he's head over heels in love with you now."

Therese studied Child's eyes, his expression, and didn't know what to say or do. She didn't even know what she felt. If Child was correct, then her most precious dream had come true, but...

She frowned and let her gaze slide from Child's face, then murmured more to herself than him, "He's never said..."

Or had he?

The two recent incidents of inexplicable, uninterpretable comments from her previously faultlessly articulate husband sprang to her mind.

But he'd explained both...

No, he hadn't.

In neither case had he clarified his meaning, but uncharacteristically, in both instances, he'd waited to see how she interpreted his words, then allowed her assumption to stand.

Why? Had he been waiting to see if she would realize...what?

Therese stared blankly at Child's shoulder as she scrambled to reassemble the exact words and, even more, the context of Devlin's strange remarks.

Although Child stood directly before her, she'd forgotten him entirely —until he lightly shook her.

She refocused on his face and saw his frustration. "You infuriating female—why are you so set on not seeing what's directly in front of your nose?" When, again, she frowned at him, he hissed in exasperation and clearly enunciated, "Everything he does in relation to you springs from one emotion—love."

The door at his back opened on the last word.

Therese looked, and Child turned, too.

Devlin walked in, his face a dark mask of vengeful fury.

Beneath his breath, Child muttered, "Oh, sh—"

CHAPTER 11

*D*evlin's lips curled in a snarl, and he slammed his fist into Child's face.

Child staggered back, stumbled, and fell to the floor. "Ow!"

Open-mouthed, Therese stared at her husband, then flung herself at him and caught his right arm, clamping her hands around what felt like living steel.

His face, his features, were hewn; they made granite look soft as, his body clearly primed for further violence, he glared down at Child.

Shocked, she ducked across Devlin and caught his eyes. "That wasn't what it looked like." He'd opened the door in time to hear one word—love—and to see Child holding her by the shoulders. If what Child had told her was true, then Devlin's reaction was hardly to be wondered at. When he didn't give any sign of paying attention, she more forcefully declared, "He was telling me about you!"

That penetrated. After a second, Devlin transferred his gaze to her, and the battle-ready tension in his frame eased. He searched her eyes, her face, then blinked. She could almost see the haze of red fury ebb and subside.

"Damn it!" Sitting on the floor, Child was gingerly feeling his nose. He glowered at Devlin in transparent exasperation. "At least this time, you didn't break it." Child shook his head. "I would make a quip about you losing your touch, but…"

With an impatient gesture, Child waved them both back and clambered to his feet. He shifted his shoulders and tugged his coat into place, then turned to Therese and glared. "Please say you believe me now." He pointed at Devlin. "Why on earth do you think he—your pillar-of-rectitude husband—just behaved like that?"

Child transferred his glare to Devlin and snorted. "As for you, what the devil do you think you're about?"

When Devlin just blinked, Child flung up his hands, stepped around Devlin, and made for the door. "I wash my hands of the pair of you. You deserve each other—far more than you know. You both plot and plan to the nth degree and overthink everything. You think you can control everyone, including each other. At least now, neither of you will be able to pretend anymore. I've done my one good deed for the year. I'll leave you to sort yourselves out—just do me and everyone else a favor and do that!"

Stunned anew, Therese watched as on reaching the door, with his hand on the knob, Child paused, looked back, and stabbed a finger at Devlin. "Just remember—after this, you owe me. A lot!"

With that, Child opened the door. Therese caught a fleeting glimpse of his face as, looking distinctly pleased with himself, he walked out and shut the door behind him.

For several moments, silence held sway.

Then she looked at Devlin. "What did all that mean?"

When he didn't immediately answer, she narrowed her eyes on his face and asked the rather more pertinent question, "And why did you knock him down?"

She should probably have reacted to that moment of violence in some suitably feminine fashion, but she had three brothers; seeing gentlemen engage in fisticuffs wasn't new to her.

When Devlin studied her as if wondering where to start, she decided to state the obvious. "You have to know neither Child nor I think of the other in any improper way."

Devlin grimaced, then sighed and looked away. "I know that."

Therese peered at his face. "So what was that about?"

He pinched the bridge of his nose and closed his eyes. "I came in and saw him holding you, looking into your face and saying the word 'love'...and I overreacted."

Reliving that moment, he clenched his jaw, then opened his eyes. "Let's just call it a moment of temporary insanity." Not an inappropriate description for the blind rage that had erupted and taken possession of him, body and mind.

He glanced at Therese and met her eyes. Watchful, waiting eyes. He was fairly certain Child had dropped him squarely in it; he didn't know if that was a good thing or… "What did he tell you?" He needed to learn what options Child had left him or whether now, he had only one way forward. When she didn't immediately answer, he recalled Child's words and amended, "What was it he wanted you to believe?"

She studied his face, then folded her arms. Regarding him steadily, she replied, "He told me that you loved me and insisted he was correct."

She'd said the words in an even tone, as a matter-of-fact statement, yet he heard the question behind them, the lingering uncertainty she harbored—that she still wasn't sure whether to believe and was half expecting him to deny Child's insight and laugh the notion aside…

He searched her face, and something with claws gripped his heart and squeezed. Behind the silver blue of her eyes lurked a raw vulnerability that was all his fault. Before he'd even thought, he shifted to face her and took her hands in his. "He was right. I do love you."

Emotion—fragile hope—flared in her lovely eyes, but she held it back, her fingers lying passively in his, while with a hint of desperation, she searched his eyes, his expression.

He'd done an excellent job of convincing her otherwise; with a conscious effort, he lowered every last emotional shield he'd erected between them and, with his eyes steady on hers, hoping equally desperately that she would see the truth, quietly said, "I don't know how or why it happened, only that it did."

With a faint, rueful twist of his lips, holding her gaze, he raised one of her hands and lightly kissed her fingers. "I look at you, and my love for you is simply there, an inescapable part of me. It influences everything I do that in any way impinges on you. When it comes to you, love is and will always be my guiding light."

He read in her eyes, in the sudden tensing of her fingers on his, that she was listening, watching, analyzing—wanting to believe, yet still uncertain. Still wary. The sight spurred him on. "I know the reality of what I feel for you, and I wanted you to know it, too, but I feared that, after all this time, if I simply came out and said the words, you wouldn't believe me."

An expression that translated to *What did you expect?* infused her fine features. "We've been married for five years."

"Exactly. So given that words wouldn't work, over these past weeks, I've been trying to open your eyes by finding ways to unequivocally show you what I feel for you." He paused to search her eyes. "To make you understand that I love you."

She continued to examine his features while hers revealed that she yearned to believe, but was still hesitating.

He'd known this wouldn't be easy.

He dragged in a breath and went on, "Just so you know, acknowledging that I love you won't make me easier to live with." He tipped his head toward where Child had landed. "As you just witnessed. When I heard and saw Child, I was overtaken by an instant, unreasoning, and ungovernable reaction. No matter what my rational mind knew, something inside me didn't stop to think but reacted to what, in that instant, I perceived as an unendurable threat. A threat to me, to us, to our life together—to what I want that life to be."

Gripping her fingers more firmly, he dipped his head so he could look directly and deeply into her eyes. "You and I—over the past five years, we've fitted so well together. In so many ways, we are each the perfect complement for the other. You *are* my wife, my countess, the mother of my children, my helpmate, and so much more. You are my lover in truth, in every way encompassed by the human condition." He paused, then voice deepening, said, "You are the only woman I want or need in my life because you fill every corner of my existence."

Her gaze locked with his, Therese saw his sincerity, read and accepted the unadorned, inherent honesty in his words, and above all else, heard the emotion underscoring his deep tones and knew beyond question that he—her perennially calculating and collected husband—was speaking from his heart.

Please believe me was blazoned in his eyes. An unvoiced plea from a nobleman who could command almost everything else in his life.

Something shifted inside her, like a protective grille sliding aside. She slipped her fingers from his and, almost tentatively, raised her hands and framed his chiseled cheeks. She stared into his eyes, held by the unwavering steadiness of his hazel gaze, and finally set aside her wariness, her hesitancy, and allowed herself to believe…all he had said.

"You love me." She whispered the words even as she confirmed that truth in his eyes. "You *love* me." Wonder filled her, and she felt her heart, freed of chains she hadn't even realized had shackled it, start to rise, then take flight.

He read her response—her acceptance—in her eyes, in her face, and the unforgiving harshness that, until that moment, had invested his features eased. "I do." He drew her closer, and she sank against him. He stared at her face as if memorizing every detail, then he bent his head, and she raised her lips.

In the instant before their lips met, he breathed, "I love you, Therese, and I always will."

Then he closed the gap, and their lips touched, pressed together, then fused. A second later, she parted hers and invited him in, and as boldly and challengingly as ever, he thrust in, stroked, and claimed.

To her escalating wonder, she could sense the difference him owning to love had wrought, even in something so simple as a kiss. If earlier, she'd identified a lowering of some screen, now that screen had been completely set aside, done away with, and there was nothing left to mute or veil the undeniable promise of something precious and wonderful or the yearning joy of a love undisguised, a love fully revealed.

A love fully reciprocated.

Her heart beat faster, and her senses rejoiced. Her hands had come to rest against his chest; she slid both up to curve about his nape and let her own love rise through her to meet and merge with his.

He reacted, deepening the kiss, transparently hungry for more, and she gave it eagerly, gladly, letting her love for him well and pour through the increasingly ardent exchange.

The engagement continued, neither willing to call any halt, too immersed and engrossed in exploring this novel landscape, familiar yet so much brighter, more entrancing, bathed in and illuminated by a newfound golden glow.

She hadn't expected any such change, yet she welcomed it, joyously embraced it with her whole heart, and so did he.

Their tongues dueled.

Their lips commanded and demanded, turn and turn about.

His hold on her tightened, then his arms circled her, cinched, and crushed her to him.

Giddy and glorying, even through the layers of gown and stays, she felt the rigid rod of his erection hard against her stomach and wantonly sank more evocatively—more provocatively—against him, pressing her body to his in flagrant encouragement.

He dragged his lips from hers on a shaky gasp, then as if helpless to resist, trailed his lips along her jaw. "God, how I want you! But..." He raised his head and closed his eyes.

Passion starkly etched his features.

Sanity trickled into her mind. "But we aren't a pair of giddy young lovers." If they were discovered, or even if such an interlude between them here, after five years of marriage, was suspected...

She hauled in a tight breath, then eased her arms from about his neck and sank her fingertips into his shoulders, trying to steady her whirling wits. Her lips throbbed. "We're not even older lovers engaged in an illicit affair."

Apparently striving to slow his breathing, he nodded. "The gossip-mongers would have a field day."

He breathed in deeply, then opened his eyes and met her gaze. His eyes were dark with desire. "Can we leave?"

She took half a second to recall what had gone before, then smiled with blatant anticipation. "Yes, let's—it's late enough." It had to be midnight at least. Stepping back, her eyes locked with his, she seized his hand. "Now."

His answering smile was edged with intent.

Delighted, laughing, she towed him to the door.

Very much like the illicit lovers they weren't, by mutual accord, they skirted the ballroom and found their way by minor corridors and secondary stairs to the front hall. Fighting to maintain their customary façade of haut ton dignity, they donned their evening cloaks, and Devlin collected his hat. Their carriage was summoned, and they waited with barely concealed impatience, with desire threading through them and tightening their nerves, and the instant their carriage rolled up before the Cassington House steps, Devlin escorted her across the porch, down the steps, and into the carriage.

He followed on her heels.

She waited only until he sat beside her and the carriage door clicked shut, then flung herself at him.

He caught her, and she kissed him, and he palmed her head and held her steady as he ravaged her lips.

The kiss turned incendiary, setting spark to their already smoldering desires. Within seconds, greedy flames licked over their skins. They seized each other, wanting, claiming, and possessing. Need glowed, then caught alight and flared.

Through the fine silk of her bodice, his clever fingers clasped her breast, then found the tight bud of her nipple and flicked, and she gasped. She closed her fists in his lapels and hauled him to her, into a ravenous kiss, only to tip back and back, until with a smothered shriek, she overbalanced and landed on her back on the padded seat with him looming over her.

He chuckled, the sound dark and laden with desire, then he dipped his head and set his lips to her collarbone and, with his tongue, traced the delicate curve, and she held him to her and shuddered and closed her eyes.

Only to feel her hunger surge as her sensitivity to touch dramatically heightened.

She felt every evocative caress he pressed on her swollen, already aching breasts. Her nerve endings sparked as if lightning danced over them. Then with one hand, he followed the long line of her bent leg, then rucked up the silk of her skirts and petticoats and, setting his hard, hot palm to her silk stockings, traced upward...until, above her garter, he met the hem of her silk drawers and, beneath that, bare skin.

She shivered; she felt his intention to further explore as if it were her own, and anticipation leapt, but then the carriage rocked and swayed, turning a corner, and he froze.

Cassington House stood at the southern end of South Audley Street. While they were so hotly engaged, the carriage had rolled sedately north, presumably passing the darkened expanse of Grosvenor Square... It had just swung left into Upper Grosvenor Street.

They had only minutes before the carriage drew up outside the door of Alverton House and the footman opened the door.

Devlin swore, his voice a gravelly rumble. Therese knew how he felt. He withdrew his warm hand from beneath her skirts, sat back, and hauled her upright.

"Quickly," he murmured, glancing out of the window at the houses sliding past while he rapidly straightened his cravat, coat, and cloak.

Smoothing down her skirts, she softly laughed, then grasped the upper edge of her bodice and wriggled it to resettle her breasts. "I'd forgotten how...limited moments like this tend to be."

There'd been a few such incidents when they were courting, but back then, she hadn't known what the ultimate destination on their sensual road actually was. Now she knew, and greedy need fizzed in her veins. If the journey had been longer...she really didn't think she would have had to argue to get Devlin to appease their mutual need. Thinking of what that would have entailed, as the carriage turned in to Park Lane, from beneath lowered lashes, she slanted a glance at him.

He must have felt her gaze; he turned from the window, scanned her face, then mock growled, "Damn it—stop that. I'm having a difficult enough time reining in my lust without you doing your best to ignite it. We have to get past Portland first—at his age, we can't afford to shock him into a heart attack."

She laughed, even while, at the mention of his lust, something inside her purred.

"Don't forget," he muttered as the carriage turned in to the Alverton House drive, "Portland's known me since I was a boy."

She leaned close to whisper in his ear, "Exactly. Which is why I can't imagine he would be shocked at all."

He looked at her, then huffed.

The carriage halted, and before it had even settled on its springs, Morton had dropped down and swung open the door.

Devlin rose and descended to the gravel, then reached back and gave her his hand. She gripped his fingers and climbed down, then released her skirts and straightened, and with her head held at her usual confident, faintly haughty angle, she took the arm Devlin offered and walked beside him up the steps.

Portland had the door open before they reached the porch. They swept inside, followed by Morton; as the door closed, Therese heard the rattle as the carriage drove off to the mews.

Portland approached to relieve her of her cloak. "I trust the evening went well, my lady?"

"It did, Portland. Exceedingly well." It took effort to keep her soaring delight over the evening's outcome from her face and voice. As for her expectation of what was yet to come, the bubbling anticipation streaking through her veins was increasingly difficult to contain.

Portland lifted the heavy velvet cloak from her shoulders, and from the corner of her eye, in the hall mirror, she saw the butler's gaze rise to her hair and, for a moment, halt.

Only then did she remember the feathered headdress—such adornments being currently all the rage—anchored above the knot of her chignon. It was now in a sorry state; presumably, her and Devlin's wrestling in the carriage had crushed it. As no plausible excuse sprang to her tongue, she blithely pretended nothing was amiss and, with her customary assurance and a restrained "Goodnight," made for the stairs.

Having been relieved of his cloak by Morton, Devlin, too, bade the staff an urbane goodnight and followed at her heels.

Therese climbed the stairs as quickly as she dared; she could sense

Devlin at her back, a sensual predator with whom she couldn't wait to tangle.

The instant her foot touched the gallery floor, she broke and, grabbing up her skirts, valiantly struggling to smother her laughter, raced down the corridor toward her room.

He caught her before she reached her door, spun her around, backed her against the panelled wall, and kissed her to within an inch of her life.

She gave as good as she got, and he seized her and held her, and she wrapped her arms about his neck and clung—to the kiss and to him.

After several seconds of a rapacious exchange, without breaking the kiss, he swung her up into his arms, juggled her, then walked the few paces to her door. He managed to open it and strode through, then kicked the door shut behind them.

Warm lamplight, soft and golden, engulfed them.

Devlin halted in the middle of the room and, on a gasp that came as much from him as from her, broke the voraciously greedy kiss. He raised his head and released Therese's legs, letting them swing down.

Once her feet touched the floor and she stood of her own accord, he raised both hands, speared them through her hair, then cupping her face, drew her up to her toes, drew her lips back to his, and—letting fall each and every rein that, with her, he'd always endeavored to retain —devoured.

Tonight, his hunger had scaled new heights. He angled his head and, with her open and avid encouragement, steered the kiss into still deeper, even more turbulent waters. Waters that churned with a deeper longing, a more profound yearning than anything in his previous experience had prepared him for.

He wanted, desired, *needed* so much more acutely. The intensity, the longing, the raw desire that infused his very soul was far beyond anything he'd previously known.

The only difference was love—that he'd confessed to loving her. And consequently, no longer needed to maintain the control he'd previously exercised over his deep-seated, unruly emotions.

His most powerful emotions.

Although he'd never consciously examined it, he'd innately known and had always recognized that love—true and pure, the sort of love he felt for Therese—was the greatest, most powerful emotion of them all.

All else bowed before it; that had been his principal reason for hiding it.

Tonight, he'd finally, irrevocably, traded his shield for all that love, an acknowledged love, could bestow. Until now—until the moment when he stood with Therese's lips plundering his and the flames of passion licking over them both—he hadn't realized that, in making that trade, he'd also surrendered control.

There was no way to halt the conflagration that seized them both. Not that he wished to, but even steering it, slowing or guiding it, was beyond him.

All he knew was the unquenchable desire to join with her. To love her in the fullest sense.

Driven, compelled, as need welled and urgency built, he felt just this side of possessed.

He divested her of her bodice, her skirts, and petticoats, allowing the garments to fall where they may. The feathered headdress tumbled from her hair, dislodged as he speared his fingers through the long, silken tresses, freeing them to lie in a rippling waterfall over her bared shoulders.

She seemed equally obsessed with stripping away his clothes. She yanked his cravat free and flung it aside, then fell on the buttons closing his shirt, all but ripping them free.

In short order, he shrugged off his coat, waistcoat, and shirt, then hissed in a breath as her palms made contact with his chest. For long seconds, he clenched his jaw and let her sculpt and caress, then he hauled in a tortured breath, spun her around, and fell on her corset's laces with the avidity of a man one tiny step from demented.

The last lace snapped beneath his fingers, and he stripped the stays away and sent them flying. Before she could turn, he reached around her, yanked the drawstring at the waist of her drawers loose, and sent the silky fabric slithering down her still-stockinged legs.

She stepped free of the pooling silk and spun to face him—and he caught the hem of her gossamer-fine chemise and hauled it off over her head. Obligingly, she raised her arms, but the instant she drew her hands free, she fell on the buttons closing his trousers. With quick, practiced flicks, she had them free.

Then her greedy little hands pushed past the gaping fabric and found him. He groaned as she wrapped her long fingers about his girth and artfully stroked, then claimed and possessed.

Jaw clenched, he tipped back his head as she played.

His lids had spontaneously fallen; he forced them up enough to look at her face.

What he saw there sent lust boiling through him, set passion pounding through his veins. She looked as fixated, as committed to the moment as the overriding compulsion so dramatically heightened by his declaration of love left him.

This was different; even in the torrid heat of the moment, he paid attention and took note. As she worked her hand and made him ache, the expression of devotion, her commitment to his pleasure, had never been so stark, so uncompromisingly clear. It seemed his declaration had opened a door to another plane of engagement. Another level of shared pleasure.

He gritted his teeth and endured...

Until he couldn't deny the driving beat welling in his blood any longer.

Without disturbing her focus, he thrust his trousers down his thighs, and she helpfully adjusted her hold on him enough to allow him to dispense with his underdrawers.

He toed off his shoes and stepped free of the debris; she shifted with him, then before he could react, she sank to her knees and, with practiced alacrity, slid his throbbing member between her lips.

He froze, then clenched his jaw and tipped his head back again as, with a devotion impossible to mistake, with her lips and tongue and the hot heat of her mouth, she lavished pleasure upon him.

She was thorough, and he'd taught her well. With slow rasps and long licks punctuating the strong suction when she drew him deep, she pandered to his senses with wanton abandon. Helpless to deny her, he reached for her, threading his fingers through the thickness of her hair to cup her head as she steadily ratcheted his tension higher.

Tighter.

He let her play for as long as he dared, then forced himself to find balance enough to lift one foot, bending his leg and reaching back to strip off his sock. First one, then the other. He would need the purchase of bare feet on the polished boards for what he had in mind.

Once the soles of his feet were planted on the floor, he steadied himself, then dragging his senses from wallowing in the sensations engendered by her ministrations, he gathered every ounce of willpower he could summon. Hauling in a quick breath, he slid a thumb into the corner of her lips, releasing the mind-numbing suction she'd been so artfully applying, withdrew his turgid erection from her mouth and, in the same movement, crouched, splayed his hands over her hips, gripped and seized, and as he straightened, lifted her—not to her feet but high against his chest.

She uttered a surprised squeak, and as he settled fully upright, she instinctively draped her arms about his shoulders and, encouraged by his hold on her hips and upper thighs, wound her long, supple legs about his hips.

He gave himself a moment to drink in her expression—one reflecting as much heated need as he felt thrumming through him. In the golden lamplight, she stared down at him even as her breasts rose and fell inches from his face.

He smiled, intent yet teasing, deliberately letting all he was imagining show. She saw and understood, and her breath hitched, then resumed a touch faster. Just a tad shallower.

He held her gaze while he adjusted his hold, freeing one hand, then bent his head enough to extend his tongue and lick one distended ruby nipple.

Her breath shuddered out, and her lids fell.

Supporting her weight on one arm, with his other hand, he caressed one perfect globe of her derriere, then slid his fingers inward, between her widespread thighs, and found her softness gratifyingly wet and wanting.

For several seconds, he played, and she quivered in his arms.

He couldn't wait any longer. Filling both hands with her hips, he adjusted their bodies until the head of his erection found her slick flesh. He pushed in, then tightened his grip and drew her down as he thrust home.

The sound that purled from her lips was half moan, half pleasured cry.

He raised her, then brought her firmly down, marveling at the heated clamp of her inner muscles around his rock-hard cock.

He wanted to slow and savor the sensation, but the urgency, the compulsion to have her, to take and possess, rose in an unstoppable wave and roared through him.

What followed was a barely controlled frenzy; he lifted her and thrust into her scalding heat, and she used her strong thighs to lever herself up and ride him, her inner muscles clamping and releasing, spurring him to ever more rapid and powerful thrusts. At one point, she caught his face between her hands and kissed him, initiating a searing exchange that whipped fire through them, relentlessly driving them on until their bodies were slick and their muscles were trembling, and they still hadn't had enough of each other.

She gasped and clung and urged him on—wanting, demanding, unendingly giving.

Struggling for breath, he crossed the few paces to an expanse of uncluttered wall, braced her spine against the silk wall covering, and pounded into her.

She raised her head, desperate for air as he pushed her up and on. Her hands turned into claws, her fingernails sinking into the backs of his shoulders.

From beneath weighted lids, he watched her face as he pressed deeper between her thighs and thrust harder, faster.

And finally, on a gasping scream, she shattered and flew.

The wash of ecstatic joy that passed over her features nearly brought him undone.

Determined to wait, to make the moments last, on a shuddering breath, he thrust deep and buried himself inside her—and held still. He bent his head and pressed his face into the scented silken mass of her wildly disarranged hair.

His breath was coming in rasping pants; he breathed deeply, the swell of his chest cushioned by the firm mounds of her swollen breasts. Every muscle he possessed remained as rigid as iron.

Wanting.

Waiting.

She was close to boneless in his arms. Gathering his wits, he plotted his next move.

He was fairly certain that conventional wisdom held that one did not engage with one's wife in such intemperate fashion. Luckily, he gave not a whit for conventional attitudes, not with her, not in this.

Then she drew in a deeper breath, and her hands, until then lying lax on his shoulders, drifted in a gentle caress.

Strengthening his hold on his ravenous impulses, promising himself that satiation would not be long delayed, he tightened his hold on her and straightened, lifting her away from the wall.

She murmured incomprehensibly and pushed her arms farther over his shoulders, helping him balance her weight as he carried her to the bed.

The mattress was high; he'd long ago ensured it was just the right height.

He set her hips on the edge, then reached for her arms and drew them from his shoulders.

On a soft huff of delight, she obligingly fell back to sprawl across the silk counterpane. A knowing little smile of anticipation curved her swollen lips, and he caught the silver flash of her eyes from beneath her long lashes.

He grasped her hips and anchored her as he rolled his hips, seating himself more fully between her widespread thighs. Her smile deepened, and she started to lift an arm as if to beckon him close, but he withdrew from her heat and thrust home again, and she caught her lower lip between her teeth.

He repeated the movement, powerful and sure, and her hand fell limply back to the counterpane, and her features smoothed as, in response to his call, desire again welled and her body rose to meet his.

During all such encounters to date, as far as possible, he'd kept the reins in his hands, but tonight...there were no reins. He'd thought he was plotting their play, but as instinct claimed him and his body reacted, he realized he'd already been swept away, his will suborned by a power, a need, he had no hope of controlling.

Obeying the compulsions that pounded through him, he leaned forward, planted his hands on either side of her shoulders, and leaned his weight on his braced arms. Hanging over her, his body plunged deeply, rhythmically, into hers, and she responded and writhed, then raised her knees, wrapped her legs about his hips, set her hands to his chest, and with reckless abandon, drove him on.

Sensation swamped him, and he struggled to draw breath past the vise locked about his chest.

Need soared, and passion seared and whipped and demanded.

Never had the moment—the ineluctable drive for completion—been more intense. More fundamentally important.

More all-consuming.

He tipped his head back and gave himself up to it—surrendered to what now lived within him.

Anchored beneath him, her body dancing to the rhythm of his thrusts, Therese watched in fascination as passion claimed his features. Claimed his wits, his mind. His surrender was there, in the planes of his face, in the tautness of his features, writ large and displayed for her to see, and he made no effort to hide it.

Her lids were too heavy to lift more than a fraction. From beneath the fringe of her lashes, even as sensation raged and caught and claimed her flesh, she watched and marveled. They'd shared so many passionate interludes, she would have sworn there could be nothing new, nothing more she had yet to experience with him.

Yet tonight…this felt different.

She'd always embraced the physical side of their marriage, had always gloried in the intimacy of these moments. And while she'd initially assumed that his declaration of love wouldn't change her, she'd been wrong.

His words had made her stronger in herself, more certain, more confident—more assured of her position by his side—and in this arena, such escalating self-confidence had consequences. Her emotions had heightened, broadened, deepened, and strengthened until it seemed they'd broken onto some higher plane.

Some higher level of existence.

Transparently, his declaration had changed him, too. Never had she sensed him so deeply sunk in the moment, so unshielded and committed, so devoted to all the act could be.

So committed to wringing every last iota of togetherness and mutual pleasure from it.

As, with him, she rode the crest of sensations he expertly called forth, a surging, building crescendo of senses-searing, rapturous delight, with joy rising in her heart, she embraced the change and reveled in it.

Passion, desire, and need raked them, then as if those emotions were tangible forces, they clashed and battered in furious demand, then merged and exploded in a firestorm that cindered every last thought and had them both surging anew, locked together in passionate harmony and desperately striving to reach the final peak.

Seeking to claim the physical solace only the other could give.

Then the moment was upon them, and they held fast to each other as the world gave way.

Release hit them, first her, then him, and they gasped and groaned as reality fractured and ecstasy rushed in and claimed them.

Her heart pounding, spent and drained, she sank deeper into the mattress, and he surrendered to her wordless tug and slumped on top of her.

Pleasure and peace burgeoned within her and spread beneath her skin, infusing every limb with the indescribable warmth that inevitably welled in the aftermath of the ultimate delight.

Gloriously replete, sated to her bones, she rejoiced in her husband's heavy, helpless weight. She wrapped her arms about him and held him while their hearts thundered and their breathing gradually eased.

Slowly, thoughts seeped into her mind, prompted by innate curiosity rather than anything else. This encounter was so very distant from their first—five years and more of active married life removed—yet as her natural inquisitiveness inevitably compared previous interludes with what had just occurred...in terms of intensity and the depths of soul-shaking completion they'd attained, this interlude had been a first.

Lovemaking made new.

Or was it love renewed?

Renewed by love?

Regardless, as sleep stole over her, she—her mind—saw one fact clearly.

Despite all the years of having told herself that she was happy and satisfied with a one-sided, half love-match, this, tonight, was what, in the depths of her Cynster heart, she'd always wanted and hoped to have.

This, tonight, had been her heart's true desire made real.

This, tonight, had been a dream come true.

CHAPTER 12

*T*herese woke to the sensation of a large, warm palm gliding over her naked hip.

She blinked her eyes wide and stared across the room to the window, where daylight seeped between the curtains.

Stunned, she twisted her head and looked over her shoulder, confirming that the large male body stretched behind hers was, in fact, her husband's. She blinked again. "You're still here."

He'd been watching his hand lazily caressing her. He raised his gaze, and his hazel eyes met hers. "I thought…" He looked down for a second, then his hand closed over her hip, and he bent his head and brushed a warm kiss to her bare shoulder. His lips quirked upward as he met her eyes again and murmured, "That perhaps you might like to try this."

Her body leapt to life. "This what?"

She tensed to turn, but he leaned closer and prevented it. "No. Like this. Let me show you…"

He showed her the joys of waking up together, of meeting the morning as one.

He showered her with sensations—sharp, sweet, and laden with pleasure.

His every touch struck her more acutely, her reactions stronger, more powerful, more intense. Her perceptions expanded, and she drank in every tactile joy he lavished upon her.

When he joined with her, spooning her and pressing deep, she lost her breath, smothered by glory. By the golden depths of what surged between them, so much more—so *very* much more—than before.

They rocked together, not so much driven as devoted. Assured of who and what they were and where they were going.

Committed, hand in hand, they trod the path to ecstasy. He worshipped her with his body; that was the only way she could think to describe the focus he brought to the act.

This was real—their new reality. With every touch, every surging, rolling thrust, he assured her of that.

In wordless reply, she tightened about him, holding him for a heart-beat before easing her muscles and letting him draw back.

They rode on, steadily, unhurriedly, with passion and desire and need and hunger riding beside them, yet for once, not overwhelming them.

When, finally, the compelling force rose to a level impossible to deny, they surrendered and let the wave of their own making sweep them up and away.

They shattered on the rocks of a glorious passion and lay wrecked and open as, bound up with ecstasy, joy, and delight, satiation and completion rolled into and over them.

As she sank beneath the wave, she knew she was smiling. Devotion, commitment, and worship—a practical definition of love made manifest.

Eventually, Devlin stirred. He drew back, then leaned over her to brush his lips to the corner of hers.

"I love you." The whispered words fell by her ear.

Eyes still closed, her lids too weighted to lift, she smiled and murmured back, "And I love you."

Even though she couldn't see him, she sensed his pleasure, there in his touch as he brushed a last caress over her shoulder.

"I have to go. I'll see you later."

"Hmm."

She felt him leave the bed, then move about the room. She stirred, then languidly stretched and looked, and saw him—gloriously naked—bending to pick up his coat and waistcoat. Appreciatively, she watched lean muscles shift beneath his skin as he collected his clothes, then walked to the door to his rooms.

In the doorway, he paused and directed a knowing glance her way.

She smiled delightedly.

Looking smug, he saluted her, and she waved him on his way.

He turned and left and closed the door behind him.

Therese sighed, then raising her arms over her head, stretched again, then relaxed. She stared up at the canopy as his "I love you" replayed in her brain.

She remembered the self-insight that had surfaced in the immediate aftermath of their nighttime engagement. She examined the thought, the conclusion, anew and couldn't fault it.

In marrying Devlin, she'd resigned herself to never being loved in return, not in the same, all-consuming way that she loved him. She'd consigned her girlish hopes—or so she'd labeled them—to the unrealistic, never-to-be-realized pile of discarded dreams.

Last night, those girlish dreams had been resurrected and given back to her.

And their interaction that morning had confirmed that.

Her deepest, oldest, most personal dream—the one she hadn't allowed herself to pursue—was no longer merely a possibility.

Devlin had made it a reality.

Somehow, love had worked its magic and handed her all her heart had, for so very long, secretly desired.

The glory of that welled and washed through her, leaving joy more profound than she'd ever felt—ever dreamed could be—in its wake.

Smiling softly, feeling that joy sink to her bones, a tangible and reassuring presence, she pushed back the covers and rose, ready to face the day. Her first day of true married life.

∾

Later that morning, Devlin sat behind the desk in his study and diligently worked through the reports from his estates. The harvests were largely in, and he needed to get a firm idea of the productivity they'd achieved before starting to work with his estate managers on their plans for next year.

Even while he tallied and collated, again and again, he found himself smiling. Besottedly. That really wasn't his style—or at least, it hadn't been. Apparently, it now was, even though he hadn't set eyes on Therese since he'd left her room an hour after daybreak.

The hand holding his pen paused, hovering over his sheet of calculations as the memories rolled through him. Finally—*finally*—he'd been able to experience the joy of waking his wife in the most pleasurable of ways.

She'd been most appreciative, which had set the seal on his delight. On his happiness.

The word gave him pause. Was he truly happy? Happy in his marriage?

He hadn't ever imagined applying the word in that way, but he had to admit it fitted. The quiet delight that coursed through his veins and left him feeling as if he was glowing was, indeed, happiness.

The ink had dried on the nib. He laid the pen aside and, accepting that he was thoroughly distracted, sat back and allowed his mind to roam the re-formed landscape of his and Therese's marriage. What in their day-to-day lives might change?

Of course, from now on, he would sleep the entire night beside her, but other than that, there was a limit to how much time a couple married for five years could spend in each other's pockets, no matter their inclination. And he definitely didn't want to shock the staff, especially because, generally speaking, the smooth running of the household was Therese's responsibility, not his.

Once they removed to the Priory, expectations of behavior would be rather more relaxed. He should plan on making whatever changes were possible there, before they returned to Alverton House in early spring. Until then...

He'd breakfasted as he usually did, earlier than Therese ever appeared downstairs. Ladies always took ages over their morning toilettes, and he liked to commence his day with a ride in the park, preferably before there were too many others about. That morning, he'd spent half an hour galloping along Rotten Row, then had returned to the house and repaired to his study to deal with estate matters.

He glanced at the clock on the mantelpiece. It was only just after eleven o'clock. He scanned the letters before him; he should be finished in time to join Therese for luncheon—perhaps even in time to go up to the nursery and indulge himself by watching her with the children while the imps ate. Luckily, he hadn't arranged to meet James and Cedric or any of his other friends that day, but as the week rolled on, he'd have to show his face at sufficient gentlemen's functions to avoid setting tongues wagging.

Despite all commonly espoused beliefs, in his experience, the gentlemen's clubs were as much hotbeds of gossip as any grande dame's drawing room.

Lately, he'd been scheduling business meetings primarily in the mornings or the later afternoons, freeing him to spend more time with Therese if the opportunity presented; he resolved to continue that practice, more or less matching his schedule to hers.

He pondered that plan, such as it was, and decided it was a reasonable start. Until he learned how Therese felt about him spending more time with her, he shouldn't push too hard.

His gaze returned to his yet-to-be-completed tally of grains produced by his farms. Grimacing, he picked up the pen, cleaned the nib, dipped it into the inkwell, and continued his calculations.

Some time later, Portland tapped and entered, ferrying in the morning's mail on a silver salver.

"Ah—thank you, Portland." Devlin laid down his pen and, after Portland had placed the small stack of letters on the blotter, reached for them. "I've several matters pending that I'm hoping to wrap up in the next few days."

"After the exhibition ends, my lord?"

Devlin nodded. "Just so."

"I hope the news is good, my lord." With that, Portland bowed and departed.

The first letter was from the manager of Devlin's hunting box, reminding him of an earlier discussion about increasing the size of his stable there. He set that aside for further deliberation, then picked up the other letters and leafed through them.

Examining one simple envelope, he grunted with satisfaction. After pushing the other letters to one side, he reached for his letter knife, turned the folded paper over, and broke the nondescript seal.

He spread the single sheet, read the close lines inscribed by a cramped hand, then slowly smiled. "Excellent!" Still smiling, he leaned back in his chair. "The timing couldn't be better."

He tapped the edge of the sheet on the blotter. Everything was falling into place. "I can call at the bank after lunch, then go on from there."

He scanned the letter again, then folded it and slid it into his pocket. Briefly, he glanced through the other letters, confirming none required immediate attention, then with his interest in finishing his calculations reinvigorated, returned to the estate reports.

Early that afternoon, in an excellent mood after enjoying an hour of her husband's company over the luncheon table, Therese decided that she really ought to start acquiring items for the children's Christmas gifts.

With that goal in mind, she summoned the town carriage and, judging that Noah's Ark's wares would be more suited to the boys in following years, directed Munns to drive to the Strand. A particular toymaker whose wooden wares the boys found enthralling had his shop on the south side of the street, by the corner of Beaufort Street.

As the carriage rattled down Park Lane and turned in to Piccadilly, Therese was rather relieved that no one could see her or the beaming smile she was having such difficulty banishing from her lips.

Before they'd enjoyed their private luncheon, Devlin had appeared in the nursery, much to the children's delight. He'd occasionally done so before, but over recent weeks, he'd more frequently turned up and, subsequently, escorted her to the dining room. Thinking back over the past days, she'd realized just how inventive he'd been in finding ways to spend more time with her—walking in the park, the zoo, even the opera. All outings, she suspected, arranged by him to give them time and opportunity to draw closer.

Not that she was complaining—quite the opposite! She was delighted to welcome him into her life and to more definitely share in his, as, under what she now realized had been his direction, they'd been doing at the social events they'd recently attended. Even at church.

While all that was true, her mood was further buoyed by the realization that, now he and she had confessed—freely and openly and in simple, unambiguous words—to loving each other, there was no impediment to further developing the day-to-day closeness they'd started to enjoy over recent days.

Clearly, realizing he loved her had freed Devlin from conventional constraints over spending time with her, which left her looking forward to a future richer and more rewarding than she'd imagined might be.

Her expectations of their shared life had risen to a degree that left her joyously eager and almost giddy with hope.

And hope of that sort felt simply wonderful.

It was hardly surprising that she couldn't stop beaming.

The carriage slowed as Munns negotiated the traffic around Trafalgar

Square. Refocusing on her errand, Therese peered out at the façades as the carriage rocked, then rolled more freely into and along the Strand.

Rather than attempt to halt on the Strand itself, amid the constant traffic, Munns sensibly turned in to Cecil Street and drew up by the curb there. Dennis handed Therese to the pavement, and she directed him to follow as she walked around the corner and along the Strand to the toymaker's shop.

Once inside the cavernlike shop, filled to the rafters with wooden toys, she realized that having Dennis accompany her had been inspired; although an adult in years, he retained enough boyish enthusiasm to provide a useful barometer for her sons' likely interests. Together, she and Dennis spent an enjoyable half hour picking out toys for all three children.

After chatting with the toymaker—an older man of Germanic extraction—and complimenting him on his wares, Therese directed him to add the sizeable total of her day's purchases to the Alverton account she'd previously established, then with Dennis, now loaded down with brown-paper-wrapped packages, following at her heels, she stepped out of the door the toymaker held for them.

It was midafternoon, and the pavements were bustling, yet the gentleman who straightened from lounging against the wall just along from the door was instantly recognizable.

Therese returned his smile. "Child." As he ambled to her, she looked up at the toymaker's sign swinging above her head, then lowered her gaze to meet his. "What on earth has brought you here, my lord?"

Child grinned and tipped his head toward the shop beyond the toymaker's. "My watchmaker. He's been repairing an old timepiece of mine. I called in to fetch it, glanced into the toymaker's on my way past, and saw you."

With Dennis juggling packages and hovering behind her, they were disrupting the flow of pedestrians. Therese turned to the young footman. "Go ahead. I'm sure Lord Child will escort me back to the carriage."

Child half bowed and murmured that he would be delighted.

With a nod of dismissal, Therese sent Dennis on, then took the arm Child offered, and together, they strolled leisurely in Dennis's wake.

Child studied her face. In light of the situation when they'd last parted, she wasn't the least surprised when, albeit cloaking his curiosity in a veneer of polite boredom, he asked, "So, how are you and Devlin getting on?"

She tilted her head to a jaunty angle and let her beaming smile resurface. "Very well—indeed, *exceedingly* well." Glancing at Child, she met his eyes. "Thank you for your..."

"Intervention?" He arched a brow. "Wise and sage advice?"

She laughed and tipped her head in acknowledgment. "All that and more." She owed him as much as Devlin did.

Child continued to study her face. She was blissfully certain he would be able to see the verification of her answer in her expression...

On a flash of insight, she realized that, while her and Devlin's complementary admissions had freed Devlin to more openly show his love for her, the new reality those admissions had created had also freed her.

Now he and she had owned to love, she could let her love for him show—openly, without restraint.

She glanced at Child, met his eyes, and simply said, "I'm happier than I ever thought to be."

Child's aristocratic features softened, and he faced forward. "I'm glad."

Given his and Devlin's supposed rivalry, she felt she ought to be surprised, yet she honestly wasn't. She pondered the fact, then accepting that, quite aside from being a neighbor in the country, Child would likely continue to feature in her and Devlin's life, she asked, "You seem to derive almost as much joy from Devlin's success as he does."

Child's lips quirked; he met her gaze and raised one hand in a fencer's gesture, acknowledging a hit. "You've seen through my mask. The truth is that I wish him nothing but the best, and beneath our incessant banter—"

"Your bickering?"

He tipped his head. "However you wish to describe our habitual sparring, I know that he wishes the same for me."

Therese recalled their earlier exchange. "You truly are like brothers."

Child lightly shrugged. "I'm closer to him than to my brother, and he's closer to me than to his. It's our similar ages and, I suspect, similar characters and dispositions, and naturally, that combination also engenders a certain competitiveness. And of course, if I see an opportunity to tweak his tail, I will." He grinned. "Truth be told, as between us, he's usually the leader, the latter is rarely difficult."

Trying to mute her smile, she humphed in mock disapproval, and he laughed.

They were approaching the corner, and Therese waved down the minor street. "My carriage is waiting along there."

As she looked back at Child, she noticed a gentleman descending from a hackney on the opposite side of the Strand. She halted, and her beaming smile rebloomed. "Look! It's Devlin."

Child obediently stopped and looked. "So it is."

There was too much traffic streaming along the Strand to hail Devlin, and indeed, he'd already turned away and started walking up Southampton Street, toward Covent Garden and the flower market.

Buoyed on her newfound feelings, heightened by sighting the object of her love, impulsively, Therese drew her arm from Child's. "I'm going to go after him." The notion of stealing an unexpected hour or two with Devlin—or learning more about his business interests—was a potent temptation, one she saw no reason to resist. Out of habit, by way of excuse, she offered, "The house could do with some fresh flowers."

The look Child threw her stated he wasn't fooled by her sudden interest in blooms, but he closed his hand around her wrist and drawled, "I suppose I'd better come with you. Allow me to escort you across."

Therese suspected that, quite aside from his innate chivalry, Child had an interest in seeing if the situation gave him an opportunity to, as he'd put it, tweak Devlin's tail.

She didn't care; Devlin was more than a match for Child and his machinations, and she was sincerely grateful for Child's assistance in crossing the bustling thoroughfare.

By the time they'd gained the opposite pavement and started up Southampton Street, Devlin was some way ahead.

"Come on!" Once more on Child's arm, Therese stepped out briskly. Without argument, Child kept pace.

Ahead, Devlin reached the end of Southampton Street. The market with its long rows of stalls and barrows lay directly in front of him and stretched away to his right.

Without pause, Devlin turned left. Away from the market.

Beside Therese, Child slowed.

Curiosity stirring, Therese drew her hand from Child's arm and forged on. "I wonder where he's going?"

Child drew level but, with his gaze fixed on the end of the street, insisted on walking more slowly. "He must be off to some business meeting. I suspect we shouldn't interrupt."

Considering that, Therese slowed for a moment, then frowned.

"It's an odd place for a business meeting." She glanced back toward the Strand. "But he dismissed the hackney, so presumably he intends to call at some address around here." She faced forward and walked on.

They'd nearly reached the end of the street. She glanced at Child, but his expression had blanked.

Abruptly, he halted. Reaching out, he caught her arm. "Therese, I really think we should leave Devlin to…whatever business he's engaged in. He won't expect to see us, and in business, one can never tell how such an unexpected surprise will play out."

Gently but insistently, he tugged to draw her back.

Therese sighed and rotated her arm, deftly breaking his hold. "Very well—we won't go any farther than the corner. But I would like to see where he goes." Rapidly, she took three quick steps and halted in the shadow cast by the building to her left and looked down the street in the direction Devlin had gone.

The famous Inigo Jones Church of St. Paul lay across the street, facing the market stalls. Unsurprisingly, Devlin hadn't stopped there. He'd walked farther along the street and had crossed to the north side, where, beyond the rear of the church, a long row of old town houses stood.

As Therese watched, Devlin paused outside one such house, then trod up the three steps to the narrow porch and, raising his cane, beat a tattoo on the door.

He stepped back, straightened his coat, and waited.

Child plucked at her sleeve. "Therese—"

"In a minute. I want to see—"

The door opened. A beautiful black-haired woman appeared, her face lighting in welcome.

Even from that distance, Therese could see the charming, almost joyous smile her husband bestowed on the lady. They exchanged a few words, then the lady, all delighted solicitousness, stepped forward, linked her arm with Devlin's, and led him inside.

He went without the slightest hesitation.

The door closed behind him.

Therese hadn't thought that hearts could actually break, but in that instant, hers did. A huge gaping wound appeared, and ice poured in, glacier cold, until she—every last emotion she possessed—was frozen over.

She couldn't feel anything—not her hands, not her feet, nothing of her body or even her mind. Her thoughts had shut down. She couldn't think.

Beside her, Child softly swore. Her hearing, then, was still functioning.

Warily, fearing she might fall if she moved too quickly, she slowly turned and, with carefully measured tread, started to walk down Southampton Street.

Child walked beside her. She felt his gaze searching her face. They neared the Strand, and he hesitated as if about to speak, but instead, from the corner of her eye, she saw his lips set grimly, and as they halted on the edge of the pavement, he shook his head.

Without a word, he offered his arm. When she stared at it, without inflection, he said, "At least let me see you across the street and to your carriage."

Gingerly, feeling as if touching any man at that point might see her break, she lightly laid her fingers on his sleeve.

He said nothing more, just guided her across the street and to her waiting carriage, then helped her up and instructed Munns to drive to Park Lane. Then to her surprise, Child climbed up and sat beside her.

She couldn't summon the energy to protest. Instead, she kept silent, and blessedly, he did the same.

~

By the time the carriage drew up beside the steps of Alverton House, Therese knew what she needed to do.

Rigidly contained, as soon as Dennis opened the door, she preempted Child and stepped down unaided. Head high, her face a carefully controlled mask with features set in stone, she walked swiftly up the steps and through the door Portland swung open.

She halted in the hall and started tugging off her gloves.

Footsteps had followed her from the carriage.

"Lord Child."

"Good afternoon, Portland."

"It's a pleasure to see you again, my lord."

"Thank you."

Despite Child's exchange with Portland, Therese knew Child's gaze had remained locked on her; he was worried, but unsure what to do. *Good.*

Having succeeded in removing her gloves and bonnet, with them in her hands, she faced both men. "Portland, please inform the relevant staff that I intend leaving for the Priory immediately, on this evening's train." Her tone had Portland coming to attention. "My lady?"

Ignoring the butler's surprise and spiking concern, she handed him her bonnet and gloves and, her tone even, uninflected, and imbued with an ice-clad iron will, continued, "Naturally, the children will travel with me. Please inform Nanny Sprockett immediately." She glanced at the clock on the nearby wall. "Send a footman to reserve a compartment. As well as the children, I'll take Nanny and both nursemaids, Parker, Morton, and Dennis—instruct whoever you send to get tickets for us all. And I suppose Cook had better prepare a basket of food for the children —we'll be traveling over their dinnertime."

Portland slid a look at Child, then returned his gaze to her and ventured, "My lady, perhaps—"

"*Immediately*, Portland." No one—*no one*—argued when she gave orders in that tone.

Portland's expression blanked, and he bowed. "Of course, my lady." He, too, glanced at the clock.

"I wish to depart the house by five o'clock," she stated. "I want to reach the terminus in good time to find our compartment and settle the children." Focusing on the practicalities of the journey helped keep a lid on the tumultuous, turbulent emotions raging inside her.

She couldn't deal with them, not now, not when she couldn't even think about what she'd seen without feeling helpless and nauseated and so *hurt*. So stupid.

So betrayed.

She hauled her mind back from the edge of the vortex waiting to suck her down. If she let herself fall into it, she would be ranting and raving, but she had children and a household to manage; she couldn't afford to succumb.

At least not until I'm safe in my room at the Priory, out of sight and sound of everyone.

"Tell Parker I won't be changing—I'll go as I am. She'll know what needs to be packed."

"Yes, my lady."

Portland bowed, and without acknowledging Child at all, Therese turned and made for the little reception room she used as her private sitting room.

Behind her, she heard Child murmur something to Portland, then Child strode after her.

With her lips set in an uncompromising line, she reached her sanctum, opened the door, and walked in, leaving the door swinging. She headed for the desk on which her diary sat, open to the page for the current week.

Child followed her into the room and shut the door. "Therese—"

"I would rather not speak about what we saw." She rounded the desk and halted and, in the same rigidly controlled and distant tone, added, "And you have no authority or right to interfere in whatever I choose to do."

"No, I don't." Child drew in a breath and carefully said, "All I can do is ask you to think things through."

She looked down at her diary, scanning the entries for the next week.

He stepped closer. "Please. If you think about the possibilities—"

"I can't." She'd replied without glancing up. When she did, she saw Child frown.

"Can't what?" he asked.

"Can't *think*." Looking down again, she confirmed that there was no event she'd agreed to attend over the coming week for which she couldn't easily write an apology. She shut the diary, picked it up, and faced Child. "I can't think, not about that. If I do, I'll..." Her hold on the tempest inside her wavered. She sucked in a quick breath, held it, and pushed the roiling emotions down. She waved one hand and, in a weaker voice, said, "Explode. Shatter into a million pieces."

Alarm flared in Child's eyes. He searched her face, pressed his lips together, then offered, "Then let me think for you. What we saw..." He drew in a breath. "There has to be some rational explanation. Something other than the conclusion you've obviously leapt to."

"Not unless business is now being conducted by beautiful women out of houses in Covent Garden—" She broke off, then head tipping, admitted, "Well, I suppose it could be said that there is at least one business beautiful women have long been known to conduct from houses around Covent Garden."

Child's jaw clenched. "I've known Devlin all my life. Ladybirds and opera dancers were never his style."

She arched her brows. "Really? But then you haven't known him for the past umpteen years. Now he's married, who knows what his *style* is?" Temper stirring, she met Child's eyes. "You certainly don't."

Child shut his lips, pressing them tight.

She nodded. "Just so." She stepped around the desk and started past him. "Now, if you'll excuse me—"

He swung around and caught her sleeve. "Therese, please—"

"No!" She halted and closed her eyes, jaw tight as she fought to rein in her temper—and failed. But this was a different sort of temper, one without heat. A cold, raging fury, it erupted and filled every corner of her mind. She was hurt, *wounded*, and she no longer cared if it showed.

She opened her eyes and rounded on Child. Whatever he saw in her face, in her eyes, had him releasing her and taking a step back. She narrowed her gaze on his face. "Yesterday, my husband told me he loved me. For the first time. He told me, and he made me believe it. He repeated that vow this morning and convinced me that I could finally have"—her voice broke, but she forged on—"something precious that I hadn't even known I'd yearned for for years."

She hauled in a breath and held it; she'd been right in her description —she felt as if she was breaking into sharp, jagged, frozen pieces inside. The churning fury in her mind thrust a single burning question into her mouth, and she skewered Child with her gaze. "Can a man truly love two women at the same time?"

Faced with such incandescent fury and instinctively knowing he couldn't reach her, with exasperated candor, Child replied, "Don't ask me. I haven't fallen in love with one woman, let alone two."

Her eyes blazed. "Even if he does think he loves me, I wish he hadn't told me, because clearly, what he means by love isn't what I thought! I would rather have continued in blissful ignorance. What does he expect me to do?" She fixed her burning eyes on Child. "Share him?"

There wasn't any viable answer to that.

Feeling utterly helpless—and very glad she was not his wife—Child was cravenly grateful when a tap on the door had her swinging around and icily demanding, "Yes?"

Portland entered, armored in the unshakeable imperturbability of an experienced ton butler. "My lady, Nanny Sprockett wishes to inquire how long you expect to remain at the Priory. Also, Dennis has returned with the required tickets, and he confirmed that the train is scheduled to depart at five minutes after six o'clock."

Therese nodded curtly. "Thank you. Please tell Nanny Sprockett to prepare for at least two weeks in the country. Call me when everyone is in the hall and ready to leave."

"Yes, my lady." Portland bowed and retreated.

Child wished he could retreat, too, but the compulsion to plead his old friend's case hadn't eased its hold. When Therese turned back to him, he tried again. "Therese, you must see that there's a definite chance that you've leapt to an entirely erroneous conclusion. And yes, I admit that I can't offer you an alternative explanation for what Devlin was doing, but at least wait until he comes home and give him a chance to explain."

Her eyes, until then as hard as ice, glimmered alarmingly. "When he returns after being with her?"

The pain underlying the words sliced into him. He breathed in slowly, then pressed, "The pair of you need to learn to talk to each other—you don't seem to have been succeeding on that front all that well."

She gathered herself—he could almost see her reining in and shackling her emotions, fusing them into a carapace, a hardened protective shield surrounding her innermost self—then she raised her gaze to his face. "If Devlin wishes to speak with me, he'll know where to find me, but at this moment, I need to leave—to put space between us so I can calm down and think." She sent a cold glare his way. "Isn't that what you want me to do—think?"

"Yes, but—"

Her temper sparked anew; he saw it in her eyes. "Can you give me any other likely explanation for what we saw?"

When he hesitated, she snapped, "And don't say 'business.' I've learned enough about his business interests to know that none of the enterprises he engages with would have offices in Covent Garden."

Again, she made him feel helpless. He fell back on adamantly assuring her, "There will be some reasonable explanation."

When she shot him a dismissive look and started to turn away, stung, he blurted, "I know, absolutely and beyond question, that he wasn't lying when he said he loved you."

Half turned from him, she froze.

Therese closed her eyes. She breathed in and tried to wrench her awareness from the seething turmoil inside, tried to do as Child had demanded and think, but as she'd earlier confessed, she simply couldn't. Her shock—her hurt—had pushed her past rational thought; at that moment, all she could do was feel. And everything she felt only fed the instinctive imperative to flee—flee to the safety she'd always found at the Priory.

She knew she was running away, but at that time, that was all she could manage.

Perhaps, once she'd had a chance to examine and tend her wounds and build sufficiently strong walls around her heart, she would be able to face the prospect of meeting and listening to Devlin.

At the moment, every time she thought of him, the image of him smiling so charmingly at the woman in Covent Garden and the look on the woman's face blazed in her mind.

And her hurt deepened.

She had to get away.

"Listen." Child had moved closer. "I know I've only recently returned, but it's plain as a pikestaff that you and Devlin...have the chance of something special in your lives. Something not all of us get a chance to have. All I want to say is don't throw that away."

She drew in a breath, then opened her eyes and glanced at Child.

A tap fell on the door, distracting her, and Portland called, "Everyone is ready, my lady, and the carriages are at the door."

"Thank you." Without meeting Child's eyes, she walked to the door.

Child heaved a resigned sigh and followed.

Therese walked into the hall and found everyone waiting. Her mask softened as the children looked up at her eagerly. For them, she managed a smile. "We're off to the Priory, my darlings."

With a nod to Nanny Sprockett, Therese accepted her bonnet from Parker and put it on, then tugged on her gloves.

Turning to the children, she smiled again. "Are we all ready?"

"Yes!" the boys answered and dove to claim her hands.

She included Horry, who was safely anchored on Nanny Sprockett's ample hip, with her smile, then allowed the boys to drag her forward.

With her entourage preparing to fall in behind her, she started to turn toward the door, and her gaze fell on Child.

He'd halted farther back in the hall, his expression frustrated, but also troubled. Clearly, he thought she was making a mistake.

That's as may be.

Therese faced forward and let her sons lead her out of the house, across the porch, and down to the carriage.

From the shadows of the hall, Child watched the company pile into the carriages that would take them to the railway terminus. Reluctantly, he accepted that there was no way he could prevent Therese's departure, even though everything a lifetime had taught him about Devlin insisted that this was all a horrendous misunderstanding.

He firmly believed Devlin would have a perfectly rational and acceptable reason for visiting a beautiful woman in Covent Garden. Alone, in the middle of the afternoon.

Inwardly, he shook his head and admitted he was looking forward to learning what that explanation was.

He watched the small cavalcade roll off.

When Portland stepped back and shut the front door, then turned to Child, Child flung up his hands in defeat. "I'm going to wait in the library. When Alverton gets in, please tell him I'm there."

Portland bowed. "Indeed, my lord. Should you require anything, please ring."

With a nod, Child turned toward the library.

Little had changed since he'd last been in the house. He'd been much younger then, and so had Devlin.

In those days, they'd been carefree gentlemen on the town. Now...

The tantalus was in the same spot in which it had always stood. Child poured himself a healthy measure of Devlin's whisky, then walked to one of the large leather armchairs angled before the hearth and slumped into its comfort.

He sipped and waited and brooded on his old friend's situation.

Drama of this sort usually sent him running. But this was Devlin, and he had to admit that despite her attempts to steer him toward a suitable wife, he'd grown rather fond of Therese and her often-acerbic observations.

When it came down to it, he didn't, exactly, believe in love, yet he'd told Therese the truth—he didn't want her and Devlin to senselessly pass up the chance of having a love-based marriage.

He dwelled on that darkly for several minutes, then grumbled, "Be damned if I give up on them now."

He raised the tumbler and took a long sip. He flatly refused to let them fail, not if he could help it.

CHAPTER 13

$\mathcal{D}$evlin arrived on his doorstep at twenty minutes past five o'clock, clutching the well-wrapped package he fondly believed would make the perfect gift for Therese's birthday, ten days from now.

He located his latchkey and quietly let himself into the house. After carefully easing the door closed, doing everything possible not to alert any of his staff, he silently walked down the hall and slipped into his study.

Closing the study door, he exhaled. Smiling at his efforts to keep the package a total secret, he walked past his desk to the wall behind it and swung the picture that hung there aside, revealing the safe.

After fetching the key from his desk, inserting it, and releasing the lock, he manipulated the latch and swung the heavy door open. He placed the package inside, then stood back and looked at it.

He couldn't help but feel smug. Everything was falling into place.

He swung the safe door shut, pulled the latch down, locked the safe, and removed the key. He turned to the desk and replaced the key in the secret drawer. As he pushed the drawer shut, a sound like a snort had him glancing up.

The door between the study and the library was open, and Child lounged in the doorway. He had a glass of what Devlin suspected was his prize whisky in one hand.

Before he could inquire what Child was doing there, Child pushed away from the doorframe and waved his glass. "I have news you're not going to like, old man. Your wife has left you."

Devlin stared at Child as he ambled forward, then evenly asked, "How much have you drunk?"

"Trust me, not nearly enough." Child collapsed in a sprawl in one of the armchairs facing the desk, and Devlin saw that his old friend's expression was abnormally stern and his amber gaze was steady and almost accusatory. "Let me tell you what's happened." Child pointed one long finger at the chair behind the desk. "I suggest you sit down."

Devlin studied Child for an instant more, then slowly complied. He narrowed his eyes on Child's face. "What did you mean about my wife having left me?"

"I mean that she's taken the children and run away to the Priory."

"What?" Devlin stared. He...couldn't take that in. A strange sensation opened in the pit of his stomach, but... Mystified, he shook his head. "Why?"

"Permit me to explain," Child glibly replied. "I went to my watch-maker's on the Strand and noticed Therese in the toy shop next door. She came out shortly after, and we met and chatted—naturally, she's curious about you and me—and then we saw you getting down from a hackney on the other side of the road."

Frowning, Devlin nodded. "I'd been to the bank."

"Well, the point that interested your wife was not where you'd been but where you were going. She said something about catching up with you and getting some flowers for the house, but it was obvious to the meanest intelligence that the 'catching up with you' bit was what mattered to her. I helped her negotiate the traffic and ambled along beside her. We had you in sight farther up Southampton Street, but instead of turning toward the market stalls, you turned left."

A sinking feeling was expanding in Devlin's gut. His jaw setting, his gaze on Child, he nodded. "Go on."

"I tried to stop her, but she wouldn't have it. She insisted on seeing where you were going."

"And?"

"She saw you knock on the door of a town house and a rather lovely, dark-haired lady greet you like a long-lost friend—"

"I'd only just met the woman!"

"Be that as it may, it appeared she was delighted to see you. Exceedingly delighted, if I may say so, and you smiled charmingly, allowed her to take your arm in a very friendly not to say familiar manner, and went inside with her."

"Of course she was damned delighted to see me! I had a draft for a thousand pounds in my pocket."

Aghast, Child stared at him. "A thousand?" He blinked. "I know I haven't been in London for a while, but that seems a trifle steep for such a lady's services."

Devlin closed his eyes, then raised a hand and pinched the bridge of his nose. His life was careening out of control, and of course, Child was there.

After a second, Child dropped his act. "Talk to me, old man. What's going on?"

Devlin gritted his teeth and ground out, "She wasn't that sort of lady."

"So I supposed."

He snapped his eyes open. "And you didn't tell Therese?"

"I tried." Child's expression turned grim. "Heaven help me, I did— several times. She wasn't having it."

Devlin knew his wife had a tempestuous temper, but he'd never seen her lose it to the point of not listening to reason. "I told her...only this morning, I told her I loved her." He couldn't stop his features hardening. "And hours later, she saw what she did and instantly believed the worst of me."

Child tipped his head consideringly. "She mentioned your confession, but from what I could gather, she interpreted it more along the lines of 'he told me he loved me, but in reality, he loves her more—or at least as much.'"

A vise had locked about his chest and seemed to be tightening with every breath. "She thought I was betraying her." Betraying her love. How could things have gone so wrong?

Child was watching him over the rim of the glass. "You still haven't said who the lovely lady was."

"She's Madame Faberge, the wife of one of the Russian jewelers who came to show their wares at the exhibition." Briefly, Devlin outlined why he'd gone to the town house in Henrietta Street. He paused, then said, "They would have had to rent a place, and like most foreign tradesmen visiting London, they would have discovered their budget didn't stretch to lodgings in any of the better areas."

Child nodded. "And this present you fetched—that was what you put into the safe?"

"It's a fabulous piece. I wanted to surprise her." The reality that Therese was no longer in the house sank in.

But his sense of ill-usage was growing, the anger that rose in its wake a hard emotion that sealed off all softer feelings. He couldn't swallow the fact that even after his confession of the morning, she hadn't trusted him —not even enough to give him a chance to explain what it was she'd seen.

Child had been studying him. Devlin had no idea what his childhood friend could read in his face, but after a moment more, Child stirred and said, "I admit I don't know her well, but..." He paused, staring into his empty glass as if seeking guidance from the dregs. "When we got back here, she seemed to be...encased in ice. Frozen inside and out. I managed to get her alone for a moment and tried to plead your case." His lips twisted in a self-deprecatory grimace. "I tried to make her think things through, but she told me she couldn't." Child looked up and met Devlin's eyes. "That she couldn't think. That if she did, she would shatter into a million pieces."

Child pulled a face. "You know me—I thought she was being overly dramatic, and I pushed. I told her that you hadn't been lying when you'd told her you loved her." Child met Devlin's eyes. "I don't know what's been going on between you—why it's taken so long for you to admit to loving her when clearly you do and have done for years—but what I glimpsed inside her..." Child's features tightened, and he sat up, carefully placed the empty tumbler on the table by the chair, then looked directly at Devlin. "Damn it, man! She was so damned *wounded*."

The kaleidoscope of fact and conjecture whirling in Devlin's brain stopped. And he saw...

He felt the blood drain from his face, along with all expression.

"What?" Child demanded.

His mind racing, assessing all he could now see, Devlin slowly said, "I don't know exactly why, but the issue of me loving her is...a very raw point for her." He paused, acknowledging that truth, feeling his way forward. "I knew convincing her that I did wasn't going to be easy, even with me demonstrating how I felt as far as I was able and telling her so in words impossible to misconstrue." He took a second to consider all that, then admitted, "I thought I'd succeeded, but..."

She'd been very ready to leap to the conclusion that despite his protestations, despite his behavior, he didn't truly love her at all.

Because I hid my love for her for five long years?

It had to be that—his years-long deception—and its deep-seated, lingering effects. Effects he'd underestimated. He hadn't yet revealed that he'd loved her from the first, which made their present situation, their mutual pain and anguish, all his fault.

Jaw clenching, his gaze unseeing, he stated, "This is my fault."

"Well, I can't say that surprises me," Child quipped. "But the question now, boyo, is what you're going to do to put things right."

Devlin barely heard the words. The vise about his chest had tightened to a near-unbearable degree. Because of his cowardice, everything —*everything* he'd wanted and worked for, so much that was now so very precious to him, and more than anything else, the future he'd wanted so very much to share with her—was now at risk.

No. That was one failure he couldn't accept. He would do anything and everything he possibly could to save his—and her—dreams.

He needed a plan. Struggling to get his mind to oblige, he reassessed what Child had told him of Therese's reactions… "She loves me. If she didn't, she wouldn't have acted like that."

Child snorted. "You've only just worked that out?"

Devlin ignored him.

After a moment, he refocused on Child. "Did you see what team was hitched to the coach?"

Child frowned. "Chestnuts, I think. But why is that important? They were only driving to the terminus." He glanced at the clock. "They must be nearly there by now."

"The train?" Aghast, Devlin stared at him. "She's taken the train?"

"Yes, didn't I say? She had Portland get tickets for the train."

Devlin growled and swung to look at the clock. "Damn it!" He pushed to his feet and strode for the door.

Child twisted around and watched him go. He heard Devlin shouting orders in the hall, then the scurrying rush as the staff responded.

Relaxing in the chair, Child looked at the glass he'd set aside, then picked it up and drained the very last drops.

Lowering the glass, he shook his head. "If that's what happens when one falls in love, I'm exceedingly glad I've avoided the malaise."

Devlin drew his team of matched bays to a snorting, stamping halt by the curb outside the London Terminus of the Great Northern Railway. Before the curricle stopped moving, he tossed the reins to his groom, Mitchell, leapt to the ground, and bolted into the station.

Dodging porters and passengers in the main hall, he made for the single outbound platform. He raced onto the gray expanse, only to see the rear of the train vanishing in a cloud of steam.

"Damn!" He slowed and pulled up. Chest heaving, he leaned a hand against a post and fought to regain his breath, a task made more difficult by the steadily cinching band of iron clamping about his lungs.

The stationmaster had noticed his mad dash and, recognizing him, came hurrying up. "My lord, if we'd known you wished to catch that train, we would have held it back."

Devlin battled to summon some civility. He and Therese alternated between taking the train and taking the coach to the Priory—the train was faster, but not by much, as they needed to take a carriage from the station at the other end—but the station staff recognized him more for being one of the major shareholders in the railway company.

He waved, attempting to project unconcern. "It's all right. I wanted to catch the countess for a word, but..." He glanced at the man. "When is the next train due to leave?"

Earnest and eager to please, the stationmaster replied, "At ten o'clock tomorrow morning, my lord. If you wish, we would ensure it waited for you..."

Devlin considered. Portland had told him that Therese had taken her usual complement of staff for the journey. She and the children would be safe enough and would reach Alverton Priory at about ten o'clock that night.

It was already dark; if he headed up the Great North Road now, it would be the small hours before he reached the Priory.

The sensible thing to do would be to wait until morning and take the next train north. He would be at the Priory by early afternoon.

Too late.

Every instinct he possessed was very sure of that. He needed to see Therese tonight—or at least before the next dawn. He couldn't let her misapprehension—and the vulnerability that drove it—remain unaddressed for a moment longer than necessary; he was unutterably certain of that.

And he did have the most up-to-date driving lamps installed on his curricle.

He shook his head and refocused on the stationmaster. "No. Don't hold the train for me." The man's face fell, and Devlin managed a weak smile. "No doubt you'll see me and the countess when next we head north."

Reassured, the man smiled and bowed. "We'll look forward to it, my lord."

Devlin reined in his impatience and allowed the man to deferentially escort him from the platform and across the hall before firmly taking his leave beneath the ornate entrance.

Finally free, he strode to where Mitchell waited, chatting to several urchins who, attracted by the show of prime horseflesh, had drawn close enough to pepper the groom with questions.

Mitchell saw Devlin coming and saluted.

The urchins took one look at his set face and scattered.

He returned to the curricle's seat and, when Mitchell offered them, retook the reins. He settled the ribbons in his hands as Mitchell swung up behind, then set the horses trotting toward the road.

Once he'd turned in to the traffic heading west, Devlin called over his shoulder. "Are you up for a run to the Priory? Or would you rather I drop you off farther along, and you can take a hackney back to Alverton House?"

He didn't need to look to know that Mitchell blinked in surprise. "What? Now, my lord?"

Devlin merely nodded.

Mitchell huffed, apparently faintly offended by Devlin's suggestion. "If it's all the same to you, my lord, I'd rather not leave you to be forced to rest these beauties in some stablemaster's care while you take a break. I'll stick with you."

Devlin faintly smiled. He'd expected as much, but had felt he should ask. Given he was driving his cherished bays, he would have to manage them over the distance. Under those circumstances, it would take at least eight hours to reach his country home.

But that was neither here nor there. He fully intended to be reunited with his wife before tomorrow dawned.

～

In their compartment in the third of the first-class carriages rattling north-ward along the rails, Therese leaned back against the squabs and tried to relax.

Spencer and Rupert sat opposite, on the rear-facing seat, with Spencer leaning forward alongside Rupert to press his nose to the window in a likely vain attempt to spot the usual landmarks the pair knew bordered the tracks as the train chuffed out of London.

Out of habit, Therese took visual stock of their small party. On the seat opposite, Nanny Sprockett's comfortable bulk filled the spot beside Spencer, with Horry wedged between Nanny and Gillian, the slighter of the two nursemaids; Gillian was playing a quiet game involving fingers, which fascinated Horry and kept the little girl amused. Therese herself sat beside the window on the forward-facing seat with Parker beside her, and red-haired Patty, the other nursemaid, filling the spot closest to the compartment's door.

Morton and Dennis had seats in the second-class carriage immediately behind the one in which Therese and the footmen's other charges sat.

Feeling sluggish and dragged down, Therese shifted her gaze to the window and stared past her sons' heads at the backs of houses, barely discernible in the darkening night. There were no lamps in the compartment —within the train, the only light came from tiny lamps in the corridor along-side—and the occasional gleam from a lantern or streetlight outside illumi-nated little of the drab scenery, leaving her with no distraction. Nothing to prevent her thoughts from turning inward, nothing to block awareness of her bruised and battered heart from rising and swamping her mind.

The pain—a dull, throbbing ache—was real. She'd always dismissed as a melodramatic metaphor the notion of one's heart being physically hurt by emotional events, but she could now testify that heartache was a very real affliction.

The train clattered on, and the boys gave up peering into the night in favor of eating the bread, fruit, and cheese Cook had packed for their supper. While waiting for the train to arrive, they'd consumed the pies provided for their main meal. Grateful for the distraction, Therese took Horry onto her lap and, in the dim light, fed her daughter bits of bread, apple, and cheese. Once their stomachs were full, the children grew sleepy, and between them, Therese and Nanny Sprockett settled the three to nod and nap, with Rupert and Spencer curled up opposite Therese and Horry snuggled down on Nanny Sprockett's ample lap.

Therese sat back. As the compartment quieted, she gazed unseeing at the darkness beyond the window, and inevitably, her inner tempest rose to the forefront of her brain.

It took some time and an effort of will to force her mind to focus on the happening—on the singular moment in time—that was the source of her anguish, her emotional turmoil. Every time she brought the image to the fore, her mind balked, and her wits skittered and tried to shy away; grimly, she tightened her mental grip and pushed herself to look again and see.

She forced herself to replay the brutal moment, to observe, recognize, and catalog all she'd seen. The beautiful, quietly voluptuous, dark-haired woman with her face lighting in joyous welcome at the sight of Devlin. She forced herself to note again the quality of the charming smile he'd bent on the lady in reply.

Ruthlessly, she forced herself to view it all, to examine and analyze every second, no matter how painful. It had happened. She'd seen it with her own eyes, and now, she had to find some way to deal with the outcome—to deal with all she felt.

She drew in a deep, unsteady breath.

She'd told Child the unvarnished truth—she wished Devlin had never claimed to love her. If he hadn't told her that and made her believe it, learning what she had that day would still have been painful, but the damage would, relatively speaking, have been minor, nothing like the raw, gaping wound she currently bore.

If he hadn't told her he loved her, the entire episode wouldn't have been so emotionally catastrophic.

The train rattled and swayed while she dwelled on that...until a connected thought arose, one that made her inwardly frown.

Why had Devlin told her he loved her?

Why bother if he didn't? Why make the effort that, looking back over recent weeks, she could see he had to spend more time with her, hours during which he'd encouraged her to draw closer and become more immersed in his life and, conversely, had seized every opportunity to draw closer to her?

Her frown materialized. That made no sense, yet above all, Devlin was a highly rational man.

He'd also never been a cruel man. She wouldn't have said he had it in him.

So why tell her something he knew wasn't true? Why tell her something he didn't believe?

She blinked and raised her head as another thought rose above the miasma of hurt and misery fogging her faculties. He hadn't simply told her he loved her; he'd shown her as well. And some of those incidents—such as him punching Child—had been as much a surprise to him as to her.

Was she reading too much into his behavior? In those incidents, large and small, had he been motivated by jealousy or merely by possessiveness? She was well aware that the latter didn't necessarily stem from love, especially within the aristocracy.

Yet still...why, after five years of marital harmony, had he gone out of his way to rock their boat and change her understanding of the basis of their marriage?

As far as she could see, he'd had no reason to do so.

She still felt deeply hurt but, now, also puzzled and confused. She'd lived alongside Devlin for five and more years; she couldn't have so completely misread his character over all that time. Could she?

Then she recalled their lovemaking of the previous night. She remembered the sense of increasing closeness, of escalating intimacy and deeper, more intense emotional connection. And the sure and certain feeling that he'd dispensed with some emotional shield.

She hadn't imagined that. Hadn't mistaken or misinterpreted what had been between them in those long, heady moments.

And *then*, to cap it all, he'd deliberately and with intent broken the habit he'd established and clung to for all the years of their marriage and remained by her side to wake her at dawn...with love. With an intense demonstration of his love for her and hers for him.

Why, why, why?

Nothing any longer made sense.

A horrendous squealing *screech* split the night, high-pitched and drawn out.

CRASH!

She was flung violently forward. Instinctively, she spread her arms to shield the children. The cases and small trunks they'd stored in the luggage racks rained down on her back and head.

A horrible grinding, groaning mingled with a succession of loud bangs and a series of shuddering, juddering thuds.

Then everything stopped.

For an instant, the only sound to reach her ears was the pervasive hiss of escaping steam.

Then screams rent the night.

Pandemonium followed. Shouts and yells came from farther up and back in the train, and footsteps pounded along the corridor outside the compartment door.

Therese hauled in a breath and started to slowly straighten, then Parker was there, lifting the cases and small trunks that had landed on Therese's back and stacking them on the seats she and Therese had occupied until Therese could draw back enough to check the children.

Nanny Sprockett had clutched Horry to her cushioning bosom; the little girl's eyes were wide, drinking in all she could see, but as no one in their compartment had started screaming, she hadn't, either.

Therese switched her gaze to Spencer and Rupert, hoping she hadn't hurt them when she'd fallen on them. Both stared back at her, as wide-eyed as their sister and—*thank God*—transparently unharmed. Therese swallowed a rush of near-debilitating relief.

Someone ran down the corridor, banging on each compartment door. "Everyone out! Everyone out!"

"Mama?" Spencer whispered.

Therese managed a reassuring smile and leaned forward to drop kisses on his and Rupert's foreheads. "Hold on, my darlings." She glanced briefly at her staff; blank-faced, Parker was busily stacking the fallen luggage on the seat, while Nanny was speaking bracingly to the nursemaids, instructing both girls on what they should carry when leaving the train. Therese looked at Spencer and Rupert and met both boys' eyes. "All of us are all right. We'll get out shortly, and you must be sure to stay with Nanny and Gillian and Patty. Can you be brave and do that?"

Eyes huge, both bit their lips and nodded.

Warily, Therese pushed upright and, with Parker's help, got to her feet.

"Here, my lady." Parker handed Therese her bonnet. "Safest place for it's on your head."

"Indeed." Therese settled the bonnet and, ignoring a twinge at the back of her head, quickly tied the ribbons beneath her chin. All of them struggled into their coats and bundled the children into theirs. "Now." Therese surveyed their company. Parker and the nursemaids had gathered the luggage. Like her, the other women were shaken, but uninjured.

From the wails and screams coming from outside, not everyone had been so lucky.

Therese didn't want to subject her children to the mayhem outside, but there was nothing for it; they had to leave the train. She nodded to Gillian and Patty. "Let's see if we can open the door."

Her phrasing proved prophetic; the door slid a few inches, then stuck.

The girls struggled to jiggle and push it on, then a dark-coated figure appeared in the gap. "My lady?"

"Morton." The relief in the compartment was palpable.

"Is everyone all right?" Morton asked.

"Yes," Therese replied. "We're all unharmed. How are you and Dennis?"

"Just a few bruises, my lady. Now, if you and the ladies will just sit tight, Dennis and I will take care of this door. The conductors are getting everyone off the train."

Therese debated, but couldn't not ask, "What happened? Do you know?"

Morton and Dennis were poking at the base of the door. "Not sure, my lady," Morton huffed. "A collision of sorts. The carriages ahead of this one are crumpled, and I heard one of the conductors say the engine's off the tracks."

The pair used something to scrape at the door's base, then they grunted and heaved, and with a gravelly grating noise, the compartment door finally slid open far enough for those inside to squeeze out.

People, mostly men—some of whom looked as if they shouldn't have been in the first-class carriage—were scouting up and down the narrow corridor. Therese gave them the benefit of the doubt; they might have been trying to help others get out.

Therese took charge. She instructed Morton to use his bulk to block the passageway heading to the front of the train, then sent Parker, carrying several small trunks and cases, to lead the way down the corridor to the external door at the end of the carriage. Therese took Spencer's and Rupert's hands and followed Parker, with Nanny Sprockett falling in behind her, leaving Gillian, Patty, Dennis, and Morton, all ferrying the rest of the luggage, to bring up the rear.

Parker reached the outer door, looked down at the ground below the iron steps, then the experienced and unflappable dresser calmly set the luggage she carried on the carriage floor, swung around and went quickly down the steps, then dropped the last few feet to the ground. Parker held up her arms. "If you'll pass me the cases, my lady?"

Releasing the boys' hands, Therese did so, then she told the pair to wait and went down the steps herself. Like Parker, she had to drop the last little way to the ground.

Immediately, she looked up and held up her hands, beckoning the boys to her. Bravely, they sat on the threshold, then at her signal, one after another, they pushed off and dropped into her arms. She caught first Spencer, then Rupert, and lowered them safely to the ground.

Nanny Sprockett took their place. The older woman bent and held Horry out and down to where Therese could almost reach her. When Therese was ready, Nanny Sprocket let go, and Horry fell the last few inches, and Therese grasped her daughter's little body and quickly drew the girl into her arms. Holding Horry close, Therese stepped back to stand with the boys; she was reassured to feel their hands clutch her skirts while Parker helped Nanny Sprockett to descend.

In short order, the rest of their party got out of the carriage. They gathered the luggage and quickly moved away from the carriage steps, allowing others to climb down. Therese recalled that the train had been fairly full.

Carrying Horry, with the boys still clutching her skirts and pressing close on either side, she crossed a roughly flat space to the bottom of the slope of a rising embankment. Their small company halted there, several yards from the tracks. Looking around, Therese swiftly took stock.

A nightmarish scene met her eyes. They were out in the country, and the sky wasn't clear; there wasn't even faint moonlight or starlight to alleviate the pitch-blackness of the surrounding night.

A cacophony of sounds enveloped them, shouts, commands, wails, and crying overlaying the persistent hiss of escaping steam. The tang of hot metal and the sulfurous stench of burning coal wafted from the front of the train.

Someone, presumably the train conductors, had set lighted storm lanterns on the ground along the line of carriages, and people were gathering around each lantern, using the light to examine injuries and, in some cases, bind up wounds. Those circling the lanterns constantly cut off the light, then revealed it again, playing havoc with people's night vision.

Therese put her back to the carriages and looked sideways toward the front of the train. The noise from that direction was ten times worse. Increasingly, people were drifting that way, forming a milling rabble. She peered past the shifting bodies and the splotches of lanternlight; what she saw made her blood run cold.

Some way ahead, the massive locomotive that had pulled the long train lay on its side, angled off the rails, the underside of the engine facing the rest of the train. Steam hissed and sputtered from the massive boiler, creating acrid clouds that hung over the scene, lending it a surreal quality. The coal car that had followed the engine had sheered off the rails in the other direction; she could see only a rear corner of the coal car, but the leading first-class carriage had clearly plowed into it and was now a crumpled mess of twisted and buckled iron and steel, precariously tilted half on and half off the rails. The second passenger carriage had run head-long into the first. The front of the second carriage was concertinaed, but the car remained more or less on the rails. The third carriage, the one they'd been in, had butted into the rear of the second, but wasn't terribly badly damaged.

The human toll in the first carriage and even in the second would be substantial.

"We were lucky," she murmured. *So lucky.* Only because the trip had been a last-minute decision had they been in the third of the three first-class carriages.

She glanced at her staff and saw that realization mirrored in their faces; it would be some time before any of them took the train to the Priory again.

"My lady, I think it'd be best if we move to the top of the embankment." Morton pointed up the slope.

Therese looked and nodded. "Yes, you're right." She wanted the children away from the melee.

Their company gathered themselves and their luggage, then Therese handed Horry to Nanny Sprockett and took Spencer's and Rupert's hands. "Ready?" She smiled encouragingly, but wasn't surprised that while the boys nodded, neither smiled back.

As a group, they started up the incline. Given they'd been traveling from one house to another, they were carrying with them only the things they habitually took from place to place. Parker had Therese's trunk-like dressing case as well as her own smaller case. The nursemaids carried the children's cases, while the footmen carted the staff's bags.

The embankment was steep in sections, but not too high and reasonably grassed. They reached the top easily enough and found themselves on a narrow, beaten path that meandered along the embankment to both right and left. About one hundred yards to their right, the path met a lane, which crossed a stone bridge under which the railway ran.

Therese looked around. Fields stretched before them. On the other side of the railway cutting, more dark fields stretched away, although in the far distance, a few lights glimmered. "Where are we?" She glanced at Morton. "Do you know?"

"We'd passed through Potters Bar, ma'am, so I'd say we're some ways south of Hatfield. I heard one of the conductors say that there's a village up farther—Welham Green—but that Potters Bar is closer. Bigger, too. More likely to have carriages and doctors and such."

"Have they sent someone to raise the alarm?"

"That they have, my lady," Dennis replied. "Seems there's a farm not too far back. They sent a man running for it."

Therese nodded. "In that case, help should arrive soon." She glanced toward the lane, along which it seemed likely that help would come. Others who, like them, had toiled up the embankment had started to head in that direction. "We may as well go to the lane and wait there until help arrives."

The others agreed. They gathered the luggage and the children and were about to start walking when a pained cry rang out from the crowd around the first carriage. Along with everyone else, Therese paused and looked in that direction.

From the vantage point of the embankment, they could see a seething mass of humanity shifting and surging around the wrecked carriages, and from the yells and calls and loud arguments that were erupting, distant but carried on the breeze, it was plain that panic had started to take hold.

Therese was a born organizer—everyone said so—and the authority she instinctively wielded had always served her well in such situations.

She looked at her children. They were safe. Other families' young ones might not be, but hers were and would remain so, and she could, she knew, make a difference. Briskly, she gave orders for Morton, Nanny Sprockett, and the nursemaids to take the children and all the luggage to the lane.

She crouched beside Spencer and Rupert and met their eyes. "I'm going to help the people down there. They're frightened and hurt, and Parker, Dennis, and I know a thing or two about what needs to be done." She rose and turned the boys toward Morton and the nursemaids. "I want you to go with Nanny and Gillian and Patty and wait by the lane. When help comes, Morton will come back and fetch me and the others." She met the boys' wide, questioning eyes. "Can you be brave boys and do that for me?"

They blinked, then quietly said, "Yes, Mama."

"Good lads." She eased them toward the nursemaids, then dropped a kiss on Horry's curls. "Be good for Nanny, poppet." Horry was struggling to keep her eyes open; she sleepily patted Therese's cheek.

Therese waited while Parker and Dennis distributed the cases they'd been carrying among the others, the boys each took the hand of one of the nursemaids, and the little cavalcade moved off along the lane, joining the stream of other passengers slowly making their way in that direction, then she drew in a breath and turned to face the challenge down in the cutting. Lips setting, she started down the embankment. "Come along. Let's see what we can do to help."

On regaining the flat at the bottom of the embankment, Therese approached the chaos surrounding the two badly damaged passenger carriages.

It quickly became apparent that no one had taken charge, much less made any decisions, and the need for clear directions to calm people enough to get those most in need to where their injuries could be examined was blatantly evident.

Therese halted at the edge of the shifting throng. "Dennis, I need to speak to one of the conductors—as quickly as you can fetch one. Use my title and his lordship's as well. "

"Yes, my lady." Dennis plunged into the melee and, in seconds, was lost to sight.

He re-emerged a minute later, dragging a conductor who looked to have reached his wits' end.

The conductor executed a shaky bow. "Countess, I don't know as I can help." He gestured weakly at the milling throng. "It's bedlam."

"Indeed." Therese's voice carried the authority that derived from centuries of forebears who had all been accustomed to lead. "That is precisely why I am here. First, who is the head conductor?"

The man had responded to her high tone and, instinctively, had drawn himself up. "I am, my lady."

"Excellent. You're precisely the man we need to bring this situation under control. I will give the necessary orders, and you and your conductors will carry them out." She paused to meet the man's eyes, her own gaze challenging. "My husband, the earl, is a major shareholder"—she'd learned that through listening to Devlin's business discussions over the past weeks—"and he would expect nothing less." Whether of her or the conductors, she didn't specify; in her mind, she meant both.

The man's eyes widened, and he looked faintly panicked, but "Yes, my lady" was all he said.

Therese nodded approvingly. "Now, the first thing we need to do is to form all these men and women into lines to help the injured out of the second carriage. We'll start there—the least grievously wounded will be there—and move forward."

Under her direction, the head conductor summoned as many of his men as he could find. Therese repeated her orders, adding more detail, and at first rather hesitantly, then with greater confidence as the crowd responded to their clear directions and fell into line and the chaos subsided, the conductors marshaled the shifting throng into good order.

Walking along the rapidly forming lines, Therese said to the head conductor, who was trotting by her side, "We need to pick out teams of men able to go into the carriages and help the injured out." She halted at the head of one line, close to the rear steps of the second passenger carriage. "Stand here." She pointed to the bottom of the steps. "I'll pick out the most suitable men and send them to you. Put them in teams of four, give one a lantern, and send them in to free and carry out the first injured person they see." It seemed likely that those who were in any way mobile had already left the crumpled carriage.

Without waiting for any agreement, she started down the line. Men and women looked at her curiously, but her innate air of command stood her in good stead. "You. And you." She tugged the sleeves of two young men who looked strong enough and wore coats that suggested they were solicitors' clerks. She was looking for men with gentle hands. "Report to the head conductor"—she pointed up the line—"over there."

She progressed down the lines, dispatching more men to the task of removing those trapped, then with Parker, Dennis, and the other conductors assisting, she formed those left into teams to receive those brought out and carry them farther down the line to where two doctors, who had been traveling in second class, had set up by the side of the train to do the best they could for the injured.

The task proved a trial for everyone involved, especially when they moved into the first carriage.

Watching for signs of collapse in the young men she set to retrieving what were increasingly the dead, Therese switched them for others who had yet to confront the grisly duty.

Flanked by Dennis, who acted as her messenger, and assisted by Parker, who, even more than Therese, had some understanding of injuries, Therese checked each person extracted from the wreckage, telling those who would carry the usually unconscious person to the doctors as much as she could ascertain of their condition. Some, she knew, were more likely to survive than others. She didn't feel qualified to pass judgment on the dead; she sent them to the doctors to deal with as well.

The minutes dragged by. Gradually, the ranks of those helping to carry the injured and the bodies back along the track dwindled; many had been searching for employers, friends, or family, and once they found them at the makeshift clinic, they didn't return.

By the time they'd cleared all the bodies they could find from the first-class carriages, only three young men and the conductors remained.

Warily, they approached the locomotive.

They were ten yards away when the head conductor halted and turned to Therese. "Please, ma'am, wait here, if you would." He glanced at Parker and Dennis. "You and your people. You've been of untold help—we would never have managed as well as we have without you. But that boiler's still hot, and pipes can burst and steam escape at any time." He gulped, then looked at the other men, who had halted a little farther on. The head conductor straightened. "We'll go in and find them and bring them out."

"How many men were in there?" Therese asked.

"Four, ma'am. Two drivers and two stokers."

Therese nodded. "We'll wait here."

Clearly relieved—the thought of a countess coming to harm under his watch was too much for him to bear—the head conductor gathered his men, and the three passengers freely offered their help. In a small band, they warily clambered around the still-hissing engine.

Therese, Parker, and Dennis waited. In the end, of the four men who had been inside the engine car, only one of the stokers, who had been flung clear, had survived. Flanked by Parker and Dennis, Therese followed the somber line of men who carried the wounded and the dead to the doctors.

Once there, Therese stood back for a moment. Her gaze traveled over the many injured laid out along the lower edge of the sloping embankment. The dead had been taken farther down the tracks; she couldn't see clearly that far away. Most of the lanterns had been brought closer to help cast light on the wounded.

Cold started to seep into her bones, and a sudden bout of weakness swept over her. But she was hale and whole and her people were safe, and there was surely more she could yet do. Stiffening her spine, with Parker and Dennis trailing after her, she walked up to one of the doctors, who was tending a young woman who was clutching what looked to be a broken arm. When the doctor glanced up, Therese asked, "What can we do to help?"

CHAPTER 14

*D*evlin drove as quickly as he dared up the Great North Road. The new lamps he'd had fitted to his curricle lived up to their claim of lighting his way well enough to allow him to keep his bays pacing at a halfway decent speed.

Nevertheless, he had to rein in his impatience and battle the urge to trust in the surface of the macadamed highway and whip up his horses. As he kept telling himself, it was simply too dark and therefore too dangerous to risk that.

They'd left the outskirts of London at least half an hour ago. Now that the night had closed in, there was very little other traffic, allowing him to keep the carriage bowling smoothly down the center of the road, while he constantly scanned ahead for any unexpected obstacle, like a farm wagon ambling along.

They were nearing the stretch where the railway line veered to within distant sight of the highway, off to the right, when ahead, across the dark fields to the right, he saw what appeared to be clouds of fog billowing slowly upward, oddly lit by lights from below.

Even as he stared, the lights bobbed and shifted.

Mitchell, behind him, was peering in the same direction, then he stiffened. "My lord, I think that's the railway line."

Devlin had come to the same conclusion. With his heart suddenly lodged in his throat, he set his jaw and urged the horses faster. "Look for a turnoff to the right."

Mitchell knew the road even better than Devlin. "There should be a lane—Hawkshead Lane—coming up ahead. I think it crosses over the railway."

A few minutes later, Mitchell squinted over Devlin's shoulder. "There it is."

A signpost pointed down a lane. Devlin slowed his horses and confirmed that the lane was, indeed, Hawkshead Lane. With his features grimly set, he negotiated the turn, then urged the bays to a rapid trot.

Half a mile along, they saw the first passengers, drooping by the side of the lane.

"They'll have sent for help from Potters Bar," Mitchell said. "There'll be wagons coming, sure enough."

Devlin's mind had seized. He couldn't think beyond finding his wife and children. Straining to see, he tried to make out features and figures amid the clumps of people dotted along the lane, many of whom glanced up at the sound of hooves, then on realizing it was only a curricle, returned to looking searchingly up the lane or talking among themselves.

"There they are!" Mitchell pointed over Devlin's shoulder.

Looking in the direction Mitchell indicated, Devlin saw the group waiting patiently by the side of the lane. Spencer, Rupert—where was Horry? Then he saw the bundle Nanny was cradling against her bosom, and relief hit him.

Only to evaporate as he realized Therese wasn't there. Nor was Parker or Dennis.

Devlin slowed his horses and halted the carriage opposite the group. He flung the reins at Mitchell and stepped down while the curricle was still rocking on its springs.

"Papa!" Spencer and Rupert rocketed to him.

Devlin crouched, spread his arms, and gathered them to him. He hugged them hard, then eased back and met eyes that, in the diffuse light from the carriage lamps, seemed tired but excited rather than frightened.

"The engine crashed!" Rupert told him.

Devlin swallowed and managed a nod. "So I supposed." He looked at Spencer. "Where's your mama?"

Spencer turned and pointed into the cutting. "She went to help with the wounded down there."

"She wasn't hurt?"

Both boys shook their heads, and Devlin finally drew a decent breath.

"None of us were hurt," Spencer informed him rather proudly. "Mama asked us to be brave and stay here with Nanny and the others, and we did."

Devlin released them, rose, and ruffled both boys' hair. "Good men. Now"—he ushered them back to where Nanny, the nursemaids, and Morton waited—"I need you to continue to be brave and wait here, with Horry and the staff, while Mitchell goes and fetches some carriages and I go and find your mama."

Plainly reassured by his presence and his plan, the boys willingly settled to wait with Nanny.

In a low voice, Morton confirmed what Spencer had told Devlin. "The first and second carriages are a mess, my lord. Luckily, our party was in a compartment in the middle of the third carriage so escaped serious harm. Her ladyship sent us to wait here and turned back to help." Proud approval tinged his tone. "She was unhurt but shaken, like the rest of us. She took Parker and Dennis with her, my lord."

Devlin nodded. He wasn't surprised that Therese had chosen to assist the rescue effort; it was the sort of response the public expected of the aristocracy and, indeed, that they expected of themselves. In times of crisis, leading others was second nature to Therese, as it was for him. She'd seen to the safety of their children and their people, then turned to help others as she could. Much as a part of him didn't like it, he couldn't fault her for that.

He swung to Mitchell, who was waiting by the horses' heads. "Drive back to Potters Bar and make sure the alarm has been raised. Tell them there are"—he glanced around—"about a hundred stranded passengers as well as an unknown number of injured and dead. They need to send wagons as soon as possible—the night's already chilly, and the temperature's dropping. Use my title freely. Then hire the largest carriage you can find, with an experienced driver and a good team, and lead the coach back here."

"Yes, my lord." Mitchell saluted, climbed into the curricle, swiftly turned it, and drove back the way they'd come.

Devlin spoke briefly with his sons, dropped a kiss on his sleeping daughter's curls, then leaving them in the safe care of Nanny and Morton, strode quickly along the path that followed the top of the embankment.

Below, he could just make out the dark bulk of the derailed locomotive. It had come off the rails a little before the bridge. The sight of the wrecked carriages, sides buckled and frames twisted, made his stomach clench; his family had survived more or less unscathed, but how many others hadn't?

Only a few dimmed lanterns had been left to light the damaged portion of the train. In the ghostly light, Devlin saw that the front of the third passenger carriage was somewhat crushed, but the carriages in front had borne the brunt of the impact. From the fourth carriage on, the train appeared largely undamaged. *Thank God.*

Farther along, toward the rear of the train, unshuttered lanterns blazed, illuminating a scene that had more in common with war than with people journeying in their own country in peacetime.

Devlin went quickly down the embankment and strode into the circle of light. A conductor was struggling to ease a man with a badly broken leg, roughly splinted and bound, down to the ground to sit. Devlin couldn't walk by; he detoured and, being much stronger than the slight conductor, assisted the wounded man to the ground.

His face pinched with pain, the man lay back with a shaky sigh. "Thank ye, sir."

Devlin patted the man's shoulder, straightened, and turned to the conductor, who was regarding him in puzzled fashion. "I'm Alverton. I've sent to Potters Bar and asked for wagons to be dispatched as quickly as possible."

The conductor's relief was palpable.

Devlin briskly continued, "I'm looking for Lady Alverton. Have you seen her?"

The conductor blinked. "The lady who's been helping us?"

"One of them, at least."

"If she's the lady who took charge"—the conductor pointed down the train—"she's along there, with the doctors."

Devlin nodded his thanks and was turning away when, in a tone tinged with awe as much as with gratitude, the conductor added, "Don't rightly know as we'd have managed without her."

Devlin stored that morsel up to relay to Therese later. He strode on, skirting the wounded laid out on the flat between the tracks and the rise of the embankment. Several times, he stopped to help those who plainly needed it. He'd never been in a war, but this appeared much as he imagined a field hospital behind the front lines would look, and no more than Therese could he turn away from those in need who were weaker and less able than he.

As he continued toward the center of activity, he acknowledged that attitude as yet another trait he and she shared.

He came upon a man who was clearly one of the doctors, leaning down and speaking with a wounded woman.

As, plainly exhausted, the man patted the woman's hand and straightened, he weaved.

Devlin caught the man's elbow and steadied him.

The man turned to thank him, but paused, blinking at Devlin, presumably recognizing him as someone with authority who hadn't been around earlier.

Devlin said, "I'm looking for Lady Alverton."

The man blinked again, then glanced farther down the train. "The only lady still down here is helping my colleague with the last of the wounded. All the other ladies are either among the wounded themselves or too weak to be of much use. However, if your lady is she, Lady Alverton has been a Trojan. You might think otherwise, but I thank God that she was on the train. She organized the conductors and able-bodied men to ferry out the wounded and the dead." He glanced around. "What we have here is bad enough, but without her leadership, it would have been much worse."

Devlin faintly grinned. "She's very good at organizing people." That was such an understatement, if they heard it, her brothers would fall about laughing. Everything Devlin was hearing suggested that Therese was well and busily rising to every challenge.

The doctor nodded down the train. "See that spot where the light is brightest? Last time I saw her, she was there."

Devlin nodded. "Thank you. I sent my man back to Potters Bar to ensure help was coming as fast as possible."

"Thank you for that." The man looked around and sighed. "Regardless, it's going to be a long night."

Devlin dipped his head in farewell and walked on.

He was still some yards from the brightly lit area when Therese, who had been crouched by the side of a wounded youth, rose and straightened. Devlin's gaze locked on her, racing over her, confirming that she appeared entirely unhurt.

The relief that hit him was even more intense than what he'd felt on seeing the children. So intense, it forced him to slow and pause and *breathe.*

Breathe past the constriction that had locked about his chest and absorb the reality that she was hale and whole and well.

Feeling suddenly freed of a crushing weight and significantly more lighthearted than he had been, with his features easing, he walked toward her.

∽

Therese glanced along the row of injured lying along the rise of the embankment. She had, she thought, done everything she could. Her heart was starting to thud strangely—not racing but rather the opposite. Each beat seemed abnormally deep and slow.

She raised her head and forced herself to breathe deeply, but that didn't help. For the last while, she'd pushed aside the steadily ballooning tiredness dragging at her limbs; she would have plenty of time to rest later. But now her hands were icy; looking down, she spread her fingers and frowned as she noted that her nails appeared leached of all color.

Now she thought of it, her whole body felt chilled.

She didn't know what made her glance toward the front of the train, but she did and, through the fading chaos of the night, saw Devlin walking toward her.

He'd come.

Her heart—stupid organ—leapt, at least as much as it could manage. She might have been wrong in thinking what she had—she still wasn't sure about that—but Child would have told Devlin why she'd rushed off, why she'd run away, and yet, here he was.

Regardless of whether he loved her or not, he'd come after her, and she had no doubt whatsoever that, now he was there, everything would be all right.

She could relax, set down the burden of caring for all these people, and let him pick it up. She knew he would.

A smile blooming on her lips—the first in hours—she shuffled to face him and started to raise her hands, extending them in welcome.

Abruptly, the energy that had been holding her upright drained to her soles.

"Oh." She swayed.

She blinked and saw Devlin's expression, which had been affectionately amused, transform to one of flaring concern, and he started to run toward her.

Her vision turned hazy, then blurred.

And she realized she was falling, crumpling where she stood.

The last touch she registered was Devlin's strong arms wrapping about her, then he swung her up, into his arms.

The last thing she heard was his voice as he said, harsh and insistent, "I've got you."

Then the world faded, and impenetrable blackness swallowed her whole.

~

Devlin searched Therese's chalk-white face and softly swore. Shock? Delayed shock? Was that all this was?

Or was it something more sinister?

He held her in his arms and felt utterly helpless.

Parker rushed up, closely followed by Dennis.

"Oh, dear." Parker caught one of Therese's limp hands and started chafing it. "She seemed perfectly all right, my lord. Shaken at first, of course, but once she started helping, she seemed right as rain."

Dennis nodded. "She was giving orders right and left, like she usually does."

"Let me take off her bonnet." Parker deftly undid the ribbons tied beneath Therese's chin.

Devlin adjusted his hold to allow Parker to ease off the bonnet, with its wide flared brim that, until then, had partially shaded Therese's face.

As Parker drew the bonnet away, Devlin stared at features that were achingly familiar but, surely, far too pale? Therese's complexion was normally creamy, not alabaster white.

"Oh, my Lord!"

Parker's shocked exclamation had him glancing at the dresser. She was staring down at the bonnet in her hands, at the silk lining, which was soaked in blood.

Therese's blood.

Dennis blanched. Devlin was certain he did, too. He raised Therese's shoulders and tried to examine the back of her head. All he could make out was that a large patch of golden-blond hair was dark and matted with blood.

Parker shook herself out of her frozen state and crouched, carefully searching, gently touching, then straightened. "It's a gash, my lord. Across the back of her head. It doesn't look to be still bleeding."

It probably wouldn't be; it had been at least an hour since the crash.

"How did it happen?" He looked around, trying to spot one of the doctors.

Parker frowned, clearly thinking back. "It had to have been during the crash, before she put her bonnet back on, but she didn't say... I'm sure she didn't know." Then her face cleared. "I was sitting next to her, and when the crash occurred, we were flung forward, and the cases fell on top of us —some on our backs, but others struck our heads." Parker raised her gaze to Devlin's face. "Her dressing case fell on her head. I remember lifting it off her. And it has those metal corners. One must have struck her."

Devlin fought to rein in the panicked desperation that had sunk steel-tipped claws into his soul. With Therese in his arms, he turned. "Find one of the doctors. She was helping them—now they can help her."

Parker and Dennis darted away.

Devlin grimly hung on—to his temper, to his wits; inwardly, he repeated, over and over again, that Therese was merely wounded, that she was alive and would remain so. That he hadn't lost her and wouldn't lose her.

Never in his life had he felt like this.

After several minutes, when incipient anguish rose almost to the point of making him howl, he switched to sternly reminding himself that he couldn't afford to indulge in such histrionics, that she needed him now— she, and the children and his people.

Never before had he so resented the demands of being an earl.

Then Parker and Dennis returned with an older man. He took one look at Therese's face and said, "Oh, dear."

Devlin clenched his jaw.

"Let's see." The doctor shifted and crouched as Parker had done. From beside him, Parker whispered about what she'd found and pointed, and he looked, then nodded and straightened.

The man met Devlin's eyes. "It's a nasty gash, my lord, but please remember that head wounds always bleed copiously." He glanced again at Therese's face. "She's been pushing herself hard, so even though I doubt she's lost that much blood, the loss nevertheless has taken its toll." He glanced around, then lowered his voice and again met Devlin's eyes. "The wound needs to be washed, but we have no clean water. I wouldn't want to attempt to tend her ladyship's wound here—the risk of infection is too great."

He glanced at Therese's face again. "My humble opinion is that, as I judge she's not in any immediate danger, you should remove her to where she can receive appropriate treatment."

Devlin stared at the man, analyzing his words, then forced himself to nod. "Thank you. I'll do as you suggest."

The man bowed. "My lord." He straightened and added, "Her ladyship was of great help to all those here. I'll pray for a speedy recovery with no complications."

Devlin stiffly inclined his head, then settling Therese more securely in his arms, turned and carried her out of the harsh light, then started climbing the embankment.

Parker and Dennis flanked him, walking close enough to be able to steady him if he faltered.

In one corner of his mind, he was relieved and grateful that Therese, the children, and the staff had survived the crash unharmed, but most of his mind was swimming with dread, a dark emotion that inexorably tightened the vise clamped about his heart.

Regardless of what the rational part of his mind reiterated, his emotions were in tumult and refused to settle, to believe.

All he could focus on as he carried Therese along the path toward the lane was that he absolutely couldn't lose her.

If he did, he'd lose himself.

~

London's bells were tolling for midnight as Devlin carried Therese's limp form up the steps of Alverton House.

By the time he'd reached Hawkshead Lane, Mitchell had returned with an old but well-kept coach, large enough to fit most of their party inside. But the boys' distress on seeing their mother draped lifeless in Devlin's arms had convinced everyone that it would be better for the children and the staff to travel back to London in the slower coach while Mitchell drove the much faster curricle back to the capital, with Devlin as passenger, holding Therese on his lap.

As he waited for Portland to answer Mitchell's demanding—panicked—summons, Devlin studied Therese's face in the light of the gibbous moon that had belatedly appeared, but her features remained as lifeless as they had throughout the fraught journey.

He'd held her cradled against his chest the entire way, cushioning her poor head as best he could against the inevitable jolts. The decision to race ahead hadn't been hard; the sooner he got her into her own bed and summoned Sanderson—their family doctor—to see her, the better.

The door finally opened to reveal Portland, managing to appear magisterial even in his dressing gown, backed by two sleepy footmen, who on sighting Devlin with Therese in his arms, immediately came to round-eyed attention.

"My lord!" Shocked, Portland swung the door wide.

Grim-faced, Devlin strode in, and Mitchell followed.

Portland quickly shut the door. "An accident, my lord?"

"Of a sort." Devlin turned to look at Mitchell.

His groom preempted him. "Dr. Sanderson in Harley Street, my lord?"

Devlin nodded. "As fast as you can. I don't care where he is or what he's doing. We need him here now."

Mitchell bobbed his head. "I'll fetch him."

As Mitchell returned to the door and slipped out, Devlin glanced at Portland. "The train derailed, and her ladyship sustained a deep gash on the back of her head. She didn't realize she was bleeding and spent the next hour taking charge and helping everyone else before she collapsed." He hauled in a breath and reached for every iota of control he possessed. "The others are following in a hired coach. We'll need to pay off the coachman."

"I'll see to everything, my lord." Gently, Portland ushered Devlin to the stairs. "And I'll send Mrs. Portland and some of the maids up to tend to her ladyship. You'll want her settled before the doctor arrives."

He supposed he did. Devlin allowed Portland to escort him up the stairs, along the corridor, and into Therese's room. Instinct prodded him to take her to his room—it was bigger—but he quashed the urge; she would be more comfortable in her own room, in her own bed.

She'd never been in his—another facet of the idiocy he'd allowed to rule him for far too long.

He halted beside the bed and waited while Portland rounded it and lit the bedside lamp on the opposite side, then guided by the soft light, gently laid Therese down, careful to ease his arm from beneath her shoulders in a way that didn't impinge on her wound.

He straightened. Portland, who, for the first time in all the years Devlin had known him, sounded faintly flustered, excused himself and left to summon his wife.

Devlin stood and, in the gentle light, stared at Therese's still face, willing her to wake or even stir.

But she'd been unmoving and entirely silent all the way home and remained so.

Helplessness welled and swamped him.

Then Mrs. Portland bustled in, along with two wide-eyed maids.

Devlin felt Mrs. Portland's gaze on his face, then the motherly house-keeper laid a hand on his sleeve and gently eased him away from the bed. "Portland was called to the door, my lord—the footman said a coach had just turned in."

The maids had left the door ajar, and Devlin caught the distant sounds of people in the front hall.

"Perhaps, my lord, you should check on the children. Even though her ladyship will be fit as a fiddle come morning, I daresay the poor mites will be upset." Letting her hand fall from his sleeve, Mrs. Portland added, "You know you can safely leave her ladyship in our hands. We'll make her comfortable, and I'll sit with her until you return."

Devlin didn't want to go, but he knew Therese would want him to, and Mrs. Portland was right. He needed to behave with confidence so the children wouldn't grow overly anxious. He drew in a breath, then nodded and forced himself to turn from the bed and cross to the door.

Mrs. Portland followed, and after he stepped into the corridor, he heard the door softly close.

He didn't look back and forced himself to breathe—in and out—as he strode to the stairs and went quickly down them.

Just as well he did; his sons were refusing to budge from the hall until they learned how their mother was.

Given his recent behavior, he could hardly fault them for that.

Schooling his features to project an assurance he didn't feel, he smiled at the boys, shrugged out of his greatcoat and handed the garment to Port-land, then crouched before his sons. "Your mama will be all right." He met Spencer's gaze, then Rupert's and prayed the prediction would come true. "I've sent Mitchell to fetch Dr. Sanderson. He'll come and bind up Mama's head, and after she rests, she'll be right as rain."

The boys looked back at him, then Spencer quietly said, "She was very still, before. Did she wake up?"

Damn. "No, but that's not to be wondered at." Even though that specific point was the source of his own escalating anxiety. "She worked very hard to help the people injured in the crash and most likely wore herself out. She might sleep for a while before she wakes up. But"—he glanced at Nanny Sprockett, who was holding a thankfully sleeping Horry, then looked back at the boys—"when she does wake up, she'll want to see you both, so as she's still sleeping, perhaps you'd better sleep, too, or else you'll be yawning when she comes to see you."

Rupert was the first to nod and mumble an "All right," then more reluctantly, Spencer followed suit.

"Good men." Devlin stood and ruffled their hair. Normally, he would have handed the pair over to the waiting nursemaids, but whether in response to their need or a need of his own, he offered his sons his hands. "Come along." As they slid their small hands into his, he added, "As your mama is asleep, I'll come and tuck you in."

Nanny Sprockett threw him a grateful look. Hefting Horry, she followed him and the boys up the stairs to the nursery. The nursemaids and footmen followed, carrying the assorted cases and bags.

Ruthlessly suppressing his welling need to return to Therese, Devlin forced himself to spend the next twenty minutes hiding his concern for her behind a reassuring mask.

Finally, the boys were tucked up in their beds. Almost immediately, sleep rolled over them, and they relaxed and surrendered.

For one last moment, Devlin hovered in the doorway of their room, watching the blankets rise and fall, then he stepped into the corridor and quietly shut the door.

He looked in on Horry.

Nanny whispered that she hadn't stirred.

He nodded and brushed a kiss to his precious daughter's forehead; she was so much like Therese, not just in appearance but also in character, that just looking at her squeezed his heart. She continued to sleep peacefully, but as he left the nursery, he knew that, once the children woke, Horry would be the loudest in demanding to see her mother.

He prayed Therese would wake soon. Even if she slid back into sleep —or was it unconsciousness? He didn't know, but if he could tell the children their beloved mother had opened her eyes and spoken to him, that would at least hold their fears at bay.

He re-entered Therese's room. Both bedside lamps had been lit, turned low, and moved to chests farther from the bed, leaving most of the room in shadow.

He approached the bed, where Therese was lying on her side beneath the covers, facing his way. She'd been stripped of her clothes and lay sheathed in a crisp white nightgown with a wide neckline. Beneath her head and shoulders, a thick white towel had been spread over the pillows, its pristine color starkly contrasting with the darkened blood matting the hair at the back of her head.

Beyond the bed, close by the wall, Mrs. Portland rose from the straight-backed chair in which she'd been sitting. "My lord, as Dr. Sanderson's been summoned, I deemed it wisest not to attempt to wash the wound. I daresay the doctor will want to do that himself."

Recalling the comment of the doctor at the crash site regarding the risk of infection, Devlin nodded. "Indeed. I believe that's so."

Mrs. Portland inclined her head and waited, clearly uncertain whether to sit again or leave.

Devlin managed to arrange his features into a softer expression before he looked at his housekeeper. "Thank you for your help—you can go. I'll sit with her ladyship for now, and Parker will, no doubt, be along shortly."

Both of them knew Parker would insist on watching over her lady, of whom she was exceedingly fond. As, indeed, the entire household was.

"My lord." Mrs. Portland bobbed a curtsy.

Devlin nodded vaguely and returned his gaze to the silent figure in the bed. A moment later, the door clicked shut.

He paused for a moment, then slowly walked to the side of the bed and stood looking down at Therese's still face. An emotion—a fear—he'd never felt before gnawed with jagged teeth at his heart. Once again, he had to remind himself to breathe.

He filled his lungs, then exhaled and allowed his gaze, again, to trace her features. So silent, so still, so lacking in all animation, her face seemed devoid of the softness, the life—the love—he was accustomed to seeing behind her every expression.

It was as if she was holding her face in a deliberately blank mask, as if, even in her present state, she felt pain and sought to hide it.

After uncounted minutes, he drew a tortured breath and looked around. Wreathed in shadows, an armchair stood a little way from the bed. He reached out and drew it to him, then tugged it still closer to the bed and sat. Then he leaned forward and took one of Therese's cold hands in his. Gently, he chafed her icy fingers between his palms.

And prayed to every deity he knew that she wouldn't leave him.

He was still sitting in the armchair, staring at Therese's face, when the door opened and Sanderson walked briskly in.

Glancing at the clock on the dresser, Devlin rose; he felt stiff all over, but although it felt as if hours had passed, in reality, it was barely past one.

Sanderson's gaze had gone straight to Therese. "I came as soon as I could." His eyes narrowed, and he rounded the bed, going to the other side. Placing his black bag on the coverlet at the foot of the bed, he said, "I'll need better light."

Devlin looked at Parker. As he'd predicted, she'd slipped into the room some minutes ago and taken up the position vacated by Mrs. Portland. Without waiting for his order, Parker went to one of the lamps left on a nearby chest, turned up the wick, then carried the lamp to the bedside table next to where Sanderson stood, his gaze on Therese. Parker set down the lamp, angling it so it threw light across the bed, illuminating the back of Therese's head.

Devlin stirred and opened his mouth, but Sanderson held up a hand. "Wait. Let me examine the wound first."

He leaned forward, reaching across the bed and gently easing aside the matted clumps of pale-gold hair so he could study the injury.

After a moment, he glanced at Parker, who had remained by the lamp. "Raise the lamp, to about your head height."

Parker obliged; the lamp and the light it cast wobbled, but then she settled her grip, and the flame steadied.

Sanderson leaned farther across the bed, peering intently before gently probing, then he huffed and straightened, letting Therese's bloodied hair fall from his fingers. "All right. Now I've seen the damage, what happened?"

"She was in a railway compartment on the train to Alverton Priory when the engine derailed and crashed," Devlin said.

Sanderson's gaze flicked up to his face. "How close was she to the point of collision?"

"Three—no, four—carriages from the engine, if you count the coal car."

Looking down at Therese, Sanderson frowned. "Do you know what happened to give her that gash?"

Devlin looked at Parker.

"I was sitting beside her." Parker carefully set down the lamp. Sanderson looked her way, and she continued, "She and I were on the forward-facing seat. When the crash occurred, we were flung forward, onto those sitting opposite—the children and Nanny Sprockett—and the luggage that had been on the rack above us tumbled down on our heads and shoulders."

Parker paused, her gaze on her mistress. "My lady's dressing case landed on the back of her head. I'm sure it was that, because I helped lifted it off her. That case was the heaviest, and it has metal corners." She straightened, clasping her hands before her. "I didn't notice anything amiss at that point. We got to our feet, and I handed her her bonnet... I told her it was safer on her head, and she put it on and tied the ribbons."

Parker's voice wavered on the last words, and Sanderson murmured, "Perfectly sensible." He glanced at Devlin.

Parker wrung her hands. "But if I hadn't given her the bonnet and told her to put it on, we would have seen—"

"You can't know that." Devlin forced himself to speak in an unflappable tone. "Given the lack of light in the train and outside, it's not certain anyone would have noticed the bleeding, at least not immediately." He caught Parker's anguished gaze and more gently said, "No one could have foreseen this. It's not your fault, Parker."

Sanderson nodded. "Indeed." He returned his gaze to his patient. "So when did she notice the bleeding?"

"She didn't." Devlin, assisted by Parker, explained how Therese had helped organize getting the injured and dead out of the wreck. He concluded, "It wasn't until right at the end, when she'd done all she could and I finally found her, that she fainted."

"Hmm. So when she stood back from action, as it were." Sanderson nodded as if that was somehow significant. "Right, then." He looked around. "I need a basin of hot water and clean cloths and bandages."

Devlin arched a brow at Parker, and with her customary rigidly controlled demeanor back in place, she bobbed and went to pour into a bowl the hot water she'd already brought to the room.

After ferrying various towels, cloths, and prepared bandages to the bed, she carried the bowl to Sanderson's side.

Sanderson picked up a thick white towel, folded it, then knelt on the bed behind Therese. "If you could lift her slightly, Alverton?"

Devlin slid one hand beneath Therese's shoulder and spread his other palm beneath her head and carefully eased her up.

"That's enough." Quickly, Sanderson thrust the more thickly folded towel beneath her head and shoulder, on top of the single thickness already spread there, then nodded. "Set her down."

Devlin did, then watched as Sanderson, after adding some tincture to the water and stirring it in, dipped in a cloth and started gently sponging the blood from Therese's head.

Sanderson worked slowly and methodically.

A gentleman's son, Sanderson was about ten years Devlin's senior and had attended Eton, where he'd met and become firm friends with Lord Ryder Cavanaugh. Sanderson had gone on to medical school and had eventually hung up his slate in Harley Street as a specialist in births and ladies' health. Regardless of his specialty, Sanderson had also become known as an excellent, no-nonsense, all-around family physician, his easy manner working as well with children as with their parents. He'd remained a close friend of Ryder, now the Marquess of Raventhorne, and courtesy of Ryder's marchioness, Mary, who'd been born a Cynster, using Sanderson's services for her confinements, he'd become a sought-after doctor to the ton and was now the physician of choice for all the Cynster ladies. Therese had insisted on engaging Sanderson for her confinements, and Devlin had been glad he'd agreed.

Even in this instance, he doubted Therese could be in better hands.

With Parker assisting, Sanderson washed, dried, and anointed the gash on Therese's head. All Devlin was called on to do was help lift her when Sanderson changed the soiled towel beneath her.

As, apparently finally satisfied with his handiwork, Sanderson straightened and reached for the bandage Parker held ready, he met Devlin's gaze. "I removed as little of her hair as possible." He waved at Therese's long locks, now spread in a golden mass over her shoulder and across the pillow. "Given her mane is so bountiful, I seriously doubt it will show." He glanced at Parker and smiled. "And I'm sure Parker will know how to dress her mistress's hair so the bare patch won't be visible." Sanderson unrolled the bandage and bent again to his task. "Of course, in time, it'll grow back, but she's bound to notice and wail—they always do."

Devlin saw Parker prim her lips, but she didn't—probably couldn't—contradict Sanderson.

At last, Sanderson straightened and stepped back from the bed.

He walked to where another bowl sat by the pitcher of warm water and proceeded to wash his hands. Parker took him a clean towel. Sanderson accepted it, dried his hands, then handed the towel to Parker and walked back to the bed, this time to stand beside Devlin.

Devlin watched Sanderson study Therese's face, then he bent over her, raised one of her lids a fraction, and let it fall.

As Sanderson straightened, Devlin asked the question he'd been waiting to ask since the doctor had arrived. "Will she be all right?"

Sanderson glanced at Parker.

Devlin raised his voice. "Parker, please take the bowl and the soiled cloths away. I'll ring when we're ready for you to return."

The dresser threw him a look, all worry and concern, but did as he'd asked. After collecting the cloths and putting them in the bowl, she carried the bowl to the door.

When the door closed behind her, Devlin returned his attention to Sanderson. "Well?"

His gaze on Therese's face, Sanderson folded his arms. "I can't say I'm pleased that she's remained unconscious for so long. Against that, however, I know for a fact that she's in excellent health overall."

He paused as if searching for words in which to explain his thinking.

Devlin didn't speak, and eventually, frowning slightly, Sanderson went on, "I wouldn't have expected such an injury to send her into so deep a faint. Not in any usual circumstances. I can only conclude that the physical effort she expended while helping at the crash site plus the effect of the blood loss—and on top of that, it must have been chilly, and the cold wouldn't have helped—combined to send her into what we term 'shock.' In her case, I suspect she was in shock and feeling the effects for some time before she succumbed."

Sanderson nodded as if satisfied with that explanation. "If that's so, then her remaining unconscious is her body's way of ensuring she rests enough to properly recover."

Devlin stirred. "So what's your prognosis? When will she wake?"

Sanderson's lips tightened, and Devlin's blood chilled, then he firmed his jaw and stated, "The truth, please. I would rather know…"

Sanderson briefly met Devlin's eyes, then blew out a breath. "All right. The worst prognosis first. Her skull might be fragile, and if that's so, it's possible she will never wake. But," he rushed to say, "in my view, that's highly unlikely." He paused, studying Therese, then went on, "That's the very worst prognosis I can imagine. At the other extreme, which is the outcome I would wager on, if her skull is half as hard as I've always thought it, she'll wake soon enough and, other than having a sore head for a few days, will suffer no lasting effects."

He exhaled, then in what seemed an afterthought, added, "Sometimes, with injuries such as this, there's some underlying trauma that means the patient doesn't actually want to wake up—to return to life, as it were—but"—he glanced again at Devlin—"in Therese's case, she has everything to live for—her children, her marriage, her households, and more. On that score, I'm confident that she won't choose to slip away."

Still regarding his patient, Sanderson lowered his arms. "That leaves me with my original prognoses, and I've told you which I strongly favor." Sanderson turned from the bed and, smiling faintly, met Devlin's eyes. "I'd place money on her waking later today—although possibly not before midday. More likely, she'll sleep deeply into the afternoon."

Devlin dragged in what felt like his first breath in hours. "And once she awakes?"

Sanderson grinned. "Knowing her, you'll have to work to keep her resting. And she'll be hungry, but she should only have broth to start with. Parker and your housekeeper will know what to send up for her."

"So she should remain abed?"

"I would prefer that she rest quietly for the remainder of the day, but again, knowing Therese, I suspect that's too much to hope for, but do your best." Sanderson walked to the end of the bed, collected his black bag, then arched a brow at Devlin. "The children?"

"Entirely unharmed and sleeping—I hope, soundly. As Parker said, they were on the seat opposite Therese, and her being flung forward protected them. I didn't see so much as a bruise."

Sanderson snorted and hefted his bag. "That will make her happy."

Devlin managed a nod; he needed some time to decide what to make of Sanderson's predictions. He waved toward the door. "I'll see you out."

He rang for Parker before following Sanderson into the corridor. They passed the dresser in the gallery as she hurried to return to watching over her mistress.

Adopting his customary urbane mask, Devlin accompanied Sanderson to the front hall.

As Sanderson shrugged on his coat, he met Devlin's gaze. "If you have any lingering concerns over Therese's recovery, or the children's, come to that, don't hesitate to send for me." He paused, then more quietly added, "Sometimes, injuries aren't evident immediately."

Devlin nodded.

Portland had a hackney waiting. Devlin walked with Sanderson onto the front porch. He shook the doctor's hand and told him to send in his account. He waited on the porch and raised a hand in salute as the hackney rattled off, then turned and went inside.

He paused in the hall, trying to fix in his mind all that Sanderson had said, then with a nod to Portland, along with a recommendation that the butler should return to his bed, Devlin headed for the stairs, intending to return to Therese's room and his vigil by her bed.

But at the foot of the stairs, he paused. For a long moment, he stared blindly before him, then he changed direction and made for his study.

CHAPTER 15

$\mathcal{F}$ ifteen minutes later, Devlin quietly opened the door of Therese's room and walked inside.

By the wall, Parker sat rigidly upright on the straight-backed chair, her gaze locked on Therese's still figure.

Devlin left the door ajar and walked to the side of the bed. Halting before the armchair he'd previously occupied, he confirmed that Therese hadn't shifted so much as an eyelash since he'd left the room, then he glanced at Parker. "Go to bed, Parker. The doctor doesn't expect her ladyship to wake this side of noon, and you'll be no use to her if you're exhausted. You were in the crash, too. Even if you don't want to think it, your nerves must need a rest." He gazed at Therese. "I'll watch over her through the night. I'll ring for you if she wakes."

From the corner of his eye, he watched Parker wrestle with what was, in essence, an order, no matter how civilly couched. In the end, her training triumphed, and she rose and dipped in a curtsy. "If you're sure, my lord?"

He nodded. He continued to study Therese's face as Parker quietly left the room and closed the door behind her.

He held still for a moment more, then exhaled.

Then he raised his right hand, the one that, as he'd entered, Parker hadn't been able to see and, moving to the bedside table, carefully set down the figurine he'd fetched from the safe.

Sanderson had left Therese lying on her side, the better to keep all pressure off the surely painful wound; although the lamps had again been moved away from the bed and turned low, Devlin could see every line of her face. He spent several seconds adjusting the position of the figurine so that as soon as she opened her eyes, her gaze would find it.

Or so he hoped.

The figurine was in the shape of a rearing dragon about to launch into flight. A fierce defender, just like Therese herself. He'd thought of her the instant he'd seen it, when they'd paused at the Russian jeweler's stand on the opening day of the exhibition. He'd been intrigued that she had also been drawn to the finely worked statue. Knowing that she had been attracted to it—drawn to it, it had seemed—had made it the perfect gift for her.

Ironic that securing the perfect gift for his wife should have caused so much heartache and pain.

If he hadn't gone to fetch it, she wouldn't have seen him and thought...and she wouldn't have been on the train when it crashed.

He'd debated whether to bring it there—even whether to give it to her at all. While he hoped it would stand as visual proof of his explanation of what she'd seen in Covent Garden, he worried that it might, instead, forcibly remind her of what she'd imagined and felt on seeing him go into the Russians' lodgings.

Would she view it the way he hoped she would—as a heartfelt gift— or as a reminder of a moment of wretchedness?

In her mind, would the dragon symbolize love or pain?

He stared at the figurine. Even in the weak light, the gold of the body gleamed, the enameled panels were vivid with color, and the gems dotted about the dragon winked and sparkled. The little creature was exquisite and seemed almost alive.

In the end, he'd allowed instinct to guide him and had brought the dragon to her.

Slowly, he sank into the armchair. He sat back, his gaze resting on her face.

Having to deal with the children and Sanderson had forced him to stay focused, to maintain outward control, but now, he had no reason, no incentive, and little remaining strength he could muster to suppress the cauldron of feelings roiling inside him.

As he sat and stared at her, those feelings surged anew. They swelled and grew, then erupted; caustic and powerful, they poured through him, scouring and stripping away all pretense and leaving him—his inner self —starkly exposed.

Fear, guilt, and frantic worry flooded him until he felt in danger of drowning.

He forced in a breath, then exhaled and breathed in again, deeper, longer, before exhaling again. He repeated the exercise until the raging tumult calmed to a sullenly surging sea.

There was no sense in wallowing in guilt over the game he had played with their lives—with their marriage, with their love. No sense in regretting the effort he'd put into maintaining the fiction that he wasn't in love, his futile yet steadfast attempt to deny reality. There was no point in railing at his own cowardice in refusing to acknowledge what he'd always known was true.

His gaze steady on Therese's unmoving features, he vowed that, when she woke, he wouldn't hesitate—wouldn't allow himself to put off the moment no matter what justification his mind supplied—but would tell her all. He would own to it all—to the breadth, depth, and overwhelming power of his love for her.

His lips tightened as memories of the last hours washed through him; in truth, he knew all about the breadth, depth, and power of his feelings for her—the emotions that had battered him had been stronger, more intense, more fundamentally shattering than any he'd ever felt before.

In starting down the path of admitting his love for her, he'd freed the genie from its bottle, and there was no way to put it back, no way to retreat.

Not that he wished to go back to the way things had been between them. These last weeks had held a promise so golden, so precious, he couldn't imagine turning his back on it. Everything in him wanted to seize and secure that golden future for him, her, and their family.

Openly loving Therese might leave him vulnerable—more vulnerable —to horrendous grief and misery, to pain, anxiety, fear, and the terror of impending loss, but against those negatives, balancing them and tipping the scales heavily to the positive, were the unrestrained joy, the sunshine of happiness, the glow of warm elation, and a deeper, richer, more profoundly glorious satisfaction that, in the absence of acknowledged love, simply did not exist in life.

Love, in all its many facets, wasn't to be underestimated. It was, he now firmly believed, fundamental to the human condition. Without it, one couldn't and wouldn't experience all there was in life.

Unbidden, his gaze traced Therese's features, drank in the beauty of her face—a beloved image.

Sanderson's words seeped into his mind. *"Sometimes, with injuries such as this, there's some underlying trauma that means the patient doesn't actually want to wake up."*

He told himself that, as Sanderson had pointed out, that wouldn't apply to Therese. She was the sort who worked through difficulties and managed. Sadly, worry was an unreasoning beast, and it had taken dogged root in his mind.

To counter it, he reminded himself of her temper. Although it didn't erupt often, when it did, it manifested with elemental force; on several occasions over the years, he'd had to hold her back from some reckless action...

Was that why she'd run for the Priory? In the grip of her temper, had she, perhaps, concluded that he'd raised her hopes regarding love purely on a whim, only to cruelly dash them by consorting with another woman?

He forced himself to face the prospect that she might have decided to cut him out of her life.

It was a battle to haul himself away from the abyss that notion conjured. He managed it only by reminding himself—again—that Therese was far more likely to confront any demons that dared block her path rather than run screaming from them.

He allowed his gaze to roam her face and, deliberately steering his mind in what he hoped would be a more profitable direction, wondered how best to proceed when she awoke. That left him reviewing what he'd wanted to achieve in starting down the track of openly acknowledging that their marriage was a love-match. Put simply, he'd done it because he'd wanted more; he'd wanted to claim what he'd realized was there to be claimed.

He'd wanted all the benefits other Cynster couples had seized and made theirs, with their love for each other openly acknowledged and embraced by both husband and wife.

That initial motive might have been selfish, but he'd known even then that, once she understood that the possibility was there, Therese would want to claim that prize every bit as avidly as he.

Wanting more; it all boiled down to that. Looking back over the past weeks, cataloguing her encouraging reactions, he felt confident that she, too, yearned to achieve the same, utterly compelling goal.

A shared purpose, then, one focused on recrafting their union from what it had been into what it could be, which encompassed and promised so much more.

When she woke, he would have to convince her of that—of their "shared purpose" and all aspects of that "more." To do so, he would need to reveal all, the complete and undisguised truth of their marriage.

Under his unwavering gaze, her lashes fluttered. Her lids tightened as if she was about to open her eyes.

Hope surging, he sat up, but before he could reach out and take her hand, her lids eased, and her lashes stilled, and she sank into deep slumber once more.

With his gaze locked on her face, he waited, but she didn't stir again.

He sighed and slumped back in the armchair.

No more prevarication, no more oblique and ambiguous utterances.

If he had to bare his soul to convince her of the truth—that he had always loved her as she'd loved him—he would. That was all the plan he needed.

Consciousness returned to Therese in a long, slow slide as if she—her mind—was falling into place after having been absent for quite some time.

She was warm and comfortable; for long moments, she didn't move, then slowly, she raised her lids.

The first thing she saw was entirely unexpected. A dragon statue...no, it was the dragon figurine she'd seen on the first day of the exhibition!

She blinked and focused on the dragon, poised to launch into the air, flames curving from its nostrils, its wings spread wide. She drank in the superb craftsmanship, displayed not just in the golden shape but also in the exceptional coloring of the iridescent enamel scales and the glittering jewels artfully embedded here and there, scattering the light.

Unable to help herself, she freed a hand from the covers and reached out to turn the figurine so she could admire the coloration on the dragon's back. The colors coruscated like living fire—yellows, oranges, and every shade of red.

Running a fingertip down the dragon's spine, she smiled. Then she wondered how it came to be there. She knew Victoria had noticed the little dragon, even before Therese had; she'd seen Victoria ahead of her, examining the statue, and she'd assumed Prince Albert would buy it for the queen. Apparently not; after all, there had been many exquisite items displayed to catch the queen's eye.

Still smiling, Therese remembered talking to the Russian jeweler. Among other things, he'd assured her the figurine was one of a kind. Yet here it was; she stroked the dragon again, confirming that it was in no way a figment of her imagination. At the exhibition, while she'd admired the statue, Devlin had been watching and waiting on her a few yards away. Given it was on the table by her bed, presumably he had bought it for her.

Her smile deepened; her birthday was nearing, and he must have remembered...

But why give it to her now?

She blinked, then blinked again as more-recent memories flooded into her brain. Events unfurled in a rush, then a torrent.

She remembered the crash. Remembered what followed. In her mind's eye, she saw Devlin walking through the chaos of the aftermath toward her and experienced again the huge upswell of relief...before she'd weakened and fallen.

Her last visual memory was of Devlin's face—of his relief, so deep and utterly unshuttered on first seeing her, being overtaken by, then erased by, concern for her.

Her last tactile memory was of his strong arms catching her as she'd sagged toward the ground.

She frowned. Why had she been on the train? Had they been traveling to the Priory? She couldn't remember...then the murky mists clouding her memory thinned, and she did.

She remembered it all.

How she and Devlin had grown closer, how happy she'd been about that, what he'd said early that morning, and what she had said in reply... then she'd seen him with the woman in Covent Garden. The emotions that had erupted in that moment remained sharp and clear, but now lacked the power they'd earlier possessed, the immediacy and urgency and sheer *painfulness* that had derailed her mind and sent her running in full-blown retreat.

In hindsight, her reasons for taking the train to the Priory were no longer as obvious, as convincing and compelling, as she'd thought they'd been.

She blinked and refocused on the dragon. The spine had warmed where her finger had been stroking.

Why was it there?

Puzzled, she glanced around, confirming that she was, as she'd assumed, in her own bed. The room was dim, with the curtains tightly drawn, but the quality of the light seeping past them told her it was full daylight outside.

Frowning, she returned her gaze to the figurine, then looked past it. Shrouded in gloom, Devlin sat slumped in an armchair.

His eyes were closed, and his chin rested on his neckcloth. His hands were clasped over his waist, and his chest rose and fell in a slow, regular rhythm; he was fast asleep, but that wasn't what caused her to stare. His coat was rumpled and smudged, his linen looked limp, his hair bore evidence of him having raked his hand through it multiple times, leaving it badly tousled, and his chin bore the dark shadow of a beard.

He looked more disreputable than she'd ever seen him, as if he hadn't left the room since, presumably, he'd carried her there.

She straightened her legs and turned the other way—to check if there was anyone else present—only to feel a stabbing pain at the back of her head. Raising her other hand, she encountered a bandage. Gingerly, she traced the band, then warily prodded the wound it covered and quickly thought better of that. Carefully, she returned to her side and her previous, unpainful position.

Her gaze went to Devlin, and she saw his eyes were open. But other than lifting his head to look at her, he hadn't moved.

He caught her gaze. "We think you were struck by your dressing case, when it fell on you during the crash."

"Oh. Yes." Her voice was scratchy. She swallowed and managed, "The children? The staff?"

"All are well." His hazel gaze appeared dark in the gloom. "Bar a few bruises, no one was hurt except you." He paused, then added, "We think the loss of blood, compounded by the effort of helping and organizing everyone, was what caused you to faint and slide into unconsciousness."

Without shifting her eyes from his, she reached out to the dragon, again stroking the line between the flaring wings with one fingertip. "And this?"

His gaze deflected to the figurine.

Her voice strengthened. "How does it come to be here?"

For a moment, he watched her stroke the dragon, then he hauled in a huge breath, sat up, and scrubbed his hands over his face. Then he lowered his hands; letting them dangle between his knees, he met her gaze. "I hope you like it. I saw you admire it at the opening of the exhibition, and"—his lips twisted wryly—"perhaps unsurprisingly, it reminded me of you, so when, last week, I saw it was still unsold, I made the jeweler an offer. He waited until yesterday, the exhibition's last day, in case someone else was willing to pay more, then he sent me a message in the morning, and in the afternoon, after visiting the bank, I went to his lodgings to pay the sum I'd offered and fetch it."

She stared at him. In her mind, she saw him enter the house near Covent Garden...

Her wits lurched, and her heart sank, then abruptly rose. She suddenly felt lightheaded again. "Where was the jeweler lodging?"

"He, his wife, and his assistants had rented rooms in a house in Henrietta Street." When she blinked, he elaborated, "Just west of Covent Garden market." As if only then remembering, he patted his coat pocket, then drew out a crumpled sheet. He glanced at it, then held it out. "Here's his letter accepting my offer. The address is there."

Her wits reeling, her emotions in turmoil, her thoughts in utter disarray, she stopped touching the dragon and took the note.

Ignoring the twinges from her head, she shifted and wriggled up to sit against her pillows, raised the note, and read it.

She looked at Devlin. "*That's* what you were doing in Covent Garden. Buying me the dragon." There was no question in the words.

Her gaze flicked to the dragon, but immediately returned to him in time to see him wryly wince.

"It seemed like a good idea at the time."

Feeling helpless and hating that he had no idea how to manage this conversation, Devlin leaned back in the armchair and met her eyes. All he could do was tell her the truth, all of it. "I'd been trying to find ways to show you that I loved you. When I saw that the dragon was still unsold, it seemed...fated, somehow. I wasn't surprised that Monsieur Faberge waited until the last day to accept my offer, but I hadn't expected him to be leaving for the Continent so soon." He tipped his head at the note she still held. "As you saw, they hoped to be away by dawn today. I think the cost of putting up in London was more than they'd anticipated, which was why they'd ended staying in Covent Garden."

He paused, then his face hardening, went on, "The woman you saw greet me was Madame Faberge, and given what I'd agreed to pay for the figurine, it wasn't surprising that she smiled on me with such delight. I gathered she was hugely relieved to have secured a decent price for the dragon, rather than have to take it home and pray they could sell it somewhere else. Faberge had made it specifically for the exhibition, hoping to sell it to the queen, only she was more interested in diamonds."

Therese had lowered the letter. When she continued to stare at him as if she wasn't seeing him so much as working her way through his words, he drew in a slow breath, waited until she refocused on him, and locked his gaze with hers. "I told you I loved you, and I do. Totally, unreservedly, and irrevocably, with all my heart. And I know—have always known—that you love me, and I value your love more than words can say. If you believe nothing else, accept nothing else, please understand that I would never, ever, do anything to in any way damage what we have, what we share." He paused, then voice lowering, amended, "What I desperately hope we still share."

She blinked, and apology—deeply felt, urgent, and transparently sincere—filled her face, her eyes. Releasing the note, she reached out to him. Instinctively, he took her proffered hand, and she clutched his fingers. "I am *so very sorry* that I doubted you." She blinked again, and he realized tears were brimming in her eyes; he'd hardly ever seen her cry.

Before he could do more than tighten his grip on her fingers, she rushed on, "I *should* have known better—known *you* better." She squeezed his fingers even more tightly. "I should have trusted you, especially after you'd told me you loved me. I know you never lie, not to me. My rational mind knew there had to be some reasonable, acceptable explanation. Child tried to tell me so, but I wouldn't listen—to him or to my saner self." Her gaze slid from his, and she shook her head as if, looking back, she was amazed at herself. "I couldn't think—not at all."

Her eyes returned to his face, searching beseechingly, then she shifted to bring her other hand to join the first, clasping his larger hand between hers as if through her touch, she was willing him to understand. "At the time, just the thought that you were there to visit some courtesan... Something inside me broke—shattered—and feelings rushed through and overwhelmed me. I *felt* so much, so painfully and powerfully, that I simply couldn't think at all." Her eyes steadied on his. "It was the most awful, dreadful feeling. I've never felt out of control like that, wholly hostage to my emotions. I felt so *hurt*." She pressed one hand to her chest. "So battered and bruised."

She studied his eyes, then simply repeated, "I'm so *very* sorry."

He felt her sincerity—the depth of it—and the underlying reassurance of her love washed over him. He let that sink in, then finally allowed his features to soften, his lips to faintly lift. Still holding her gaze, he quietly said, "After finding you by the side of a wrecked train and seeing you collapse"—he had to draw in a tight breath of his own—"I know all about *feeling too much*. About how emotions like love and fear can scramble one's brain. I hadn't ever felt like that, either."

He twined his fingers with hers, more firmly linking their hands. "If I hadn't had the children and the staff to see to—if I'd been allowed to think of only you and what you meant to me..." Reliving the moments all too vividly, he broke off, then raked his free hand through his hair, met her gaze, and admitted, "God alone knows what I would have done. I certainly wasn't capable of thinking rationally, not about anything to do with you."

She managed a weak, rather watery smile. "We are a pair, it seems. As Child said, we deserve each other."

He held her gaze, studying her eyes, then he shifted forward in the chair, separated their fingers, and retook her hands, one in each of his, gripping them firmly; her fingers curled over his, tightening in response. Fixing his eyes on hers, he looked deep into the silvery blue and stated, "Never doubt this. I love you. That hasn't changed over the past five and more years, and it's not going to change any time in the future. You are my world. You might not have known it, but from the very first instant I set eyes on you, you held my heart in your hands."

The words—unquestionably true and uttered with such conviction that she couldn't possibly doubt them—rang, bell-like, in Therese's ears. They sank into her, into her heart and into her soul, sending it soaring, yet at the same time, anchoring her. Grounding her. Making her whole and complete...

Then her brain caught up with the implication. She blinked, and all inclination to teariness vanished. *What?* Galvanized, she searched his eyes, but saw nothing beyond his usual, steady seriousness along with naked honesty.

His comment at Christopher's wedding popped into her mind. *"Perhaps your dear Christopher finally opened his eyes and took his cue from me."* And when she'd challenged him, he'd said, *"Oops."*

Oops because he hadn't meant to tell her what was, in effect, his truth?

She stared at him as numerous little pieces of the puzzle he'd become realigned and fell into place. Was what he'd just said the something he'd been working toward telling her with his various, annoyingly imprecise comments?

She decided she needed to hear his declaration again—and this time, clearly, without even the faintest possibility of misconstruction. She licked her lips and, her gaze still locked with his, asked, "Just what is it you're trying to tell me?"

Although his lips twisted in a faint grimace, his gaze didn't shift from hers. "I never thought to make this confession but…the truth is that I've always loved you—madly, deeply, irrevocably—from the very first. I hid it—from the world, but most especially from you—because…" His fingers tightened on hers. "Because I feared love. I feared the power love would—could—wield over me. I feared what love might do to me or, more specifically, what I might do for love."

He paused, then went on, "I thought love would change me, and in thinking that, I wasn't wrong, but I feared it would make me less of a man, when in fact, the opposite is true. Loving you made me so much more—made me into the man I could and should be. Loving you made me grow."

Caught in the moment, in the raw honesty of his revelations, she watched as his gaze grew distant and he seemed to search for words.

Eventually, he said, "The reason I was so misguided as to believe that love for my wife was something I should never own to…was that I took my parents' marriage, or at least how I saw it, as a pattern card. I knew my father loved my mother to distraction and that she loved him in return, but to me, it always seemed that his love for her made him weak. Less. That loving his wife prompted him to behave in ways that diminished him —in my eyes and, I assumed, in everyone else's."

He grimaced. "More recently, that everyone else who knew them seemed to see their relationship in a different, far more positive light made me question my conclusions. I was a child when I formed them, then I was away at school for a decade, and they'd both died by the time I came home from Oxford. From childhood, I never spent much time around either my father or my mother, and hardly any time at all with them together—possibly not enough time for an older, more mature me to open my eyes, see and realize, and adjust my thinking."

Somewhat ruefully, he refocused on her. "All of which is to say that I now accept that my child's view of my parents' marriage was false, a nonsense, and that the error was purely mine." He paused, then added, "Unfortunately, James and Veronica's tempestuous union only served to bolster my by-then-fixed antipathy over acknowledging love for one's spouse."

She squeezed his fingers. "But you were wrong about them—or at least, not right."

He nodded and looked at their linked hands. "I can see that now, but when I first met you, my antipathy was deeply rooted, and in using it to guide my interactions with you, I felt completely and arrogantly justified. I was confident I saw things clearly and that my path was the correct one to take."

She studied his for-once totally unguarded expression and took note of the self-annoyance, tinged with self-disgust and self-blame, that was so clearly etched in his features. The compulsion to ease some of that self-recrimination grew. Gently, she said, "Children tend to see things in black and white. Your sons certainly do, and I suspect your daughter will be even worse. Children make up their minds based on how they interpret what they think they see and hear, and they are always very certain they are correct, but children aren't adults—they lack an adult's sophistication at all levels of personal interaction. Children don't hear the nuances or see the shades of gray that adults routinely employ in dealing with each other."

He met her eyes; relief that she understood showed in his. "I always thought that my father gave way to my mother—acceded to her wishes over his own—far too often. It never occurred to me that he might have been perfectly willing to do so because he regarded her wants and needs as more important than his." He grimaced. "And my own character probably colored my judgment. By all accounts, I was a hedonistic little lordling. I never liked not getting my own way, so I never imagined that he—my father—might see things differently."

She smiled gently and held back words to the effect that he still didn't appreciate not getting his own way.

He looked at their hands again, then drew in a breath, blew it out, and said, "So that's why I approached our marriage as I did." Fleetingly, he glanced at her. "You thought I was only marginally interested—attracted to you, yes, but not looking for a wife, and that you had to pursue me and show me how perfect you would be in the role and badger and hound me until I agreed to front the altar."

Tilting her head, she studied his eyes. "And that was...not how it was?" She couldn't keep her tone from rising. She wasn't sure if she was aghast or amused. How many more secrets did he have?

He shook his head and returned his gaze to their hands. "That was me manipulating you. I know you thought the shoe was on the other foot"— he started absentmindedly playing with her fingers—"but it wasn't. From the moment I set eyes on you, I knew you were the one for me, but with my oh-so-entrenched position about not acknowledging love, I had to find some way to get you to the altar without admitting I loved you. You were a Cynster—I assumed you would demand some declaration of love, one I wasn't willing to give, so"—he threw her a sheepish look she was far more familiar with receiving from his sons—"I had to find some way around that. I asked about you and watched from afar until I felt I understood you and your reactions well enough to make a bid for what I wanted. I'd heard and seen you summarily reject any suitors who approached you in a conventional fashion—in fact, you turned a cold shoulder to any gentleman who pursued you. So I decided I would engage with you, but decline to pursue you and see if that piqued your interest."

"And it did." She regarded him with fascinated awe as the events of their courtship rolled through her mind, her perceptions shifting with the knowledge that it had been his hand steering them along, rather than, as she'd always believed, hers. The sheer audacity of it took her breath away. But then she refocused on him and the truly important point. "So all that time...?"

He understood what she was asking; steadily holding her gaze, he replied, "All that time, I was in love with you—head over heels, completely in thrall. It was frightening, truth be told, powerful and exhilarating and utterly compelling. I'd never felt anything like it, and of course, that only emphasized how dangerous love was and underscored how correct was my approach to marriage. I was convinced beyond question that I would be a fool—more, that I would be inviting disaster—if I admitted any of what I felt to you. Or to anyone, for that matter."

"So you hid it." No question; he had, extremely effectively. She studied him, feeling as if she was seeing him properly for the first time. "I never suspected, not even a little bit."

He grimaced and squeezed her fingers apologetically. "I know. I made sure that, from the first, you saw only what I wanted you to see and that you felt totally confident that you knew exactly what our marriage was based on. I was over the moon and so very grateful when I realized you loved me. It seemed that even Fate had decided to support my plans."

Gently, she reminded him, "I never said the words."

"I did everything I could not to let you—I didn't dare risk it. I feared that if you ever did say those three little words, something in me wouldn't be able to resist saying them back to you."

She studied him, sensing something of what, through the years, he'd battled to hold back, to rein in, and admitted, "I put the recent changes between us down to a maturing of our relationship." She tipped her head, her eyes steady on his. "That wasn't entirely wrong, was it? I just hadn't correctly seen the point we'd started out from."

His lips twisted in a faint grimace, and he nodded. "You thought I was coming to love you, when in fact I've loved you all along."

After a moment, he shook his head. "Where was I? Oh yes. From the beginning and through the early years of our marriage, I worked diligently to plant in your mind and nurture and establish the fiction I wanted you and everyone else to believe." He pulled a face. "And trust me when I say that my success in doing so has haunted me over the past months, ever since I realized that I would never be truly happy—that we both would never be as happy as we could be—until I made you understand what the actual reality of our marriage was and that I loved you in exactly the same way that you loved me. Only after I convinced you of that truth would we be able to claim the sort of marriage that, five years ago, I'd so stupidly turned my back on."

Her heart was giddily dancing, yet she remained utterly fascinated by his revelations. "What changed your mind?"

He looked at her with fond resignation. "Need you ask? Cynsters."

When her expression conveyed her bewilderment, he explained, "Your cousins and connections and their marriages. We've attended so many weddings and family events, and I saw—there, enacted in front of me—the reality of what love-matches could and should be. How strong and joyous and supportive such marriages are." He paused, then more quietly went on, "I felt such a coward for what I'd done to us, to our marriage. All of them had had the courage to embrace love, with all the joys and potential sorrows it can bring, but I...I'd hidden my love and refused the challenge. And that also meant that I'd kept you from having what you deserved."

Her heart somersaulted, but before she could respond, he continued, "I can't remember exactly when it happened, when the compulsion to rescript our marriage took unrelenting hold. It was before Christopher and Ellen's wedding, certainly, although that proved the last straw."

"That was why you made that strange comment at the wedding breakfast."

He looked sheepish again. "I didn't mean to say that—to blurt out those particular words. I..." He shrugged, looked down, then admitted, "Through these past weeks, while I've been trying to forge a path to my —our—new goal, sometimes, it's been as if some power inside me got impatient and, when an opening occurred, pushed me to simply speak and tell you, but another part of me kept getting in the way, and instead of being clear, I'd be..."

"Obfuscating, oblique, elliptical?"

He grimaced. "Yes. All that."

Truly puzzled, she shook her head at him. "Why didn't you simply tell me?"

He raised his gaze from their hands and met her eyes. "Would you have believed me? Or would you have thought I was up to something in trying to make you believe in a scenario that you were convinced beyond question wasn't true?"

She blinked at him. He waited. He'd been blatantly honest; she had to be, too. "I...don't know." After a moment, she grimaced and acknowledged, "Probably not."

He nodded. "And if you didn't believe me, there wouldn't have been any easy way to win back the trust I would have lost by trying." He drew breath and went on, "So reasoning that actions spoke louder and more convincingly than words, I set out to show you that I loved you." He arched a brow at her. "Did I succeed? Before my declaration of yesterday morning?"

The events of the past weeks flowed through her mind, and she smiled. "Yes. Before you told me you loved me, I certainly suspected something had changed in the way you thought of me."

"Thank heaven I got that right, at least."

She smiled slightly, but the events of yesterday and all the powerful, turbulent emotions that had rushed through her had jerked open a mental door she'd firmly shut more than a decade ago. His revelations, his honesty in making them, his push to change the acknowledged foundation of their marriage to reflect what she now accepted was their true reality... all that demanded that she face her own demons.

He was studying her face, no doubt worrying over what she was thinking; when she forced herself to meet his eyes, he was frowning slightly. She drew breath and said, "As confessions seem to be the order of our day, it wasn't only you pretending to something that wasn't true— it wasn't only you keeping up a false façade."

Shaken by what she now understood of herself, for a second, she closed her eyes, then she opened them and, clinging to his gaze and the anchor of his touch, said, "Long ago—long before we met—after the end of my second Season, I made up my mind what my marriage would be like. And it wasn't a typical Cynster love-match. By then, I was absolutely convinced that would never come my way. I knew, by then, how others, but particularly the male of the species, saw me. I was too bossy, too determined, too willful, too strong-willed. Too so many things that it was clear that no gentleman would ever love me—not as I wished to be loved."

While she'd spoken, he'd shifted closer. Now his eyes flared in protest, and raising her hand, he pressed a kiss to her knuckles, but before he could speak, she rushed on, "Like you, I harbored an entrenched belief. With all the evidence around me, I had to accept that the adage that all Cynsters marry for love was true, but I'd never heard it said that we had to be loved in return, only that *we* would love. So"—she drew in a breath and forged on—"I quartered the ton, searching for the man I could and would love, and found you." She smiled rather ruefully at him. "In oh so many ways, you were *exactly* as I'd imagined you would be."

His eyes, locked with hers, widened in understanding. "My tack in pretending not to love you while you loved me fitted the prescription you'd created for your husband."

She nodded. "You were perfect in *every* way. So, you see, like you, I, too, turned my back on love—on the love-match we could have had—and happily accepted you as you pretended to be. I told myself I would be content with that and that such a one-sided love-match was all—" Her voice broke, but she swallowed and forced herself to go on, "All I deserved."

"*No*, my darling." His voice was low and fierce. "You have that wrong—every bit as wrong as I've ever been. You deserve to be loved exactly as I love you." He pressed a fervent kiss to her fingers. "To madness and beyond."

A smile threatened to break through her seriousness, but determinedly, she went on, "Be that as it may, as a result of my, apparently misguided, acceptance of our half love-match, I never pressed for more in our marriage. I never looked for your love or did anything to encourage it, because that would have meant admitting that beneath my bravado, behind my attempt to dictate my own expectations, I really did want a proper Cynster love-match, one with love on both sides."

She closed her other hand over their linked fingers and looked into his eyes. "You showing me you loved me, then declaring that and convincing me you truly did, opened a door in my mind and pushed what I really yearned for into the light. Over the past day since you told me you loved me, through my assumption that you'd betrayed me, through my heedless flight and all that flowed from that, I've realized that, no matter how often I've told myself that I've been happy with the way our marriage has been, underneath, I've always craved the full Cynster experience—to love and be loved."

He searched her eyes. "That was why seeing me with Madame Faberge affected you so powerfully. You thought I'd offered you the most shining of prizes—the one that your heart has always truly craved—only to cruelly snatch it away."

She nodded. Turning her hand in his hold, she squeezed his fingers. "You've told me your truth. My truth—the one I've finally seen clearly and that I'm ready to own to—is that I *want* to be loved by you as much and to the same extent as I love you. What you're offering me now is all and everything my heart truly desires."

His smile was everything she needed it to be. Raising their linked hands, he brushed a gentler kiss to her fingers. "It seems that in the matter of loving each other, we've been playing games—two separate, idiotic, and unnecessary games—you and I."

She nodded again. "So it seems."

There was a glow in her eyes, a softness in her features, a quality in her smile that Devlin had never seen before—as if, through the exchange of their hearts' secrets, the true Therese had been freed.

Freed to love—freed to be loved.

He drew in a breath and, all but lost in the glory of her eyes, declared, "We are a pair, right enough. But our reality, my darling, is here and now. Whatever our past mistakes, our past weaknesses and shortcomings, we've seen the light. Can we go forward from here?"

Her smile conveyed all the joy and ready agreement he could wish for. "That would be my greatest, most fervent wish."

He basked in the warmth of her silver-blue gaze. "It's mine as well, so I believe that settles it." He rose from the chair and, without releasing her hand, swung to prop his hip beside her on the bed, then leaned over her and kissed the lips she tipped her head back and offered.

A long, slow, achingly simple kiss ensued, one laden with love, acknowledged and claimed, and with the shining promise of a glorious future informed by, anchored by, and invested with the irrefutable power of mutual love. The caress spun out and on, each feeding the other, each hungry and needing, until reluctantly, he raised his head.

He drew in a strained breath, glanced at the white band encircling her head, and grimaced. "Sadly, your wound precludes any immediate demonstration of our mutual ardor."

Therese stared at him. "Really?" When he tried to ease back, she gripped his hand tighter. "It doesn't hurt that much. Truly."

He hesitated, and she hoped, but then his features firmed and he shook his head. "I've no doubt that Sanderson will call later today to check on your recovery, and if he discovers his handiwork dramatically disarranged, he isn't above hauling me over the coals, earl or not."

She huffed, released him, and slumped on the pillows, openly frustrated. "He's not above lecturing me, either."

Devlin grinned. "Never mind." He leaned over her again and dropped a kiss on her nose. Sitting back, he met her gaze. "As we're already married, we can't have another wedding, but I intend to tell you that I love you several times each day—just so you don't forget—and I will endeavor to show you as well, in all that I do, every single day for the rest of our lives."

She smiled gloriously; as vows went, she was delighted with that one. She reached out and caressed the rough line of his stubbled jaw. "And for as long as we live, I'll treasure your love and love you in return, with all my heart."

"That," he said, capturing her hand and brushing a kiss to her fingertips, "is all we can do and all we can ask."

She drew in a deeper breath, then glanced at the window. "I'd better get up and get washed and dressed—and you need to wash and change as well." She wrinkled her nose at him. "I was thinking before you woke that you look thoroughly disreputable."

He laughed. "All your fault, my lady." But he obediently rose from the bed, retaining his hold on her hand to help her up.

Making use of the support, she pushed back the covers, swung her legs over the bed's side, and sat on the edge.

"How's your head?"

She looked up to see him peering anxiously at her face. "It aches a bit, but is by no means unbearable."

He didn't look convinced.

Ignoring that, she poked at the band. "What did Sanderson say?"

Devlin described the wound and Sanderson's predictions. "He said you would probably wake sometime in the afternoon."

She opened her eyes wide. "What time is it?"

He glanced at the clock on her dresser across the room. "Nearly half past eleven."

"Good Lord! The children will be wondering what's become of me." She looked at him. "Of us."

"I'm sure they will have slept in." Dryly, he added, "They had a disturbed night, if you recall."

She huffed and waved a hand at him, urging him to step back and help her up.

His lips set, but he grasped her hands and drew her to her feet.

He shifted to her side and slung an arm about her waist, clearly worried that she might faint again, but learning all she had, understanding all she now did of herself as well as him, had filled her with confidence and calmed her previously turbulent emotions. She felt strong and steady.

She smiled reassuringly, gently eased her hand from his hold, and stepped away from his hovering support. "Can you ring for Parker?"

He looked adorably uncertain, but after waiting for several moments to confirm she was steady on her feet, he crossed the room to the bellpull. "She would, of course, have been here, watching over you, but I ordered her away. I wanted us to be alone when you woke."

"Thank you," she replied with feeling. He tugged the bellpull, then she waved him away. "You'd better go and make yourself presentable, or you'll frighten the staff, let alone the children."

He hesitated; she could see him debating whether or not to stay until Parker arrived.

She hid a grin. "Go—or Parker will be shocked and then disapproving. You know she will."

He huffed, but finally turned and headed for the door to his rooms. "I'll wait on the other side of the door until she arrives. If you fall, call, and I'll come running."

She smiled.

With his hand on the doorknob, he halted and looked back. "Wait for me. We'll go up to the nursery together."

He was all earl now. Still smiling, she tipped her head in acquiescence.

As the door closed behind him, she arched her brows and murmured, "I suspect that, from now on, we'll be doing a lot of things together."

She was looking forward to forging their new, improved, love-based marriage with a full and eager heart.

Half an hour later, her hand in Devlin's, she walked into the nursery. From the petulant not to say grumpy looks on the children's faces, they remained unsettled, but the instant they spied her, their expressions transformed into ones of joy, and they pelted across the room toward her.

"Mama!"

"You're awake!"

Beaming herself, she slipped her fingers from Devlin's, crouched, and opened her arms.

"Careful," Devlin warned, and Spencer and Rupert, almost upon her, slowed enough not to cannon into her.

The pair flung themselves into her arms; carefully avoiding her bandaged head, they hugged her hard and clung. Then they paused and, with Therese, waited for Horry, squealing and toddling as fast as she could, to join them.

The curly-haired tot threw herself at Therese, and Therese laughed and closed her arms, gently squeezing all three small bodies to her.

Spencer and Rupert pressed kisses to her cheeks.

Not to be outdone, Horry planted a smacking kiss on Therese's lips.

She smiled at each of them. "Yes. I'm here."

Devlin's hand rested supportively on her shoulder. She looked up and met his eyes and saw love, unshielded, blazing there.

The response, instinctive and powerful, that welled and flowed through her, shining in her eyes and glowing in her features, spread in all its golden glory about them.

This was their new reality. This joy, this shared commitment, was the foundation on which they would build their future—one strengthened by, informed by, guided and protected by the greatest power in heaven and on earth.

Therese hugged the children to her, smiled into Devlin's eyes, and mouthed the words "I love you."

His face lit, and his features softened. "And I love you."

It really was that simple. That profound.

They'd found their way through the maze of the games they'd played with each other and, even more, with themselves. They'd won through to emerge stronger, more confident, more secure. Now, they could and would go forward and, hand in hand, create the future both craved—

loving and being loved in a marriage openly, visibly, and in every way that mattered anchored in love.

∼

By the time her birthday rolled around nine days later, Therese felt thoroughly vindicated in her belief in their new direction.

Two days after the crash, their household had traveled by coach to Alverton Priory so she could recover from her injury in the peace and quiet of the countryside. Now, after a week of recuperation and rejuvenation, as arm in arm, she and Devlin strolled the Priory lawns, watching the children—closely attended by Gillian, Patty, and Dennis, all striving to ensure that none of the three enterprising youngsters ended in the lake —Therese was ready to acknowledge that one could, indeed, be so happy, so filled with happiness, that one's heart felt as if it might literally burst.

At that moment, she couldn't imagine her life being in any way more perfect.

Over the past week, she and Devlin had steadily rescripted their lives, more definitely intertwining the individual strands to create a framework for their shared life that was significantly more solid and defined. She rode out with him after breakfast most mornings; as with all Cynsters, she loved to ride, but had never liked to ride alone, so the habit had withered over the years since their marriage. Now, alongside Devlin, she roamed far and wide, making the most of the prime horse-riding country surrounding the Priory.

While with each of them having different responsibilities both within and beyond their household, their days were still largely spent apart, their evenings had become cherished times. Especially in this season, they were most often free to dine in private and spend their evening hours together, talking of various happenings, discussing business and politics, and sharing the events, be they large or small, serious or silly, that filled their days.

And when night fell, they retired to the bedroom they now openly shared. There, the little enameled dragon stood guard by their bed, in which they came together, sharing all they felt for each other, further exploring all they had claimed, all they now so avidly embraced, with an ardor more intense than ever before, wrapped in a closeness that reached to and bound their souls as they reveled in an intimacy that grew ever more profound.

Perfect. Simply perfect.

Smiling with quiet joy, she tipped her face up to the weak sunshine. Just as he'd vowed, in everything he did, the man walking by her side showed her his love. That emotion now permeated every act, every word; it shone through—unscreened, unrestrained, unfettered.

She thought of that morning—her birthday morning—and how he'd chosen to wake her.

Her smile deepened. *Definitely unfettered.*

Devlin was about to ask Therese what had occasioned the particular smile that was curving her lips when hoofbeats coming up the gravel drive drew his attention.

A second later, Child rode into view, mounted on a glossy chestnut.

Therese had seen him, too. "He must be visiting his parents."

Both Devlin and Therese glanced at the children, then reassured that all was well with their brood, they redirected their steps to where Child had drawn rein in the forecourt.

Child dismounted, hitched his reins to the tail of one of the carved fish that graced the fountain in the forecourt, and came to meet them.

Devlin halted with Therese at the edge of the lawn.

A charming smile on his face, Child strode up, halted before Therese, and swept her an elegantly elaborate bow. "Happy birthday, dear Therese." He straightened and grinned. "I came to offer my felicitations. How's your head?"

"Entirely recovered, thank you." Therese smiled at Child with sunny assurance. "I understand I have you to thank for sending Devlin hotfoot after me."

Along with the rest of England, Child had learned of the train wreck on the Great Northern Line on the morning after the crash. Unlike the rest of England, he'd known Therese had intended to be on the train and that Devlin hadn't returned after trying to catch her and his family at the station. By midmorning, Child had been knocking on the door of Alverton House, to be told by Portland—who, Devlin had later been informed, had taken pity on Child's obvious distress—that Therese had been wounded but was recovering, and the children and Devlin himself were unharmed.

Child had called again later in the afternoon, and Devlin had descended from the nursery to reassure his old friend that Therese was, indeed, recovering, but that she was in no condition to meet anyone at that time. Child had been openly relieved and, in his usual glib manner, had waved away Devlin's heartfelt thanks for the warning Child had remained behind to deliver after Therese had quit the house.

Now, in response to Therese, Child arched his brows. "I sent him after you, yes." Child leveled a teasing look at Devlin. "The 'hotfoot' was all him."

Gloriously smug, Therese tightened her hold on Devlin's arm and glanced up at him with love gilding her features. "Yes, I know." She looked back at Child.

Devlin saw Child blink as if dazzled by the glow in Therese's face.

Her smile only brightened, and she went on, "But your help was crucial, and on my behalf and that of the children and staff, too, I thank you from the bottom of my heart."

Child looked uncomfortable and endeavored to reassemble his usual charming mask. "Think nothing of it." He looked at Devlin. "Any old friend would have done the same."

A scream of fury—from Horry—sliced through the bucolic peace. Both Devlin and Therese turned their heads to see the little mite tearfully pointing to a small toy boat drifting away from the shore and Dennis rushing up with a hook on a long pole to catch it and draw it back.

Responding to Therese's unvoiced need to return to the children, Devlin stepped back and turned in that direction, catching Child's eye as he did. "Come—walk with us."

Child readily fell in on Therese's other side, and they crossed the lawn, with Devlin and Child exchanging comments about developments in various business and investment spheres. Despite considerable subtle probing, Devlin had still not succeeded in learning exactly what business enterprise or enterprises Child had been involved with in America; indeed, for some reason, Child was keeping that particular card very close to his chest. "Why?" was the point that most intrigued Devlin.

They halted a little way from where the three children were lined up along the shore, with the nursemaids and the footman once again hovering. With the long string attached to her boat's prow restored to her chubby hand, Horry was once more all smiles and delight. Her brothers had a small flotilla of craft bobbing parallel to the shore. Devlin was pleased to see both boys try to show Horry how to make her boat sail along with theirs as they attempted to perform some complicated maneuver on the water.

Although Therese hadn't contributed to the conversation, Devlin knew she'd been listening and absorbing every comment, and it was she who finally asked Child outright, "What business did you engage in over there? Evidently, it was at least mildly successful."

Devlin didn't miss the mask that slid over Child's features, and he was sure Therese didn't, either.

Sliding his hands into his breeches pockets, Child lightly shrugged. "This and that. I moved around." His gaze shifted to the children. "I say, Devlin, are those boats the ones we used to play with?"

Devlin shared a sidelong glance with Therese as he evenly replied, "I believe so."

Unsurprisingly, Therese turned the conversation to social matters, asking after Child's parents. "They must have been so thrilled to see you," she observed.

Having visited the duke and duchess the day before, Therese and Devlin knew that Child hadn't been expected at Ancaster Park and that his appearance there would have been the first time his parents had set eyes on him for over nine years.

Child snorted, but there was affection in the sound. "Mama fell on my neck—literally—while Papa wrung my hand and thumped my back so hard I could barely stand. Then they called for the fatted calf to be slain—you wouldn't have thought I'd ever written a word, while in fact, I made sure to send letters every few months."

"What about Roderick and Pamela?" Devlin asked, referring to Child's older brother and his wife.

"They're still up north, thank heavens, but I've been warned they'll be home any day." Child sighed and met Devlin's eyes. "You know Roddy will lecture me and hold forth on issues about which he has no actual idea. My tongue's going to be black and blue from biting it to stop myself from wasting my time arguing."

Devlin smiled commiseratingly; despite Child's nine-year absence, he doubted anything between the brothers would have changed. "Sadly, I can't say that Roddy has grown any wiser over the years."

"So I had supposed," Child grumbled. He glanced at Therese. "I might have to seek refuge over here."

Something Child had always done whenever Roddy's pomposity had scaled heights too great to bear.

Therese smiled—glowingly—and reached out to squeeze Child's arm. "You know you'll always be welcome here."

Again, Devlin sensed that Child—looking at Therese, then at Devlin—was growing uncomfortable.

Before Child could respond, still smiling, Therese continued, "And as it's nearly time for tea, please do stay."

Child's answering smile was all glib charm. "Thank you, but no. I'd better get back to the Park, or Mama will start to worry that, in light of Roddy's imminent arrival, I've slipped the leash and ridden back to London."

Exchanging easy, undemanding comments about the local hunt, the three of them recrossed the lawn to the forecourt and Child's waiting horse.

Therese renewed her invitation, but Child held firm.

He swung up to the saddle, gathered the reins, and looked down at them with an easy smile.

"I daresay," Therese said, smiling serenely up at him, "that we'll see you here over Christmas, and then once we're all back in town and the Season starts, you'll have to allow me to help you find a lady of your own. I know your Mama and aunts are keen to see you settled, and you have to admit that you're not getting any younger."

Devlin couldn't help grinning at Child's horrified expression; he suspected Therese would assume it was feigned, but Devlin was fairly certain it wasn't.

"Huh." Child stared at Therese as if he'd only just noticed how supremely dangerous she might be. "You really don't need to bestir yourself on my account. After all, Roddy has two sons, so there's really no need for me to set foot in parson's snare." Before Therese could reply, Child's tone firmed. "I truly don't want, much less need, a bride."

After saluting them and wheeling his horse, as if to soften his rejection of Therese's assistance, he called, "I will, however, look you up at Christmas, and I'll certainly see you in London next year."

With a last wave, he urged his horse down the drive.

Therese watched him go, then still smiling but now rather smugly, shook her head. "He's forgotten how the ton works."

Devlin watched Child's dwindling figure as he turned his horse through the trees, heading across the Priory's park toward his family's home. "He's fooling himself." Then he glanced at Therese and arched his brows. "But who am I to cast stones?"

She laughed and squeezed his arm. "At least you saw the error of your ways—and ensured that I did, too, and also that I revised my own misguided opinions to boot." She turned him toward the house and, as they ambled in that direction, said, "Hopefully, soon, Child will see the light, too."

Devlin dipped his head and murmured, "Don't hold your breath. There's something he's holding back, and as yet, I have no clue what it is."

She met his eyes. "I've noticed the same thing, and I don't have any idea, either."

Devlin grinned rather diabolically. "That's a joint mission we can look forward to undertaking next year—winkling Child's secret from him."

"Indeed." Therese glanced across the lawn to where the children were still absorbed. "We'd better summon our brood for their tea, or Nanny will grumble."

They paused before the front steps, and Devlin called, and after entrusting their navy to Dennis and Patty, the boys came pelting across the grass, with Horry holding Gillian's hand and shrieking as she toddled in their wake as fast as her little legs would carry her.

The boys mobbed Therese, while Horry made for her father. Letting go of Gillian's hand, the golden-haired moppet wound her arms around one of Devlin's legs and clutched like a limpet. He laughed and ruffled her curls, then the crunch of boots on gravel had everyone turning to see Martin come striding around the house from the direction of the stable.

Martin's face lit. "There you all are!"

The children promptly forsook their parents and raced to Martin; he was already firmly established as their favorite relative.

He'd arrived midmorning, having driven himself from London in his newly acquired curricle, which he'd proudly displayed to Devlin, Therese, and the boys. He'd brought wishes from the rest of her family, along with a quantity of gifts, and had happily accepted Devlin and Therese's invitation to stay for a few days, admitting that he'd come hoping to pick Devlin's brain about setting up a business venture.

Keen to get the air of the capital out of his lungs, after lunch, Martin had gone riding.

While the boys grasped his jacket and pelted him with questions, Horry rushed up, holding up her arms, and Martin swooped and scooped up the little girl, settling her in his arms as he answered her brothers' eager queries.

After spending some minutes smiling fondly at the sight, Therese shooed the children toward the house. "If you don't get up to the nursery soon, your tea will be cold, and Nanny Sprockett will be cross."

At the mention of food, the boys cheered; deserting Martin, they raced up the steps and into the house. Martin handed Horry to the waiting Gillian, and once she, Horry, Patty, and Dennis had followed the boys inside, Therese, Devlin, and Martin climbed the steps and ambled into the stone-flagged hall.

Alverton Priory was a rambling old house, built around an old baronial hall that had been added to by successive generations of the Cader family until it had grown to the sprawling, comfortable home it now was.

The children's voices echoed down the ornately carved wooden stairs, the sound bringing a smile to Therese's lips, a smile she noted Devlin shared.

This was their principal home, the house in which they would live and love for the rest of their days. More than at any other of the earldom's houses, their hearts were anchored there.

They knew their greatest peace in this place, and to add yet more joy to their happiness, she and Devlin were expecting a new addition to their family next year.

She felt her smile deepen as, on Devlin's arm, she walked across the huge old hall and sensed all around her that most precious of commodities—love, open and true, made manifest in every action, in every expression. That emotion now bound them so much more tightly than it had before, spilling its glory onto every small task, filling every moment.

This was the life she and Devlin now shared. She slanted a glance at him. Even though he was conversing with Martin, the change in his face was obvious to her. He was happy, truly happy, now that they'd embraced their love and blossomed into their new reality.

She looked ahead and determinedly steered her husband and brother toward the drawing room while, in her mind, she contemplated the certainty, unshakeable and absolute, that now lived in her heart and reached deep to her soul.

For her and Devlin, *this* was their heaven on earth, and now they'd claimed it, neither would ever let go.

EPILOGUE

DECEMBER 27, 1951. SOMERSHAM PLACE, CAMBRIDGESHIRE.

*D*evlin lounged by the side of the large, third-floor nursery of Somersham Place, principal seat of the Dukes of St. Ives. With his hips propped against an old sideboard, he watched with fond amusement as Therese, seated on a battered chaise, kept a close eye on their three children, sprawled on the rug before her. All three, Horry included, were attempting to play with—or perhaps lead astray—the Carrick girls, who were two-year-old twins, four or so months older than Horry. Therese's cousin Lucilla, the twins' mother, sat beside Therese and also observed the group. Judging by the expressions that flitted over Therese's and Lucilla's faces as they exchanged low-voiced comments, they were swapping anecdotes and predictions, as fond mamas were wont to do.

Elsewhere in the large, comfortably furnished room were no less than five babes in arms, although the eldest, Richard Cynster, first child of Marcus Cynster and his wife, Niniver, was making a determined bid to walk under his own steam. Marcus and Niniver hovered, trying not to laugh at Richard's stubborn bid to master the elusive skill of balancing on his sturdy legs.

Next in age came the ducal grandson, Sylvester Gyles Cynster, currently perched on the hip of his mother, Antonia, and evidently fascinated by the pearl choker circling her throat. His father, Sebastian, in between chatting with his wife and his heavily pregnant cousin, Prudence, tried to distract his son, but Sylvester was having none of it; pearls were clearly more interesting than his papa.

Ensconced in one of the large armchairs, Thomas Carrick, the twins' father, jiggled his heir, Manachan Carrick, who was only days younger than Sylvester, on his knee. Thomas was chatting with Cleo, Michael Cynster's wife, who was standing by the armchair and rocking her sleeping daughter, Katherine Louise, in her arms. Katherine was barely three months old, but she wasn't the youngest there. That title belonged to Andrew Royce Varisey, who was not quite two months old and presently draped over the shoulder of his mother, Louisa, and sound asleep.

Given how powerful Andrew's lungs had earlier proved to be, everyone was grateful for that.

Devlin raised his gaze and surveyed the room. A gaggle of nannies and nursemaids was clustered at the far end, ready to resume responsibility for their charges when the parents were summoned downstairs for the massive celebratory luncheon. The huge, sprawling house was packed to the rafters with family and connections; the Somersham Place Cynster family Christmas gathering was not an event one missed, not if one wanted to remain in the good graces of Honoria, Duchess of St. Ives, and her socially powerful, grande-dame cronies, chief amongst whom was Therese's mother, Patience.

On Devlin's left, Christopher, Therese's older brother, was chatting to Michael, the current duke's second son, while on Devlin's other side, Deaglan Fitzgerald, who had married Prudence Cynster earlier that year, was swapping tales of—of all things—goats with Ellen, Christopher's recently acquired wife.

While 1851 might have been a year of births within this group, there were already three more happy events slated for the year to come. Deaglan and Prudence were preparing to welcome their first child in February, and Christopher and Ellen hoped to do the same in the middle of the year. Added to the son or daughter Devlin and Therese anticipated adding to their brood, plus the likelihood of further additions to the tally as the months rolled on, the coming year looked set to further expand the ever-widening circle of the family.

Drake Varisey, Marquess of Winchelsea, ambled up. He nodded to Devlin and turned to stand beside him, ostensibly surveying the room. Devlin wasn't surprised when, after Drake confirmed that his wife, Louisa, was engrossed in a discussion with Marcus and Niniver, Drake shifted his gaze to Devlin and asked, "How's your brother?"

Devlin smiled. "Enjoying his customary untrammeled health and his equally customary unfettered existence. He's taking his ease at the Priory at the moment. Or at least, he was there when we left."

"Melrose is how old now?"

"Twenty-nine."

"What are his interests?"

"I'm not sure he has any." Devlin grinned. "At least, none that would be of much use to you."

Drake sighed. "It's been made clear to me—by several forces of nature I would rather not cross—that I should limit my recruiting of eyes and ears to those of our ilk who are yet to marry. Consequently, I'm forced to go fishing."

Devlin was a few years older than Drake, but prior to his own marriage, he'd helped Drake out by trawling for information on certain secretive business deals and the movement of monies that had bordered on the treasonous. He knew what Drake and his band of helpers—the "sons of the nobility," as Louisa had dubbed them—did, because he'd been one of them.

Leaning against the old sideboard alongside Devlin, Drake went on, "I have Toby, but given he's already worked so many missions, I have to be cautious over what spheres I use him in. It's not helpful if those I'm seeking information on recognize him as one of mine on sight."

"I would have thought the Cynster horde plus your own relatives would supply you with enough agents."

"Up to a point. But then there's the matter of their surnames, and even if they try to conceal those, most of them are recognizable as belonging to one or other of the families."

Devlin couldn't help his grin. "The physical traits do tend to breed true, at least among the males."

"Exactly. So I'm widening my net." Drake met Devlin's eyes. "I heard that Child has returned."

"He has, but if you have ambitions in that quarter, you'd better act quickly, because Therese has plans for Child come next Season—and that assuredly means your fair wife will get involved as well."

Drake narrowed his eyes on his wife. "I'm going to have to have a discussion with Louisa over her edict of me using only bachelors while, meanwhile, she does her damnedest to marry them all off."

"Have you spoken with Martin yet?"

Drake shot Devlin an arrested glance. "Not yet. Should I? He's only just returned to England, and he's what? Twenty-four? Has he found his feet yet?"

"Twenty-five, I believe, much the same age as Toby, but I wouldn't judge Martin's caliber by his years—any more than I would Toby's. In Martin's case, his time away from society, earning his living, has matured him far more than had he spent those years in the ton. I would have more confidence in Martin behaving decisively and appropriately in any situation than I would have in Melrose. But more to your need, Martin's moving to establish a metalworks manufactory. He knows quite a bit about up-and-coming developments in that area—I don't need to tell you how much activity there is in those industries, how fast they're expanding, and how vital they are to our collective future—and Martin has contacts in the business side of that world that I quite envy."

"Has he now?" Drake had started smiling.

Devlin turned to Drake. "Now I think of it, you should definitely have a word. Martin had a run-in with some Germans over an invention offered through the exhibition, one Martin eventually secured."

Drake stilled for an instant, then nodded decisively. "Thank you. I'll definitely sound him out."

The underbutler appeared at the nursery door. When several of the adults looked his way, he drew himself up and announced, "The duchess requests your presence in the dining hall."

That was the signal that the nannies and nursemaids had been waiting for. They streamed forward to relieve the parents of their bundles of joy, allowing the ladies to straighten their skirts, resettle their jewelry, and tuck strands of hair back into place.

Along with the other husbands, Devlin ambled to wait by the door for their wives to join them.

He watched, smiling, as the group of lovely, lively women, their faces alight with expectation, swept up to claim the appropriate arms. He welcomed Therese with a smile he reserved just for her. She beamed at him and linked her arm with his, and they followed Drake and Louisa out of the nursery.

From elsewhere in the house came the sounds of thundering feet and male and female voices as the other groupings that had been scattered throughout the huge old mansion—the bachelor gentlemen, the unmarried young ladies, the smaller number of youths and children of the older Cynster couples—rushed or sauntered or walked demurely to join the stream of family members heading for the formal dining hall downstairs.

As the line of couples from the nursery progressed along the corridor to the stairs, Louisa, on Drake's arm, turned her head and fixed her wide, curious, and faintly amused pale-green eyes on Devlin. He withstood her scrutiny with a faint lift of one eyebrow and a gentle, entirely confident smile.

He knew what she was looking for, and he knew what she would see.

What she would do...

To his relief, Louisa beamed delightedly at him, then transferred her gaze to Therese and pronounced, "Wonderful!"

And with that, Louisa faced forward.

Devlin met Therese's laughing eyes and, smiling back, arched his brows resignedly.

As far as he and she were aware, none of the others had ever known of her belief or his attitude regarding their marriage. Being wrapped up in the reality of their own, openly acknowledged love-matches, the others had never questioned the foundation of Devlin and Therese's marriage, and he and she had never so much as alluded to it.

Now...while the change between them was obvious to them, there in the quality of the smiles they shared, the more confident and more relaxed connection between them that showed itself in so many little ways, such as how close they stood, how often Devlin's hand found Therese's, how frequently she briefly rested her head against his shoulder—all the little touches that spoke of their love—he doubted the majority of their peers had noticed or would notice anything different about them. Nothing that clashed with what they thought they'd been seeing all along.

That said, it was inevitable that those more highly alert to and aware of the emotional currents between partners, those expert in reading them —like Louisa, her sister-in-law Cleo, and Lucilla—would notice. But all, Devlin noted, had, as Louisa had just done, merely smiled catlike smiles and, transparently, bestowed their blessings without actually saying anything.

He was distinctly relieved and entirely content with that.

They reached the massive dining hall—originally a baronial hall— and filed in. The long table had been fully extended and would, that day, sit close to a hundred hungry souls. Decorations abounded, with boughs of fir and pine scenting the air and red, green, and gold ribbon rosettes and bows liberally distributed along the board.

Just inside the door, a small phalanx of older ladies had taken up posi- tion in such a way that they more or less forced all those entering to run what amounted to a gauntlet under the knowing eyes of experience, allowing mothers and grandmothers to run either approving or critical eyes over their children and grandchildren, to share kisses and squeeze hands, tweak lapels and straighten lace, and commend or instruct as they felt necessary.

As Devlin had expected, here, too, there were some who saw deeper than the surface. Horatia, Therese's grandmother, took one long look at him and Therese, then beamed and congratulated them on having come to their senses.

After duly kissing Horatia's proffered cheek, as he and Therese moved on, he caught her eye with a look of mock alarm, but she only laughed and patted his arm. "You knew that was coming."

Just as he'd known that they would never get past Therese's great-aunt Helena and her bosom-bow, Lady Osbaldestone, without some comment. Both were ancient, and in Devlin's opinion—shared by all the males present—nothing, but nothing of significance escaped Helena's pale-green gaze, much less Lady Osbaldestone's basilisk black eyes.

The pair were unquestionably the most unnerving and awe-inspiring grandes dames in the ton, but today, after scrutinizing him and Therese, the old ladies smiled and nodded in gracious approval and regally extended their hands for him to kiss. He complied with all due deference, while Therese kissed their lined cheeks.

"I hear you have another young one on the way." Helena's eyes twinkled. "A true celebration, yes?"

Rather more terrifyingly, Lady Osbaldestone declared, "We have always wondered if the pair of you would ever sort yourselves out—it's commendable that you have managed to do so entirely on your own."

Devlin kept his relaxed smile in place, but a glance at Therese's widening eyes confirmed that, yes, he'd interpreted that pronouncement correctly. If they *hadn't* sorted themselves out soon, something would have been done. Smoothly, he inclined his head. "Thank you, ma'am."

Before he could lead Therese away—and escape—Lady Osbaldestone commandingly tapped her cane to the floor. "Now, tell me, how is that reprobate Child?"

On entering the dining hall with Jason and Henry and the other bachelors his age, Martin had to bear up under particularly close examination. Somewhat to his surprise, the older ladies focused more on his social plans—as his grandmother phrased it, "Now that you're back in civilized society"—rather than upbraiding him over having vanished from their orbit for eight years.

"We'll be keeping an eye on you," Lady Osbaldestone unnecessarily informed him, her gimlet gaze locked on his face.

His great-aunt Helena smiled in her usual sweet way and disconcertingly said, "And of course, we will expect great things."

He'd anticipated rather more complaints and was very happy to escape their censure, enough to admit under further questioning that he'd done rather well for himself and planned to invest in manufacturing. He even uttered the words he knew would put a smile on their faces by saying he expected to "settle down in a few years, once I've found my feet."

With that admission made, he was allowed to escape.

"Phew!" He dropped into the chair Jason had saved for him at the long table. "That went better than I'd hoped."

Henry, seated opposite, grinned. "They've decided to forgive you because—courtesy of being away for so long—they no longer know you, so you've piqued their interest. They're looking forward to learning all about you, while they already know everything about us."

Jason nodded. "You're a fresh new prospect to be observed and analyzed."

Toby dropped into the vacant seat beside Henry. "Heigh-ho, Martin, my lad. How's things?"

Martin grinned and laughed, and in that instant, he knew he'd come home.

Farther along the table, Gregory sat surrounded by his own group of Cynster peers. At thirty years of age, he, Justin, and Aidan were the oldest of the unmarried Cynster males, with Nicholas and Evan, at twenty-nine, just behind. At family events such as this, all five of them did their best to fade into the woodwork, actively avoiding the notice of their mothers, aunts, grandmothers, and great-aunts. Regardless of their success in that, they all felt as if they were living on borrowed time.

Justin slanted glances up and down the table; the older generation were clustered about the table's ends, one set of couples on either side of Devil, the duke, at the table's head, and the others flanking Honoria, his duchess, at the table's foot. "How long do you think we have? I mean, surely they'll hang back until we're at least thirty-three?"

"I wouldn't bet on it," Aidan returned.

"I suspect," Nicholas said, "that it'll be more a case of how long their patience lasts rather than how old we are."

"Don't say that." Evan turned a mock horrified glare on Nicholas. "At least your mother has had one wedding to enjoy so far." He looked at Justin and Gregory. "And so have yours. But our fond mama"—he pointed at Aidan, his brother—"has started looking at us as if we're deliberately withholding the only thing that will ever make her happy again."

Soberly, Aidan nodded. "It's almost enough to make one want to go out and start looking around."

"Almost," Evan agreed, "but not quite."

They all shared commiserating looks, then the conversation turned to their favorite topic, horses.

Gregory contributed where appropriate while trying to quell the inner restlessness—the dissatisfaction with his life—that, over the past year, had built and built.

It was becoming a near-constant distraction.

After considerable soul-searching—not an activity that came naturally to him—he'd identified the source of his malaise. Put simply, he lacked a purpose. When it came to his life, he had no aim, no goal that called to him, no ambition to achieve…anything.

He only needed to look about him—at his three siblings for a start— to understand that lack was something peculiar to himself. Christopher had always had the manor and the associated acres to run, the family fortune to marshal and grow; he'd been focused on that from his early teenage years, and now, with Ellen by his side, he was in full control of his future and was unrelievedly happy. Therese had always been set on marriage, and she'd applied herself to the task, landed Devlin, and now had an earldom as well as her husband and family to organize and care for; that had always been her dream, and she'd achieved it and was, transparently, going from strength to strength. She and Devlin both now radiated contentment.

As for Martin, Gregory had thought that after returning from the presumed dead, his younger brother would be as aimless as he, but no. Martin was focused on building a life for himself in manufacturing and was already taking steps to making his envisaged future a reality.

Gregory was the only one in his immediate family without a clear path before him. He'd never been attracted to farming or good with that sort of management; he could have learned alongside Christopher and bought his own acres, but there was no point in that when his heart wouldn't be in it.

Somewhat unexpectedly, he'd come to realize that having sufficient funds to do whatever he wished in life wasn't the unmitigated blessing most imagined it to be. His comfortable financial position provided zero motivation to explore the sort of avenues that had fired Martin's enthusiasm. On top of that, he had a sneaking suspicion that he would never be any good at business or investments, as some of his peers were proving to be.

So where did that leave him?

What could he do?

How could he occupy his time?

He'd been searching for an answer for the past twelve months.

As for marrying, he was firmly of the opinion that he would be one of the rare unmarried Cynster males, a bachelor uncle to his nephews and nieces. Indeed, with his mind engrossed with his thus-far-fruitless quest, he felt zero inclination to idle away hours in the company of gently bred females. To what end?

Marriage, he felt increasingly certain, would never be for him.

Aside from all else, if he continued in his aimless rut, no lady worth marrying would marry him.

He refocused on the company as the first of the courses, a rich lobster bisque, was ferried to the table. The laughs and cheers and comments that abounded about the table, the very real happiness and joy surrounding him, weighed on his shoulders.

He felt like an interloper, but pasted on a smile and chatted and joked with his peers while, inside, a sense of failure gnawed at him, pushing him to seize the very first opportunity and flee as soon as he possibly could.

∼

December 27, 1851
Ancaster Park, Lincolnshire

In midafternoon, still replete after another interminable family luncheon, Lord Grayson Child returned from the stables to the house, having excused himself from repairing to the drawing room on the grounds of checking on his newly acquired hunter. He entered what he affectionately thought of as "the old pile" through a side door and, walking silently into the front hall, swiped up the last of the newspapers lying on the hall table and, instead of making for the drawing room, cravenly diverted to the library.

Gray knew his father and brother, who, by now, would have pried themselves from the clutches of their wives and Roddy's two sons, would have sought refuge in the smoking room, there to enjoy the cigars his father favored. While Gray didn't indulge in the practice himself, he had nothing against cigar smoke, but he harbored no wish to indulge in the usual inane conversation his father considered appropriate for such interludes, much less subject himself to more of Roddy's pompous posturing. The three hours of luncheon had been more than enough; Gray's temper needed a respite.

On reaching the library, he opened the door, checked that the room was unoccupied, then slipped inside and shut the door.

He crossed to the alcove at the far end of the room, where, from experience, he knew the weak late-afternoon sun would slant through the nearby window, creating a pocket of diffuse light in the otherwise gloomy chamber.

The curtains were open and, sure enough, what sun there was illuminated the spot. Gray dragged up one of the wing chairs, positioned it with its back to the door, and slumped gratefully into the cushioning comfort.

"At last." He unfolded the paper and flicked it out—only to discover that it was what was commonly termed a gossip rag. "Not quite *The Times*," he muttered as he glanced over the front page. His father and brother must have snaffled all the copies of the more serious publications.

"Beggars can't be choosers, I suppose."

He spent the next minutes perusing the main story—that of some unnamed gentleman caught with his hand in the till of some insurance company. Gray snorted. "That's hardly news."

That acknowledged, the article was surprisingly well-written, more as a story—a cautionary tale—than in the lurid and sensationalist style he'd expected. He glanced again at the masthead. *The London Crier.* He arched his brows. "As in town crier, I assume."

That was, he supposed, an apt name for a publication that, according to the subtitle running below the name, prided itself on being "The Voice of Revelation."

As if in support of that claim, the other two articles on the front page covered a series of relatively mild but entertaining misadventures at a ball in London and the rather more scandalous goings-on at a country house party held somewhere in the Cotswolds. Of course, in keeping with the time-honored practice of scandal sheets, no names of people or places were printed.

None of the revelations was any surprise to Gray, yet he found himself drawn into the game, artfully designed by the writer, of trying to identify the various personages who were referred to by sobriquets such as Hooknose and Puce-Waistcoat. While he could think of several males who might be Hooknose, the person referred to was female. Gray wondered who Lady Hooknose was and whether she would recognize herself in the printed account.

He was almost certain Puce-Waistcoat was Lord Farquhar-Mallet; although Gray had been back in England for only a few months, he'd seen the dandy mincing down Oxford Street and parading in the park, invariably wearing a quite startling puce waistcoat.

Gray grinned. No doubt his mother had requested that the *Crier* be delivered to the house, and he could understand why. As a means of alleviating boredom, it was remarkably effective.

He was about to turn the page when a small column at the bottom right corner caught his eye.

From the editor's desk:
An Upcoming Exposé
Which scion of a noble house, after
a lengthy sojourn in far-flung lands,
has recently returned to these shores a
veritable Croesus, yet is being exceedingly
careful to hide his remarkable wealth
from the eyes of the world?
More details will be revealed in coming editions.

Gray stared at the notice, then roundly swore.

～

～

Dear Reader,

The exchange between Therese and Devlin in the epilogue of the previous book (*The Inevitable Fall of Christopher Cynster*) set me the challenge of working out how Therese and Devlin had got themselves to that point—namely, five years married yet with Therese unaware of the true nature of Devlin's regard for her. Once I'd understood that and also Devlin's new direction, steering the pair of them to their happy ending was quite a feat!

I have to admit that I particularly enjoyed learning all about the Great Exhibition and the history of the edifice known as Crystal Palace as well as exploring all the outings and excursions a family with young children might have enjoyed in the London of 1851.

Of interest to some might be the mention of Faberge. Gustav Faberge had, indeed, set up business in the 1840s and was already making a name for himself with his particular style of enameled, jewel-encrusted pieces. I could not discover whether he and his firm and his wife attended the Great Exhibition, as I have postulated, but considering the situation, it would have been strange if they hadn't.

I hope you enjoyed reading of Therese and Devlin's journey to claiming a love that was, in effect, always there. If you feel inclined to leave a review, I would greatly appreciate it.

As is my habit, the last pages in this book switch our focus to the subject of the next novel in the series, but in this case, it wasn't who I thought would be next—Gregory, Christopher's and Therese's brother. Instead, Lord Grayson Child, recently returned old friend and sometimes-bane of Devlin's existence, waltzed onto the page and immediately commanded so much attention that I couldn't resist seeing what Fate had in store for him.

Consequently, Child's story—*The Secrets of Lord Grayson Child*—is scheduled for release in July 2021, only four months away!

And by popular demand, October 2021 will see the release of the long-awaited romance between Miss Melissa North, one of Lady Osbaldestone's granddaughters, and Julian, Earl of Carsely (previously Viscount Dagenham)—a treat for you to enjoy in the lead-up to the festive season.

With my best wishes for unbounded happy reading!

Stephanie.

For alerts as new books are released, plus information on upcoming books, exclusive sweepstakes and sneak peeks into upcoming novels, sign up for Stephanie's Private Email Newsletter http://www.stephanielaurens. com/newsletter-signup/

Or if you don't have time to chat and want a quick email alert, sign up and follow me at BookBub https://www.bookbub.com/authors/stephanie-laurens

The ultimate source for detailed information on all Stephanie's published books, including covers, descriptions, and excerpts, is Stephanie's Website www.stephanielaurens.com

You can also follow Stephanie via her Amazon Author Page at http:// tinyurl.com/zc3e9mp

Goodreads members can follow Stephanie via her author page https:// www.goodreads.com/author/show/9241.Stephanie_Laurens

You can email Stephanie at stephanie@stephanielaurens.com

Or find her on Facebook
https://www.facebook.com/AuthorStephanieLaurens/

COMING NEXT:

A Cynster Next Generation-connected novel
THE SECRETS OF LORD GRAYSON CHILD
To be released on July 15, 2021.

Lord Grayson Child rushes to London to halt the publication of an exposé that he fears will make him the prime target of every matchmaking mama in the ton, let alone every shyster and Captain Sharp, only to find himself astonished, astounded, and wrong footed on every count.

Available for e-book pre-order in mid-April, 2021.

RECENTLY RELEASED:

The fourth instalment in Lady Osbaldestone's Christmas Chronicles
LADY OSBALDESTONE'S CHRISTMAS INTRIGUE

#1 New York Times *bestselling author Stephanie Laurens immerses you in the simple joys of a long-ago country-village Christmas, featuring a grandmother, her grandchildren, her unwed son, a determined not-so-young lady, foreign diplomats, undercover guards, and agents of Napoleon!*

At Hartington Manor in the village of Little Moseley, Therese, Lady Osbaldestone, and her household are once again enjoying the company of her intrepid grandchildren, Jamie, George, and Lottie, when they are unexpectedly joined by her ladyship's youngest and still-unwed son, also the children's favorite uncle, Christopher.

As the Foreign Office's master intelligencer, Christopher has been ordered into hiding until the department can appropriately deal with the French agent spotted following him in London. Christopher chose to seek refuge in Little Moseley because it's such a tiny village that anyone without a reason to be there stands out. Neither he nor his office-appointed bodyguard expect to encounter any dramas.

Then Christopher spots a lady from London he believes has been hunting him with matrimonial intent. He can't understand how she tracked him to the village, but determined to avoid her, he enlists the children's help. The children discover their information-gathering skills are in high demand, and while engaging with the villagers as they usually do and taking part in the village's traditional events, they do their best to learn what Miss Marion Sewell is up to.

But upon reflection, Christopher realizes it's unlikely the Marion he was so attracted to years before has changed all that much, and he starts to wonder if what she wants to tell him is actually something he might want to hear. Unfortunately, he has set wheels in motion that are not easy to redirect. Although Marion tries to approach him several times, he and she fail to make contact.

Then just when it seems they will finally connect, a dangerous stranger lures Marion away. Fearing the worst, Christopher gives chase—trailed by his bodyguard, the children, and a small troop of helpful younger gentlemen.

What they discover at nearby Parteger Hall is not at all what anyone expected, and as the action unfolds, the assembled company band together to protect a secret vital to the resolution of the war against Napoleon.

Fourth in series. A novel of 81,000 words. A Christmas tale of intrigue, personal evolution, and love.

The fourth and final volume in the Cavanaughs
THE OBSESSIONS OF LORD GODFREY CAVANAUGH

#1 New York Times bestselling author Stephanie Laurens concludes the tales of the Cavanaugh siblings with the riveting story of the youngest brother and his search for a family of his own.

The scion of a noble house who is caught in a storm and the lady who nurses him back to health strive to unravel a web of deception that threatens her family and ensnares them both, forcing them to fight for what they hold most dear—family, each other, and love.

Lord Godfrey Cavanaugh has no thoughts of marrying as he drives into North Yorkshire on a plum commission for the National Gallery to authenticate a Renaissance painting the gallery wishes to purchase. Then a snow storm sweeps in, and Godfrey barely manages to haul himself, his groom, and his horses to their destination.

Elinor Hinckley, eldest daughter of Hinckley Hall, stalwart defender of the family, right arm to her invalid father, and established spinster knows full well how much her family has riding on the sale of the painting and throws herself into nursing the initially delirious gentleman who holds her family's future in his hands.

But Godfrey proves to be a far from easy patient. Through Ellie's and her siblings' efforts to keep him entertained and abed, Godfrey grows to know the family, seeing and ultimately being drawn into family life of a sort he's never known.

Eventually, to everyone's relief, he recovers sufficiently to assess the painting—only to discover that nothing, but nothing, is as it seems.

Someone has plans, someone other than the Hinckleys, but who is pulling the strings is a mystery that Godfrey and Ellie find near-impossible to solve. Every suspect proves to have perfectly understandable, albeit concealed reasons for their behavior, and Godfrey and Ellie remain baffled.

Until the villain, panicked by their inquiries, strikes—directly at their hearts—and forces each of them to acknowledge what has grown to be the most important thing in their lives. Both are warriors, neither will give up—together they fight to save not just themselves, not just her family, but their futures. Hers, his, and theirs.

A classical historical romance set in North Yorkshire. Fourth novel in The Cavanaughs—a full-length historical romance of 90,000 words.

PREVIOUS CYNSTER NEXT GENERATION RELEASES:

THE INEVITABLE FALL OF CHRISTOPHER CYNSTER
Cynster Next Generation Novel #8

#1 New York Times *bestselling author Stephanie Laurens returns to the Cynsters' next generation with a rollicking tale of smugglers, counterfeit banknotes, and two people falling in love.*

A gentleman hoping to avoid falling in love and a lady who believes love has passed her by are flung together in a race to unravel a plot that threatens to undermine the realm.

Christopher Cynster has finally accepted that to have the life he wants, he needs a wife, but before he can even think of searching for the right lady, he's drawn into an investigation into the distribution of counterfeit banknotes.

London born and bred, Ellen Martingale is battling to preserve the fiction that her much-loved uncle, Christopher's neighbor, still has his wits about him, but Christopher's questions regarding nearby Goffard Hall trigger her suspicions. As her younger brother attends card parties at the Hall, she feels compelled to investigate.

While Ellen appears to be the sort of frippery female Christopher abhors, he quickly learns that, in her case, appearances are deceiving. And through the twists and turns in an investigation that grows ever more serious and urgent, he discovers how easy it is to fall in love, while Ellen learns that love hasn't, after all, passed her by.

But then the villain steps from the shadows, and love's strengths and vulnerabilities are put to the test—just as Christopher has always feared. Will he pass muster? Can they triumph? Or will they lose all they've so recently found?

A historical romance with a dash of intrigue, set in rural Kent. A Cynster Next Generation novel—a full-length historical romance of 124,000 words.

A CONQUEST IMPOSSIBLE TO RESIST
Cynster Next Generation Novel #7

#1 New York Times bestselling author Stephanie Laurens returns to the Cynsters' next generation to bring you a thrilling tale of love, intrigue, and fabulous horses.

A notorious rakehell with a stable of rare Thoroughbreds and a lady on a quest to locate such horses must negotiate personal minefields to forge a greatly desired alliance—one someone is prepared to murder to prevent.

Prudence Cynster has turned her back on husband hunting in favor of horse hunting. As the head of the breeding program underpinning the success of the Cynster racing stables, she's on a quest to acquire the necessary horses to refresh the stable's breeding stock.

On his estranged father's death, Deaglan Fitzgerald, now Earl of Glengarah, left London and the hedonistic life of a wealthy, wellborn rake and returned to Glengarah Castle determined to rectify the harm caused by his father's neglect. Driven by guilt that he hadn't been there to protect his people during the Great Famine, Deaglan holds firm against the lure of his father's extensive collection of horses and, leaving the stable to the care of his brother, Felix, devotes himself to returning the estate to prosperity.

Deaglan had fallen out with his father and been exiled from Glengarah over his drive to have the horses pay their way. Knowing Deaglan's wishes and that restoration of the estate is almost complete, Felix writes to the premier Thoroughbred breeding program in the British Isles to test their interest in the Glengarah horses.

On receiving a letter describing exactly the type of horses she's seeking, Pru overrides her family's reluctance and sets out for Ireland's west coast to visit the now-reclusive wicked Earl of Glengarah. Yet her only interest is in his horses, which she cannot wait to see.

When Felix tells Deaglan that a P. H. Cynster is about to arrive to assess the horses with a view to a breeding arrangement, Deaglan can only be grateful. But then P. H. Cynster turns out to be a lady, one utterly unlike any other he's ever met.

Yet they are who they are, and both understand their world. They battle their instincts and attempt to keep their interactions businesslike, but the sparks are incandescent and inevitably ignite a sexual blaze that consumes them both—and opens their eyes.

But before they can find their way to their now-desired goal, first one accident, then another distracts them. Someone, it seems, doesn't want them to strike a deal. Who? Why?

They need to find out before whoever it is resorts to the ultimate sanction.

A historical romance with neo-Gothic overtones, set in the west of Ireland. A Cynster Next Generation novel—a full-length historical romance of 125,000 words.

The first volume of the Devil's Brood Trilogy
THE LADY BY HIS SIDE
Cynster Next Generation Novel #4

A marquess in need of the right bride. An earl's daughter in search of a purpose. A betrayal that ends in murder and balloons into a threat to the realm.

Sebastian Cynster knows time is running out. If he doesn't choose a wife soon, his female relatives will line up to assist him. Yet the current debutantes do not appeal. Where is he to find the right lady to be his marchioness? Then Drake Varisey, eldest son of the Duke of Wolverstone, asks for Sebastian's aid.

Having assumed his father's mantle in protecting queen and country, Drake must go to Ireland in pursuit of a dangerous plot. But he's received an urgent missive from Lord Ennis, an Irish peer—Ennis has heard something Drake needs to know. Ennis insists Drake attends an upcoming house party at Ennis's Kent estate so Ennis can reveal his information face-to-face.

Sebastian has assisted Drake before and, long ago, had a liaison with Lady Ennis. Drake insists Sebastian is just the man to be Drake's surrogate at the house party—the guests will imagine all manner of possibilities and be blind to Sebastian's true purpose.

Unsurprisingly, Sebastian is reluctant, but Drake's need is real. With only more debutantes on his horizon, Sebastian allows himself to be persuaded.

His first task is to inveigle Antonia Rawlings, a lady he has known all her life, to include him as her escort to the house party. Although he's seen little of Antonia in recent years, Sebastian is confident of gaining her support.

Eldest daughter of the Earl of Chillingworth, Antonia has abandoned the search for a husband and plans to use the week of the house party to decide what to do with her life. There has to be some purpose, some role, she can claim for her own.

Consequently, on hearing Sebastian's request and an explanation of what lies behind it, she seizes on the call to action. Suppressing her senses' idiotic reaction to Sebastian's nearness, she agrees to be his partner-in-intrigue.

But while joining the house party proves easy, the gathering is thrown into chaos when Lord Ennis is murdered—just before he was to speak with Sebastian. Worse, Ennis's last words, gasped to Sebastian, are: *Gunpowder. Here.*

Gunpowder? And here, where?

With a killer continuing to stalk the halls, side by side, Sebastian and Antonia search for answers and, all the while, the childhood connection that had always existed between them strengthens and blooms...into something so much more.

First volume in a trilogy. A Cynster Next Generation Novel – a classic historical romance with gothic overtones layered over a continuing intrigue. A full-length novel of 99,000 words.

The second volume of the Devil's Brood Trilogy
· **AN IRRESISTIBLE ALLIANCE**

Cynster Next Generation Novel #5

A duke's second son with no responsibilities and a lady starved of the excitement her soul craves join forces to unravel a deadly, potentially catastrophic threat to the realm - that only continues to grow.

With his older brother's betrothal announced, Lord Michael Cynster is freed from the pressure of familial expectations. However, the allure of his previous hedonistic pursuits has paled. Then he learns of the mission his brother, Sebastian, and Lady Antonia Rawlings have been assisting with and volunteers to assist by hunting down the hoard of gunpowder now secreted somewhere in London.

Michael sets out to trace the carters who transported the gunpowder from Kent to London. His quest leads him to the Hendon Shipping Company, where he discovers his sole source of information is the only daughter of Jack and Kit Hendon, Miss Cleome Hendon, who although a fetchingly attractive lady, firmly holds the reins of the office in her small hands.

Cleo has fought to achieve her position in the company. Initially, managing the office was a challenge, but she now conquers all in just a few hours a week. With her three brothers all adventuring in America, she's been driven to the realization that she craves adventure, too.

When Michael Cynster walks in and asks about carters, Cleo's instincts leap. She wrings from him the full tale of his mission—and offers him a bargain. She will lead him to the carters he seeks if he agrees to include her as an equal partner in the mission.

Horrified, Michael attempts to resist, but ultimately finds himself agreeing—a sequence of events he quickly learns is common around Cleo. Then she delivers on her part of the bargain, and he finds there are benefits to allowing her to continue to investigate beside him—not least being that if she's there, then he knows she's safe.

But the further they go in tracing the gunpowder, the more deaths they uncover. And when they finally locate the barrels, they find themselves tangled in a fight to the death—one that forces them to face what has grown between them, to seize and defend what they both see as their path to the greatest adventure of all. A shared life. A shared future. A shared love.

Second volume in a trilogy. A Cynster Next Generation Novel – a classic historical romance with gothic overtones layered over a continuing intrigue. A full-length novel of 101,000 words.

The third and final volume in the Devil's Brood Trilogy
THE GREATEST CHALLENGE OF THEM ALL
Cynster Next Generation Novel #6

A nobleman devoted to defending queen and country and a noblewoman wild enough to match his every step race to disrupt the plans of a malignant intelligence intent on shaking England to its very foundations.

Lord Drake Varisey, Marquess of Winchelsea, eldest son and heir of the Duke of Wolverstone, must foil a plot that threatens to shake the foundations of the realm, but the very last lady—nay, noblewoman—he needs assisting him is Lady Louisa Cynster, known throughout the ton as Lady Wild.

For the past nine years, Louisa has suspected that Drake might well be the ideal husband for her, even though he's assiduous in avoiding her. But she's now twenty-seven and enough is enough. She believes propinquity will elucidate exactly what it is that lies between them, and what better opportunity to work closely with Drake than his latest mission, with which he patently needs her help?

Unable to deny Louisa's abilities or the value of her assistance and powerless to curb her willfulness, Drake is forced to grit his teeth and acquiesce to her sticking by his side, if only to ensure her safety. But all too soon, his true feelings for her show enough for her, perspicacious as she is, to see through his denials, which she then interprets as a challenge.

Even while they gather information, tease out clues, increasingly desperately search for the missing gunpowder, and doggedly pursue the killer responsible for an ever-escalating tally of dead men, thrown together through the hours, he and she learn to trust and appreciate each other. And fed by constant exposure—and blatantly encouraged by her—their desires and hungers swell and grow…

As the barriers between them crumble, the attraction he has for so long restrained burgeons and balloons, until goaded by her near-death, it erupts, and he seizes her—only to be seized in return.

Linked irrevocably and with their wills melded and merged by passion's fire, with time running out and the evil mastermind's deadline looming, together, they focus their considerable talents and make one last push to learn the critical truths—to find the gunpowder and unmask the villain behind this far-reaching plot.

Only to discover that they have significantly less time than they'd thought, that the villain's target is even more crucially fundamental to the realm than they'd imagined, and it's going to take all that Drake is—as well as all that Louisa as Lady Wild can bring to bear—to defuse the threat, capture the villain, and make all safe and right again.

As they race to the ultimate confrontation, the future of all England rests on their shoulders.

Third volume in a trilogy. A Cynster Next Generation Novel – a classic historical romance with gothic overtones layered over an intrigue. A full-length novel of 129,000 words.

If you haven't yet caught up with the first books in the Cynster Next Generation Novels, then BY WINTER'S LIGHT is a Christmas story that highlights the Cynster children as they stand poised on the cusp of adulthood – essentially an introductory novel to the upcoming generation.

That novel is followed by the first pair of Cynster Next Generation romances, those of Lucilla and Marcus Cynster, twins and the eldest children of Lord Richard aka Scandal Cynster and Catriona, Lady of the Vale. Both the twins' stories are set in Scotland. See below for further details.

BY WINTER'S LIGHT
Cynster Next Generation Novel #1

#1 New York Times bestselling author Stephanie Laurens returns to romantic Scotland to usher in a new generation of Cynsters in an enchanting tale of mistletoe, magic, and love.

It's December 1837 and the young adults of the Cynster clan have succeeded in having the family Christmas celebration held at snow-bound Casphairn Manor, Richard and Catriona Cynster's home. Led by Sebastian, Marquess of Earith, and by Lucilla, future Lady of the Vale, and her twin brother, Marcus, the upcoming generation has their own plans for the holiday season.

Yet where Cynsters gather, love is never far behind—the festive occasion brings together Daniel Crosbie, tutor to Lucifer Cynster's sons, and

Claire Meadows, widow and governess to Gabriel Cynster's daughter. Daniel and Claire have met before and the embers of an unexpected passion smolder between them, but once bitten, twice shy, Claire believes a second marriage is not in her stars. Daniel, however, is determined to press his suit. He's seen the love the Cynsters share, and Claire is the lady with whom he dreams of sharing *his* life. Assisted by a bevy of Cynsters —innate matchmakers every one—Daniel strives to persuade Claire that trusting him with her hand and her heart is her right path to happiness.

Meanwhile, out riding on Christmas Eve, the young adults of the Cynster clan respond to a plea for help. Summoned to a humble dwelling in ruggedly forested mountains, Lucilla is called on to help with the difficult birth of a child, while the others rise to the challenge of helping her. With a violent storm closing in and severely limited options, the next generation of Cynsters face their first collective test—can they save this mother and child? And themselves, too?

Back at the manor, Claire is increasingly drawn to Daniel and despite her misgivings, against the backdrop of the ongoing festivities their relationship deepens. Yet she remains torn—until catastrophe strikes, and by winter's light, she learns that love—true love—is worth any risk, any price.

A tale brimming with all the magical delights of a Scottish festive season. A Cynster Next Generation novel – a classic historical romance of 71,000 words.

THE TEMPTING OF THOMAS CARRICK
Cynster Next Generation Novel #2

Do you believe in fate? Do you believe in passion? What happens when fate and passion collide?
Do you believe in love? What happens when fate, passion, and love combine?
This. This…

#1 New York Times *bestselling author Stephanie Laurens returns to Scotland with a tale of two lovers irrevocably linked by destiny and passion.*

Thomas Carrick is a gentleman driven to control all aspects of his life.

As the wealthy owner of Carrick Enterprises, located in bustling Glasgow, he is one of that city's most eligible bachelors and fully intends to select an appropriate wife from the many young ladies paraded before him. He wants to take that necessary next step along his self-determined path, yet no young lady captures his eye, much less his attention...not in the way Lucilla Cynster had, and still did, even though she lives miles away.

For over two years, Thomas has avoided his clan's estate because it borders Lucilla's home, but disturbing reports from his clansmen force him to return to the countryside—only to discover that his uncle, the laird, is ailing, a clan family is desperately ill, and the clan-healer is unconscious and dying. Duty to the clan leaves Thomas no choice but to seek help from the last woman he wants to face.

Strong-willed and passionate, Lucilla has been waiting—increasingly impatiently—for Thomas to return and claim his rightful place by her side. She knows he is hers—her fated lover, husband, protector, and mate. He is the only man for her, just as she is his one true love. And, at last, he's back. Even though his returning wasn't on her account, Lucilla is willing to seize whatever chance Fate hands her.

Thomas can never forget Lucilla, much less the connection that seethes between them, but to marry her would mean embracing a life he's adamant he does not want.

Lucilla sees that Thomas has yet to accept the inevitability of their union and, despite all, he can refuse her and walk away. But how *can* he ignore a bond such as theirs—one so much stronger than reason? Despite several unnerving attacks mounted against them, despite the uncertainty racking his clan, Lucilla remains as determined as only a Cynster can be to fight for the future she knows can be theirs—and while she cannot command him, she has powerful enticements she's willing to wield in the cause of tempting Thomas Carrick.

A neo-Gothic tale of passionate romance laced with mystery, set in the uplands of southwestern Scotland. A Cynster Next Generation Novel – a classic historical romance of 122,000 words.

A MATCH FOR MARCUS CYNSTER
Cynster Next Generation Novel #3

Duty compels her to turn her back on marriage. Fate drives him to protect her come what may. Then love takes a hand in this battle of yearning hearts, stubborn wills, and a match too powerful to deny.

#1 New York Times *bestselling author Stephanie Laurens returns to rugged Scotland with a dramatic tale of passionate desire and unwavering devotion.*

Restless and impatient, Marcus Cynster waits for Fate to come calling. He knows his destiny lies in the lands surrounding his family home, but what will his future be? Equally importantly, with whom will he share it?

Of one fact he feels certain: his fated bride will not be Niniver Carrick. His elusive neighbor attracts him mightily, yet he feels compelled to protect her—even from himself. Fickle Fate, he's sure, would never be so kind as to decree that Niniver should be his. The best he can do for them both is to avoid her.

Niniver has vowed to return her clan to prosperity. The epitome of fragile femininity, her delicate and ethereal exterior cloaks a stubborn will and an unflinching devotion to the people in her care. She accepts that in order to achieve her goal, she cannot risk marrying and losing her grip on the clan's reins to an inevitably controlling husband. Unfortunately, many local men see her as their opportunity.

Soon, she's forced to seek help to get rid of her unwelcome suitors. Powerful and dangerous, Marcus Cynster is perfect for the task. Suppressing her wariness over tangling with a gentleman who so excites her passions, she appeals to him for assistance with her peculiar problem.

Although at first he resists, Marcus discovers that, contrary to his expectations, his fated role *is* to stand by Niniver's side and, ultimately, to claim her hand. Yet in order to convince her to be his bride, they must plunge headlong into a journey full of challenges, unforeseen dangers, passion, and yearning, until Niniver grasps the essential truth—that she is indeed a match for Marcus Cynster.

A neo-Gothic tale of passionate romance set in the uplands of southwestern Scotland. A Cynster Next Generation Novel – a classic historical romance of 114,000 words.

And if you want to discover where the Cynsters began, return to the iconic

DEVIL'S BRIDE

the book that introduced millions of historical romance readers around the globe to the powerful men of the unforgettable Cynster family – aristocrats to the bone, conquerors at heart – and the willful feisty ladies strong enough to be their brides.

ABOUT THE AUTHOR

#1 *New York Times* bestselling author Stephanie Laurens began writing romances as an escape from the dry world of professional science. Her hobby quickly became a career when her first novel was accepted for publication, and with entirely becoming alacrity, she gave up writing about facts in favor of writing fiction.

All Laurens's works to date are historical romances, ranging from medieval times to the mid-1800s, and her settings range from Scotland to India. The majority of her works are set in the period of the British Regency. Laurens has published over 75 works of historical romance, including 40 *New York Times* bestsellers. Laurens has sold more than 20 million print, audio, and e-books globally. All her works are continuously available in print and e-book formats in English worldwide, and have been translated into many other languages. An international bestseller, among other accolades, Laurens has received the Romance Writers of America® prestigious RITA® Award for Best Romance Novella 2008 for *The Fall of Rogue Gerrard*.

Laurens's continuing novels featuring the Cynster family are widely regarded as classics of the historical romance genre. Other series include the *Bastion Club Novels*, the *Black Cobra Quartet*, the *Adventurers Quartet,* and the *Casebook of Barnaby Adair Novels*.

For information on all published novels and on upcoming releases and updates on novels yet to come, visit Stephanie's website: www.stephanielaurens.com

To sign up for Stephanie's Email Newsletter (a private list) for heads-up alerts as new books are released, exclusive sneak peeks into upcoming books, and exclusive sweepstakes contests, follow the prompts at http://www.stephanielaurens.com/newsletter-signup/

To follow Stephanie on BookBub, head to her BookBub Author Page: https://www.bookbub.com/authors/stephanie-laurens

Stephanie lives with her husband and a goofy black labradoodle in the hills outside Melbourne, Australia. When she isn't writing, she's reading, and if she isn't reading, she'll be tending her garden.

www.stephanielaurens.com
stephanie@stephanielaurens.com